W9-CBB-056

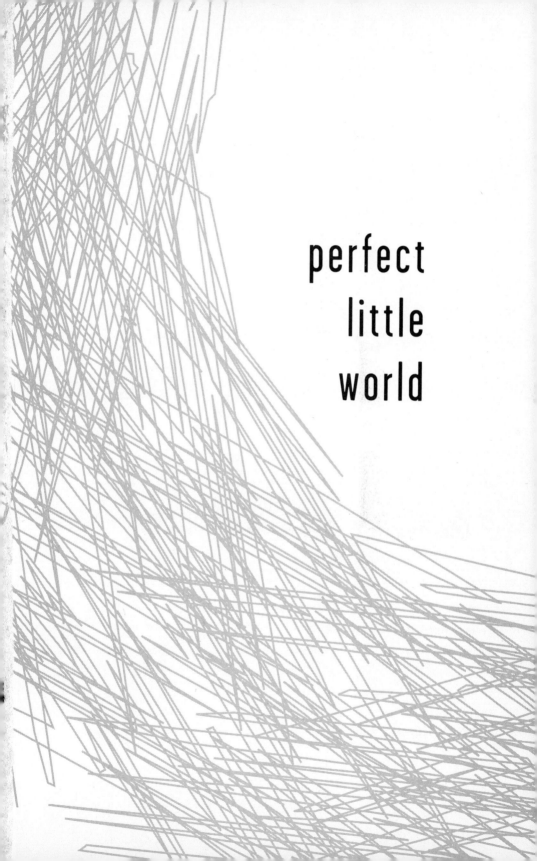

perfect
little
world

perfect
little
world

kevin wilson

An Imprint of HarperCollins *Publishers*

PERFECT LITTLE WORLD. Copyright © 2017 by Kevin Wilson. All rights reserved.
Printed in the United States of America. No part of this book may be used or repro-
duced in any manner whatsoever without written permission except in the case of
brief quotations embodied in critical articles and reviews. For information address
HarperCollins Publishers, 195 Broadway, New York, NY 10007.

HarperCollins books may be purchased for educational, business, or sales promotional use. For information please e-mail the Special Markets Department at
SPsales@harpercollins.com.

FIRST EDITION

Designed by Suet Yee Chong

Library of Congress Cataloging-in-Publication Data has been applied for.

ISBN 978-0-06-245032-6

17 18 19 20 21   LSC   10 9 8 7 6 5 4 3 2 1

for Griff and Patch

We were a large family once, you recall, a large and happy family.

—Shirley Jackson, *We Have Always Lived in the Castle*

We are the gardeners who might have been the garden.

—Leigh Anne Couch, "Obsolescence"

the infinite family project

DR. KALINA KWON

DR. JIL[...]

ISABEL "IZZY"
POOLE

|

CAP
POOLE

LINK
+
JULIE HOWSER

|

ELIZA
HOWSER

HARRIS
+
ELLEN TILTON

|

MARNIE
TILTON

KENNY FLOYD
+
CARMEN RIVERA

|

MAXWELL
FLOYD

DAVID PARTI[...]
+
SUSAN LIN

|

IRENE
PARTIN

BRENDA ACKLEN

DR. PRESTON GRIND

ATTERSON

DR. JEFFREY WASHINGTON

ASEAN
+
NIKISHA WATTS

CARLOS
+
NINA TORRES

PAUL BROCK
+
MARY
HUBBARD

JEREMY
+
CALLIE
GIPSON

BENJAMIN
+
ALYSSA
RAYMOND

JACKIE
WATTS

GILBERTO
TORRES

LULU
BROCK

ELI GIPSON

ALLY
RAYMOND

perfect
little
world

prologue

Izzy was suffering from a dull, rattling hangover on the morning of the formal introductions. It had been too much for most of them, the years of anticipation for this very moment so overwhelming that they'd resorted to a few bottles of bourbon, which while certainly not forbidden was rarely encouraged.

"What would the children think?" Julie had said, deep into her third tumbler; her husband, Link, was playing a fast, carnivallike rendition of "She'll Be Comin' Round the Mountain" on his banjo. Izzy had started singing along, trying to keep up with the music, but found she couldn't remember what the woman would be doing other than coming, forever coming round the mountain, never quite there, so she gave up and focused on the reassuring taste of alcohol, the thick coat it put on her tongue like gold plating.

"What would the doctor think, more importantly?" Harris said, who then adopted the tone of the young doctor. "Not in terms of bad and good, please," he said, a fair imitation of Dr. Grind, "only kind and unkind."

"Well, this bourbon is kind, that's for sure," Ellen said, giggling, none of them really trying to keep their voices down in the courtyard, not caring about the other couples who wanted a good night's sleep before tomorrow.

"How different will it be, really?" Kenny said. "I know it's important; it's the most important thing, I guess, but I can't wrap my head around what it will actually feel like."

The men and women got quiet, allowed themselves the momentary lapse of imagining the future, and then collectively refilled their glasses, regardless of how much they actually wanted or needed.

Izzy was too smart to say it aloud, but she had an idea of what it would feel like, the way that giving something a name, whatever that name was, changed the way you felt when you touched it. She considered all the hugs and kisses that had come before, and how this would inevitably be different because the contact would expand their idea of the world. What had been known as one thing would become another thing. It would be terrifying and thrilling and, if she had her wish granted, worth everything that had come before.

Now, sitting in the classroom, all of them uncomfortably positioned on the floor because the chairs were too small for adult bodies, they waited for Dr. Grind to appear. There were nineteen of them, their names and faces so familiar to Izzy that she actually did think of them as her brothers and sisters, or, at the very least, as her extended family. However she defined them, she felt an intimacy with these people that never touched desire, thank god. There were nine couples and then Izzy, who came to the group alone. The others assumed she would meet someone, eventually marry, but Izzy had not considered it. There was something more important at stake, Dr. Grind always reminded them. They had to be fluid and open and no longer dependent on the expectations of their former lives, before they had come together.

In this cheery, brightly colored room, Izzy tried to focus, tried to ignore the creeping feeling that she was not just hungover, but was actively ill, in danger of, at any moment, throwing up on her shoes and ruining the moment. She willed herself into a position of strength, which was her greatest talent, how she steeled her weaknesses into something that could protect her and those around her.

Dr. Grind finally appeared, a weak smile on his face, as if his own happiness made him embarrassed just in case other people weren't in a good mood and had to witness it. He was dressed in a white short-sleeve dress shirt with a red tie, gray slacks, and gray running shoes. It was a good look for him, his constant uniform. It wasn't so stiff as to seem scientific or eggheaded and not so rumpled and absentminded that she worried about placing her trust in him. He was comfortable and clean. He looked much younger than his thirty-four years, childlike but serious. Was it any wonder, as he shuffled into the room, that Izzy was possibly in love with him?

"I'm not going to spend a lot of time talking about family and our purposes here and all that stuff we talk about all the time," he said. Julie, who was also showing severe signs of a hangover, started to cry, and both Dr. Grind and her husband quickly leaned over to comfort her. She apologized, gathered herself, and the doctor stood up again to address the group.

"It's a lot to process, no matter how much time you've spent thinking about it. I'll let you guys move to the selected rooms and you'll wait for the kids. Now, be prepared. As momentous as this is for you, these are five-year-olds and it will not be as momentous for them. Just remember that the important thing is not what happens today, but what happens after, for the rest of our lives, okay? You'll have about thirty minutes, maybe a little more, and then the kids have a nature walk today, and we'll have to round them up. Just remember, everybody," he said, holding up his hands as if to show that there was no big secret here, nothing he was withholding from them. "Your kids are wonderful and they love you and you love them and nothing that happens today changes that." He smiled again, now beaming with genuine affection, and then left the room. This was the power of Dr. Grind, always making meaningful speeches, always radiating kindness and capability, and then striding out of the room and leaving them alone again.

The staff met up with the adults and started leading them out of the classroom. One of the staff members, Roberto, who taught the children Spanish and was in charge of physical education classes, touched Izzy on the shoulder and gestured toward another room in the complex. She took a deep breath, took his offered hand, and stood up, ready for whatever came next.

She was in the dining hall, the big room empty and echoing. They had been instructed not to bring gifts, no pictures or candy or anything that might distract the children from the moment. But she wished she had something in her hands, something to occupy her nerves.

Of course she had seen him almost every day, had hugged him, had rocked him to sleep, but it would be different now. It would forever be different and yet, hopefully, the same as ever. She wished, not for the first time, that she had someone with her, a partner. Then, immediately, she shook off that hope; she wanted this moment just for herself, as it had always been, no one but her.

The door opened and Roberto looked in, flashed a thumbs-up sign, and Izzy nodded in response. Roberto disappeared from view and, suddenly, there he was. A little boy stood in the doorway. Her little boy. Her son.

He walked into the room, already waving, already smiling, but then stopped short when he saw her.

"Izzy?" he said, his face curious and open.

"Hi, Cap," she said, the shock of seeing him standing before her, just the two of them, almost too much to process.

"You're my mom?" he asked, tentative, afraid to come too close to her, which broke her heart in the places it had always been broken.

"I am, sweetie," she said, smiling.

"You made me?" he asked, moving a little closer to her.

"We all made you," she said, a mantra of the group, but she then added, "but I made you the most."

"Mom," he said, a statement of fact. He waved to her again and she waved back.

"I'm your mom," Izzy said, another statement of fact, holding her breath.

"Good," he finally said, smiling, and he stepped into her arms and let her hug him for what felt like the first time.

"It is good," she said, this boy in her arms, the son she had given up and yet managed to keep, the child she had not wanted and yet could not love more than she did.

"We are a family," he said, and she knew that he meant everyone, the other children, the other parents, Dr. Grind, but she pretended that he meant only the two of them.

"We are a family," she responded, still hugging him so tightly, "we are the best family in the whole wide world."

part
one

chapter one

Three hours after she had graduated from high school, Izzy sat on a park bench next to her art teacher, Mr. Jackson, and told him that she was pregnant. Despite the awkwardness of the confession, she felt a buzzing excitement that kept pushing against her dread. She had graduated from high school, had hated almost every minute of it; now she was on the other side and free, those four years simply a scar that would add character in the long run. She was wearing the best dress she owned, a thin summer dress from the Target in Murfreesboro, green and white, like the flag for some exotic African nation. It went well with her deep, crowded freckles; her light brown hair cut short for the ceremony; and her round, bright face. She looked better than she felt, and this gave her some kind of invincibility that she worried would crumble the minute it was put to the test.

She was holding the cap from graduation in her hands, playing with the tassel to help calm her nerves. When all the other students had thrown their caps into the air, she'd held on to hers for reasons she couldn't understand other than her inability to ever fully celebrate around other people. Happiness, she believed, was small and quiet and you expressed it when no one else was around. She had not, in fact, experienced enough of the emotion to support this firm belief that she held as fact.

Mr. Jackson had been her favorite teacher; he was in his thirties, had not yet entered into that phase of teaching when every other sentence was sarcastic and without genuine emotion. Before he'd come to Coalfield High School two years before, he'd been an actual artist, with an exhibition in Europe, and had the slightest degree of fame. He came from one of the richest families in the state. And, yet, here he was teaching dumbass kids at a nowhere high school, which made Izzy confused as to whether he was noble or stupid or, perhaps most important, damaged goods.

On the first day of Advanced Art, her senior year, he put an empty vase on a stepladder and asked the class if this vase was art. Most people said no. Then he put some flowers in it. "How about now?" he asked. Fewer people said no. He removed the flowers and then said, "What about if I urinated into the vase?" Nobody, including Izzy, said a word, but they certainly paid more attention to their teacher, who was wearing paint-spattered khakis and a worn, faded-blue chambray shirt, a pack of cigarettes in his front pocket. His face looked like an old-time movie star cowboy, lean and rugged but not from actual hard living. His close-cut hair was prematurely gray and made him seem even wiser. "The answer," he said to them, smiling, "is that everything is a work of art, kids." He then let the students offer examples to see if it passed his test. "What if you smashed it to pieces?" someone asked, and Mr. Jackson said that this was art. "What if you fucked it?" one of the stoner kids said, his friends making that awful "huh-huh-huh" sound that passed as laughter. "Especially then," Mr. Jackson replied.

Izzy, before she could even think about it, asked, "What if you didn't want it to be a work of art?"

He turned to her, his face open and inviting. "What do you mean?" he asked her, and she felt the embarrassment of having the entire class waiting for her to respond.

"What if you specifically told people that the vase was just a vase and not a work of art?"

Mr. Jackson's eyes seemed touched with sorrow, as if he understood exactly what she meant, and he seemed reluctant to say what came next. He continued to look at her, the silence growing palpable. "Even then, Izzy," he finally said, his shoulders softly shrugging, "I'm sorry to say that it would still be art."

It was then that she fell in love with him, the tenderness of his answer. In that moment, the future spilled out around her: she would become his secret lover; they would spend most of the entire year wrapped around each other; she would now be pregnant with his child.

"I'm pregnant," she said to Mr. Jackson, who had been sipping from a nostalgic glass bottle of grape soda. He went out of his way to find things that tasted better because they were rare. In response, he took the half-full bottle of soda and hurled it into the grass in front of them, the bottle breaking heavily into two pieces.

"That's not good, Izzy," he said, his head twisting to the side as if suddenly embarrassed, one of the warning signs that intense anger might follow.

"I know it's not good," Izzy told him, a little angry at his response. She had expected this, but she had hoped, deep down, that he would embrace her, tell her it would all be okay, and that they would be a happy family, the three of them. Hope, goddamn, she hated it, that tiny sliver of light that you believed could fill your heart. "I know it's not good," she repeated, "which is why I'm telling you, because the two of us made this happen, and now we need to figure out what to do."

"Are you sure?" he asked. The desperation and the cliché of it.

"I'm as sure as you can be without getting other people involved," she said. Five pregnancy tests, all stolen from the drugstore because they were more expensive than anything that depressing should ever be. Let the people who wanted a baby pay for them.

He was twitching like a cornered animal. Even now she felt a tenderness for him. She touched his shoulder, and with that, the slightest pressure against his body, he cracked open and began to cry, deep sobs like someone had dropped a boulder onto his chest. Izzy dropped her graduation cap and placed her hands on his face, willing him the strength to recover. It was confusing, she decided, which one of them needed more help. The point, she had realized quite some time ago, was that both of them needed help and how wonderful and lucky it would be if each could be the one who could save the other.

Mr. Jackson composed himself. His moods were a constantly shifting weather pattern. "I'm sorry," he said. "I'm making this about me, I understand that."

"It's okay, Hal," she said. "I understand."

As if electrocuted by a hidden truth, his posture became rigid, and he stared into her eyes. "Is this why you still refuse to go to college?" he asked.

Why was it impossible to focus on the pregnancy? Izzy wondered. Was it so hard to accept the fact that she had gotten pregnant because they had spent a fair amount of her senior year having sex and that now the obvious problems of this pregnancy needed to be addressed, one way or the other? Did they need to bring other elements into this already combustible situation, just to see how they might interact?

"It has nothing to do with that," she replied, removing her hands from his face, remembering that they were in public. "I never wanted to go to college, I've told you a million times. You thought I should go to college, but I never considered it. The baby is just our own singular bad luck."

"Okay, okay, fine," he said, waving her off. "Okay, let's just think." He paused. He reached into the backpack at his feet and produced a greeting card envelope. "I got you a graduation card," he said, holding it out for her.

She slapped it out of his hand. "The baby, Hal. Jesus. Can we talk about the baby?"

"Is it a boy or a girl?" he asked, his face so open and sad.

Once again, she felt dizzy. It was so strange, how tenderness and mania could exist in one imperfect body.

"I have no idea," she said. "I think it's too early for anything like that."

"What do we do, then?" he asked, and Izzy was relieved to see that he was finally addressing the issue, the elephant in the womb.

"I know what I want to do," she said, "but what do *we* want to do?" She wanted, the minute the first test came back positive, to find some way to keep the baby, to raise the baby, to transform her unbelievably dim life into something beautiful because of this baby. But to say that out loud, to say it to Mr. Jackson, to Hal, seemed beyond her. She could not remember the last time she had asked for something and been anything other than disappointed. This time, she would keep her intentions hidden and see if they were granted as if by magic.

"That's unfair," he said. "Why can't we just talk about what we want to do, honestly?"

"We can. I just want you to go first."

Mr. Jackson looked down at the card again, lying in the grass at their feet. It was as if the answer was written on the inside of that card. "There's fifty dollars in there for you," he said.

"C'mon now."

"I'm just saying we need to remember to get it before we leave," he said. He stared out at the empty park, a pathetic excuse for a park, just a few benches, lots of trees, and a walking trail that had not been kept in walking order. They had met here dozens of times over the past year, one time, though not the time that created this baby, having sex on this very bench in the middle of the night. The recklessness of their actions, Izzy now considered; how had they not expected some kind of reckoning?

"All things considered," Mr. Jackson finally said, drawing out each word, searching her face for emotion or guidance, "we should probably think really hard about . . ." He paused and took a deep breath. "We should probably think about not . . ." He again looked for any sign from her, but she was good at this, was as skilled as a robot at hiding her emotions. "Well, we should probably just go ahead . . . and just have this fucking baby, I guess."

It was the least romantic, least touching way that the sentiment could have been delivered, but Izzy, at this point, was willing to accept it in any form. She did not need a heartfelt and life-affirming speech about their destiny together. She needed this baby, for reasons she was still hoping to understand. She needed this baby, and he had given it to her, again.

She kissed him, pressed her body as close to him as physics would allow, holding on to that kiss as if to keep any possible reconsiderations at bay. She let that kiss linger, forgetting, or really just ignoring, the fact that they were in public and they were a secret couple. Or perhaps that didn't matter anymore, the secrecy. Pretty soon, she would be showing and he would be holding her hand in public and things would simply take care of themselves. She felt, in that quick moment, her entire life bend and shift by such a number of degrees that she felt nauseous from the new possibilities. She was, fuck it, as happy as she might ever be.

"What do we do now?" he asked.

"Let's go see a movie," she said, bending down to pick up the graduation card. She ripped it open and, without reading the card, produced the two twenties and single ten. "I'll pay for it," she offered, still smiling.

They drove for forty-five minutes into Georgia, their typical routine for any kind of public date, a habit they had no desire to break just yet. Izzy's father would expect her to be out with her friends, unaware that she had none, to celebrate graduation, so she could be out late tonight without consequence. Izzy was not someone to show much affection, hated the obviousness of any romantic action that didn't take place in private, but she kept resting her hand on Hal's leg as he accelerated the car to where they wanted to go. She tried to focus on the good while keeping a realistic view of the possible disaster heading their way.

Hal had not said a single word since they got into the car. His jaw was tight and sometimes his lips pulled away from his teeth like a cornered dog showing its fangs, one of his nervous habits. Hal was a series of nervous habits, each one working in an ever-increasing symphony of compulsion. Sometimes his neck twitched, sometimes he bared his fangs, sometimes he shouted nonsense in ragged bursts of breath, sometimes his muscles stiffened so violently that it seemed as if he was having a seizure, sometimes he smashed his head into walls without warning. Izzy's job was to try to anticipate these tics and direct them toward some goal. Usually, that was sex. Tonight, it was a movie. Whatever it was, she needed it to happen before he got too worked up.

Though it was still early and she wasn't about to ruin the satisfaction of Hal's allowance of the pregnancy, there had been no discussion about how they would make this happen. There had been no talk of moving in together. No talk of making their relationship known to the town, though it seemed impossible to keep it hidden much longer. There had been no talk of marriage, as strange as that discussion would be. She had hoped that perhaps some of these issues would be handled here, in the car, on the way to the movies, but Hal was working himself into a state of agitation. She simply stared ahead and hoped that, as the miles accumulated, they would find themselves changed.

Izzy had been a straight-A student in high school, so whip smart, seemingly without effort, that the teachers simply forgot about her. She showed so little enthusiasm for the subjects that her perfect scores on every test were seen as an anomaly and the teachers focused instead on the smart enough students who begged for attention. From her junior year until graduation, the guidance counselors assured her that she could receive a full ride to any of the state universities, but she informed them, politely, quietly, that she had no interest. She was smart and she wasn't apologetic about it, but the studying and the memorization tore something loose in her each time, the fear that she was devoting her life to something that did not entirely interest her and would, ultimately, disappoint her. She imagined herself at a job making only slightly more than the minimum wage, as fucked as if she hadn't spent four more years in school. Maybe, if things didn't work out, she allowed, she would try community college, but for now she would continue to live with her father and keep working in the kitchen at the Whole Hog BBQ, which she'd been doing since she was fourteen. It was, she had to tell herself almost every single morning and every single night, a good enough life.

And then, Hal Jackson had appeared, or had at least made himself known to her, and, while she didn't dream of altering her future for him, she allowed for an alteration to her present. She'd gone to him after school one day, a month after he had first shown signs of tenderness toward her, and had laid out her plan for him. The problem was this: She knew that she was the top student in the senior class. She had a perfect GPA, the highest average, and she did not skimp on the few AP courses the school offered, even if she had no intention of going to college. The problem, she now realized, was that the valedictorian, shit, even the salutatorian, had to give a speech at graduation. She could not do this. She could not imagine what that speech would sound like coming from her stunned lips. What could she possibly say that wouldn't draw unnecessary and unpleasant attention her way?

Mr. Jackson had not understood the problem. "Just flunk a few classes," he said. "I can't do that," she informed him. When he asked why not, she couldn't give a satisfactory answer. "I guess I just can't do it that way," she finally said. "I have some pride, I'm finding out." Mr. Jackson asked what he could do about it then. "You could fail me," she responded, smiling.

"Actually, I'm going to give you an A plus just on the first month alone."

"But I want you to fail me. I'm asking you to fail me."

"Well, I just won't do it," he responded, folding his arms over his chest.

"If you don't fail me," she said, "I'll just stop trying in your class."

"So you will fail on purpose?" he asked.

She knew that she had walked into a trap, though she wasn't sure who had set it. "I guess I will, yeah."

"Do you understand why I'm confused?"

She nodded. She wasn't asking him to understand; she was asking him to help her. "I don't want to give that speech. I don't want people to look at me. I don't want them to wonder why I'm the valedictorian and I'm not even going to college."

"Wait, why aren't you going to coll—" he began to question, but she cut him off.

"The point is, I'm asking you to help me. You're my favorite teacher, the best teacher I've ever had, and I'm asking you to please help me. I'll do my very best in your class and you'll give me an F and everything will be fine."

She could tell that he had no idea what was going on. She watched the confusion and consternation disappear from his face with such suddenness that she was afraid of him for a brief moment.

"Okay," he said. "I'll do it."

"Thank you," she almost shouted. "Thank you so much, Mr. Jackson."

"But I won't fail you. I can't do that. I'll give you a D. I'll give you a D minus even, but I'm not flunking you." He smiled, and she felt, again, the warmth of his kindness.

Without thinking, or perhaps thinking so forcefully that she made her fantasies come true, she put her arms around him and kissed him. When it was over, something entirely new having begun, he looked into her eyes and she smiled without reservation.

"Congratulations," he said. "For reasons beyond me, you are no longer the smartest person in this school."

"It's nice to hear," she said. "It feels so good to hear that."

In Georgia, Izzy used some of the money from the graduation card to purchase two tickets for a movie that was so layered and complicated that it offered, according to reviews, at least three mind-blowing twists in the first hour. She chose it because she hoped the difficulty of the plot would force Hal to focus on the movie instead of the pregnancy. Of course, it could backfire and he would completely ignore the movie and simply vibrate with anxiety about his role, past, present, and future, in Izzy's condition.

She ordered a bucket of soda so the sugar would keep them alert.

She assumed that caffeine and sugar were bad for the child but it was so early in the pregnancy that she believed there must be some kind of grace period. It had been hard, in this first week after realizing that she was pregnant, to think of the baby as a thing separate from herself. She kept imagining the baby as simply some newly discovered muscle or bone in her body and that it didn't require any alteration in her lifestyle. She did not want to acknowledge that the baby would demand attention to her own body in order to keep it safe. Throughout her adolescence, she treated her body as a damned vessel that she would pilot until it exploded or sank, without any upkeep or care. Once she paid for the soda, she asserted her belief in a grace period and took a long, satisfied sip, fighting back the hiccups that came immediately after. Hal, either in solidarity with Izzy or simply working himself into a smaller and smaller box within his mind, did not say a thing about the soda.

They found seats directly in the middle of the theater, space all around them, and Hal immediately took out his cell phone and popped the battery out of it. He was terrified of being a public nuisance, the mere idea of his phone ringing during a movie making him so scared that he did not trust even the act of turning it off. To suggest setting the phone to vibrate would send him, she imagined, into a fit. He handed the battery to Izzy, who had left her own phone in the car, prepared for this phobia of Hal's. She put it in her purse so as to keep the phone and battery as far apart as possible. Still, fidgeting in his seat, Hal next removed his wallet and change and lip balm and placed them all at his feet with the hollowed-out cell phone. For anything that required relaxation, Hal had explained to Izzy that he needed to do a fair amount of prep work to even consider the prospect, and she was as fine with it as a person could be, because she actually liked watching the way, as he literally stripped the distractions from his body, that he gradually calmed himself. It was like viewing some strange, unsanctioned form of yoga. He handed his ring of keys to Izzy because they would make a jangly sound if his feet accidentally touched them on the floor. Now, his pockets emptied of objects, finally free to focus on the movie, he kissed Izzy on the cheek, the first sign of affection since they'd left the park. Just then, two young men shuffled into the seats directly behind them, jostling her seat as they sat down. She registered Hal's irritation, the fact that any stranger would choose to be near another stranger, but he calmed just as the previews came on, and she watched the green glow of the screen reflect across Hal's face and his eyes widen with anticipation. Whatever came next, his body seemed to suggest to her, he was ready.

Once Izzy and her teacher became a couple, in perhaps the loosest form of that word, her understanding of him both expanded and deflated in the most thrilling of ways. He was as kind and as funny and as knowledgeable as he seemed in class; the things she found to be interesting about him in that hour of class each day compounded and became solid. His considerable monetary wealth, a never-ending trust fund from his parents, gave him access to a world that Izzy found bizarre, even if she didn't get to actively participate in it. She could not accompany him to Nashville for gala benefits for the Tennessee Arts Commission. She could not travel to Belgium for the week of spring break for the singular purpose of attending the opening of a famous artist's exhibition. She could, however, hear about these things, the casual way that he mentioned these amazing occurrences, the casual way he accepted the fact of them. He was a high school art teacher and yet he was a millionaire bon vivant. It made him as close to a superhero with a secret identity that she could ever hope to know.

Being his lover, god, the awfulness of that word, the refusal on Izzy's part to think of herself as anything other than his *pal,* as if she was in a 1930s comic strip, she also gained access to the secret diminishments of his life. He was a high school art teacher because his art career had dissolved almost immediately. He was not talented, he readily admitted, his famed European exhibition having been only a single painting displayed alongside a dozen others in a government building in London, and he was teaching only because his parents had forced him, after his aborted attempt to become a serious artist, to attend college and actually do something with his adult life. He was, he believed, a failure, albeit an insanely wealthy failure thanks to his family's fortune. More troubling to Izzy, although she also found it soothing in some strange ways, was his obvious mental health issues, bouts of extreme depression offset by incredibly manic periods. All of this was supposedly controlled by medicine and therapy, but he sometimes ignored both and seemed to dare himself to fall into craziness. It was not immediately noticeable at school, his classes strange and offbeat even when he was in the best state of mind, but as she spent more and more time with him, especially in his private moments, she noticed the signs of instability and found herself shocked by the force of them. Some nights, after she had slipped away from her house or from the restaurant, she would drive to his farmhouse, acres of privacy yet she still had to park her barely running truck in the garage just in case, and find him slightly drunk and already bemoaning the awful fact that this illicit affair was ruining her and further ruining him.

"I'm doing my best here," he once told her, "but I feel like, no matter how this plays out, I'll make you hate the world."

She kissed him, flipped through the complete series of Criterion Collection movies that he owned, films stranger than porn to her, and she said, "I already hated the world. You make me hate it less."

Sometimes she could snap him out of it, but other times, when the depression turned into something more combustible, he would reach for whatever was close and smash it against the stone floors of his house. He would break things until the world was tiny and jagged and understandable again to him. Then he would grow sheepish and try to clean it up. The next time she was at his house, it never failed, he would stroll barefoot through the house and then wince when he stepped on a tiny shard of pottery or glass or plastic that his broom or vacuum had not found. These moments gave her pleasure, to watch the reminders of his behavior bite into him. She always, always, wore her shoes in that house.

Her own mother, who had died of heart failure when Izzy was thirteen, had been undiagnosed and unmedicated but so terrified of the world by the end of her life that she would not, except on the rarest of occasions, leave the house. Izzy was so used to mental instability she began to assume that everyone except herself suffered from it. Hal's psychological problems were not a surprise but rather the eventual revelation of what she already knew. He was artistic; he was a failure in developing his artistic abilities; he taught at a public high school; he was in love with her, an eighteen-year-old girl; of course he was crazy. Sometimes she believed she was immune to psychosis, that she had spent so much time in its presence that she had built up defenses against it. And then she saw the multiple positive pregnancy tests, and she felt the strange, sweeping panic of unchecked emotion, and she knew that she had been foolish to believe that she, tiny and ridiculous, was anything close to invincible.

The movie was as complicated as advertised, so twisty that Izzy felt her mind constantly juggling the possible motives of the characters, never able to consider one long enough before she had to deal with another. The two guys behind Izzy and Hal had spent a good portion of the movie discussing, in voices just below a conversational volume, their theories as to what might happen next.

"That dude is bad, bet on it," one of them said.

"They want you to think that dude is bad so that, like, when the real bad guy shows up, you won't notice."

"That's why he'll end up actually being bad, just to blow your goddamned mind."

Hal, who had been twisting a napkin into tiny, sweat-dampened bits of confetti, finally turned to the guys and said, "Could you guys not talk about this, please?"

"Sorry, man," one of the guys said, and Izzy quickly grabbed Hal's hand and gave it a reassuring squeeze. Even in the dim light, she could see him force a tight smile for her benefit. Five minutes later, the two men started up again as if nothing had happened.

"His car is gonna run out of gas, bet on it," one of them said, a little louder than before, as a matter of fact. "Why show the needle of the gas gauge unless he's going to run out of gas later?"

"Well, of course it's going to run out of gas, shit, man, that's a given."

Hal turned around again and whispered, his voice cracking a little with exasperation, "Guys? Could you not talk?"

"Why don't you and your daughter move to another seat if it's bothering you so much, man?"

Hal, his twitchiness and anxiety sometimes obscuring the fact that he was solid and fairly tall, stood up and turned to face the still-seated men. "Why don't I fucking move you guys out of the fucking theater," he said.

"C'mon, Hal," Izzy said, immediately pulling on his arm, which he snatched from her grip. "Let's just move." She tried to calm him while knowing, the way he kept snapping his head to the side, that he was already well on his way toward that frightening stage of his mania, where he smashed something into tiny pieces.

"Jesus, man, relax," one of the men said, smirking. "We're sorry, okay? We'll shut up."

Izzy leaned toward Hal and said, "Let's get the heck out of here, please?"

Hal kissed her and then turned back to the movie. "I cannot fucking figure this thing out to save my life."

Less than a minute later, just enough time to believe that order had been restored, disaster narrowly averted, the man sitting behind Hal kicked viciously at the back of the seat. As if coiled in anticipation of this very action, Hal snapped around and punched the man squarely in the face. The man recoiled from the impact and slumped in his seat, stunned by the act. Before the other man could even react, Hal had jumped over the seats and was on top of him; they were wrestling and Hal kept grabbing for leverage while the man shouted, "Take it easy. Take it easy, man. Take it easy."

Izzy didn't realize it, but she was pounding on Hal's back, trying to get him to disengage from the fight, to get his feet moving out of the theater. "Please, Hal, we have to go."

By now, the rest of the audience was turned to watch the fight. "You had to be a fucking asshole, didn't you? Like the world isn't already full of fucking assholes," Hal said, his voice still barely above a whisper, as if trying to be courteous to everyone else. Izzy nearly fell over the back of her seat trying to maintain her grip on Hal's shirt. "Come on," she said. "Let's go."

Finally, Hal pulled away after he managed to land a single punch to the man's ear, which made him howl in pain. Izzy pulled Hal down the aisle, out of the theater, not stopping to look around. The pocket on Hal's shirt was nearly ripped off, and the knuckles on his right hand were as red as raw meat, but, otherwise, there was no immediate sign of a fight on his person. No one was yet following them out of the darkened theater. They moved swiftly but calmly out of the building, past the concessions, past the ticket taker, into the parking lot. Izzy tossed the keys to Hal and they sped onto the main road, putting traffic between them and the fucking calamity that they had made.

After nearly ten minutes of uneasy silence, both of them breathing so hard and their bodies radiating so much heat that the windows constantly fogged, Hal finally said, "Are you okay?"

Izzy was still unable to speak. She just nodded, not able to look at Hal.

"I'm sorry," he said, and his foot touched the accelerator at this same moment and the car kicked forward. "Everything hit at once. I need things to hit in a sequence and things just hit all at once. I don't know how to handle myself sometimes."

"How is your hand?" she finally asked.

"It hurts, actually. I'm not going to say that I haven't punched someone before, but I don't think I've ever punched two people in the same fight. The human hand is not made for that kind of activity." He was trying to lighten the mood in the car, but Izzy would not let him. This was what always happened, the tension ratcheting up until Hal exploded and then, a mess made, he grew sheepish and conciliatory. He grew self-deprecating, not quite self-loathing, and he hoped that his renewed good humor would save the day.

"That was bad, Hal," she told him. "That was awful to see."

Hal didn't respond, just kept driving. After a few minutes, he said, "I'll be a good father, Izzy. I'll do every single thing you ask in order to be good to you. I fuck up, I know that, but I always clean up after myself."

Izzy was shocked to remember that she was pregnant, had forgotten for a few moments that a baby was inside her and waiting to make itself known to the world. She had, in that rush of violence and activity, simply been a girl who was struggling to keep up with the awful shit around her. It was familiar and she fell into it without hesitation. Now she put her hand on her stomach and felt nothing on the other side.

"Cleaning up after yourself is not the same as fixing things," she said. "It's not the same thing, Hal."

"I love you, Izzy," he said. Izzy did not like this phrase and was both upset and weakened to hear it from Hal. Her family did not say things like this and she had worked so hard to believe that it was something that she did not need. She did not value love nearly as much as she valued kindness, not knowing if they were the same thing.

"You have to try harder," she said, and Hal nodded. "More therapy. Constant medicine."

"I will," he said, his voice getting high and quick with the anticipation of forgiveness. "I will do everything to make us happy."

"You can't punch people in the face just because they're rude."

"Shit," Hal said. "That was bad."

"Well, it finally pays off that we go on dates in a different state."

"You said it," he said, and she knew that he was relaxing now. She was giving in to him, and she did not try to fight it as hard as she knew she should. He was a mess, nothing but imperfections, but he was still the most perfect thing she had ever touched. She did not need him, she told herself, but she wanted him, and so she would make the adjustments necessary to keep him.

"I better stop to get gas," he said, pulling off the highway into a gas station. As he stepped out to fill up the car, Izzy walked toward the lit-up station. "I'm going to get a soda," she said, wondering if it was better for the baby to drink regular or diet, still needing the fizz and burst of soda in her belly. "You want anything?" she asked. He shook his head and smiled. "Just come back," he said.

When she walked back to the car, taking deep sips of the bottle of soda, she saw Hal slumped against the car, crying. She dropped the soda. "What?" she shouted, now running to Hal. "What? What?"

He looked up at her, his eyes so red that it seemed a movie special effect. He held out his hands, empty. "My wallet," he stuttered. Izzy immediately felt a sickness start in her belly and paralyze her limbs.

"I left my wallet in that theater," he said and then shrugged.

His wallet, his driver's license, his credit cards, sitting untouched on the floor of the movie theater. She could see the way things would play out, were probably already playing out, the discovery of the wallet, the decision, easy enough, to press charges, the way things would get smashed apart. "God, I fucked up," he said.

"It's okay," Izzy said, stroking his hair, uncaring about what anyone at the gas station might be thinking. "It's going to be okay."

"This is bad," he said. "Everything is so fucking bad."

"No, it's not," she said, but she found that she could not muster up the force that the statement required.

Hal gathered himself, readjusted his body so that he was now kneeling, so that he could better see her. "I can't do this," he finally said.

"It'll be okay," she said.

"I don't want the baby," he said, almost breaking down again when he said the last word. "I can't do it."

"Okay," Izzy said quickly, just trying to get him to stop talking. "Okay, okay, okay."

"You deserve so much better, Izzy," he said, and she didn't even believe him for one second. She didn't deserve a fucking thing, she believed, but she would take what she could have. She reached for him and held him loosely in her arms.

What was the worst that would happen to him, rich and connected? Probation, probably, certainly not jail. Maybe another stint in a very expensive mental health facility, one where he got to wear his own clothes and have trips into town. How could he not hold it together for her? She could take anything if he had not mentioned the baby. Of course he was unfit; of course he didn't want it. She wished he was able to keep those doubts to himself and soldier on. She felt her life disentangling from him, all the tendrils being tweezered apart, leaving bruises that she knew would never heal.

"I'm a mess," he said, and she kissed him and then stood up, reached into her purse for the rest of the money from her graduation card, and walked back into the station to pay for the gas.

She would pay the man behind the counter, pump the gas, and then drive Hal back to the park, to her own truck. She would kiss him, and, as he drove away to wait for his own singular fate, she would sit on that park bench and she would play with the graduation cap and she would freak out in private, so hard and so long, until she had emptied everything inside her except the one thing that mattered, the only thing she wanted anymore. Let one person tell her she couldn't have it and she would claw them into submission. Let one more person tell her what she could and could not have, and she would smile, nod, and, without apology, do whatever the hell she wanted.

chapter two

Izzy stood over a hog that was split nearly in two, its skin so reddish-brown that it looked like the finest leather. Wearing thick rubber gloves, she reached into the pig and pulled the meat from its bones, her hands shaking, some bits of pork somehow getting into the inside of her gloves, steaming against her skin. It took every bit of strength she had to fight the nausea, the morning sickness that swirled inside her. The smell of smoked meat, she had determined, ruined her now, and it angered her that weakness crept into her body and kept her from doing one of the few things she was so good at.

She wasn't showing yet; she was tall, five feet nine inches, and skinny, and she hoped she could hold on to the familiar dimensions of her body for as long as possible. Still, even if nothing showed on her frame, something fierce was assembling itself inside her. The morning sickness spilled over into the afternoons most days, and she found a constant, buzzing irritation spiking her interactions with her father, not even close to recognizing her new state. She believed, in the most secret parts of her mind, that she could hide the pregnancy from everyone for the entire duration, simply appear one day holding a baby that people assumed she conjured up with a magic spell. Now, however, another wave of nausea washing over her, her gloved hands slippery with pig fat and juices, she realized how stupid she could be sometimes.

When she first started at the Whole Hog, she was a waitress, navigating the tables while balancing a tray filled with bucket-size glasses of sweet tea. She hated every second of it, but she needed the money, the tossed-off tips, almost always a mere 10 percent of the check. She didn't pretend that she was a good waitress; she was too shy to check her tables often enough, believing that she was always a nuisance when she stopped by to ask if anyone needed more tea, more food, or the check. She did not like being witnessed while in possession of someone else's food. The owner had given her the job as a favor to her father; the rest of the waitstaff was comprised of Mr. Bonner's daughters and nieces. And she was truly grateful for the work and steeled herself to smile more, to be charming, to flirt with the farmers and factory workers who wanted young girls to serve them giant plates of pulled pork so they could call them *sweetie* and *honey* and *baby doll*.

On her breaks, however, while the other girls went off to smoke or to talk on their cell phones, Izzy would hide in the kitchen and watch Mr. Tannehill, the seventy-year-old man who worked the smoker, prepare the pigs. She watched him rub down the lifeless carcasses of the pigs with a simple mixture of salt and pepper, watched him somehow hoist these beasts onto the smoker, and watched him mop the skin with a prehistoric-looking implement before finally tearing the pig apart into something so delicious that it was not food but a miracle. The men and boys hired to assist Mr. Tannehill were shiftless and transitory, doing the bare minimum to earn a paycheck, and so Izzy, inching closer and closer to the action over a period of months, found herself, on occasion, the recipient of Mr. Tannehill's clipped, specific instructions. He seemed pleased with the serious way she obeyed his orders, the fact that he only had to tell her something once and then she never forgot it. Sometimes, as the actual pit boys sat on a stool and read a magazine, Izzy would go over her allotted break and one of the other waitresses would yell for her to get back to work. One time, she heard Mr. Tannehill mumble under his breath when she had been summoned, "Damn it all." It thrilled her, to be of use and to be good at it. Some days she would come to work before school started or stay an hour or two after her shift had ended and simply sit by the smoker with Mr. Tannehill, neither of them speaking, tending to the fire, maintaining the exact heat that gave the pork its singular flavor.

Once a year had passed and three successive pit boys had either quit or been fired, Izzy asked Mr. Tannehill if she could take the job. He talked to Mr. Bonner, who needed convincing, but soon it was just Mr. Tannehill and Izzy in the back room, left alone to handle the pigs, alchemists in a dungeon, two lonely people who understood meat better than other people.

Izzy felt a gagging sensation stall in her throat, and she hunched over the hog and tried to reclaim her bearings. Mr. Tannehill finally spoke up, his eyes barely visible beneath the brim of his baseball cap, "You feeling poorly?"

She shook her head and then, knowing it was no use to lie, thought up a lesser lie. "Hungover," she said. She watched Mr. Tannehill wince at the admission, and she remembered, too late, the story of the man's past, his own restaurant in North Carolina, written up in magazines by enthusiasts of barbecue, and the ruin his drinking had brought down on the establishment. Still, no other choice seemingly available to her, she soldiered on. "I drank too much last night, I guess."

"Not a good habit," he said, "but sometimes a necessary one." He stood beside her and then lightly shoved her out of the way, his ancient hands, no need for gloves, tearing the meat apart. "Drink some water," he told her, and she did, running the tap and slurping from her cupped hands. She felt the water stabilize her nausea, but she hung back from the hog and its inescapable scent. Recently, she had to start washing her hair twice, scrubbing furiously, to get the smoke and fat out of her hair so that she could sleep in some state of calm.

"I'm better," she said, and she then took her place beside him, quickly working the meat from the carcass, their hands never once reaching for the same spot. Once they had finished, Mr. Tannehill cleaned the innards, saving them for the dishes that certain old-timers requested from off the menu. Izzy took a cleaver in each hand and started to chop the meat into a uniform size and consistency. She found a rhythm as the cleavers hit the wood, the knives an extension of her desires, never once betraying her. She wiped her blades clean on her apron and then sat on an overturned empty bucket of vinegar, wondering how she was going to make it through seven and a half more months of this.

"Looks good," Mr. Tannehill said to her, not smiling, but his soft tone was kind enough to show his appreciation. He once said that, aside from him and Mr. Sammy, who ran the black-owned barbecue restaurant in Coalfield and worked exclusively with ribs and chicken, that Izzy was the best barbecue person in town. She once mentioned that the two of them should do a barbecue competition, head over to Memphis in May and show them how it was done. "Too much stress for me," he said. "I don't like competition. I like to cook the pig the way it's supposed to be cooked and not worry about anything else. You get to be my age, Izzy, you just want peace and quiet." Izzy sometimes felt aged beyond her years, and it made her feel inauthentic and silly, but she could understand Mr. Tannehill's desire for solitude, to simply be allowed to do what you loved without interference.

And now, once again, she wanted to throw up. She ran out of the kitchen, into the bathroom, and dry-heaved herself rigid. She listened to make sure that no one had heard or was coming to check on her. She sat on the closed lid of the toilet and rested her head in her hands, so tired already, the uphill climb of each day since the pregnancy.

She had not heard from Hal since the night of graduation. All she had to go on were the imperfect rumors in town, but she was willing to settle for these as long as they had the slightest hint of truth. The police, apparently, had paid him a visit that same night, thanks to the wallet he'd left in the theater. It seemed either he had the charges dismissed or he was given probation, more people were saying probation. Her name was never mentioned and she was both relieved and slightly surprised by this fact; it was strange how, in such a small town, everyone seemed to know your business and yet Izzy had been carrying on an affair with her art teacher and was pregnant with his child and not a single person was the wiser. It was a testament to her cautiousness or her simple invisibility.

Hal was now spending the rest of the summer in the Northeast; his parents had sent him away to a facility to recuperate once again. She waited for a letter from him, a phone call, but none came. Either he was so dulled with medicine that he had forgotten about her or, more likely, he was ashamed of everything, the fight, the pregnancy, the affair, and he was trying to make her, the constant reminder of his bad decisions, disappear. She wanted to hear his voice, to have some reassurance that he cared for her. And, though it was crass and she did not want to think about it too much, she would have appreciated some gesture on his part, even if it was merely financial, that would help her get through this pregnancy, to show that he understood his complicit role in her current predicament. Was it so awful to hope that, having been impregnated by the wealthiest bachelor in town, Izzy could at least have the luxury of not going elbow deep in pig carcasses all summer? But there was only silence where there was once Hal, and so she focused on the baby, thinking about it all the time, hoping that it would not make itself known before she was ready to reveal it.

The next day Izzy woke up to hear her father in the kitchen, banging around for something to eat that would soak up the alcohol from the night before. She looked at her clock and saw that it was six o'clock in the morning; she pulled the covers over her head and wallowed in her misery. A few minutes later, her father walked into the room, eating a Pop-Tart, shaking her exposed foot to wake her.

"Dad, please. I need sleep," she said.

"When did you get home?" he asked.

"Late."

"I didn't even notice you come in," he replied. He had been passed out in his easy chair, the TV volume eight clicks too loud, when she crept into the house. Ever since her mother died, her father had slept on the couch, in the easy chair, or sometimes on the front porch when it was warm enough. The bedroom had turned into his closet, a place he entered only to change clothes.

"Well, you got something in the mail," he said, tossing a letter onto the bed. "Return address is some city in Massachusetts. Who you know in Massachusetts?"

Izzy quickly propped herself up in the bed, staring at the envelope. There was no name on the return address, but she knew it was Hal. The morning sickness turned into a solid chunk of stone, a temporary relief.

"It's just a friend. She's at a camp up there," Izzy said. Her father, true to form, asked no further questions. With her father out of her room, Izzy still held the secret of her pregnancy within her.

She opened the letter, ripping the envelope nearly in half, which momentarily distracted her, as if she'd ruined a keepsake. Inside the envelope were two sheets of unlined white paper, with Hal's messy half-cursive, half-print handwriting in blue ink. When Izzy was eight, her mother taught her, forced her actually, to speed-read because of her love for John F. Kennedy, who was a proponent of speed-reading. Even though Izzy found it to be less than what her mother had promised, the practice was now ingrained, and it took Izzy a considerable amount of time to adjust, to slow down and subvocalize and actually consider what Hal was telling her, no matter how painful it might be.

She had read the letter five times now and it did not change, which tore out something tiny and perfect in Izzy's heart. He loved her. He said this five times in the letter. He loved her more than anyone or anything else in the world. He was getting help and, though he had to be realistic about his situation, he thought it was going to help him function more easily in the world. He would be better to her, he promised. He wanted, and this lodged in her throat as she sounded it out, to marry her some-time in the near future, when he had proven to her that he was a good person. He had talked to his doctors and in his support meetings and he was pleased that they tentatively agreed with his assertions that Izzy was good for him, despite the age difference and the unfortunate circumstances of how they met. He would like to marry her and take his trust fund and go somewhere far from Tennessee and live happily with her for the rest of their lives. This was all on the first page and Izzy wished she could frame it or consume it or tattoo it on her skin. But. But there was that motherfucking second page.

He did not want Izzy to have the baby. He was not ready for kids, would probably never be able to handle the pressures of raising a child or, god help us, children. He wanted her, Izzy, and only her. He hoped that she trusted him and loved him enough to know that this was the right decision. They could be together, forever, but he could not handle the disappointment of how things had become ruined. Would she please agree to this? Would she write him back and let him know what was in her heart, if she understood how much he loved her and wanted everything to be good and perfect? He signed it *With Love* because of course he would, because who wouldn't say it again at the end after using it so frequently throughout the letter?

Her morning sickness, which had abated during her examination of the letter, returned in full force, mixed with her own dread for the future, and she scampered to the bathroom and dry-heaved until her neck muscles ached. This could not be normal, she thought, the morning sickness or her life. When she could stand, she got into the shower and let the hot water seep into her pores and wash away the rancid smell of pork. When she felt human, she brushed her teeth, got dressed, and then tried to imagine the rest of her day, standing over the smoker, the humidity of summer turning the smell of vinegar into something chemical and harmful. Once she lay back on the bed, Izzy understood that she could not face work, not with the letter now in her possession, her answer necessary to turn the future into the present. She understood that she needed to call in, to let Mr. Tannehill know that she wasn't going to make it into work, but the thought of that phone call, the embarrassment of disappointing him, kept her rooted to the bed. She closed her eyes and felt the ease of shutting out the world, however temporary. Sleep, the only space that did not refuse her, took over her body. Just an hour, she told herself, just two hours, just three hours, just a day, just two days, just a month, just nine months, just the rest of her life. That's all she would sleep for, the rest of her life.

When she finally awoke, it was eleven o'clock at night and she felt the strange exhilaration of having erased an entire day from her record. The problem was that now she was wide awake. Izzy listened to her heart beating inside her chest and she mistook it for the baby, wondered if there was a difference.

She rose from the bed and called out for her father, hearing no reply. Sometimes he played cards in the back of the market with some friends, drinking steadily until the next morning, when he simply took up his post once again behind the counter. She suddenly felt the claustrophobia of the house, the need to get outside it. But where could she go, what place would have her? She picked up her keys and walked outside, convinced that if she drove long enough, she would figure it out.

Izzy drove five miles per hour under the speed limit, with the freedom of having no particular destination and no one around to hurry her. After about thirty minutes of aimless cruising, she finally drove to the Whole Hog and idled in the parking lot before she cut the engine. She walked behind the restaurant, smoke forever rising from the chimney, and stared at Mr. Tannehill's trailer, which Mr. Bonner let him have rent free so that he could tend to the smoker at all hours. The trailer was dark, but she took a deep breath and allowed herself the rare luxury of intrusion, of needing someone. She knocked on the door and it was a full minute before Mr. Tannehill, still wearing his gray coveralls, appeared in front of her, his eyes wide at the sight of her. The only detail that suggested she had interrupted a private moment was that the front of his coveralls was unbuttoned enough that she could see a yellowing undershirt beneath it.

"What in the world are you doing here, Izzy?" he asked her, looking past her as if some irresponsible person had put her up to this.

"I'm in a bad situation, Mr. Tannehill," she said. "I don't know what to do."

Mr. Tannehill had an expression that suggested that he did not want to know her trouble but could not figure out how to politely deny her. Finally, he readjusted his baseball cap and then gestured toward the restaurant. "Well, come check the pig with me," he said, but she held up her hands and replied, "I better not. The smell of barbecue is making me sick these days."

Mr. Tannehill considered her and then shook his head. "That is a bad situation, then," he said. "Do you mind sitting on the steps here? I haven't had another person in this trailer since I moved in and it's a damn mess."

They situated themselves on the steps and Mr. Tannehill said, "I figured something was going on with you when you didn't turn up today. You've been out of sorts lately."

"I'm pregnant, Mr. Tannehill," she said.

"Oh lord, Izzy," he said, shaking his head. "I was hoping you just needed to borrow some money."

"I'm only a couple months along. I haven't told anybody else."

"Well, everybody else will find out soon enough, I reckon," he replied. They sat in silence; Mr. Tannehill took off his cap and held it in his hands, fiddling with the band.

"I'm really, really scared," Izzy said.

"I understand why, Izzy," he said. "It's a hard thing even in the best of situations." He paused, and she noticed that he was blushing, fighting with himself to be polite but to also be her friend. "I imagine," he said and then stuttered for a second before righting himself. "I imagine you know who the daddy is?"

"I do," she said.

"And he's gonna help out?" he asked, and Izzy shook her head.

"It doesn't seem like it," she said.

"And you," he stuttered again, and then coughed. "Sorry about this, but I'm just wondering if you still think you want to keep it."

"I do. I definitely do, however I can manage it."

"Fair enough," he replied. He looked at Izzy, his eyes the most unknowable shade of dark brown, not a flicker of emotion behind them. He reached for her and pulled her into an embrace, an awkward but generous hug. Izzy fell into it and closed her eyes.

"There are worse things in the world, Izzy," he said. "You're a good person and that baby will be lucky to have you. You'll be a good momma, you can bet on that."

She did not cry because she knew how embarrassed Mr. Tannehill would be to witness it. He had done her the kindness of this conversation, of his support for her desires, and she would not ask for more than that.

Having told another person, the burden of secrecy lightened by even an ounce, she could allow herself the expectation, however unsupportable, of a happy future. It made her, for the first time in weeks, ravenous. It made her want to eat the entire world and let whatever nutrients it held seep into her child. "I'm hungry," she said.

"Only thing here is barbecue," he said.

"I'll eat it," she said, staring down whatever made her sick.

They stood and walked to the back entrance of the restaurant. Mr. Tannehill made her sit at the card table while he heaped a plate with barbecue and topped it with two slices of white bread. He placed it in front of her and she asked him for the East Carolina–style barbecue sauce that no one in Coalfield seemed to prefer. Mr. Tannehill brought her a Styrofoam cup of the sauce and she built herself a disgusting sandwich, the bread soaked through with vinegar, and took such a large bite that it demolished what was left in her hands. She chewed and chewed, finally swallowing, and when she looked up from her plate, Mr. Tannehill was sitting across from her, smiling. "Eating for two now," he said.

"How many times do you think I'll have to hear that?" she asked him.

"More times than you want, I guarantee you that. Unwed pregnant girl, folks don't know how to talk to her in anything other than bland platitudes."

"This is gonna be hard," she said, not wanting reassurance, simply reminding herself of what she was getting herself into.

"You're tough," he said, and then he pushed away from the table and busied himself with wood and smoke.

She ate and ate and, only minutes after she had finished, she fell asleep at the table, listening to the faint sounds of Mr. Tannehill shuffling around the smoker, tending the fire, keeping all things in order.

chapter three

D r. Preston Grind stood in an unfamiliar forest, the buzzing of the natural world competing with the distant sound of construction that had intruded upon this space, which was to be Dr. Grind's new home for the foreseeable future. He carried his duffel bag over his shoulder, which held three identical outfits, a pair of sneakers, and a dopp kit, and he lugged a tote bag in his other hand, which held a laptop, a tablet, and three notepads. Holding the bags, it seemed like too much and too little at the same time, that for such an endeavor, he should either have nothing but the clothes on his back or one hundred steamer trunks packed with all sorts of unnecessary items.

At various times since he'd embarked on this new project, he felt like he was a pioneer, setting off into an unknown landscape that would either swallow him whole or come to bear his own name. Other times he felt like an astronaut about to board an experimental rocket ship to explore a galaxy that was only theoretically known to exist. And other times, when his loneliness and depression threatened to derail all the therapy and positive thinking, he felt like he was simply embarking on a project doomed to failure, an error in judgment so profound that it would send him so far underground that no one would ever see him again.

There were times when Preston realized that if he were to take the emotions and anxieties that were inside him and place them next to the exterior calm of his actual body, it would be terrifying to behold. That he could hold the two aspects separate from each other, or at least make them work together, was a testament to his abilities, though he worried that they would become combustible next to each other and simply vaporize, leaving him nothing.

But now, having driven along the East Coast for the past three days, he simply felt like a man who was going to try something difficult and hope that it worked, which made him no different from most of the other inhabitants of this planet. It gave him the slightest amount of strength, to believe that he was both special and no different from anyone else, and he walked the last mile down the dirt road that had been dug out of the forest and happened upon the place where he would build his new family.

The structure was awe inspiring, the way it so clearly asserted itself within the acres of woods that surrounded it. The front of the structure was a three-story building, all windows, a garden on the roof, while the rest of the buildings, all irregular heights and dimensions, were connected in a rectangular shape, a planned community, which is what it was intended to be. What made it so striking was that every exposed part of these concrete structures was covered in a specially designed olive green AstroTurf. It made the buildings seem both futuristic and camouflaged. The design had come from an architectural firm in Spain, shocked that anyone was interested in such a strange layout, but to Dr. Grind it had been perfect. It was enclosed, private, but with enough open spaces that it suggested the freedom to move around the complex without fear. The children, Dr. Grind knew from experience, would love it; the parents, well, they might take some convincing.

The foreman on the project met Dr. Grind at the front of the building and invited him to tour the grounds. There was only a skeleton crew left on-site to handle a few odds and ends with wiring, though the interiors of the buildings would have to be installed and furnished at a later date, but there was time enough for that. As he walked around and around the interior of the courtyard, he couldn't help brushing his fingertips against the AstroTurf, the way it transformed the primitive concrete walls into something that a child might dream up, all dangerous things made soft with care. He walked through every room and imagined its future use, the dreaming made easier by the absence of any real detail to impede his wishes. He stayed out of the way of the workers whenever they stepped into a room in which he was standing. By the end of the day, the light golden through the trees, fading into a dimness, the foreman asked if he needed a ride back to his car in the makeshift parking lot at the entrance of the woods, but Dr. Grind declined. He said he would like to walk around a bit more, and though the foreman hesitated, he seemed to understand that Dr. Grind was important enough that he was allowed to do whatever he desired, this being his building. Once the men had left and Dr. Grind could hear them starting up their trucks, he walked up to the third floor of the main building, each floor as large as an auditorium. He found a ladder that had been set on its side and he set it upright and leaned it against one of the concrete walls. He climbed to the top of the ladder, his hand able to touch the space where the wall met the ceiling. Steadying himself, he reached for his wallet and produced a small photo of his wife and child. In the photo, his wife, Marla, was holding on to their son's arms, spinning him around in a circle. Jody, his son, was a blur of motion, his face ghostlike and hazy, but he remembered when the photo was taken, and he knew his son was smiling, beaming with delight. He took the photo of his family, both of them now dead and gone, and he slid it into a slight, almost nonexistent space between the wall and the ceiling. He pushed the photo into the crack, little by little, until it disappeared into the structure. Though he did not believe in an afterlife, he hoped some aspect of them would filter into whatever it was he was trying to accomplish with this endeavor. He hoped, was it not too much to ask, that they would never leave him.

After he descended the ladder, finding himself relieved to be back on steady ground, he eased himself onto the floor. He sat quietly, legs crossed, and imagined what would come next, the new family he would bring into this wonderful space.

Three years ago, Dr. Grind sat in the vast waiting room of the head-quarters of Acklen Super Stores, the largest retailer in the world, lo-cated in Knoxville, Tennessee. Mounted on the wall to his left, an enormous original painting by Helen Frankenthaler was proudly dis-played, swaths of deep color that suggested a horizon. As he walked into the massive building, he'd noticed what he assumed was a Georgia O'Keeffe in the front entrance. In such a bland, inoffensive space, ev-erything bright lights and sensible carpet, the only reading material on the coffee table the Acklen Super Store newsletter, it was strange to see major works of art presented without comment. It was as if a museum had decided to start selling time-shares over the phone and simply for-got to remove the art.

In the week since he had been summoned, almost entirely without pretext or explanation, to meet with Brenda Acklen, the matriarch of the Acklen family and fortune, he'd been reading up on her life. She'd met her husband, Terry Acklen, the founder of Acklen Super Stores, at an orphanage where both were wards of the state. Her husband had quickly turned a few discount stores in Knoxville into a global concern. Though it felt unseemly, Preston had checked and rechecked the fact that Brenda Acklen, eighty-two years old, was worth over nineteen billion dollars. Though she'd let her sons run the business after her husband died nearly eight years earlier, she remained active, funding several charities for un-derprivileged children and amassing a personal collection of virtually every important female artist of the twentieth century. And now, after a series of phone calls and e-mails with both her and her assistants, Pres-ton had taken Mrs. Acklen's private jet from New York to Knoxville in order to talk about, what Mrs. Acklen had mentioned in vague terms that would be irritating if the person wasn't a billionaire many times over, something simple and elemental, something that Dr. Grind had devoted nearly all of his life toward understanding more completely: family.

Dr. Preston Grind was the son of Drs. Stephen and Wendy Grind, two of the most famous child psychologists of the 1980s and '90s, specializing in childhood trauma. Their son, Preston, had become part of the public consciousness soon after he was born, when he became the initial subject of what became known as the Constant Friction Method of Child Rearing. According to the Grinds, the world itself was harsh and unpredictable, exacerbated by human beings who were programmed to selfishly consider only their own interests. The failure of many parents, in their opinion, was that they tried to create a false and ultimately unhelpful view of the world with regard to their children, seeking at all times to provide comfort and to make life free of complication. This resulted in children who, as they became adults and were forced to interact more closely with the true world around them, were incapable of processing the actual unfairness and destructive qualities of society. In a series of landmark studies, they sought to create a world where baby Preston would exist in what they called "a state of constant friction" in order to make him more adaptable, more capable of handling whatever challenge might present itself. Instead of being swaddled and kept warm in a crib, Preston would randomly be removed from his bed at various times during the night and placed on the floor, the temperature adjusted to make sleep uncomfortable. Regular feeding times were discouraged and sometimes meals lasted mere seconds. As Preston learned to crawl, weights were attached to his ankles to make his movement more difficult. One of the most famous aspects of the study involved Preston, at age three, being handcuffed and placed in a locked room with the keys to both the handcuffs and the door hidden somewhere in the room. He managed to exit the room in less than five minutes. The only constant in the experiment was the affection of the doctors for their only child; they were never outwardly cold or physically violent with Preston and showered him with approval for his ability to handle outside impediments in order to reinforce the idea that, while the world was difficult and unpredictable, parental love was unwavering. Critics of the studies continually brought up the fact that, despite their affection and careful nurturing of the child, they were, without his knowledge, also the ones responsible for his discomfort. These experiments continued until he was eight years old, by which time the experiment had been labeled by the Grinds to be a resounding success and their book, *The Constant Friction Method of Child Rearing,* had become an instant best seller.

In the face of criticism, the Grinds frequently brought up the results of young Preston's upbringing. He showed an unusual aptitude for learning in all of their tests and recorded unprecedented IQ scores for a child so young. He skipped several grades and eventually received a B.A. at age fifteen from Brown University. He then went to Harvard and received a doctorate in clinical psychology at age twenty. He was, they reported for the rest of their lives, with no other scientific processes that would ever equal the Constant Friction Method, the greatest example of how children could be made exceptional by preparing them for the wilderness of the world into which they would enter.

An entire subculture of child rearing based on the Grinds' methods developed soon after their book was published, sometimes resulting in high-profile charges of child abuse leveled against the parents. The Grinds were frequent expert witnesses in these trials, defending the actions of the parents as the truest expression of parental love, to prepare the child for a world that was not a "fairy tale" and might not always produce a happy ending. By the early 2000s, the method had been summarily dismissed by most experts, though Preston's success always served as a rebuttal to those assertions. "The method may have been flawed," Wendy Grind once told a reporter, "but the result was perfect." As Preston set out on his own career as a child psychologist, his parents, who were both exhibiting the earliest stages of dementia, committed suicide with sleeping pills, side by side in their bed. When Preston heard the news, he felt the unwanted effect of his parents' method asserting itself, steadying his emotions, leaving him without sorrow, but with an instantaneous acceptance that his parents were no longer living, no longer with him.

One of Mrs. Acklen's assistants appeared in the waiting room. "Miss Brenda is ready to see you," she said, and Preston immediately stood, took one last look at the painting to his left, the colors deeper than bloodstains, and followed her into something of which he could not, having tried many times, anticipate the outcome.

There was no art in the room, no sign of papers or office supplies, no evidence that the room was even used on a daily basis. The only furniture in Mrs. Acklen's office was a desk with a chair on either side, one of which was currently occupied by that very woman. Though she was in her eighties, she seemed much younger, her body lean and suggesting a lifetime of good choices and moderate exercise. She wore a faded pair of red khakis and a chambray shirt with a blue-and-white bandanna tied around her neck, as if she were a cowboy in the old west. In one hand, she held a glass tumbler of what looked to be iced tea and, in the other, she held a copy of Dr. Grind's book, *The Artificial Village*.

"Dr. Grind," she said, not standing, no available hand to offer for a handshake, "I am so happy to finally meet you."

Preston replied that he was happy to meet her as well and then awkwardly sat down in the unoccupied chair and tried very hard to understand what was going on and why he had agreed in the first place to meet with her. Did he think she was going to give him a billion dollars? He did not need a billion dollars. But why else would he be here? He decided that it was simple curiosity, the hope that someone important might need his expertise. It was, after all, what he spent his life doing, offering his expertise to people who seemed to desire it. It was how he made his living, not a billion dollars, but enough that he considered himself to be fairly rich.

"I have read and reread this wonderful book of yours," she said, holding the book out to him as if she were unsure whether he was aware that he had written a book at all. "It is so enlightening and really gets to the heart of something that I care about very deeply."

"Thank you so much, Mrs. Acklen," Preston replied. "It's very gratifying to hear that."

"I wondered, if it's not too much trouble, if you might sign it for me?" she asked him.

Suddenly, it dawned on Preston that this might be the entire reason that he was summoned to Knoxville. A billionaire wanted her book signed. "I can do that, Mrs. Acklen," he said.

"Let me get you a pen," she said, opening the desk drawer and then frowning. "There's no pen in here. Well, damn it. They keep this office for me if I ever have official business, though I rarely do, but, still, someone is supposed to keep the desk stocked with supplies. Samantha!" The assistant stepped back into the room. "Yes, ma'am?" she asked.

"I need a pen."

The assistant was holding a pen, though she seemed slightly reluctant to part with it, and handed it to Mrs. Acklen, who then handed it, and the book, to Preston. With no precise idea of how to personalize the book, he merely signed it and wrote "with warm regards" and then handed the book to Mrs. Acklen and the pen to her assistant, who took it and then disappeared from the room.

Preston and Mrs. Acklen sat for a few seconds in silence, both of them smiling, the air-conditioning rattling softly. Finally, Mrs. Acklen leaned over the desk, looking directly at Preston. "I imagine you're a little confused as to why I asked to meet you," she said and then nodded as if there was no need for him to respond because she already knew the answer. Still, Preston could not help but nod in agreement. "I was wondering what the main objective might be," he admitted, "but of course it's also an honor to meet you."

"Nothing special about me," she said. "But you . . . you are something else. After I read your book, a little later than everyone else did, I admit, I knew that you were someone who had designs on improving the world, of doing something important. And, in my old age, doing something important really appeals to me."

The book she was referring to, *The Artificial Village,* sought to outline how, as nuclear families became less traditional and people were less likely to spend their lives in the same geographic location, surrounded by their relatives and neighbors whom they'd known for their entire lives, children, especially babies and toddlers, were finding fewer and fewer possibilities for meaningful human interaction. The book offered several new ways of thinking about community building, of how to create villages in seemingly inhospitable circumstances. Grind's primary focus was on inner-city and rural areas, where the need for childhood development was greatest, and he traveled the country to help government agencies design programs to encourage a more communal relationship among seemingly random families. He had met Oprah, who had endorsed his book and ideas, which was about as much fame as a child psychologist could hope to gain. When so many of his colleagues were focused on teenagers, trying to explain the rise in drug use and violence, Grind focused on toddlers, on those first five years of life, when a few adjustments could, he asserted and numerous studies had proven, make a huge difference. The worry was all about schools and how they could properly prepare youths for the future, when children from birth to age five were pretty much ignored. There had to be a way, he posited, to make the first years of a child's life as easy and as protected as possible, regardless of circumstances.

It did not escape Grind's awareness, or those who looked to write stories about him, that his work seemed to be a direct response to his own parents' methods of child rearing. "Every parent," he would often say, "believes they are working in the best interests of their children. And sometimes this is true. Sometimes it is not. Sometimes we need other people to help us."

He had received several grants, a substantial amount of money, to test his theories, and he focused on a few neighborhoods, finding ways to link new parents and their children, putting aside resources for child care and development, getting those without children or who no longer had children within the age range involved in outreach with their neighbors, and, finally, providing communal spaces for interaction and growth. Initial studies had shown significant improvement in the development of these children, regardless of socioeconomic background or family history. For Grind, however, it wasn't enough to get people to see their neighbors as potential sources of support, he wanted them to see one another as members of a singular family, but this seemed troubling to his colleagues, moving into a kind of new-age therapy, and so they continued to focus on hard data and scientific methods.

"Well," Preston replied, his pale skin, he could feel it, turning deep red with embarrassment, "I don't know how successful it ultimately will be. It requires long-term studies, and further testing has found new issues that we'll have to address moving forward."

It was a habit that he found difficult to break, the way he talked about the work as if he were still a part of it, as if he had anything to do with the studies now, having removed himself from all of it.

"I mean, rather, that someone else will have to address. I am, as you may or may not know, no longer directly involved in the Artificial Village project. My name is still listed as an advisor, but I couldn't tell you exactly what the status of the project is at the current moment. If you want to become involved in it, I know they would appreciate your support. I could put you in touch with the proper people."

"Dr. Grind, I am very much aware of your circumstances," Mrs. Acklen said. "I have quite a bit of time to devote to my interests; I do my research. No, while I think it is worthwhile and deserves attention, my interest is not with the Artificial Village project. My interest is, to be frank, with you."

Preston's face grew even hotter, a heat wave passing through his system. Was Brenda Acklen coming on to him?

"I'm flattered, Mrs. Acklen," he responded.

"Call me Brenda, please," she said, smiling.

"Only if you call me Preston," he said.

"Certainly," she replied. "No need for formality here."

"Well, I'm very honored to meet you, as I said earlier, and I'm very grateful to hear your kind words about my work. I'm just not sure what it is I can do for you, why I'm here."

Mrs. Acklen took a sip from her iced tea. "Preston, could I tell you a story? Do you have time for that?"

Preston felt like time had stopped, that he had entered some kind of vortex when he stepped into Mrs. Acklen's office. "I have time, certainly," he said.

"I grew up in an orphanage. Did you know that?"

"I read something about that, yes," he replied.

"Well, when I was four years old, my father died of a heart attack. A complete shock to the family. And my mother, in his absence, had to find work to support our family. His parents had long since died and he had no siblings. My mother's father was dead and her mother was in a state-run hospital. She also had no living brothers or sisters. She was, for the most part, entirely alone. She did her best to raise me and my older brother, but times were hard and she eventually felt that she could not take care of us. So she took us, without warning or explanation, to the Church of God Orphanage in Knoxville. I don't know if you were aware, but a good number of children in orphanages at that time were not actual orphans. It was common for parents, fallen on hard times, to give up their children. In fact, there were several boys and girls at the orphanage who would be reunited with their parents and then, six months later, brought back to the orphanage when money had again run out. But that's not entirely important, I suppose. I just thought you might be interested to hear it. The point was, Preston, that the traditional view of orphanages, especially at that time, was that they were depressing places where children were abused and neglected. And while that was quite true of some places, I have no doubt, my time at the orphanage was, frankly, a gift. My mother, bless her, had psychological problems, which were exacerbated by my father's death. She hit us and put us through quite a bit of emotional abuse. She could not care for us. The orphanage could. I loved my time there, not least because I met my husband. I truly believed that each and every child in that home was my true brother and sister. I felt a kinship greater than any nuclear family. And while the staff was by no means a substitute for a mother and father, they treated me with kindness; I was loved, in some way, by not just two parents, but by a large group of people with whom I interacted daily. In fact, once I was old enough to leave the orphanage, Terry and I moved into an apartment while he started working at the store he would eventually own, and I felt so lonely in that place, removed from all my friends. I was completely out of sorts. And when we had our children, again I felt adrift, no one to help me or show me the best way to take care of these babies that had come into my life. And though we got through it, far better than most people, and we made a wonderful life for ourselves and our children and their children, I can't help but think back on that time in the orphanage as the best years of my life. Isn't that silly?"

"I don't think so, Brenda," Dr. Grind replied, feeling something click in his brain, his affection for Mrs. Acklen growing as she voiced something that he had considered for many years now.

"Well, it feels silly sometimes, but it's true. And now, it seems like there are a large percentage of children who are unwanted and uncared for, drifting through this world, and I wish there was something in place for those children that's better than what we have now. There are safety nets, but so many children slip right through them or they never even reach them. It seems to me that there must be a wider net, to make sure that every child is loved and cared for."

"A network?" Dr. Grind offered.

"That's too formal for my tastes," she replied. "Not a network. Not even a community. Certainly not those awful communes that are just excuses for adults to remove themselves from society and do whatever they please, with no regard for the children. I'm talking about something quite different. Dr. Grind, excuse me, Preston, I'm talking about a family. I'm talking about a family that is larger than just a husband and a wife and their children. I'm talking about a place where everyone is connected and everyone cares for each other equally."

"A family," Dr. Grind then said, in agreement with Mrs. Acklen.

"A kind of family, yes," she said, smiling. "A family that will not end, no matter what the circumstances. An everlasting family. An infinite family." She reached across the desk and took hold of Dr. Grind's hand, which he willingly allowed. "And I think, Preston, that you could help me make this happen. I think you are just the person I've been hoping for."

Preston had no real idea as to what he could do to help Mrs. Acklen. In fact, what she was suggesting seemed too broad and unrealistic to ever be a reality, with no real structure for making something like this happen, at least in an organic way. But, as he held her hand, feeling the warmth of her skin and the easy way that it fit in his own hand, he could not resist her, could not deny her what she was asking for.

"Are you the person that I'm hoping for, Preston?" she asked.

"I think I might be, Brenda," he finally said, smiling, so relieved that he thought he might cry.

chapter four

In the smokehouse of the Whole Hog BBQ, Izzy mixed together salt, pepper, and vinegar in a bucket using a wooden oar while poring over a Bible-size Dr. Sears book on babies. Now three months' pregnant, Izzy finally felt like an authentic expectant mother; although it was only noticeable to her, the flatness of her stomach was becoming the slightest bit convex, something beyond her powers making itself known.

She had finally told her father; he reacted at first with an anger that Izzy had not expected, a desire to beat up whatever boy had done this to her, but that eventually gave way to a stoic acceptance of the fact and a belief that Izzy's mother, had she been alive, would have been very excited about this, though Izzy knew for a fact that her mother would have been furious that Izzy had allowed a baby to slow down her inevitable rise to greatness.

Word got out among her few friends and coworkers and, once it was clear that she was not going to reveal the father and that he was out of the picture anyway, people let it drop, or at least didn't discuss it around her. In fact, the waitresses at the restaurant now seemed more interested in talking to Izzy, as if her pregnancy finally made her normal in their eyes, and they shared numerous stories about their own experiences, most of them so unpleasant that Izzy wondered why anyone willingly got pregnant.

Mr. Tannehill refilled Izzy's cup with water; he was always making her drink water, as if he'd heard water was important to expectant mothers and this was the only thing he knew about the subject and he was going to stick with it until the baby was born. He tipped an imaginary cup to his lips and Izzy nodded and took a deep gulp of the cold water. Mr. Tannehill had also purchased a carbon-filter HEPA mask for Izzy to protect her from the smoke, but it fit strangely on her face and made her feel dizzy, the sound of her breathing always in her ears, so she took it off. Mr. Tannehill now made her take frequent breaks to walk outside and get air. And he would not allow her to lift anything over five pounds, which meant he was hoisting the pig carcasses onto the chopping block by himself, a task for which Izzy had assumed she was necessary. But she found that Mr. Tannehill could do it without much effort, which made her feel the slightest bit patronized, all those times she'd used every muscle to move the more than one hundred pounds of pig around the room, thinking she determined whether it fell to the ground or not.

One of the waitresses stepped into the back room and hollered that someone was here to see Izzy. "Who is it?" Izzy asked, but the waitress was already rushing back to her work. Mr. Tannehill was preparing a new pig for the smoker, which could hold two pigs at one time and therefore was always in use, using an electric saw to remove the head and legs. He looked over at Izzy and asked, "You need to check on that?" Izzy shrugged. "I better go check. It might be my dad." Mr. Tannehill returned to his work and Izzy walked through the kitchen, where all the frying was done and the sides prepared, into the seating area for the restaurant. She scanned the area, a huge space lined with picnic tables, but saw no one she recognized. The waitress who had called her was walking by with a tray of food, and Izzy stopped her for clarification.

"That old lady over there," said the waitress, pointing to a woman in a business suit, sipping a glass of water and looking quite worried to be in her current predicament. Izzy realized instantly who it was, Hal's mother. She felt sick and her knees wobbled for a second before she righted herself, just as the woman spotted her. Izzy placed her hand over her stomach, as if there was something to hide, and she considered going back to the smokehouse. She understood, there was no other explanation, that Mrs. Jackson knew about her and Hal. The only mystery was how much she knew. It was a strange sensation, to finally be discovered, especially since Hal was now out of her life. The woman gestured for her to come over, and Izzy found that her feet were moving without her consent, her subconscious hoping that Mrs. Jackson had a message from Hal, who had never responded to Izzy's letter rejecting him.

Mrs. Jackson had been a small-time actress in Hollywood for a few years in the fifties. She had left Tennessee to move to Hollywood and was cast in a few movies, always as a beautiful woman, always a minor character. She moved back to Tennessee and married Hal's father, Dr. Horton Jackson, a former OB/GYN who had become a U.S. senator and now worked for a lobbyist group. They were one of the richest families in Tennessee, and Mrs. Jackson, according to Hal, mostly planned fund-raisers for Republican candidates across the state. She was not, it was clear, a person who frequented barbecue joints.

Izzy stood over Mrs. Jackson who simply nodded toward the empty space on the picnic table next to her, not shaking Izzy's hand or acknowledging her in any meaningful way. Izzy sat down and stared straight ahead, afraid to even look at Mrs. Jackson.

"Do you know who I am?" Mrs. Jackson asked Izzy, who nodded. "And you are Isabel Poole, correct?" Izzy again nodded, unable to speak.

"I came here today because I need to talk to you about something very important. I'm afraid I have terrible news and it's very hard for me to do this, so I'm just going to say it. Hal died three days ago. He killed himself."

Izzy felt every available breath of air in her body condense into something solid. She felt herself tearing up, even as she admitted that Mrs. Jackson's news was an outcome that she had foreseen without admitting its possibility for as long as she had known Hal. She wanted some kind of comfort, the slightest touch, but saw that Mrs. Jackson was not offering any, which made Izzy feel embarrassed for her neediness.

"I'm so sorry," Izzy finally said.

"It is very hard for any parent to lose their child," Mrs. Jackson admitted. "Hal was a beautiful boy, but he had a difficult life. He was beset by demons and it seemed nothing my husband and I did for him ever quite helped him."

"I feel sick," Izzy admitted, realizing that she would never see Hal again, that she had been relying on the sliver of hope that he might come back to her at some point.

"He left a note and I've had a chance to read it. I'm sure you understood this when you saw me here, but I know about your relationship with Hal. And I know about the baby."

Izzy didn't know how to respond, what Mrs. Jackson wanted from her, and instead she simply blurted out, as if this were a surprise, "I'm having a baby."

"I know, dear," Mrs. Jackson replied. "And I know that the child is Hal's. And I apologize for everything that has happened to you, but I am in a state of shock and so I may not be as graceful as I would like to be about all of this."

"I'm sorry," Izzy said, still unable to form any articulate sentences, no way to express the inexpressible feelings inside her.

"And I am sorry for what Hal put you through. He meant well, I'm sure, and from what I gather from the letter, you were very special to him. But I want to know about your intentions."

"What do you mean?" Izzy asked, her brain so many steps behind this woman.

"I want to know what you intend to do with this baby," said Mrs. Jackson, tapping her hand lightly on the table as she spoke.

"I want to have it," Izzy said.

"I understand that, dear," Mrs. Jackson said, her voice showing the slightest bit of impatience. "What I want to know is what you expected of Hal and, by extension, our family."

"I don't have any expectations, I guess," Izzy responded. "I had hoped Hal would help me raise the child."

"Financially, you mean?" Mrs. Jackson said, leaning toward Izzy; apparently Izzy was starting to interest her.

"No," Izzy said, embarrassed. "I thought he would be a part of the child's life, I guess. I thought he would physically be present. I hadn't had a lot of time to think about it and Hal was in the hospital, so I didn't know what to expect, really."

"So you didn't expect to ask for child support?"

Izzy felt herself growing angry, her emotions finally overpowering her shock. Why was Mrs. Jackson talking about this? "I hadn't thought about it," Izzy said. "Not as much as you have, I guess."

"Dear, I am simply trying to figure out how to proceed. I have lost my youngest child, a child who was very important to me and caused me a great amount of emotional pain. And then I find out that he has impregnated a teenager, a student of his, and that she is going to have the baby. I did my best to help Hal, Isabel. But the Jacksons are an important family in Tennessee, with a legacy and a future that is greater than just one person. Do you understand why I would be concerned about this? I want to protect our family from any further embarrassment."

"To you and your husband," Izzy said, "I would be an embarrassment."

"You are focusing on only a small portion of what I'm saying, dear," Mrs. Jackson said. Each time she used the word *dear*, it felt like a tiny pin was being inserted into the webbing between Izzy's fingers.

Perhaps sensing that Izzy was unable to think of a response, or perhaps simply not caring what she had to say, Mrs. Jackson continued.

"Let me offer some suggestions, Isabel. I don't know what Hal told you about his finances. Hal had a trust fund, but he was quite reckless with his money. There is almost nothing left. He was borrowing money from his father and me for the past few years to pay off debts he had incurred for reasons that he did not share and we did not ask about. If you were to think about legal proceedings regarding child support, you would find very little that Hal's estate could offer. What I am offering, instead, is a lump sum to help with the initial stages of the rearing of the child, as well as a promise to pay for the cost of having the baby, any medical bills you might take on. My husband, if you didn't know, was one of the most prominent OB/GYNs in the state and he still has many contacts in the field. We want you to go to a very respectable doctor in Chattanooga, perhaps the best doctor in the state. And my husband has also set up a meeting with a researcher and doctor who might be able to help you further with your current situation. It would be beneficial for you and for, as crass as it sounds, our family."

"What kind of meeting?" Izzy asked. She thought about the offer of money, which, even with the pain of Hal's death still settling upon her, she could not ignore.

"A possible research project that would help pay for the care of your child and offer the possibility of training and a career for you, if I understand correctly, though I don't have the full details. It would be a wonderful opportunity."

"What if I say no?" Izzy said.

"Very little would change," Mrs. Jackson admitted. "You would be a single mother with very few resources trying to raise a child in inhospitable circumstances. You would only cause unnecessary emotional pain to people that Hal cared about very deeply."

"And if I say yes?" Izzy asked.

"You will find that things would be easier for you and your child. I would imagine, especially now that my son is no longer with us, that he would have hoped that you would take care of yourself and this baby."

"Hal didn't want me to have the baby," Izzy said.

"That was not up to him, frankly. It was not his position to demand that. I love my son, but he did not behave honorably. If you want to have the baby, I would not dream of trying to dissuade you. I'm only trying to find a way that everyone benefits from these awful circumstances."

"I can't think about this right now."

"Not right this minute, I understand. I want you to take my number and we can talk about this in the coming weeks."

Izzy took the slip of paper from Mrs. Jackson and put it in her pocket. She realized how long she'd been away from the smoker, from her work. She stood up to leave and Mrs. Jackson, for the first time, reached for Izzy's hand.

"I'm so sorry, Isabel," Mrs. Jackson said. "I know that you loved him, and so, since I loved him, too, I know this is very difficult to deal with."

"It's awful," Izzy admitted. Mrs. Jackson's face was blank, with the slightest hint of exasperation, which suggested to Izzy that she did not entirely understand or believe in her son's love for Izzy.

"There will be a funeral, dear," Mrs. Jackson continued, "but I hope you might give our family the space to grieve in our own way."

"I have to go," Izzy said, pulling her hand away from Mrs. Jackson. She thought Mrs. Jackson said something else, but she was already out of earshot. Jessica, the waitress who had been watching them, came over to Izzy.

"You okay, sweetie?" she asked.

"I'm okay," Izzy said.

"Who was that?"

"Nobody. Friend of the family. Somebody we know died."

"She looks familiar."

"She's nobody," Izzy said, and Jessica shrugged her shoulders as if giving up the matter, and then patted Izzy on the shoulder.

Izzy kept moving, back through the kitchen, to the smokehouse, where Mr. Tannehill was standing over the opened Dr. Sears book, biting his thumbnail, nodding his head in agreement with whatever he had just read. He still had not noticed her, and Izzy composed herself in that moment. When he finally looked up, he gestured to the book and said, "How can something be so simple and so complicated at the same time?" She shook her head. She had absolutely no idea, no concept of how anything in this world truly worked.

The next night, after she had returned home from work, she took a small washbasin from under her bed and filled it with warm water from the bathroom sink. She tipped a few drops of peppermint oil, seven dollars at the health food store in Chattanooga, into the tub and carefully carried it back into her bedroom. She took off her shoes and socks, her feet slightly swollen and aching from standing all day long, and soaked them in the tub. She leaned over to open her nightstand drawer and produced a notebook, the front of which simply read *Baby* in black Magic Marker. She had seen a pregnancy journal at Walmart, but it was eighteen dollars, and so she found a reasonably similar template online and copied it into this blank notebook, saving herself more than sixteen dollars. She flipped through the pages until she found today's date at the top and then listed all the food she had eaten that day, her weight and waist size, and then looked at the question that she had written in the middle of the page: *What were the best things about your parents as parents?* Her pen hovered over the page, unsure of how to proceed.

Izzy's mother had been a beauty queen, Miss Tennessee in 1985; her talent, though she had a beautiful singing voice, was a ventriloquist act featuring her dummy, Miss Tenny C, who told beauty pageant jokes. Her mother was so beautiful in her youth that people would stop her on the street to tell her this fact, but she was also slightly weird, spending a good portion of her free time in high school reading UFO journals and seeking to debunk questionable sightings. She was studying veterinary medicine at Middle Tennessee State University when she and Izzy's dad, who had been a high school baseball star and was now playing Single-A ball in Tampa, Florida, found out that she was pregnant with Izzy. Catherine, Izzy's mom, dropped out of college and, as if ordained by god, Izzy's father tore up his pitching arm and was forced to give up baseball and move back to Coalfield, where they took out a loan to open the market where her father still worked. And in the months leading up to Izzy's birth, her mother rarely left the house, and started smoking even more, weighed down by a kind of pre-partum depression. After Izzy was born, though, it seemed to rejuvenate her mother, finding a child who might be able to fulfill the dreams she had missed out on in her own life. Izzy's mother taught her how to read at age three, had her writing complete sentences the year after that. While her father was at work, Izzy and her mother spent the days engaged in a strenuous, though un-structured, lesson plan. Whenever Izzy complained, her mother would kiss her, pull Izzy into her considerable bulk, as if trying to smother her child, and say, "You are special, Izzy. That means life will be harder for you than other people. It's even worse because we're your parents and we don't have much to give you." Izzy would tell her mother that she didn't mind, didn't need to be special, which would make Izzy's mother grind her teeth and shake her head. "You do need to be special, sweetie," she would say. "Being special is what's going to save you."

Izzy's mother was working on a vague, book-length manuscript de-bunking history's most famous UFO incidents, staying up well into the early morning hours, taking diet pills and amphetamines to stay awake, before she continued her homeschooling of Izzy during the day. Izzy asked to participate in the research, to at least sort the piles of pamphlets and weird photocopies of government documents that came in the mail, but Catherine gently refused, saying this work was hers alone. When Izzy asked why UFOs were so important to her, Izzy's mother replied, "I don't like the idea that there are other worlds where life could be better for me. I want to make sure they aren't there, that this is all I have."

When Izzy was thirteen, her mother died of heart failure brought on by her morbid obesity and her use of stimulants. Izzy was, thank god, not the one who found her, slumped over her desk, pictures of UFOs taped to the wall. She woke up one morning and her father was standing over her, two policemen and an EMT behind him. "Where's Mom?" she asked, and not a single one of the men responded.

After her mother's death, Izzy went into the attic and retrieved Miss Tenny C, who looked vaguely similar to Izzy's mother when she was a teenager. She would sleep with the dummy, carry it everywhere with her, making it talk, saying the things that Izzy's mother no longer could. While she and her father would sit in the living room, eating lukewarm fish sticks and watching late-night TV, Izzy would operate the dummy, Miss Tenny C saying, over and over, "You are special, Izzy. You are so, so special."

Izzy looked at the question one more time and then wrote: "They loved me without reservation and tried their best to make me happy." The way she answered, it sounded like both of her parents were dead, but she decided not to rewrite the answer. She skipped ahead a few pages and looked at the next question: *What role do you see your family playing in your baby's life?*

Izzy slammed the journal shut and placed it back in the nightstand drawer. She pulled her feet out of the tub, her toes pruney and pale white and soft. Once again, she asked herself how in the world she was going to do this and, once again, she had no real answer.

She wished she knew Hal's thinking in the lead-up to his suicide. Had he made a logical and evenhanded assessment of his life and made the judicious decision to end it, or had he simply read Izzy's letter, torn it into pieces, written his own suicide note, and then waited for the chance to finally enact his own death? Was death preferable to a life with Izzy and the baby they had made together? Was death preferable to any life? Izzy wondered. She opened her laptop and checked Google again for any mention of Hal's death, using different search terms to narrow the results for Hal Jackson. She found nothing of note, but then simply typed his name into the search engine and added the word *art*. On the image search, she found several examples of his paintings and she stared at them for at least thirty minutes, clicking back and forth among the images.

In Hal's earliest work, before he started painting portraits, his method was to set different objects on fire, take a detailed and close-up photograph of the slow, controlled burn, and then turn that photo into a painting. Canvas after canvas of white and orange and red, as if the image could incinerate what was special inside you. She had asked Hal about the paintings and he just shrugged his shoulders and said, "I keep thinking I can find the moment when the object is not what it once was,

but it also isn't ash yet. I want to find the moment that the fire trans
forms us. I never do, though."

She closed her browser and opened a file folder called *Finances*. Sh
hated looking at the spreadsheet, but couldn't look away. She looked a
her annual income, at the minimum wage, of nearly $13,000, befor
taxes. She looked at her expenses, even considering the fact that she di
not have to pay rent because she still lived with her father. She looked a
the payment plan she'd worked out for the $2,000 in prenatal care witl
the OB/GYN, no real belief that she could pay it off in a timely fashior
She didn't even try to add up the cost of diapers and formula and all th
things a baby demands. Nothing matched up; the equations did not ex
ist that would allow for Izzy's financial comfort.

Mrs. Jackson's phone number was on the desk next to Izzy's com
puter. She looked at the numbers, imagined what would possibly tran
spire if she called it. Hal was gone. There was nothing she could do t
bring him back. The Jacksons were going to pay her in order to sav
them some measure of embarrassment. They had so much money that
no matter what Izzy hoped, taking it would not be a punishment fo
them. Izzy knew what was happening, the way she was allowing weak
ness to override her sense of pride. For Izzy, there was no direction le1
to her but forward, away from Hal and into something new and un
known. Like any journey, she needed supplies to help her get there. Sh
called Mrs. Jackson, happy that at least it was late enough that it woul
interrupt the woman's peaceful, dreamless sleep. Izzy waited for her t
answer, knowing that she would take whatever Hal's family would giv
her, whatever she could snatch from their hands and make her own.

chapter five

zzy lay on the examining table, her shirt pulled up to her chest, her belly exposed. The technician, an unsmiling woman wearing Hello Kitty scrubs, held a bottle of gel and asked Izzy, "You nervous?" Izzy nodded. "Don't be," the woman continued. "This is the easiest and best procedure in your entire pregnancy." The woman squeezed a glob of gel onto Izzy's stomach, which wasn't nearly as cold as she'd been led to believe, and spread it around. The technician gently moved the transducer over Izzy's skin, but Izzy focused instead on the screen, the weirdest movie she would ever watch. As she listened to the baby's heartbeat, cloudy and rapid, she watched as the gray smudges on the screen eventually, without warning, turned into the shape of her baby. She gasped; it was as if she had been looking at a Magic Eye poster and had suddenly seen the image appear out of the random patterns. There, on the screen, was the shape of the baby's head.

"You want to know what it is?" the technician asked.

"You can tell already?" Izzy replied.

"With this one I can."

"Okay then."

"Well, you're gonna have a little boy," the technician said, her face still without emotion, as if the news of a boy was a disappointment to Izzy. Izzy had not cared either way, had not been able to wrap her head around the specificity of a boy or a girl, thinking of the child only as a baby, as an *it*. The baby had been, up to this moment, merely a ghost that was haunting her, but now it had a shape and a sex, and Izzy felt relieved to know that all of this was real, was worth the sadness and uncertainty.

"A boy," Izzy replied.

"By the measurements here," the technician continued, "a perfectly normal, growing baby boy."

"Good," Izzy said, taking a certain pride that her body could form and house something perfect.

"Just one," the technician said.

"Even better," Izzy replied.

"The doctor will be here in a few minutes to go over the results and talk to you. Have you met Dr. Kirwin?"

"No," Izzy admitted. "I just moved over to him recently; I'd been seeing a different doctor."

"Well, he's very energetic, just so you know," the technician said, and she abruptly stood up, handed Izzy a paper towel for the gel, and then turned away from Izzy to type some notes on the computer. Izzy had a hard time conceptualizing what was meant by *energetic*. She imagined the doctor jogging in place during the entire visit, doing jumping jacks as he discussed her placenta.

"This the mom?" Dr. Kirwin asked as he pushed open the door.

"Yes, Doctor," said the technician, not even looking at him.

"She's too young to be a momma," he replied, smiling so broadly that it seemed to Izzy that she was on a very easy game show. "She's a kid."

Dr. Kirwin was in his late fifties or early sixties, the size and dimensions of Uncle Fester from the Addams Family, a bald, big-eyed chunk of a person. He was, Izzy had to admit, terrifying in an enclosed space.

"I'm nineteen," Izzy offered, as if hopeful that Dr. Kirwin was simply confused and anticipating a different pregnant girl.

"Well, that's not so young, these days," he offered thoughtfully. "Not so different from fifty years ago, truth be told. People always have babies and a lot of them are too young to be having them."

"Doctor," the technician said, a warning note, though she still wasn't paying him much attention.

"Sorry. I get going and it's hard to stop. Now, let me see," he said, looking over her meager chart. "Oh, you're the girl that Dr. Jackson sent my way. How is Horton these days?"

"He's fine," Izzy said, not sure what the doctor or Mrs. Jackson had told Dr. Kirwin.

"He's a damn sight better than fine, I imagine. Saint Horton, I call him. Richer than god, he is. Well, let's look at this baby."

He looked briefly at the results, seemingly uninterested in the numbers and measurements. "Okay, okay, okay. You got a good womb, darling. You have a healthy baby in there and your placenta looks good and we're just fine and dandy here."

"Thank you, Doctor," Izzy said.

"Just go home and tell your husband that things are good."

"Doctor," the technician said, another warning note in her voice.

"No husband? No boyfriend?" the doctor asked Izzy, who was caught off-guard by the question. When she'd filled out the forms, as instructed by Mrs. Jackson, she put *Unknown* when asked for information about the father. Izzy hated doing it, the way it made it seem that she had slept with so many men that it was impossible to pin down the father or that she had immaculately conceived.

"No," Izzy said, her face feeling warm.

"Not a problem," Dr. Kirwin replied, his face still stuck in that weird rictus of a grin. "Once you get pregnant, no real need for the man, truth be told. They just get in the way." He winked at Izzy and then turned to leave. "Be good to that baby, Isabel," he said, and then he was gone.

The room was silent until the technician, her face softening for the first time all day, lightly rubbed Izzy's shoulder and said, "Dr. Kirwin is probably the most respected OB/GYN in the state, sweetie."

"I've heard," Izzy admitted.

"He's a complete doofus in all other respects, but he'll make sure that baby is safe and sound, I promise you."

Izzy nodded in thanks, unable to say anything, and then the nurse handed her some photos of the ultrasound. "These are for you. A couple pictures of the baby. On this one," she said, pointing to one of the pictures, "I circled the penis so you could show people the evidence."

"Thank you," Izzy said, perhaps the strangest reason she'd ever had for thanking someone.

She placed the pictures in her purse, another clue that would eventually lead her to solve the mystery that was unfolding around her, and she walked out of the room, down the hall, and into a waiting room filled with women in her same situation. She could not determine, as she moved out of the room to leave, if it made her happy or sad to be in their company.

Izzy sat on a bench in Coolidge Park. She had time to kill before her next appointment, the meeting she'd been both dreading and desiring since it had been booked.

True to the Jacksons' word, Izzy had been recommended for this new study, a possibility for financial aid and job training, things Izzy realized that she now desperately needed before the baby arrived. Right after she had received a packet in the mail from The Infinite Family Project, its logo that of a tree whose roots eventually formed the infinity symbol, she went online and found what little information was available. The main article she referenced had appeared on the front page of the Science section of the *New York Times,* with the headline "Odd Couple Seeks to Redefine Family Values." It talked about a billionaire, Brenda Acklen, who owned Acklen Super Stores, and how she had now initially funded, to the tune of nearly two hundred million dollars, a private, long-term study on child development. The article also mentioned her partner in this project, Dr. Preston Grind, a famous child psychologist and researcher who would be heading the project. The focus of the study seemed to be about communal parenting, though both Acklen and Grind were vague on the details, which was a foreign concept to Izzy, and she read about the huge complex that was being constructed to house the experiment. Everything about this study seemed grand and mysterious, which both intrigued and terrified Izzy. The project was in its infancy, and no other Web sites or articles had any new information, only a regurgitation of the facts, either heavily for or against. The main takeaway for Izzy had been that the study would cover all costs for the participants for the duration of the study. It was a testament to her desperation for something to help add clarity to her future that she would endure any number of tests if it meant she and her child were taken care of. She had already filled out dozens and dozens of online forms and surveys for The IFP, wanting to know all manner of family history, financial standing, and personal information. It had all the makings of a low-level scam, but Izzy dutifully filled out every single question, including those that asked for her favorite short story ("A Rose for Emily" by William Faulkner) and song ("Rocky Raccoon" by the Beatles), knowing intrinsically that, if nothing else, her participation was connected to the Jacksons' good faith deposit of $20,000 in her bank account, a penny of which she had promised that she would not touch until the baby was born. It did not help that the meeting was taking place at the Chattanooga Public Library and not a hospital or doctor's office.

Izzy finished her sandwich, heavy on the peanut butter, which she craved constantly since she became pregnant, and reached into her messenger bag for her pocketknife. She flicked open the blade, sharp as anything in the known world, and then produced a little piece of basswood that had recently, in Izzy's own hands, taken on the shape of a duck. She started to make a pull stroke to further define the duck's shape, working carefully, not even worried about cutting herself. She loved the way it relaxed her, to carve into a formless block and make it something tangible and specific, as if the shape had been there all along.

She had recently learned the hobby from Mr. Tannehill, who would often whittle intricate shapes out of the scraps of hickory that weren't used in the smoker. It was a way to pass the time while the pig took on the properties of good barbecue. After Izzy showed an interest, Mr. Tannehill, unceasingly kind, had brought a cloth drawstring bag filled with blocks of basswood ("It's the easiest wood to work with," he told her) and her own knife, a Case & Sons model that looked both antique and brand-new at the same time. After that, Izzy and Mr. Tannehill would silently carve, occasionally offering up their work for the appraisal of the other. It had taken Izzy a while just to get the wood to make the shape that she desired. Now she was able to add the slightest of detail work, good enough that she could, if she wanted, offer them for sale at a craft festival and not feel totally embarrassed. Mr. Tannehill, on the other hand, could whittle an unbroken wooden chain with his eyes closed. He had already made two ball-in-a-cage carvings for the unborn baby, smoothed as soft as a river stone with sandpaper. The hobby was, Izzy understood, anachronistic for someone her age, another aspect of herself that she modeled on people much older and more grizzled than she was. It was an affectation that separated her from the other kids her age, though one that she was growing to love, turning into habit. This was how things worked, Izzy believed, you pretended to love the thing in front of you until it really happened. If this wasn't the case, then Izzy was in deep trouble. She had predicated any chance of being a good mother on this principle.

She made another delicate cut with her knife and found the duck's shape to be slightly off, asymmetrical. It did not worry her in the least, her hands knowing by now that she could make adjustments, worry the shape until it was finally correct, no matter how small it became in the process.

In the downtown branch of the Chattanooga Public Library, Izzy followed the signs (EXPECTANT FAMILIES STUDY) that led to a small waiting area on the second floor. Understanding that a public library was not the place for wood shavings and a sharp knife, Izzy instead took out a copy of Grace Paley's *The Little Disturbances of Man* from her messenger bag and began to read, for the umpteenth time, the story where a man gives his wife a broom for Christmas. Paley had been her mother's favorite writer, and Izzy had been made to read all of her work, even her poetry, as soon as she could properly read and write. "If you combined a thousand male writers, they still wouldn't know as much about women as Grace Paley does," her mother told her. Izzy used a pencil as a guide to fly through the story, her brain knowing the word that would follow before she saw it on the page. When she was done, still alone, she started over and read it again.

Finally, she saw the door to the meeting room open and a His-panic couple, not much older than Izzy, walked out of the room with smiles on their faces. This, more than anything else, reassured Izzy that she wasn't entering into something very stupid and regrettable. The woman, her hand resting on her stomach, nodded to Izzy in the way that all expectant mothers seemed to do, a secret acknowledgment of their shared state. Izzy nodded in return and then looked up to see an Asian woman, apple shaped, slightly overweight, though quite pretty, walking toward her.

"Are you Isabel?" she asked. Izzy noticed how striking she looked, her face perfectly round and her skin almost glowing, her eyes obscured by a pair of thick-framed rectangular eyeglasses.

"I go by Izzy," Izzy responded, again wondering if she would ever use her real name, which seemed to be reserved for a princess or a wood-land fairy. Izzy, she always imagined, was the name of a shortstop for a ragtag bunch of Little Leaguers who played by their own set of rules. It was the name of a slightly dense cartoon character who winningly always came out ahead of her antagonizers.

"Okay, Izzy," the woman said. "I'm Dr. Kalina Kwon. I'm a postdoc-toral research fellow for this project and I'm going to be interviewing you today."

Izzy followed the woman into the meeting room, which was bare except for a laptop, a stack of file folders, and a dozen or so bottles of wa-ter. At this point, Izzy decided to stop expecting some kind of scientific formality, lab coats and surface disinfectants. She began to think of it more like a focus group for a new brand of potato chip.

Dr. Kwon motioned for Izzy to sit down and then took her place at the head of the table, partially obscured by the opened laptop. She typed a few things into the computer, frowned, skimmed her finger across the tracking pad, and then smiled. "Okay," she began, "we'll start the interview now. I'm recording this on my laptop, unless you have any objections."

"That's fine with me," Izzy admitted.

"So, I work with the Early Childhood Foundation, which is funding a new initiative to focus not only on the development of children, but also on helping to prepare parents for the rigors of parenthood." Izzy nodded. She had seen all of this information on the countless cover sheets and e-mails that she had received.

"Now," Dr. Kwon continued, "you've been diligent in filling out these countless surveys and forms, and I'm wondering what, exactly, your expectations are. Why are you doing this?"

Izzy paused. She wanted one of the bottles of water, but it was out of arm's reach and it seemed rude to stand up and procure one. "I'm going to be a single mother," Izzy finally said, and Dr. Kwon nodded, smiling. "My mom died when I was young, so I know the effects of a childhood without one of your parents. I don't have much support, emotionally or financially, from my family and friends, and I'm worried about how I'm going to care for my child. I want to be a good mother. I want that more than anything in my life so far. I thought that this project could help me do that."

Dr. Kwon continued to smile, as if this question had a right answer and Izzy had provided it. "That's totally understandable and commendable," she said. "Let me ask you this. If I can be a little more personal, I've studied all of your information. In all the questions that pertain to the father of your child, you've given very little information. Is there a reason for that?"

Apparently, Izzy was taking too long to answer, or revealed some kind of emotional discomfort, as Dr. Kwon leaned forward and said, her voice soft and reassuring, "I'm sure this is a difficult thing to talk about, but I just want you to help me fill in a few blanks."

"He's not alive," Izzy finally said. "He didn't want me to have the baby. I said I was going to have the baby. He killed himself."

"I'm very sorry, Izzy," Dr. Kwon said. "Do you think you can tell me just a little bit about him?"

"He was older than me. He was an artist, a painter." With each new detail, Izzy felt strangely elated, as if she was reconstructing Hal, bringing him back to life. "He was also a teacher. He was well educated, a B.F.A. and an M.F.A. in art from Yale. He was a very good cook. He had traveled a lot."

"Was he married? To someone else, I mean."

"No."

"And you were his girlfriend?"

"Sort of. Yes, I think so."

"And why don't you want to mention his name on the forms?"

"He didn't want the baby," Izzy said, feeling as if she was also explaining this to herself for the first time. "I don't want to involve him in any of this if I don't have to."

"And his family? How much do you envision them playing a part in raising your child?"

"None," Izzy said, feeling strangely exhilarated. "They do not want any part in raising the child."

Dr. Kwon flipped through the pages in what Izzy assumed was her own personal file. "Well, could you tell me a few of the skills you possess that you would like to pass on to your child?"

"What do you mean?" Izzy said, feeling quite certain that she had no skills that any child would want.

"When your child is developing and becoming his or her own person, what aspects of your own life do you hope to instill in him or her?"

"It's a him," Izzy said. "I just found out today."

"Congratulations," Dr. Kwon replied. "Well, what things about yourself do you want to pass on to him?"

"I guess a love of literature and art," Izzy said cautiously.

"Do you write or paint, Izzy?"

"Not really. I just appreciate it."

"What else?"

"I don't know, to be honest. I haven't thought about this. I just want him to be kind. I want him to be kind to other people and I want him to be happy."

"Okay, let me ask you in a different way. If someone asked you to brag about yourself, what would you offer them?"

"I would not offer anything. I wouldn't brag."

"Just suppose you had to."

"I'm a hard worker."

"Okay. That's important."

"Um." Izzy could not believe that this was all, but it seemed like this was the sum total of what she had to offer.

Dr. Kwon offered her hand, palm out, as if to beg forgiveness. "We can move on, Izzy."

"I can barbecue."

"Excuse me?"

"I'm really good at barbecue. Whole hog. I can prepare a pig and smoke it and serve it. It's very good. I'm actually a fairly good cook across the board."

"That's wonderful. That's what I'm looking for, Izzy. Great."

"I can speed-read."

"Excellent. That's very useful, I would imagine. I wouldn't mind having that skill."

"I can whittle," Izzy said.

"What does that mean?" Dr. Kwon asked, genuinely puzzled, it seemed.

Izzy reached into her messenger bag and produced the unfinished duck. She gently skidded it across the table to Dr. Kwon, who picked it up and inspected it.

"How did you make this?" she asked.

"I carved it with a knife."

"This is impressive."

"Thank you."

"You're more talented than you gave yourself credit for."

"I guess so," Izzy said, feeling slightly embarrassed that she was offering up these ridiculous talents as if they meant something. She felt like she was three years old, but she couldn't stop herself.

"Can I keep this, Izzy?" Dr. Kwon asked, holding up the duck.

"It's not finished," Izzy said.

"I think it's wonderful."

"Well, yeah, you can have it."

Dr. Kwon ran her thumb along the wooden animal and then placed the object in the pocket of her business suit.

"I know you've been reading about child development in preparation for the birth of your child, especially about attachment parenting, and I'm wondering if you have any fears or concerns about what you've been reading."

"I'm terrified of just about all of it, really," Izzy replied. The fact of the matter was that Izzy was already at a disadvantage, no husband to help shoulder the load, and she knew this. She knew what the books said about how important the early stages of childhood were and she knew that she was all alone in making this happen for her child.

"Why are you terrified about it?" Dr. Kwon asked.

"I have to work, have a job, in order to raise this baby," Izzy continued. "I don't have anyone else to help me. I can't be there for the baby in the way that I think I should be. I'm going to always be deficient when it comes to caring for him. It makes me nervous."

"This is an entirely personal view, Izzy, and it's probably not professional behavior for me to interject those feelings into this conversation, but I'm going to do it anyway. You are going to be a wonderful mother, Izzy. I've got so much information and data here that I've studied and you are thoughtful and kind and you will do fine, no matter what happens."

Izzy just nodded, grateful for those words, knowing, however, that they meant nothing once the baby arrived and Izzy was forced to care for him.

"Okay, I just have a few more questions, Izzy. If you and your child were chosen for the project, would you be willing to move? The project will be located in La Vergne, which is just outside Nashville, so could you foresee yourself moving in order to participate?"

"I guess I could do that. I'd at least be willing to consider it."

"Great. And your father? How problematic would it be to see less of him?"

"I see him every day. I live with him."

"If the project required you to move, would you be able to handle not seeing him every day?"

"We live together, but he's not an active part of my life, unfortunately. He helps me with money sometimes and gives me a place to live, but we don't interact all that much. It's been that way since my mom died. He's a little afraid of me, I think."

"Okay. I have to say, Izzy, that you offer a very compelling case study for the project. I've very much enjoyed talking to you and I hope we'll be in touch in the near future."

"Is that all?" Izzy asked. "You don't have anything else to ask me?" Izzy wasn't sure if she was happy or disappointed by this possibility.

"That's all for now. I just wanted to meet you. You've been very helpful with the information that you've already provided, so this interview was just to have a face-to-face meeting and clear up any outstanding questions that I had. Thank you very much for coming. And good luck with the baby. You look great, by the way."

Dr. Kwon stood and walked over to shake Izzy's hand. Izzy stood and followed Dr. Kwon out of the meeting room, past the sofa and chairs where now a new couple, two pale, towheaded teenagers who looked like brother and sister, were waiting. Izzy nodded in solidarity to the pregnant girl, and felt awful when the girl's face blazed red with embarrassment. Izzy kept walking, down the stairs, out of the library, and into the parking lot, where she finally stepped into her truck and began to breathe as calmly as she possibly could.

She still had no idea what was going on, what the project entailed, but Dr. Kwon was so kind, so patient, that Izzy felt very strongly that she wanted to be a part of the study. She wanted, after a long stretch of being avoided and ignored, to be desired by someone with good judgment. She wanted to believe that, inside her, there was something of great importance to the rest of the world. Was that so hard to believe, she wondered, as she started her truck and headed back to her normal life, which was patiently waiting for her, would always be waiting for her, she imagined.

chapter six

r. Preston Grind sat at the table in the meeting room of the complex, surrounded by file after file of people who, under no circumstances, would be a part of the project. Either their familial connections were too strong, their value systems regarding traditional families too ingrained, or they were doing well enough on their own and could not be induced to listen to him. His three postdoctoral research fellows, Jeffrey Washington, Kalina Kwon, and Jill Patterson, had each compiled ten prospective families that they believed best fit the profile for the project, and they were now making their cases to Dr. Grind.

"Carmen and Kenny fit perfectly into the socioeconomic parameters that we've targeted," Jeffrey continued, a series of bullet points appearing on the screen for everyone to follow along. "They have already begun to tentatively espouse the desire for alternative methods for child rearing, and they lack almost any familial connections that would offer support once the baby is born. And, of course, they fit the time line regarding due date." Jeffrey offered a pained smile, which seemed to be the only way he could express happiness; he was obviously convinced that he had found a compelling case for Dr. Grind to consider. Jeffrey, more than the other two fellows, was the most reluctant to accept Grind's theories on the project, and seemed concerned that they were entering into something that could blow up in their faces and leave their reputations beyond repair. It was one of the reasons that Grind had selected him, his skepticism. It was helpful, Grind believed, to constantly be aware of the fact that he might be making a huge mistake.

"And," Jeffrey then offered, "if we care about racial diversity, and I know that we do, then this couple helps with that complexity." Jeffrey's thesis at Texas Tech had focused on the disparities in childhood development among socioeconomic classes, focusing closely on race. As the only African American involved in the project thus far, Jeffrey wanted reassurance that Dr. Grind wasn't simply going to put ten white families into a house and think that the data gathered would ultimately matter. Grind had assured him several times that racial diversity was a necessary component of the study, and, now, he agreed that Carmen and Kenny were perfect. Dr. Grind moved their folder onto the very slight *yes* pile and then turned to Dr. Kwon.

"Your next couple, Kalina?" Dr. Grind asked.

Kalina took the cord that had been connected to Jeffrey's laptop and now attached it to her own. On the screen, there was a single photo of a young woman.

"It's not a couple, actually," Kalina said, smiling, radiating confidence. "It's just a mom."

"Okay," Dr. Grind said, interested in hearing Kalina's case. They were now in their third hour of deliberations and yet, to Dr. Grind, it felt like no time had passed at all. They were making something, he told himself. They were mapping out the years of their own lives, and the lives of perfect strangers. It was exhilarating.

"Isabel Poole, nineteen years old."

Dr. Grind thought for a second and then remembered the name. This was the girl who had been recommended by Dr. Horton Jackson.

"She's perfect," Kalina said. "She's absolutely perfect."

Things had moved quickly for Preston after his initial meeting with Brenda Acklen. After a career spent begging for money, scraping together grants or university funding, he was shocked by how easy it was when you had access to billions of dollars, the power behind that money that induced people to do whatever you said. There were no committees, no advisory board. Mrs. Acklen had no interest in these formal proceedings. "Who knows how long I'll be on this earth," she told Preston. "I want to make this happen right now."

So it was just Preston and the theories he was developing, in consultation with Mrs. Acklen, no stopgaps or oversight. Preston asked for something, postdoctoral fellows for research, a full staff of nurses and child care professionals, a complex to house the families, money to take care of these children, Mrs. Acklen wrote a check or called her lawyers or just said, simply, "Okay then."

During one of his many visits to Brenda's home in Knoxville to discuss the project, she asked him, "Have you decided on the name yet?" Branding was important to her, she reminded him, had been one of her husband's greatest interests in business.

"I think so," he replied. "The Expanded Family."

"Oh, yes?" she said, still smiling, but the light had gone out behind it. "You like that?"

"I think it encompasses what we're doing here, not just an extended family, but an expanded one, moving out in all directions."

"Well, it is straightforward," she said. "But can I offer some constructive criticism?"

When he nodded, now afraid, she continued, "It's got to be memorable. It has to ring true but also suggest something more than what they had already suspected."

"Who is *they*?" he asked her, and she replied, "Everyone in the world."

"Well," Dr. Grind said, now completely flummoxed, "do you have any thoughts on it?"

She smiled again, the light returned. "I do. I thought back to something we had discussed when we first met, the idea of boundlessness, of how this will continue from family to family, forever."

"Well, technically, it's going to end after eight—"

"No, Preston. No, it won't. Even if that's true, we won't say it. This will outlast both of us, will be our true gift to the world."

"I see," he said, not totally seeing.

"The Infinite Family Project," she said, her hands out in front of her like she was offering it to him.

"I see," he said.

"I like that," she said, as if he had been the one to suggest it, her voice ringing with certainty. "That will certainly look good on a T-shirt."

Dr. Grind smiled and nodded. She had the money. She got to name it. It was only fair.

Mrs. Acklen had initially worried about the study being connected to the Acklen Super Stores brand. "My sons, honestly, would have a conniption fit if they knew I was fully funding a study to redefine traditional family values. They were, god bless them, raised with every need and want fulfilled. To them, things work just fine as they are. They don't know what it's like to be totally lost, to have no idea how to get from one day to the next." In the end, however, it seemed advantageous to the project, and Preston's ability to bring in talented people, if her name, and her money, were attached to The Infinite Family Project. Two days after she agreed, her publicity department had contacted the *New York Times* and an article had been written. "The sons are not happy," Mrs. Acklen had reported to Preston by e-mail. "Oh well."

Mrs. Acklen's lawyers created the Early Childhood Foundation, which would house The IFP, and transferred an initial deposit of eighty million dollars into the account. More would come, Mrs. Acklen assured Preston, as needed. Almost immediately after he was able to utilize the money, he hired these three fellows, all incredibly talented and perceptive and willing to enter into this unconventional study because he could offer them three times what they would make elsewhere. And, of course, there was the chance to do something entirely unique, to make something brand-new and see if it worked.

"I don't think, honestly, that the project has done enough to take into account the challenges that face single mothers," Kalina said. Kalina's research at Harvard had focused on the implications of attachment parenting for feminism. She had argued, and her study had supported, that attachment parenting actively inhibited the agency of mothers from a societal, philosophical, and emotional standpoint. She argued for cooperative child rearing as a more progressive model; she was the first fellow whom Dr. Grind sought out. "We've talked about low-income families, but at least those couples have each other. Single mothers are forced to navigate these issues entirely on their own; that's coupled with the unrealistic expectations of modern parenting. I think we owe it to ourselves to include a single parent in the family."

"Well, I think that's a reasonable request, though it means one less parent involved in the day-to-day activities of the larger family."

"That seems to be a fair trade-off," said Jill, from Duke University, who specialized in gifted children, the markers of child prodigies, and Jeffrey agreed as well.

"So, why is Isabel the single parent that we choose?" Dr. Grind asked.

"She's quite young, nineteen, but she scored a 138 on the Stanford-Binet IQ test, the highest score of all the parents that I screened. She has esoteric talents for someone so young, as well. Of all the parents with whom I corresponded, she was the most comprehensive in her answers."

"What about the father?" Jeffrey asked.

"He committed suicide after Isabel became pregnant," Kalina answered.

"Jesus," said Jeffrey, shaking his head.

"Her mother also passed away when Isabel was thirteen."

"Well, she's certainly deserving of something good in her life after all that," Preston replied. "But do you think someone so young, without a partner, would fit into the project?"

"Isn't that the whole point of the project?" Kalina asked. "To provide a cooperative parenting model that would benefit people exactly like Isabel?"

"Let me see the folder," Preston said, and Kalina slid it across the table. He looked at the data, her history. He remembered Dr. Horton Jackson's insistence that Isabel be considered for the project before he agreed to help facilitate the search for prospective parents. Brenda Acklen had contacted Jackson early in the process; apparently Mrs. Acklen had been a vocal supporter of his congressional run and had been a prime donor, and he orchestrated Preston's unfettered access to so many OB/GYNs in Tennessee. His name had opened doors and had given legitimacy to Preston's project in the early stages. It wouldn't hurt to take this girl, whom Dr. Jackson had referred to as a friend of the family, in order to show his appreciation.

He stared at the photo on the projector; the girl was quite pretty, tomboyish and freckled, though there was something mysterious, something serious and dark, behind her eyes, something beyond what a teenager would or should possess. Her eyes, emerald green and hypnotic, reminded him of his wife. He thought about Marla for perhaps the fifth or sixth time that day, and he smiled. He noticed then that the fellows were all staring at him in silence, waiting for his answer. Dr. Grind nodded in approval.

"Okay," he said. "She's in." He placed her folder on the stack and then looked toward Jill. "Who's next?" he asked, and waited for someone else to make themselves known to him.

Preston met Marla Starr when he was living in Cambridge in the mid-1990s, getting his Ph.D. but not even old enough to drink yet, ostracized, understandably, by the other doctoral students. He had begun the program when he was barely a teenager; his youth made it easy for him to communicate with the children whom he was studying, but in all other respects, his age was a severe hindrance, his self-possession and intelligence coming off as creepy when housed in such a slight frame. For Preston, the work was easy enough, almost too easy, and so he was left with so much time and, his parents back in New York, no friends to speak of, no one to talk to. He was also teaching a section in Contemporary Issues in Psychology to undergrads at Harvard, most of the kids as old or older than he was and, when the class ended for the day and the students left, he had the weird sensation of wanting to follow them to wherever they were going next, hoping they might lead him to something that seemed normal.

Marla was one of his students, a sophomore from Atlanta, Georgia, majoring in psychology; she was short and stocky, her brown hair obscuring her face, which was dotted with acne. Her eyes, green and depthless, would unsteady Preston if he ever looked her way during class, which was often. She came to his office hours frequently, though she made perfect grades on all the exams, seemingly without effort. She flirted with him, though he had trouble deciphering exactly what it meant or how to respond. She called him *Professor Kid Genius* and liked to punch his arm, which hurt more than she intended, or perhaps just as much as she intended. After she finished his class in the fall, she returned to his office the next semester and gave him a flyer for a show at TT the Bear's that weekend. "I'm playing," she said. "I'm really good. I want you to see that I'm really good at something."

"I already know you're good at something," he said. "You were the best student in my class."

"I want you to know that I'm good at something important, Professor Grind," she said, rolling her eyes. "Something that matters."

They were an all-girl punk band made up of Harvard undergrads called Plug It Up, who had just self-released their first album, *Blood in the Rafters*. "We love that movie," she said, and when he seemed not to understand, she continued, "*Carrie*? It's like the best movie of all time. All of us in the band, we all think we're Carrie." That night, he rented the movie and felt slightly disturbed by Marla in the best possible way.

When Preston showed up for their set that Saturday, the band opening for Sebadoh, which even he knew was a big deal, he stood near the front of the stage and watched as Marla carried out her drum kit and set it up. "You came!" she said when she saw him, doing a strange little jig as she ran over to the edge of the stage and waved to him. "You're going to love this," she assured him, and he began to feel certain that he would.

Their set lasted only twenty minutes and yet they managed to play every song on their album, a wave of sound that finally crashed over the audience only after the girls had already left the stage. The set had ended, Preston finally determined, not because their slot was over, but because they had no other songs to play. Though no one in the band seemed to have any formal training, Marla seemed the least interested in technique of all of them, her rickety drum kit held together with duct tape, always seemingly about to collapse under the burden of her intensity. It seemed, from Preston's vantage point, that she had four or even six arms when she played, the sound so jarring and fast. She also sang backing vocals, without the need for amplification, her hair whipping around her head, blood seeping from under her fingernails, an unstable element under intense pressure. Preston fell in love with her, her wildness that he did not possess, without reservation or concern for how he would win her heart.

After their set, while Sebadoh was playing, Marla came over from their merch table and punched Preston in the arm, her teeth chattering with excitement. "I told you I was good," she said, smiling. "You were the absolute best," he told her and, before he had even finished the sentence, she was kissing him.

They married once she had graduated and he had finished his Ph.D. Nine months later, they had a boy, Jody, while Marla was getting her master's in Human Development and Psychology and Preston was teaching at Stony Brook and already beginning his work toward the Artificial Village project. For five years, life was better than anything Preston could have ever hoped for, better than anything his parents had ever prepared him to expect.

And then, one night in the dead of winter, Marla and Jody were driving back from the grocery store and she lost control of the car and slid off the road, flipping over and hitting a tree. Both Marla and Jody were dead before Preston even received a call about the accident. And, as if he was three years old again, he felt the certainty of disaster, the impossibility of uninterrupted happiness. He felt every single good thing in his life evaporate into the atmosphere and he was left with his theories about family that, now, made absolutely no fucking difference to him. His family was gone. He did not need a village any longer. He needed to be alone, to let the pain seep into him. It was as deep a depression that he could imagine a human enduring, always shocking to discover that there seemed to be no bottom to it. He left the Artificial Village project, stopped appearing on TV shows and in magazines, and simply cocooned himself within his empty house, a house that creaked and settled in the middle of the night and woke him from uneasy sleep; and he was always surprised, no matter what his childhood training had prepared him for, to discover that he was all alone.

It was midnight when they had finished and now, to Dr. Grind's right, was a stack of fifteen potential families. They anticipated that, even with all the screening they'd done, a number of these families would refuse the offer once they heard the specific conditions, but they were optimistic. The complex, which felt quiet and empty with only the four of them wandering through the main building, would soon fill up with people, with children, and their real work could begin.

Unable to sleep, still burning off the anxiety of their decisions, the four of them walked around the enclosed courtyard of the complex, the stars shockingly clear in the sky.

"How many families do you really think will say yes?" Jeffrey asked Dr. Grind.

"All of them," he replied.

"Seriously," Jeffrey said.

"Maybe a dozen," Preston finally offered, an optimistic number but he felt he had to combat some of Jeffrey's inherent pessimism for the project's future.

"We should take a bet," Kalina offered. "Dr. Grind says a dozen. I say ten. Jill?"

"Eight, maybe?" Jill offered.

"Three," Jeffrey said, his voice flat with certainty.

"If there are only three families," Dr. Grind said, "then I won't need any fellows to help me."

"Okay," Jeffrey then said. "Four."

They walked the length of the complex. The AstroTurf that covered the buildings, so vibrant and whimsical in the daytime, felt like a living, breathing organism in the dark. They sat on benches situated around one of the three playgrounds, the ground soft and rubbery with a special polymer made to lessen the impact on children's bones while playing.

"I just have to ask one more time," Jill said. "We definitely aren't going to allow pot within the complex?"

"Not again," Jeffrey said.

"It just seems like maybe it wouldn't be the worst thing in the world if people were allowed to smoke a joint every now and then."

"When you say *people,* who do you mean exactly?" Kalina asked her.

"Not just me," Jill replied. "I'm sure others will wonder the same thing."

"No drugs," Preston said, again. "This is a scientific endeavor. It's not some hippie commune."

"Sometimes it feels like it," Jill said, and the rest of them sat in silence, considering the truth of this statement.

For Preston, this had been one of the guiding principles of the study. The Infinite Family Project would focus on communal parenting, but he wanted to remove the ideological stumbling blocks that had hampered so many American communes in the past. No religion, no "back to the land" ecological bent, no sharing of sexual partners. He had, in several interviews, stated that this would be a true experiment in communal parenting, but the goal was not to isolate themselves from the outside world. Eventually, he asserted, the parents and their children would be returned to society, stronger than they would have been otherwise, not broken by the failure of the communal experience. He had no idea, truth be told, if any of this would actually work.

Two days later, Mrs. Acklen came to visit the complex, the first time she had set foot on the property since the project began. "Good lord," Mrs. Acklen said when she saw the AstroTurf. "It looks wilder in person than it does in pictures."

Dr. Grind walked over to Mrs. Acklen and she kissed him and then held one of his hands. He introduced her to the fellows and then took her on a tour of the facilities. As they walked, Mrs. Acklen said, "My husband bought this tract of land about thirty years ago. He just told me it was a good deal and someday he'd get around to figuring out what to do with it. I think maybe he envisioned a hunting lodge or maybe a wildlife preserve. I can assure you, he did not envision this." Once they'd finished the tour, Mrs. Acklen hugged Dr. Grind. "It's perfect. It's a perfect little world that you've got here. I really think this could work."

"I very much hope it does, Brenda."

"When do you talk to the families?" she asked him.

"Next week. I will personally speak to each prospective family and tell them everything about the project, all the parameters and financial incentives that we've discussed."

"Preston," she said, gesturing for him to come closer to her. He stepped uncomfortably close and listened intently. "Do you remember that baseball movie with James Earl Jones in it?"

"I never saw it, but I know what you're talking about. *Field of Dreams.*"

"That's it. You know that guy builds a baseball field in the middle of nowhere and the line is, 'If you build it, he will come.'"

"Yes, I've certainly heard that line before."

"Well, my husband hated that movie. It was irrational, but that line just made him so irritated. He would always tell me, 'By god, it's not enough to just build something. You have to give people a reason to stay.' That's what he thought with the stores, that you had to sell people on something that they may or may not have known they wanted, because, ultimately, it's best for both you and them if they believe in it."

"I imagine that I understand that logic, Brenda," Dr. Grind answered, wondering if the long car ride had unsteadied Mrs. Acklen's faculties.

"You need to make these families understand that we're doing something important. That this is going to make their lives so much better than they would have been otherwise."

"I'll do my best. I promise you."

"I know you will, sweetie," she said, and kissed him one more time.

He walked her back to the car, where her assistant and the driver were waiting, making small talk with the fellows. As the car drove away, and they waved good-bye, Jeffrey asked Dr. Grind, "What happens to us if she dies?"

Before Dr. Grind could answer, Kalina said, "She won't die. That much money, you get to live for as long as you want."

"There are measures in place," Dr. Grind assured them, though he had no idea if this was true. It seemed in poor taste to mention the likelihood of the study outliving the donor, especially when so much money was at stake. And what he didn't say, though he understood from his own experiences, was that there were no measures that truly protected against disaster; you simply held on to what mattered and hoped that you found your way to the other side.

They all turned and walked back into the complex, the buildings blending into the woods that surrounded them, keeping their existence a secret until they decided it was time to be known.

chapter seven

zzy was wearing clothes too nice for chopping up steaming piles of pig meat, so Mr. Tannehill had taken a black garbage bag, cut holes for her head and arms, and pulled it over her head. Izzy made a face of extreme embarrassment, and Mr. Tannehill threw up his arms. "What?" he asked. "What's the problem?"

"Wearing a garbage bag defeats the purpose of wearing nice clothes," she said. "I think it'd be better to have grease stains on my blouse."

"Do what you want, Izzy," he said, "but you look pretty even in a garbage bag, so don't think too much on it."

Izzy went to work with her cleavers, using one to chop and the other to move the meat around on the block. She loved the reassuring thunk the cleaver made as it turned the meat into something perfect. She had kicked off her sneakers and was standing in a tub of ice-cold water, which Mr. Tannehill refilled every two hours to help with the swelling that came from standing around all day in a dry, hot room.

"I'm just nervous," she said to Mr. Tannehill once she had finished with the pig. Dr. Preston Grind, the head of The IFP, was meeting her in less than an hour to discuss her future, or, rather, for him to outline her future. She had once again Googled his name the night before and found more information than she could process. She gave up halfway into a YouTube video of him on *Oprah,* surrounded by children, his manner easy and untroubled as he gave himself over to their pleas for his attention. He was legitimate, that was all she cared about at the moment. He was real, and he thought she was special enough that he was coming to see her.

She was overtly pregnant now, six months into the process, no hiding what would be coming. She knew that she made Mr. Tannehill nervous, the thought of having to deliver her child in a smokehouse, but she needed the work to keep her mind occupied. At all times, the baby was in motion. She felt the rhythmic lurch in her belly, the baby's hiccups, and on a few occasions while resting in bed at night, she watched the baby push against her belly, fetal movement, and she would sit in controlled stillness, hoping to see it again. She was, for the first time in her life, infinitely interesting to herself, not a single change in her circumstances going unnoticed.

When she first became pregnant, all she could think about was the strange fact that a living thing was inside her, some kind of horror movie. Each week that passed, she appreciated how many of the pregnancy sites online compared the size of the fetus to food, starting with a mere poppy seed and then moving to a grape and then a lemon. It made her feel like she wasn't having a baby at all, merely growing a vegetable in her belly, an organic garden housed within her own body. But as the baby asserted itself, began to move and flip and test the limits of the space it had been given, she grew irritated with the fruit comparisons. Fuck it, she thought, she was not having an avocado, she was making a baby. She wanted the power of creation now, to own the fact that she was making something tangible and beautiful. It was a rare feeling of satisfaction, from her experience as a teen mother, because everyone seemed to assume that you'd made a terrible mistake and that the baby's development was just a harbinger of doom to come. People either avoided talking about it or made faces of the most punch-worthy suggestions of sympathy. Why, she now wondered, when a woman became pregnant, weren't people lining up on either side of her as she made her way through each day, wildly cheering her on like she was running the most important marathon in the world? Other days, a fair number of days perhaps, she wanted simply to be invisible, to crawl into a cave with her baby and wait for it to come, far removed from anyone who thought they knew their future.

"Your shift's done," Mr. Tannehill said to her, and Izzy awkwardly struggled to lift the garbage bag over her belly and then to free her head from the black plastic. "Now, you're sure you don't want someone to be there with you? Just to have somebody else to listen?"

"I'll be fine," Izzy assured him, and she laced up her sneakers and walked through the kitchen and into the dining area, seated herself at a table, and waited for the doctor to arrive.

Dr. Grind was exactly on time, to the second, and he pushed open the door and stood, searching for her. She had the power, though it was fleeting, the last time she would be the one who knew something that he didn't, and she relished his uncertainty for a second, two seconds, and then she raised her hand, caught his attention, and waved him over to her table.

There was no way around her surprise at his youthfulness; she had seen images of him, but in person it was hard to shake the notion that he was a child impersonating an adult. He was in his thirties, but he looked younger than she was, his face free of stubble, his body undefined by fat or muscle. He wore sneakers, gray New Balance running shoes, and this calmed her, his lack of formality. Dr. Grind smiled at her and walked with an unhurried gait toward her, his hand still raised, as if he was expecting, at any moment, to run into an invisible wall.

"Izzy?" he said, and it made her happy that he had not used her given name, had prevented her from the awkwardness of correcting him.

"That's me," she replied, absentmindedly patting her stomach as if to affirm her identity. It felt like a date; she could not shake this feeling as he took a seat beside her, not across from her.

"I'm Dr. Preston Grind. I've heard a lot about you, Izzy, and I'm so happy that we finally, after all this time, have the chance to meet."

"Me, too," she replied.

"Do you mind if I eat something?" he asked. "I skipped breakfast and, anyway, I was hoping to try some of the barbecue here. I'm from New York; we have barbecue there, but not like this."

Izzy just nodded. Her nerves were just beginning to spike, in trying to act like she wasn't terrified about what was going to happen to her, and, as if he could read her mind, he set down his menu, smiled again, and said, "Just to be entirely upfront, Izzy, I want you to know that I am here to ask you and your child to be a part of our project. I'm going to do my best to convince you to say yes. I think, we all think, that you are a very special person and that you'd be a great asset to our study. I have so much information that it's impossible for it all to make sense, but I have all the time in the world and I'll answer every question you have until you feel comfortable making a decision, one way or the other."

"I'm nervous," Izzy admitted.

"I'm more nervous than you are," he said. "Believe me." Izzy was grateful for the sentiment but knew it was total bullshit.

Dr. Grind ordered a barbecue sandwich and a sweet tea. The waitress took his menu and walked off; Izzy noticed that all the waitresses were throwing glances at her. She imagined that they were debating whether or not this was the father of her child. Of course, they would never ask her. Izzy's awkwardness, which manifested itself as intensity, repelled all inquiries into her private life. It did not help her paranoia, however, to be left out of the conversation. She wished now that she had met with the doctor at a park or library, somewhere quiet and private.

"I have some pictures," Dr. Grind said, as if he'd just thought of it, and reached into his army green tote bag, which had The Infinite Family Project logo on it in silver ink. He produced a stack of photos of buildings that looked alien, interdimensional, at first glance. It was huge, so much space, so new and clean, surrounded by woods. It felt private and yet teeming with activity.

"It's beautiful," Izzy said.

"I'm happy to hear you say that," Dr. Grind replied. "This is the site of the project. It sits on about four hundred and fifty acres, if you can believe that, so we have a lot of space, lots of trails for hiking and running, but we're close to supermarkets and a hospital, all the things you could want in a town. And we're about thirty minutes from Nashville, so there are lots of opportunities there, as well."

He showed her pictures of the interiors of the buildings and it seemed to Izzy like a day care center for billionaires, lots of electronics and lighting and soft colors. "This is where I would live?" Izzy asked, almost ashamed to be considered.

"You would have your very own place, but you'd also have access to the rest of the complex, a swimming pool, a full-size restaurant-quality kitchen, a dining hall where we take all of our meals, a number of gardens, and lots of spaces that are as yet undefined. For instance, if someone needed a studio space for their art, we could accommodate that. The complex is designed to grow alongside the residents, so as you learn more about what you need, we have the resources and space to make that available to you."

"This does not feel real at all," Izzy said.

Dr. Grind's food arrived and he gestured to the plate in front of him, asking for Izzy's permission to eat. She nodded, embarrassed, and he smiled, rubbed his hands together, and picked up the sandwich, bits of meat falling from the bun. He took a large bite, chewed, and then set the sandwich back on the plate. "This is the best thing I've ever eaten," he said.

Izzy smiled; he had a faint ring of grease around his mouth, but he made no move to wipe it away. "Try some of this sauce on it," she offered, and handed him a squeeze bottle of the vinegar sauce. He obeyed her orders and took another bite. "You made this, Izzy?" he asked. She nodded with great certainty. "I could eat this every day for the rest of my life," he said. He took four more huge bites, barely chewing, finished the sandwich, and then held out his hand. Izzy took it and he gave her an approving shake. "Thank you," he said. Izzy felt the slightest twinge of love for Dr. Grind.

"Izzy, there's a lot of information to go over and much of it is rather complicated. Still, the basic idea, as you've learned from the information we've been sending you, is that we're trying to explore new ways to help children develop. It's said over and over, but the first few years of a child's life are incredibly important. The problem with that statement is that it puts a lot of pressure on the parents. There's an overriding fear that, if a child doesn't receive the right amount of care or is neglected in any way, then they'll be at a disadvantage for the rest of their life. And that's simply not true; however, I do think that our country could do a better job of addressing the needs of both children and parents in order to help them with what is admittedly a very difficult task."

"Okay," Izzy said, hearing nothing that was out of the ordinary, waiting for the bizarre to arrive, knowing it was coming or else Dr. Grind wouldn't be sitting beside her, offering her this opportunity.

"So often, parents are left to fend for themselves, to figure out how to raise their children, and I think, and my work has reflected this, that there needs to be a level of investment in each child's life, a community-wide interest in the fate of every child who is born into this world. If two parents is the traditional ideal, then why not four parents? What could you gain if there were now four people heavily invested in that child's future? Why not six? Why not a situation where every child feels an attachment to all the adults in their lives? My work, for the past ten years, has focused on helping parents and their children in neighborhoods and communities receive support from their fellow man, a village of sorts, created to help raise each child so they feel loved and respected and have opportunities that they wouldn't have otherwise. Now, The Infinite Family Project is different. What we're trying to do in this case is to build a communal setting where a group of parents and their children have access to every possible advantage, to group families right at birth to see if we can improve the way in which we raise children. If my previous work sought to encourage all adults to feel connected to the children around them, then this project seeks to turn every possible adult into an actual parent. We want to create a scenario where every child feels that every adult is, in essence, one of their parents and cares about them without hesitation or reservation. Does this make sense, Izzy?"

"Not entirely, if I'm being honest, Dr. Grind," she replied. "It sounds like some kind of commune."

"Well, not exactly," Dr. Grind replied. "It's not exactly a commune, it's a scientific family."

"That sounds like a cult, no offense," Izzy said.

Dr. Grind smiled. "That's very perceptive," he said. "That's good." He took a sip of his tea, winced at the sweetness of it, and then stared at his hands for a good five seconds. It seemed like Izzy had inadvertently created a riddle that Dr. Grind was now trying to solve.

"How about this, then," he continued. "I am in the process of finding ten families for a ten-year study. Those ten families will live together in the complex and have access to the very best in child care, child development, and child education. These children, instead of being only children within their traditional families, will now have nine brothers and sisters and they will live together in the complex and spend their early childhood feeling that companionship. And the parents of these children, in exchange for their time and their hard work, will have access to their own opportunities for education, job training, and parental support, things that they would have struggled to obtain on their own, weighed down by the responsibilities of parenthood. Beyond the actual families, we will have trained specialists in every available field ready to help meet the challenges of raising a child. Our hope is that, by the time the project has come to an end, the children will have received a level of care unlike anything they would have received otherwise, and the parents will be better prepared and more stable for the future. All that I'm asking in return is for you to open up your belief system to include a more communal style of parenting, to make room in your heart and mind for not just one child, but many children. The hardest part of this entire project, for the parent at least, is that you will not be defined as the child's primary parent for a portion of the project's duration. You will always see your child and interact with them on a daily basis, but they will only think of you as one of their many parents. It's a necessary component for the early years of the child's development, until they are ready to accept the fact of their biological link."

Izzy felt her skin instantly turn to goose bumps, but she tried to disguise her discomfort by looking as thoughtful as possible, as if she was merely comparing Dr. Grind's ideas to her own scientific methods for raising children. She felt that perhaps this was more than she could handle, but then she worried that this was part of the test, to judge her ability to accept new ways of thinking. If she wavered, even for a second, the offer would be rescinded, and she would never know what her life could have been. With a primitive instinct, she held on to her emotions until they flattened out, until she felt capable. She looked up at Dr. Grind, whose expression had not changed, with no sign of discomfort. Izzy nodded, slowly, and Dr. Grind nodded in return. A code she could not understand, the gesture nevertheless gave Izzy the confidence to speak, as if talking could make her come to terms with what Dr. Grind was offering her.

"Dr. Grind, I want my kid to have access to everything you're talking about. I want to be able to provide for him and to be a better parent. But I don't know if I can do what you're asking. I'm a lonely person, a solitary person, I guess is a better term. I just don't know if I can walk into some new space and be surrounded by people who are now supposed to be my new family and be expected to love them and care for them. I'm worried about taking care of one kid. I can't take care of ten kids."

"You won't have to, Izzy. That's the beauty of this project. You will never, for as long as you live with us, be alone again. You will be surrounded by people who care for you, who will do everything they can to help you become the person you envision. It will be so strange. I can't deny that. I'm asking you to love other children as if they are your own. I'm asking you to support the other parents as if you are their sister or best friend or partner. I'm asking you to accept a nontraditional family dynamic. Your child, as much as you love him, will no longer be entirely your own. He will be a part of a larger family. But I wouldn't ask you to do this if I didn't think that, ultimately, it was going to change your life for the better."

Dr. Grind was looking at Izzy with an intensity that she never experienced in relation to herself. It was a crazy idea to be included in something so obviously flawed and yet so idealistic and beautiful. She imagined her son, nothing but a blur at this point in her mind, surrounded by other children, every day a chance to be exceptional. She thought, for the millionth time, of her future as it lay before her without the aid of this project, working two jobs to make ends meet, her son in the cheapest day care she could find, so tired at the end of the day that her baby felt like an unbreakable curse, failing each and every day until the bottom fell out of the world.

She knew, without reservation, that her own mother would have chosen this project for Izzy. It had all the markings of something her mother would love, a woman who desired equations and routines to ensure excellence. The buildings themselves looked like an alien planet, something her mother would have drawn on a sheet of paper during a fever dream. Was she using the ghost of her mother to justify a life-changing decision? Maybe. But it wasn't difficult for Izzy, who had always kept her mother's ghost right at the edges of her life, to imagine that this felt preordained in some weird way.

She picked up the photos from the table and flipped through them again. It was a fantasy, science fiction, to think that this could be her home.

"Okay then," she said.

Dr. Grind's face opened up with shock. "Well, Izzy, you should think about this. I have about fifty pages of contracts and documents that you need to look at, have someone look over with you. I have about four more hours' worth of information to discuss. I want you to be a part of this project, but I want you to have the facts. This is not for everyone, not for most people, honestly. I want you to feel confident about this. It's ten years of your life. Ten years of your child's life."

"Okay," Izzy said, her face itching with embarrassment. "I'm sorry. I'll think about it more."

Izzy realized now that she had acquiesced too quickly, that she had almost missed out on hours of wooing, the unfamiliar joy of being wanted, of hearing Dr. Grind offer up even more ridiculous promises, even more pseudoscientific reasons for why her son would become a superhero, a kid genius. She would have missed out on listening to someone tell her, over and over, that things were going to be fine. She sat back in her chair, the baby happily swimming in the confines of her own body, and she smiled at Dr. Grind, who smiled back, shrugging his shoulders as if he couldn't believe this was happening either.

That night, her messenger bag weighed down with the papers that Dr. Grind had left with her after their three-hour conversation, Izzy walked into her room and locked the door, even though no one else was in the house at the moment. She took out the papers, shaggy with Post-it notes attached to where she had to sign her name, and laid them out on her bed, as if they were a code that could be broken. Dr. Grind had suggested that she have a lawyer look over the documents, as if Izzy had access to someone with a law degree, someone who could make sense of what Dr. Grind had already spent hours explaining to her. There was a fifteen-page memo that outlined the ten years of the project, but Izzy simply could not wrap her head around the next few months of her life, much less ten years into the future, as if anything would turn out the way Dr. Grind and his assistants were so confidently predicting. Or maybe they were right, maybe they had lined up the project in such a way that they really could see into the future. Her eyes wandered over the documents so that she caught snippets of the project.

> At night, the children are placed in a communal sleeping area, tended by a rotating team of nurses, caregivers, and biological parents (determined by color-coded bands).

She tried to imagine this reality, but she soon realized that the only way she would truly understand any of this would be to throw herself into it and see for herself. It was strange to realize it, but The IFP, in trying to give her a range of options in order to have a more fully realized life, was banking on the simple fact that she had almost no options at the moment, which made it impossible to refuse the project.

* * *

At 10:30 P.M., her father returned from the market, carrying two plastic bags filled with the unsold food that had been sitting under the heat lamps for hours, corn dogs and chicken fingers and potato wedges and thick, tasteless wedges of pizza. This was, and had been for years, her father's primary source of nutrition. Izzy walked into the living room and sat down on the sofa while her father eased himself into his recliner. He barely acknowledged her presence, simply nodded toward all the food on the coffee table, and bit into a corn dog. She searched through the food, already lukewarm from the drive home, and took a chicken finger for herself.

"You want something?" he asked her, when it became clear that she wasn't going to leave the room. Her father, for as long as she could remember, was a cipher to her. His face was perpetually empty of emotion, as if everything meaningful had been burned out of him. He accepted her existence, made no effort to prevent her from anything she chose to do, but he had never once offered to help her or to support those decisions. Izzy had been his wife's responsibility and, once she died, it was as if the link between him and his child had become untethered. He never hit her or yelled at her, but she also could not remember him ever saying that he loved her. Actually, if she had ever heard him say it to her, she would have had no idea how to respond. And, yet, she did not begrudge him any of this. His life was awful and she was quite sure that she, with her simple need, had made it more so for him.

"I'm having this baby," Izzy said.

"I know all about that," he said.

"Well, I've been talking to some people, some doctors, and they want to help me take care of the baby. They've offered me money and scholarship opportunities and health insurance and all kinds of things like that."

"Good for you," he said, and she felt like he genuinely meant it, even though his voice was flat and dead. "I never understood how in the world you was going to take care of that baby on your own. I sure don't have any money. I'm near underwater on just about everything."

"I'd have to go away, not far, but up near Nashville. I wouldn't be around here anymore, probably not for a long time."

"You need to do what's best for you, Izzy," he told her. "And the kid, I guess, too." He leaned over the coffee table and then chose a slice of cheese pizza. He popped the top on another beer and they sat again in silence while he watched a war movie with the volume turned way down.

"It's a hard decision," she said.

"Okay then," he told her. "You can't say I've ever stood in the way of anything you wanted to do. I don't intend to start now. Sounds like a good idea, though. Either way, you're welcome to stay here as long as you want."

This was the longest she and her father had talked in years, and she felt the strange sensation of wanting it to go on. He had partly made her, she understood this, but she had yet to figure out where the evidence was within her.

As if the force of Izzy's own need had temporarily sharpened his focus, had burned away the alcohol in his system, her father leaned forward in his chair and stared at her for a second or two, his eyes unclear and bloodshot but most certainly focused on her.

"I have never been a good father," he said, waving his hand as if to stop her from disagreeing, though she had remained silent. "I loved your mother, once upon a time, but we had you and she changed. And I blamed you for that. Then your mom died, and so much time had passed that I didn't feel like it was right to step in and try to be a dad to you. That's my fault. So, I'm sorry. I'm sorry you've had such a rough go of it."

As if every bit of breath had been sucked out of his body, he visibly sagged back into the thin comfort of his easy chair. Izzy had the distinct feeling that her father had been possessed in these moments, that someone else was speaking through him. It didn't make her love him more, but it made her understand him just a little, which was maybe all that was left in her family. She looked at him, her own father, and felt her heart constrict around the thought of what could have been.

She stood up and walked back into her room, where the papers were still waiting for her. She could not figure out why she was hesitating, other than the nagging suspicion that, once she signed the papers, she would never know if she could have done it on her own. She had a strange, unspoken pride that she could handle anything; she'd felt this way since her mother, the one person who truly loved her, had died. Ever since then, she believed that if she tamped down her emotions enough and made herself resistant to all pain, she would never need anyone's help and could be left entirely alone. To enter into this project, it felt like all of her bones would have to be broken and reset. She took a pen from her desk and, with an unsteady signature that could have been any name, she signed each and every page without reading it again, initialed where needed, and then collected the documents, shoved them into her bag, and tossed the bag under her bed. She retrieved her baby journal from the nightstand, dutifully filled out the information, and then read the question for that day. *What one thing do you want to be sure your baby has that you didn't?* She was too tired, too scared to even think about this question. She was past this kind of worry or contemplation now, was already drifting into some kind of dream that would take on the correct dimensions and shape as she lived in it. She wrote, in all caps, EVERYTHING and then put the book away and fell dead asleep.

The next morning, she drove to the hotel where Dr. Grind was staying and sat in the lobby while she called him on her cell phone. He answered and she told him to meet her downstairs.

"Hello, Izzy," he said when he walked out of the elevator, that easy smile on his face that seemed so genuine, as if the world was worthy of being loved.

"I talked it over with my dad," she said, letting the doctor believe the project had actually been discussed in detail. "I thought about it myself. I looked at the papers. I want to do it."

Dr. Grind's expression of patient kindness broke for a split second and was flooded with what looked like relief, as if he'd just defused a bomb but didn't want to make a big deal about it. "I am so happy to hear that," he said.

"Here're the contracts; I signed everywhere that it said to."

"Did you go over them? You can still have time to look at it and make sure you're satisfied with—"

"I'm sure about it," Izzy said. "I've decided."

It seemed that Dr. Grind either had too much to say or nothing else, and he stood there, looking at her with great interest. He finally took the documents from her hands and then he said, "I'm so pleased. You won't regret this."

"I'm used to regret," she said, "so it won't be a huge deal."

He laughed and then gestured to the breakfast bar in the corner of the lobby. "Are you hungry?" he asked. "I was just going to get something to eat. I'd love the company, if you can spare the time."

She nodded and they walked across the lobby, two people about to eat breakfast, the most normal thing in the world. Izzy had signed over her child to a scientific study, had entered into something that she could not explain to normal people without seeming slightly crazy. She would not think about that now, or ever again. She was moving forward into the new future that she had made, and she was ravenous.

chapter eight

Izzy was impatient. The baby was almost a week past its due date with no signs of revealing himself to the world. Back at the doctor's for yet another checkup, she listened as Dr. Kirwin, unflappable and inappropriate, kept telling her that there was nothing to worry about. "You just have a nice womb, little lady," he said, patting her stomach. "He isn't ready to come out." He told her that there were no complications and to simply relax, stay comfortable, and everything would be fine. She gritted her teeth, as if there was any way that she could get comfortable in her current state. She was dizzy, constipated, couldn't stop urinating, had constant heartburn, her breasts were killing her, her legs cramped, her feet ached, her back ached. She was a self-contained disaster, as if her body was making itself as inhospitable as possible to force the baby out of her, but it wasn't working. Aside from the terrifying jolt of Braxton-Hicks contractions from time to time, the baby showed no signs of leaving. "Let's say this," Dr. Kirwin told her. "You don't go into labor by this weekend, we'll induce. How about that?" Izzy simply nodded, had no time left for Dr. Kirwin and his jocular dismissal of her body.

Izzy, by this point, had quit her job at the Whole Hog, could no longer manage the work, and so she spent most of her time in her tiny bedroom, listening to her iPod or checking her e-mail. She had already packed up and shipped most of her clothing and personal effects, which Dr. Kwon assured her were set up and waiting for her at the complex. When she felt stir-crazy, she took walks, shuffling through the neighborhood while old women watched her suspiciously from their front porches, as if they thought that Izzy was scoping out their houses so she could come back later and give birth on their sofas. By the time she made it back to her own house, she was dizzy, short of breath, still so fucking pregnant.

Ever since she had elected to join The Infinite Family Project, Dr. Grind had included her in a Listserv with the other expectant parents. There were nine other couples, so apparently she was going to be the only single parent, the only person on her own. She would also be the youngest person involved in the project, and so the other women who had signed on were already talking to her like she was their little sister. Even though the project had yet to begin, Izzy could already see the benefits of finally having someone to talk to about the bizarre process of having a baby. Five months into her pregnancy, she had signed up for some classes at the community center, but had been embarrassed to be the only one who had come alone. Even the high school girls had managed to drag their boyfriends, one of whom refused to stop playing a game on his cell phone for the entire class, and so Izzy never went back, preferred the solitude of the Internet, which she convinced herself was just as good.

Now, however, she realized how nice it could be to have friends, or pen pals at the very least. Her favorite woman was Carmen, who was twenty-five years old and from Memphis. "I was so careful not to get pregnant, all through high school," she told Izzy in one e-mail. "Then I got cocky and let my guard down, just the littlest bit, and now here we are." She wanted to be a nurse, was currently working as a cashier at, funny enough, an Acklen Super Store. "I've worked there five years, don't even get health insurance," she wrote, "and now the lady who runs the whole joint wants to make sure I get taken care of. It's weird." It was weird, Izzy admitted; all of it was weird, and it felt good, on the Listserv, in private e-mails, even on the video chats they had set up, to hear the other men and women admit as much. They were now, for better or for worse, all in it together.

Except, goddamn it, Izzy was still pregnant. Over the past month and a half, every other woman had given birth by now, was spirited away to the complex, and, though she tried not to worry about it too much, the e-mails had come to an almost immediate halt. Carmen had finally e-mailed her a few days earlier and attached a photo of all the parents and their babies. "We pass the kids around like hot potatoes," Carmen said, "so they get used to us. Hurry up and have that baby and get over here!" Even though she'd been promised that she was now a part of something larger than herself, that she and her child would be surrounded by other people who would help her, she felt like she was already missing out. "Come on," she would say to the baby. "Come on now."

The day after her visit to the doctor, Izzy felt the contractions start around nine in the evening, and then she experienced a weird double sensation that happened almost in unison, of being able to breathe so much more easily while also needing to pee with a sudden and embarrassing urgency. She walked up and down the hallway of the house, tentatively touching her belly, as if trying to pick up frequencies from the bottom of the ocean. She hesitated calling or e-mailing anyone, felt the immediate distrust of her own body, a reluctance to believe that she was about to give birth until she had definite proof. She went to a bookmarked page on the stages of labor, read it carefully, and then turned off her computer. Her father came home, though he did not even call out to check on her, simply deposited himself on the recliner and turned on the TV. An hour later, the contractions still coming, she checked her underwear and saw blood and, almost immediately, forgot everything that she was supposed to know about childbirth. She knew that it was probably time to get to the hospital and yet something was keeping her inside the confines of her room, some irrational fear that, by stepping out of the house, everything that had been held at bay would come rushing toward her, her undefined future becoming clear and vibrant. She hunched over her bed, as if she was praying, and counted the seconds passing, reminding her that she was alive and well.

Finally, unable to put off the reality any longer, she walked into the living room. "Dad?" she said, wondering why she was being so tentative, as she softly jostled him in an attempt to pull him out of his eight-beer coma. Izzy felt the contractions again and sucked on her teeth to keep herself from making a sound. Her father's eyes were aggressively closed and his mouth was so wide open she could place her fist in it. Even if she managed to wake him, what then? He couldn't drive her to the hospital; at best she would help shoulder him into her truck and he would sleep as she drove herself to Chattanooga. Jesus, she was fifty minutes away from the hospital, she realized. She did not have time to turn her father into the person she wanted him to be.

Instead, she walked back into her room, moving so carefully, as if the slightest move could dislodge the baby and she would birth him on this filthy carpet. She shouldered her duffel bag, which she had packed nearly a month earlier in preparation for this very moment. It helped reaffirm the fact that she was a capable person, that she could do this. She walked out of the house, the stars so bright and nothing moving in the entire world except her baby. She started her truck and pulled onto the street, and then another contraction hit her and she accidentally hit the horn and accelerated without intending to do so. She started to realize that she could not drive herself; she was vibrating with a weird rush of endorphins. She could not focus. She pulled to the side of the road and tried to think. Finally, no other option available, she called Mr. Tannehill and waited for the reassuring softness of his voice.

"Who is this?" he said, not at all reassuring or kind. It was, Izzy reminded herself, two in the morning.

"Mr. Tannehill, this is Izzy. I hate doing this; I hate it so much."

"What's wrong, sweetie?" he said.

"I'm having the baby," she replied, and then she started breathing deeply, trying to catch her breath. "I need you to drive me to the hospital."

"I'm leaving right now," he said, and then the line went dead. She sat in the truck, thirty feet from her house, and regulated her breathing. For the past few weeks, she had been pleading with the baby to finally come and now, sitting in her truck, completely alone, she begged that he would hold on a little longer.

She heard the roar of Mr. Tannehill's engine before she saw the headlights. As he sped down her street, she flicked her headlights to catch his attention and he pulled alongside the truck. He threw open her door and lifted her, not a hesitation or a struggle in his movements, into his arms. He gently placed her into the backseat and she stretched out, trying to get comfortable. "My bag," she said, but he was already returning from her truck with the duffel bag. He was back in the car, shifting into gear, before she knew what was happening. "It's been a long time coming, sweetie," he told her. He reached into the backseat and she took his hand and squeezed it. "A hell of a long time coming," he said, and then Izzy focused on the sound of the engine taking her somewhere safe and clean, which was, she imagined, the most that anyone could ask for in an emergency.

When they arrived at the hospital, Izzy having notified them of her impending arrival on the drive there, Mr. Tannehill opened the door and helped Izzy onto the sidewalk. By this point, the contractions were so intense that Izzy was making a low, moaning sound like a grizzly bear, and she was hobbling toward the entrance like someone who'd learned about walking from YouTube videos. Mr. Tannehill shouldered most of her weight, his car still running, the driver's-side door wide open. "This way," a nurse who had run out to meet them said. "Let's get her a wheelchair," the nurse said, but Izzy, for reasons entirely unknown to her, refused the wheelchair. "Let me just keep walking," she said, as if she was about to finish a marathon and did not want assistance, and the nurse looked at Mr. Tannehill, shrugged, and gestured for them to follow her. When they made it to the reception desk, Izzy took the duffel bag from Mr. Tannehill and retrieved all of her information and forms for the nurse.

"Oh, I like it when they're prepared," she said to Mr. Tannehill, looking through the forms and nodding with satisfaction. "Okay, Isabel, let's get you to a room. Is your father coming with you?"

Mr. Tannehill shook his head and said, "I'll just stay in the waiting room, if that's okay. Unless you want me there, Izzy?"

Izzy did want him there, or, rather, wanted someone in the room with her, but she could not imagine the embarrassment of his presence when her private parts were exposed. "I'll be okay," she said, and tried to smile, but it was difficult since she was grinding her teeth so hard.

"You'll be okay," he said to her, and he squeezed her shoulders. The nurse led her to a room and helped her get into her robe. "That baby is coming, isn't it?" the nurse asked, and Izzy could only nod. "I'm a little scared," she admitted.

"Let's get you comfortable and you'll be less scared, I promise. The doctor has been alerted and she'll be here soon."

"She? My doctor is Dr. Kirwin."

"He's not on duty tonight. Dr. Starling is. She's very good, very capable. You'll love her."

It was a strange relief that, in her most vulnerable moment, Dr. Kirwin would not be present, that she might have this baby without a single comment about her hospitable womb or questions about her work toward finding a new boyfriend. She lay back on the bed and let the pain run through her, so intense that she felt it in her hair, in her toenails, in her rapidly beating heart. And then, good lord, all the pain was in her back and she grabbed on to the sheets underneath her and she wished that she had two tongues in her mouth so that she could go ahead and bite one of them off.

She wished Hal were still alive, if only for him to be present in this moment. She wanted to be on a team, to be a part of something, so that she could say, "I'm scared," or "This hurts," and someone who loved her would reply, "I'm scared, too," or "It will be over soon." She wished it wasn't so, but all she felt when she pictured him, sheepishly handsome and promising her all manner of good things, was disappointment and anger. There was no room left over for grieving. He was gone and she could not bring him back and, even if she could, he probably wouldn't have been in this room anyway. She got out her cell phone and sent a text message to Dr. Kwon that read *having baby,* the best she could do under the circumstances. She wondered when Dr. Kwon would see the message, if everyone in the complex was fast asleep with their children already in their arms. Or their children in someone else's arms; she imagined a huge heap of bodies, with Dr. Grind at the bottom, all of them holding on to each other like a hurricane was coming. And then another contraction hit her in the spine and she cried out a little and a nurse helped her stand so that she could try to evenly distribute the pain. "Baby, baby, baby, baby," she wheezed, the easiest mantra, and the nurse, who had a heavy Eastern European accent, said, "Not much longer now, darling."

The doctor finally showed up, the tiniest woman Izzy had ever seen pass for an adult. She was dressed in workout clothes, her eyebrows perpetually raised as if she didn't know whether Izzy was aware of the fact that she was having a baby. Dr. Starling put on a pair of gloves and Izzy allowed herself to be examined and, a few seconds later, the doctor poked her head back up and said, "This baby is almost here, okay? You are very lucky. This is going to be so easy."

"It does not feel easy at all," Izzy said, and the doctor raised her eyebrows again, smiled, and said, "Easier than it could have been."

A few more nurses came into the room and Izzy sucked on ice chips and let the pain wreck her and, though she could not have explained it, it felt like the contractions were turning into a bright light inside her. She would see her baby soon and she was not afraid. Two of the greatest things in the world would coincide, the discomfort would stop and her baby would be born. The doctor touched her thigh and paused and then told her to push, which she did, though it felt like nothing was happening. "Push," the doctor said again, and Izzy shouted, "I'm trying," and the Eastern European nurse was helping Izzy hold her legs in the right position and the doctor again said, "Push," and Izzy did, two, three more times, though it all seemed futile and stupid and yet so necessary. She kept pushing and then not pushing and then pushing again, her body finally not her body, and then, a miracle, if they existed, every sound in the room became inaudible and everything in the room became a flare of light, and then, in the silence and whiteness, she heard the sound of her baby crying, the most ragged and paper-thin sound she had ever heard, a sound that was connected by an invisible wire to all of the receptors in her body.

She was exhausted and her teeth were chattering, and Dr. Starling put the baby on Izzy's chest and she and the baby instinctively reached for each other and that was it. There was nothing that would ever be as important as this, Izzy was certain. She had made something and now it was hers and no one could ever tell her otherwise. She was not alone in the world. She had been so lonely, she understood now, and never would she be again. She held on to her baby and the baby held on to her, this wild, purple animal that she had made. "I did it," Izzy said to Dr. Starling, pitched somewhere between a question and a statement, and the doctor merely nodded. "A beautiful and healthy baby boy, Isabel," the nurse said to her. Izzy smiled and lay back against the bed and felt her body, so much stronger than she ever gave it credit for being, repair itself in preparation for whatever came next.

Izzy had trouble remembering the next day in the hospital; time became connected only to the baby's actions. Occasionally, someone would enter the room to check on her, the nurses, Dr. Starling, a lactation consultant, a woman going over Izzy's payment plan, a parade of people who affirmed that Izzy was a mother and this boy, swaddled so tightly, was hers. Izzy received a phone call from Dr. Kwon, who said that everyone was so happy and that Dr. Grind himself was on his way to see her. As soon as she was released from the hospital, she would come to the complex, and so Izzy saw her time in her little room, so clean and quiet and filled with reassuring medical equipment, as a kind of halfway house between her old life and her new one. She wanted to stay in this space for as long as possible, safe and protected from whatever lay outside those walls.

If her baby cried, she placed him on her breast and she felt proud that she could give him exactly what he needed. She changed his diapers and swaddled him and rocked him and kept taking pictures of him with her camera phone, blurry images of something that looked as much like an animal as it did a human.

Mr. Tannehill came into the room, his baseball cap in his hands. He had been in the waiting room until a nurse came out to tell him that the baby had been delivered, when he went back home, back to work, until he could make it back to her. He seemed slightly nervous to be in the room, though he admitted that it was because he'd left the new pit boy in charge and had no idea what to expect from him. He had a plastic shopping bag and he opened it to reveal ten perfect ball-in-cage carvings, the wood a rich, beautiful blond. "I figured it wouldn't be right to give it to just your baby, seeing as how this project is supposed to work," he told her, "so I made one for each baby. I hope they'll like 'em. At the very least, it'll keep those babies occupied." Izzy thanked him profusely, shaking her head at the sheer work that had been involved.

"You made a beautiful little boy, Izzy," he told her, and she held the baby out to him. She had thought he would politely refuse, but he took the baby into his arms and the baby readjusted and fell back to sleep. "You look like an old pro," Izzy told him, and then she took a photo of the two of them with her phone.

"Are you doing okay?" he asked her and she nodded.

"I keep waiting to get tired but I feel pretty excited."

"The tired will come, you can bet on that," Mr. Tannehill said. "Enjoy this time while you have it."

They sat in silence for a few minutes, Mr. Tannehill studying the baby with what looked like great affection.

"What's his name?" he suddenly asked her.

"I haven't decided yet," Izzy said, slightly chastened by the admission. For so long, she had imagined that she would name him Hal, though she now knew that she couldn't do that. It would be a sad reminder of a life that didn't happen, and she knew it would be a mistake. She had thought about Carson or Flannery, after Flannery O'Connor and Carson McCullers, two of her favorite writers, but they didn't seem to fit now, either. There were no family names that appealed to her, and it didn't seem to make sense to use them anyway, as if they had mattered to her. She had the form next to her bed, but still couldn't imagine filling it out.

"What's your name?" she asked Mr. Tannehill.

"Izzy, you know my name," he said.

"I don't, actually. I've only ever known you as Mr. Tannehill. I don't believe I've ever heard anyone refer to you as anything other than that."

He shook his head, as if he'd committed a social mistake and could not live it down. "Seems like friends should know each other's names," he said. "It's Cap. My mom's maiden name was Caplin, and Cap was the compromise between my parents."

"I like it," Izzy said. If there was a person who had been kinder to her than Mr. Tannehill, she didn't know who it was. She remembered that early morning when she had come to his trailer, had admitted to the baby, and how he had been the first person to tell her that she could do it. "Cap Poole," she said, and found that the name fit perfectly in her imagination.

"You don't want to think about it?" Mr. Tannehill asked.

"I just did," Izzy replied. "I'm going to name him after the best man I've ever known."

Mr. Tannehill teared up and then looked down at the baby in his arms. He held out his free hand and touched Izzy's own hand, gripping it tightly. "If I had any money, Izzy, I would give you every dime. I have thought of you like my daughter, if I have to be honest about it. I know I'm not your father and I don't pretend that I could be, but you've meant the world to me since we started working together. I don't entirely know what to make of this project, and I hate that you're moving away, but I hope it gives you everything that you and this little boy deserve."

"If you'd been my dad, Mr. Tannehill," Izzy said, "life would have been a lot easier for me."

"I guess you don't get to choose your family," Mr. Tannehill said, "but you get to choose your friends, and I'm glad you're my friend." The baby roused and started to cry; Mr. Tannehill seemed shocked to remember that he was holding the baby, and he handed him back to Izzy. She opened her gown to feed him and Mr. Tannehill stood to leave. "I'll give you some privacy," he said, but she asked him to stay, and he sat back in the chair. After she fed the baby, she practiced his name over and over in her mind, *Cap,* and she found that the name easily attached itself to the boy in her arms. After about fifteen minutes, a nurse came into the room and told Izzy that someone else was here to see her and the baby. Mr. Tannehill stood and then leaned over Izzy and the baby. He kissed Izzy on the forehead and then he waved good-bye to Cap. She promised that she would visit him as soon as she could, would write him letters and stay in touch, and he said he'd be happy to hear from her whenever she could manage. "Be strong, Izzy," he told her, and then he walked out of the room, his tall frame filling up the doorway.

A few seconds later, Dr. Grind appeared in her room, carrying a small basket of gifts with a blue ribbon tied to the handle. It was not his fault, of course, but his proximity to Mr. Tannehill, now the namesake of her only child, made her slightly disappointed to see him. He was a symbol of change, at the very moment that Izzy wanted everything to stay the same, frozen at this singular moment.

"Is it okay if I come in?" he asked tentatively; Izzy waved him in. He put the basket down on the chair and then went to wash his hands. When he was done, he sat beside Izzy and looked at the baby.

"He's beautiful, Izzy. Everyone is so excited and so happy for you."

"His name is Cap," she said.

"Hello, Cap," Dr. Grind said, smiling; his face had the appearance of never knowing sadness, the smoothness of his happy life. She knew it wasn't true, that he had what seemed like a horrible childhood and had his own family tragedies, but she wondered how he had gained such a calmness, a belief that every single piece of the universe fit neatly into another one.

"Are you comfortable?" he asked. "Everything is okay here?"

She nodded. "It's great," she said. "They say the baby is healthy and everything is normal."

The baby had freed his hands from the swaddle and his fingers, purple and pruney, slowly twitched in the open air. Dr. Grind placed his index finger in the palm of Cap's hand and the baby instantly tightened his grip. Izzy smiled, and Dr. Grind then said, "It's just a reflex. The palmar grasp, they call it. A doctor in the 1890s tested a newborn's grip, I think he tested around fifty babies, and found that, though their grip was uncertain, that they could let go without warning, they could also support their body weight, suspended from a stick, for as long as two and a half minutes." He observed the baby and then, suddenly, the baby freed Dr. Grind from his grasp. Dr. Grind made an inchworm motion with his finger and then looked back at Izzy. "Seems like a strange study to actually put into practice. I always imagined the job of the baby catcher in that study to be terrifyingly difficult, just hovering there, waiting for the baby to let go of the stick."

Izzy thought that it was strange for Dr. Grind to think of any newborn study as being odd. It was hitting Izzy, a weird, creeping sensation, that she was now expected to embark on this project, to take this baby boy, her son, and travel into the woods, into a mysterious complex, and surround themselves with strangers who would get to handle her baby with impunity. Her fear of being a single mom had now turned into the strangest of fears, of being only one of nineteen parents, not counting Dr. Grind.

"You'll be released from the hospital tomorrow," Dr. Grind said, and she wished he could buy into her own fantasy of never leaving this hospital room. "I'll take you and Cap to your home and we'll help you get settled."

Izzy, who never wanted to make trouble, who had assembled a life that, before she got pregnant, seemed entirely invested in leaving no trace of her existence, now felt a shaking nervousness about her future. She did not want to go home, back to the unhappy life that would await her, but she did not want to go with Dr. Grind either. "I don't know if I can do this, Dr. Grind; I feel like I'm making a mistake."

"I do not blame you at all, Izzy," he said, and Izzy noticed that Dr. Grind almost always made it a point to say her name, as if calming a wild animal. "It wouldn't be normal if you didn't feel anxiety about what comes next. But I can assure you that I am here to help you, to make your life so much better, to make Cap's life better."

"I don't think I can give him up," she said, and the baby began to stir and then cry.

"You aren't giving him up, Izzy," he replied. "You're bringing him to something wonderful."

Not thinking of Dr. Grind, to hell with being demure, Izzy opened her robe and tried to get Cap to breast-feed. The baby could not latch on, or would not, instead continuing to make a sound like a science project gone wrong. "I just don't know," Izzy said, adjusting the baby in her arms; she was leaking milk. The baby's pitch increased by a significant decibel level and Izzy felt that stab of inadequacy, which she had foolishly hoped the baby's arrival would eradicate. She softly jiggled the baby to no avail and then Dr. Grind, his face holding the most sheepish expression, offered his help, holding out his hands. Izzy reluctantly handed the baby to him and Dr. Grind took Cap into his arms, holding him close to his chest, making a soft sound with his mouth, like a little sewing machine, and he did a shuffling dance. The baby's cries softened, perhaps because of the simple transition from mother to stranger, but then he quieted entirely, Dr. Grind still buzzing away, holding the baby as if he were his own. After a minute of quiet, he returned Cap to Izzy and he smiled.

"Okay," Izzy said. "It's okay. I'll go. I'll do it."

"I'm very happy to hear that, Izzy," he replied. He sat down on the chair and blew out an exaggerated burst of air. "Was it the trick I just did with the baby that sealed the deal?" he asked, and Izzy nodded. He shook his head. "Just dumb luck, I promise you, but I'll take it." Izzy again noted how much she liked him; she found it endearing and a little odd that someone who seemed entirely without ego had constructed the Infinite Family, someone who obviously believed that he was doing something correct and true despite all evidence against it.

When Dr. Grind finally left, promising to be back the next morning, she returned her entire attention to her son, who regarded her with what she anxiously interpreted as skepticism. She kissed him, the simplest and easiest thing to do, and waited for the moment, fast approaching, when he would need her again, and she would give him whatever he wanted.

The next morning, Izzy found that whatever endorphins the birthing process had bestowed upon her had become entirely depleted. She had been up several times during the night to feed the baby, to change the baby, to rock the baby, and now, the sun up and the nurses moving in and out of her room with their assigned duties, Izzy wished for an energy drink or a coffee, an IV of fluids hooked up to her arm. She packed up her meager duffel bag and included the baby's gifts, both from the complex and from the hospital. The nurses also told her that she could keep her giant plastic mug from which she had sipped gallons of water over the past day, and she felt so happy that she immediately was embarrassed. She signed papers, thanked the nurses, and then, completely flummoxed as to why no one was stopping her, she walked out of the room with her baby, Cap Ellgee Poole, into the waiting area, where Dr. Grind was waiting for her, and then out of the hospital, still no one coming up to her to even give her a simple quiz on child rearing. Cap was hers, and no one, she realized, was going to take him away from her. Dr. Grind put her bag in the trunk of his car and then helped Izzy as they buckled Cap safely into the car seat. Izzy took her spot beside him in the backseat and Dr. Grind, after checking to make sure she was buckled up, gave her a thumbs-up sign and accelerated onto the highway. To anyone in the hospital, Izzy thought, they looked like a normal family.

After a long drive, during which Cap mostly slept, Dr. Grind finally turned onto a long, winding road that was lined with trees, bumping over the path until, like a mirage, the trees gave way and the complex took shape against its surroundings.

"Oh my god," Izzy said, shocked by the AstroTurf; the buildings looked like a computer simulation.

"Isn't it wonderful?" Dr. Grind asked, and Izzy could only nod. It was a world unto itself, and Izzy understood now that this space would be her home for the next ten years. It was as if she had fallen through a rabbit hole, into an unexplored dimension, and, as the car pulled up to the huge main building, Izzy saw the people waiting on the steps, eight or nine people, some of them holding babies, waving as Dr. Grind stopped the car and turned off the engine.

"I need a second," Izzy said. "I can't go out there just yet."

"Take your time," Dr. Grind said. "It's okay."

Izzy unstrapped Cap from his car seat and lifted him into her arms. He started to nuzzle against her chest and she felt the contained heat of his body now against her own. She held him for a moment longer, and then she nodded to Dr. Grind. He got out of the car, came around to her door, and opened it. She took a tentative step onto the driveway and she could now clearly see the faces of the men and women, all so happy and so calm, waiting for her and Cap to join them. Dr. Grind put his arm around Izzy's shoulders, like a cape of protection, and the three of them walked into whatever would come next, the family now complete.

part
two

chapter nine

the infinite family project (year one)

Izzy tilted her head and took a quick intake of breath before she re-turned to the water, her strokes heavy with intent though still lacking the perfect form she desired. She had been swimming for forty minutes, no breaks, going nowhere in the endless pool, which kept pushing her slightly back, forcing her to keep moving. She had never seen one of these pools before she arrived at the complex, the constant current letting you swim in place for as long as you wanted, but she had immediately taken to it. A swim instructor had come for a week, as if summoned by magic, to teach Izzy the proper strokes, since she'd only mastered a modified dog paddle from her time in public swimming pools. Now, it was how she greeted almost every morning, shaking off the sleep, or lack of sleep depending on the babies and their night patterns. It felt good, even though it was a losing battle, to struggle against the resistance and find herself stronger for it.

In the regular pool, standing in the shallow end and wearing weighted mitts, Asean churned the water around him. He was in his early twenties, in perfect shape, and he was Izzy's only companion in the early mornings here at the pool. She waved, and he grinned and lifted a blue mitt in greeting. "Good morning," Izzy said, and Asean simply nodded, listening to music on his waterproof MP3 player. She checked her watch; she had fifteen minutes before she was due in the nursery. She took a deep breath, willed herself to be happy. When she stepped outside, she tried so hard to keep the fear out of her facial expressions, wondering, as she did every day in this new world, if today was the day that she finally reached her limits, finally admitted that she could not live in this strange place.

It was June, not quite overwhelmingly humid, which would come in July and August, but warm enough that it felt distinctly like summer. And after the winter and rainy spring, Izzy was grateful to have more excuses to be outside. Her house was nice enough, sparsely decorated and furnished, though she sometimes counted down the minutes until she could leave it. It was strange that a lifetime of solitude, whether she wanted it or not, had now turned into a need to surround herself with other people. She knew why this was the case; it did not take scientific or psychological inquiry to find out. It was Cap; it was, truthfully, all the babies. Having them in her life, she felt slightly untethered from the world if she wasn't actively participating in their lives. And when she was alone, it was so easy to doubt herself, to worry about the smallest mistakes, so she tried to attach herself to the other people in the complex. If she could observe them and compare herself in relation to their own ability to adapt to the complex, then she could ward off any signs of disaster.

She jogged the last bit toward Main 1 and, skipping the elevator, took the steps up to the top floor where the nursery was located. She signed in, checking her wristband, which was purple, against the sheet and finding that she was in the right place at the right time. She used her key card, which all the parents and staff wore around their necks, and scanned herself into the room, where, as always, she was temporarily stunned into paralysis. It was overwhelming at first, the room swirling with activity, ten babies hidden throughout the space, so much unadorned need radiating out toward Izzy. It always took her a few seconds to accept this responsibility before she could work to meet it.

Dr. Patterson was in charge of the room today, and Izzy appreciated her presence. Of the three postdocs, Izzy felt most comfortable with Jill, who was the least formal, the one most willing to admit the strangeness of the situation and yet attempt to figure out how to work with it toward something productive. Dr. Washington was so aloof and serious that it was difficult for Izzy to ever know what he was thinking, if he even believed the project was worthwhile, and Kalina, though so kind to Izzy, sometimes had the opposite effect, of being so deeply assured of the project's superiority that it was impossible to suggest otherwise. Dr. Patterson was the happy medium, and that's all that Izzy desired, something that kept her from intense emotional swings.

Along with the doctor, there were four caregivers, highly trained and with all the necessary health certifications, as well as backgrounds in early childhood development. These three women and one man were local, from either La Vergne or from Nashville, and they seemed, at least to Izzy, to accept the unique circumstances of The IFP. In fact, they seemed fairly excited for the opportunity, and Izzy was often amazed by how calmly and easily they navigated the day-to-day activities required to keep ten six-month-old babies alive and thriving. She waved hi to Dr. Patterson, who was playing on the floor with Marnie, a cute little girl with a red birthmark on her forehead, who was gamely trying to remain upright while Dr. Patterson handed her various colored foam shapes. Eliza, the biggest of the babies, an Amazon in a diaper, was lying on her back, her ice blue eyes wide open as Shonda, one of the caregivers, sprinkled bits of red construction paper over her, the pieces floating through the air, Eliza's legs kicking in excitement. Izzy could detect the buzzing of the babies, like a machine; their happiness, to Izzy's ears, was so close to mania that she worried when it might tip over into wailing.

Izzy had noted from the clipboard that Nina, who was twenty-two and one of the youngest people in the family, and Jeremy, the oldest person in the family at thirty-six, were the other two parents in attendance for the next three-hour shift. Jeremy, ruggedly handsome like the Marlboro Man, was already holding Maxwell, Kenny and Carmen's boy, who was rubbing against the grain of Jeremy's stubbly beard. Izzy checked the dry-erase board that held the names of all ten babies to see who was asleep, who was already being attended to, and who was waiting for a caregiver. Her own son, Cap, was sleeping, as were Lulu and Eli, and the other three caregivers were each with a child, which left only Jackie, who was reclining in the automatic swing. Jackie was Asean and Nikisha's daughter, a baby with a perpetual look of practiced skepticism, and Izzy crawled on the floor, in Jackie's line of vision, until the baby noticed her and began to hold out her hands. Izzy scooped her up and bounced the baby on her hip, cooing until Jackie's raised eyebrows softened and she had accepted Izzy's presence.

Just then, Nina showed up and waved to Izzy before going to sign herself in. Her son, Gilberto, was with Marcus, another caregiver, who was reading to him from a floppy, fabric storybook filled with objects that the baby observed and then discarded. Instead of going to see her son, she followed Dr. Grind's suggestion and spent her first hour working with one of the other children, joining one of the caregivers to change Irene's diaper and then helping the baby practice rolling over. Sonny Rollins was playing softly over the speakers in the room, and Izzy set Jackie on the floor and did some object permanence exercises with some balls and cubes, which lasted for almost thirty minutes, Izzy continually amazed by the attention spans of babies; she had always imagined them as twitchy kittens, their eyes forever darting toward some new prey.

Izzy then switched with Christie, a caregiver who had also been working with the parents to teach them sign language, and took watch over Ally, a pale, blond-haired, blue-eyed baby who smiled with obvious excitement when she saw Izzy. Ally was hungry, nuzzling Izzy the moment she picked up the child, so Izzy went to the dry-erase board, saw that it was time to feed Ally, and then carried the baby over to the milk bank, where she signed out a bottle that had been pumped by Alyssa, Ally's mom.

*　*　*

There had been discussion about how the babies would be fed from the moment the families had gathered at the complex. When they first arrived, mothers breast-fed their own baby or pumped so that the father or another parent or caregiver could handle the duty. After two months of this system, Dr. Grind offered the suggestion of a milk-sharing scenario, where all ten mothers banked milk, which could be used for any of the babies, to create an even more communal style of parenting. Julie, the most forward-thinking of the parents, who seemed to have chosen The Infinite Family Project not because of circumstance, but from a genuine desire to be a part of something so unique, then suggested cross-nursing, where mothers nursed any baby that needed it, but most of the other parents, including Izzy, opted against it, either because it simply made them uncomfortable or because it prevented the fathers from taking part in the feeding process. Finally, after careful consideration, everyone having their own vote, including Dr. Grind and the postdocs, they decided that they would keep using the current system, that if they were not available to feed their child, they would pump and store that milk in the bank and it would be reserved for their own child. It did, however, make it necessary for the mothers to pump several times during the day and night. Some of the mothers would meet in the TV room to pump, the machines whirring while four or five women watched a baseball game or *The Price Is Right* on mute. Others preferred to do it privately, in their own home. Now, at any time of day, one could hear the whooshing of the pneumatic tubes that had been fitted throughout the complex, as another mother sent milk to the bank for immediate labeling and refrigeration. This was the future, Izzy decided, which was never the future you imagined.

Cap woke from his nap, wailing in a pitch that Izzy instantly recognized as being that of her own son, even over the sound of the other babies. Nina went to his crib, wrote down when he had awakened, consulted the chart once more, and then lifted him into her arms, where he burrowed into her, his sobs so aggrieved that Izzy unknowingly squeezed Ally until the child began to wriggle against Izzy's grip. Nina then walked over to Izzy and offered to switch. "It's time for him to eat," Nina said, and Izzy handed Ally over and then took Cap into her arms. Cap's tiny fists were clenched so tightly, shaking to enumerate what Izzy could not help but perceive to be his many complaints with The Infinite Family. Izzy sat in one of the rockers and hurriedly, awkwardly, unclipped the strap of her tank top, her face burning with the anxiety that everyone in the room was watching her, taking notes on her abilities; she began to feed Cap, who finally quieted, not happy but at least appeased, while Nina calmly sat beside her and rocked Ally. The jazz music stopped and then Neko Case came over the speakers, which made Ally start to bounce with excitement. Nina stood up and carried Ally to a playmat, where several other babies were lying on their backs or sitting up.

Cap ate with great intensity, and Izzy felt the familiar tugging sensation in her breast, strangely pleasant. In the feeding position that worked best, Cap was looking directly at Izzy, his eyes always wide open as he ate, which had initially disconcerted her, though now she liked these moments, when it felt like it was only the two of them in the room. If she stared at him long enough, she could signal to him, without words, that she indeed was his true mother. When he had finished, his anger a ghost that Izzy now believed she had never actually seen, and she had coaxed a burp out of him, she let him recline against her chest, facing the activity of the other babies and caregivers. He reached out for the other babies and said, "Ba-ba-ba," so far his only word or sound, and Izzy eased him onto the floor, where he lay on his belly for a few seconds and then tried to crawl toward Gilberto, who was laughing loudly as Marcus kept placing a pair of plastic sunglasses over his eyes, each time Gilberto shaking his head quickly to shed the glasses. Cap inched his bottom forward, as if trying to propel his entire body toward what he wanted, but he was still not quite ready to crawl, and Izzy helped him back to a sitting position, closer to Gilberto. The two babies observed each other and then Gilberto offered the sunglasses to Cap, who took them and then shook them with great vigor before they flew out of his hands and landed back in Gilberto's lap, which made both of them erupt in rumbly laughter. Marcus held out his hands, palms up, for Gilberto and Cap and said, "Boom, boom, boom," and the two babies slapped at his hands. Izzy held out her hand for Cap and the baby regarded it, then grabbed Izzy's thumb and squeezed it, which, as the babies did on a daily basis, sent shivers up her spine and flooded her heart. This was the way of things for Izzy at the complex, her heart seizing up with fear and then resuming its beat, even stronger than before. She kissed Cap on the head and then, as Gilberto regarded them, she leaned over and kissed Gilberto, who smiled and shook his head, as if the sunglasses had again been placed on his face.

Switching to other babies, always a different activity, a different way of interacting, often simply the mind-numbing act of holding an inconsolable baby; her shift ended and she filled out reports on her interactions with the children, noting anything of interest for Dr. Grind, who checked all the babies' reports at the end of the day. She wandered through the nursery and kissed each baby and then walked with Nina and Jeremy out of the room. It felt like she had ended a shift in a factory that had been imagined by Walt Disney, the bright colors and happy music overriding the weird fact that you were working on an assembly line that created superbabies.

At 5 P.M., the caregivers and staff headed home to their own families and Izzy and the rest of the parents met up on the second floor of Main 1, in the largest room, which functioned as both a dining hall and an indoor playground. All ten babies would now, until the next morning, be cared for by the parents, the postdocs, Dr. Grind, and three overnight nurses who helped in the sleep room. It was Izzy's favorite part of the day, all the parents sharing the space with their children, the open space of the room filled with the sounds of the adults' conversation and the babies' occasional crying. They passed the babies around, and it amazed Izzy to see how quickly the babies, when passed into a new set of arms, instantly resettled and adjusted to their new situation. She did this often, an informal anthropological study of how the babies were dealing with their (unknown-to-them) strange circumstances. And she was heartened, always, to find that they seemed either too dulled by their infancy to notice or, more hopefully, that they thrived, that Dr. Grind knew just what he was doing.

Izzy worked with Kenny to prepare dinner while Jeffrey and Nikisha portioned out the baby food that the complex's chef, who handled breakfast and lunch, had left to supplement the babies' breast-feeding. Chef Nicole, prior to the complex, had been the executive chef for the day care center at a start-up company in San Francisco before it went belly-up, probably because it had devoted quite a bit of money toward things like executive chefs for the day care center.

While salsa music played loudly through the speakers, Kenny grilled burgers and Izzy quickly chopped sweet potatoes into perfect fries before seasoning them and sliding them into the oven. Izzy had become one of the best cooks in the family, and Chef Nicole often commented on her natural skill in the kitchen. Izzy owed this to her work, of course, at the Whole Hog, but she was now working beyond pork and the occasional fried food. She had learned sous-vide, pickling, and coddling eggs, each time figuring out the process with almost no help from anyone else. It was thrilling, as if acquiring through gamma radiation a new superpower. If the fanciness of the food made her uncomfortable, she would master the means of preparing it, until it no longer had any power over her. She had done this often in her life to deal with uncertainty, to become so adept and so skilled that people assumed it must not be that difficult and left her alone. Now she delicately sliced a bowl of beets into thin circles, before topping them with some fresh herbs and goat cheese. Kenny leaned over from his work at the grill and placed a beet in his mouth before making a face of pure happiness. He nodded in appreciation and Izzy smiled.

Once dinner was ready, the adults gathered around the long oak table and placed the babies in their high chairs. Izzy set out the bowls of vegetables and a few loaves of bread while Kenny handed each made-to-order burger to the intended eater. Benjamin, who had been a car salesman in Knoxville, told a fairly long and complicated story about a difficult customer who, after finally buying a car, drove it into a ditch less than thirty yards from the dealership. Jill told the family about forgetting to put her car into reverse when leaving a drive-in hamburger stand, and smashing into a set of unoccupied picnic tables. It seemed that everyone had a ridiculous car crash story and that took up most of dinner, while the babies made their own strange sounds, occasionally demanding to be picked up and walked around the room or placed on the floor. Izzy fed the softest cubes of carrots to Marnie, Harris and Ellen's baby, the orange of the carrots so bright that they seemed to be rare gems. Izzy couldn't help but look down the table to where Cap was being fed by Callie, who cooed and smiled as Cap fixed his gaze on Callie's smile. There was the sharpest, smallest pain in Izzy's heart, and then she recovered and returned her attention to Marnie, who had managed to put her fingers in some mashed avocado and had rubbed it into her hair.

She had come to understand that her past life, all those years of living without, of removing emotion from her makeup, had prepared her for this new situation. She tried so hard to dismiss her desire to be Cap's entire world, telling herself again and again, with increasing forcefulness, that it would not change anything. Instead, she would open her heart to the world and hope that good came from it, even if there was the recurring stab of regret. She kissed Marnie on the cheek and the baby squinted and smiled, her hands reaching for Izzy, who pulled her close, the muck of the baby's dinner rubbing into Izzy's own clothes. *Good enough,* she told herself, *almost as good.*

After all the babies were washed and freshly clothed, a seemingly endless process that left Izzy wrung out and tired, she took Cap in her arms and fed him, then handed him to Carmen, one of the three parents who would take over night duties with the children. Truthfully, though she barely got any sleep, she preferred night duty, the chance to be near the children, the odd sensation of hearing them breathe in unison, the feeling that your mere presence was protecting them. Izzy kissed a few of the other babies and then bid farewell to the parents who were staying behind.

Back outside, she thought of the endless pool, but opted instead to return to her own home. When she opened the front door, she was startled by the emptiness of it, not a single sound of occupancy. She went up to her bedroom on the second floor and fell onto the bed, not even bothering to get under the covers. Another day had passed, she had seen her way clear to another morning, and now she waited for the sleep she had fought off for hours to overtake her. As the complex shifted and expanded around her, she hugged herself and let everything inside her own body become still and perfect.

Finally alone, she allowed herself to uncoil, to become ragged, and she cried without effort, almost without any emotion powering it. She cried and cried, and she pictured every single person in the Infinite Family surrounding her, watching her, telling her it would be okay. And she tried, sleep still not coming, to believe that this was good, that this was the right thing for her.

But it was a mistake. Even if it worked out, she had made a mistake, joining this project. The strangeness of it, and the way everyone worked so hard to pretend that it was perfectly normal, was going to change Izzy in ways that she would not recover from.

But Izzy was used to making mistakes. She was used to living inside it. The key, she knew, was to bend and shape and worry the mistake until it turned into something else, something that would allow her to survive.

Then she forced herself to sit up, to become tough. She willed it to happen.

She thought of where she'd be if not for the complex, living in that tiny bedroom at her father's house, her mother long dead, her father drunk and useless. She thought of how impossible it would be to sleep, the baby crib wedged so tightly into the room that Izzy could hardly move. She thought of her hair smelling of wood smoke, her eyes red with irritation. She'd have to take on another job, extra hours, a job so bad, the only thing she was qualified for, that would stretch her out so much she'd be flattened by the end of the night. She would have to leave Cap with old ladies who ran nurseries out of their own ramshackle houses, women so burned out by life that they swatted the kids into submission, charging so much that Izzy could barely afford to feed herself and her son, eating food that only slowed them down more. People in town would wonder who the father was, poor Izzy Poole, a smart girl, but such bad circumstances. Pity, she hated it. She'd come to regret Cap like she'd regretted Hal and damn near most of her life.

She would not allow that to happen, she told herself, now sitting up so straight in bed that it felt military or like very perfect yoga. She'd fought her way out of that life, had traveled so far to this place in the woods. She was scared. She was terrified of fucking everything up. It didn't matter. She would make it work. Izzy would find tiny ways to make herself essential, to succeed when it seemed so unlikely. Ten years, that's what she had. She would mine every essential element out of these ten years and she would be transformed. "Infinite," she said to herself. "Infinite. I am infinite." And so she was, and so she would be.

chapter ten

the infinite family project (year one)

Dr. Grind sat in Gerdie Kent's office on the first floor of Main 1 as she explained the finances of The IFP at the end of the first year, which seemed like imaginary numbers to him, the endowment so large that it simply was not possible that they could ever spend it all. Even so, Gerdie was frugal. It was her job to tell Dr. Grind that perhaps they did not need a full-time physical therapist to help with the babies' gross motor skill development when they could simply use an outpatient program in Nashville or bring in an independent contractor for a few months. And it was Dr. Grind's job, or one of the many aspects of his job, to defer to Gerdie's expertise. "Save more than you spend," Gerdie always told him, "and it's there when you really need it." Dr. Grind always wanted to say, but never did, that he always needed it, that there was always some aspect of the project that could be expanded in order to make life easier for the parents and children. He did not say that, if this all blew up in his face, it would probably be the end of his career. Gerdie did not care about any of that.

Gerdie was fifty-seven years old, loaded down with degrees, unfazed by the strangeness of the project. She and her husband had raised six foster children and she admitted during her interview for the job that "sometimes you gotta start with an artificial family in order to make it a real one later on." She was gruff and often seemed to regard Dr. Grind with bemusement, which he appreciated, having someone acknowledge that maybe he didn't know what he was doing, since he had to radiate confidence to everyone else in the complex.

"We spent just under what we had budgeted for the first year, though of course that number is going to increase quite a bit now that we'll be funding the parents' educational and occupational endeavors and hiring some extra staff to make up for their absence within the complex. It would help to try to cut back in other ways, which I've outlined here." Gerdie handed Dr. Grind a sheaf of papers that would have taken him days to read.

"Just be honest with me, Gerdie. We've spent enough time together. You know what I'm trying to do here. Are any of these cuts going to make me feel bad?"

"Any cut would make you feel bad, Preston. But these will make you feel the least bad."

"Okay, then. Let's move forward."

They went over each parent's allocation. For some, such as Susan Lin, it was easy enough, as she wanted to be a homemaker, and so she would take on more responsibilities within the complex, and she would take some outside workshops on finances, child development, and whatever extracurricular activities in which she expressed an interest. Her husband, David, on the other hand, would be entering the Peabody College of Education and Human Development at Vanderbilt University in Nashville to receive his doctorate of education in the K–12 track, and the project would entirely fund his education, including textbooks and supplies.

Jeremy and Callie Gipson, who had primarily chosen to join the project because they had lost the family farm that had been in Jeremy's family for five generations, were going to take over several acres of the grounds and begin to build an organic farm and sell their food to local restaurants, which meant that the project would be funding all the equipment and training necessary to expand their allegiance to organic farming beyond the small gardens already located within the complex.

Link and Julie Howser were interesting because they were already established within their fields and mostly just wanted the time and space to pursue their own work. Link was a fairly accomplished session musician and had toured for years with various bands; he wanted to stop touring and focus on his own music while also becoming a stay-at-home father, while Julie was a writer who had published her first novel two years earlier to some critical acclaim and was working on her second. Beyond room and board, and perhaps funds to create a studio for Link within the complex, they required no additional funding.

Harris and Ellen Tilton, who had lost their coffee shop to bankruptcy, were going to be taking classes in finance and management at a local community college and would look into starting another business later, once they had established a business model that met with Gerdie and Dr. Grind's approval.

Kenny Floyd would finish pursuing a degree in auto technology at a technical institute in Nashville and then open his own garage, while his wife, Carmen Rivera, would start nursing school.

Asean Watts was going back to college to get a degree in physical therapy and his wife, Nikisha, who had already finished college, would be starting a graduate program in library science at MTSU in Murfreesboro. Gerdie was constantly pleased to remind Dr. Grind that both Asean and Nikisha would be fully funded by scholarships and financial aid, costing the project almost nothing beyond room and board.

Carlos, who had received his GED while at the complex, and Nina Torres, both only twenty-two, would be pursuing undergraduate degrees at MTSU.

Benjamin and Alyssa Raymond, who had lost their jobs at a car dealership in Georgia, simply wanted to return to the workforce and, aside from additional job training, would require almost no funding.

Paul Brock and Mary Hubbard had been living on government aid since Paul lost his job as a grocery store clerk and Mary had not been able to find a job. Both of them would be going to community college to get degrees in business administration and looking for part-time work.

Finally, Izzy Poole would be going to MTSU, no idea of a major yet; thanks to the encouragement of Chef Nicole, who believed Izzy was uniquely gifted, she would also become Nicole's assistant in the complex's kitchen.

It constantly amazed Dr. Grind, who had focused so intently on the children of these parents, how much of his time was devoted to making sure that the adults were taken care of as well. They were assigned bimonthly visits with a psychiatrist to discuss their lives in the complex, and Dr. Grind was constantly assessing how they were adjusting to life in a more communal setting. The babies were thriving, had been hitting a good number of their developmental goals, even to Dr. Grind and the postdocs' surprise, earlier than normal. One of the babies, Ally, was already talking and a few of the other babies weren't far behind. Though Dr. Grind had cautioned everyone from the postdocs and caregivers to the parents themselves that they could not expect radical advancement in the children's development in such a short time, this collective family was outpacing the work Grind had done with the Artificial Village project, and Preston believed that starting from the moment of birth had been essential to this feeling of community. During his video chats, every other week, with Brenda Acklen, she was overjoyed to hear how things were going with the children, and Dr. Grind never failed to provide her with videos and pictures of the babies, all the things they were accomplishing. Her focus had primarily been with the children, so she asked less about the parents, but he continued to provide her with optimistic information about their future endeavors. "This is your family, Preston," she would tell him time and time again. "I'm the benefactor, but you're the daddy." He was entirely uncomfortable with that logic, the patriarchal conundrum it provided, but how to explain the fact that it also thrilled him to hear it, to feel that he was, once again, a part of a family.

But it wasn't entirely true. Though he worked hard to make the experience communal by nature, he was still the doctor, an outsider by definition. When he walked into a room, the parents and the postdocs seemed to adjust their posture, as if they believed he was noting every detail of their interactions. But then, there were those moments, when one of the parents handed him a child, their own child, and trusted him to care for him or her, that made him believe that, no matter what the outcome was for everyone else, he had built something necessary for himself, and that when the ten years of the project had come to a close, he would be as rehabilitated as everyone else, although no one could know that he had changed.

After his meeting with Gerdie, he checked on the babies in the nursery, so much activity swirling around him that he was momentarily discombobulated by the sounds and colors and motion; he simply let it wash over him for a few seconds and then rejoined the world. He picked up Cap, the quietest of the babies, the most thoughtful, he had determined, who smiled as Dr. Grind rubbed noses with him. A few of the babies were sitting in a circle, each manhandling a musical instrument, everything becoming an object of percussion in their tiny hands. Dr. Grind set Cap in the circle and placed a tiny ukulele in his lap.

Marla, long after her band had broken up and she'd given up on the drums, took to the ukulele once Jody was born, singing him revised new-wave and punk songs while she plink-plunked on the flimsy instrument. Preston could still easily recall the sounds of her singing to Jody in his bed while Preston washed dishes from that night's dinner. It was the best sound of his family, his wife singing songs of distorted anger, softly pitched, his son joining in until his voice wavered and then fell away from the song entirely.

As Dr. Grind made random chords on the neck of the ukulele, he was amazed to see Cap stroke his open palm against the strings in what seemed to be a fairly smooth strumming motion, making a rickety song between the two of them. Cap had an innate sense of rhythm, or as much as a baby could have, and he played for a few more seconds, smiling with great satisfaction at the sound he was making, looking up shyly at Dr. Grind for approval, who responded with great enthusiasm. When he tired of the music, Cap pushed the ukulele entirely into Dr. Grind's hands, and then Dr. Grind awkwardly strummed some passable notes and sang gibberish to Cap, who smiled and then pointed to Dr. Grind and said, as clear as a struck bell, "Daddy."

Christie, who was playing with Marnie on a drum set, instantly turned around to face the two of them. "That's his first word," she said. Jeffrey walked over from where he'd been playing with a few of the babies and agreed. "I heard it from over there," he said. "Daddy."

As if on command, Cap said it again, "Daddy," still pointing at Dr. Grind. Christie touched her heart and oohed and aahed at the cuteness of it. "That's the sweetest thing I've ever seen," she said. Jeffrey went to Cap's clipboard and noted the new development on the sheet. Two of the parents came over to hear it as well, Cap unable or unwilling to stop now that he'd spoken aloud. Dr. Grind found that he could not let go of the ukulele, kneeling awkwardly over the little boy, who kept pointing to him. He knew that, in less than three seconds, he would start sobbing and he would not be able to explain this properly to anyone, not even himself. He simply kissed Cap on the forehead and then walked out of the nursery.

Down the hallway, safe from view, finally alone, he found that the tears now wouldn't come. He cradled the ukulele and thought of his own son and he found that he could not remember the exact moment when Jody had said, "Dad." There was no memory of it and he wondered how much else he had simply lost to time or inattention. He thought of the photo that he had hidden within the building itself, and now he wished that he could break into the plaster of the ceiling and retrieve it. Had he been so naive to think that one family could take the place of another? Or had he been so naive to think that a family, dispersed, would live forever in his mind?

After a few minutes, he felt the overwhelming emotions start to dissipate, the way his parents had taught him to deal with any stress, external or internal. You owned it, you put your hands on it and you made it a part of yourself, so that it no longer had any power over you.

He remembered when he was a small child, how his mother had placed her hand softly on his stomach and coaxed him into pulling all of his anxiety, all of his terror and uncertainty, down into his belly, the furnace for his entire being. Once trapped there, she would breathe with him, slowly, confidently, until he had vaporized those emotions. "Feel what's left?" she asked him, her mouth right at his ear. "It's nothing. It's just clouds. And when it moves through your body, to your arms and your legs and your feet and your hands, it tickles just a little bit and then it is gone forever." She pulled away from him, held his shoulders, and made him stare right into her eyes. "All of it is gone forever," she said. "And you? You're still here. You are untouched." She hugged him and he collapsed in her arms, nothing inside him that could cause pain.

Though the world tried so hard to hurt us, his parents assured him that there was nothing on the outside that could ruin what was inside. "If you do what we say," his father said, "you will be invincible." And, whether or not it was true, he believed them without hesitation.

As he stood up to continue his day, Dr. Grind whistled a Tin Pan Alley tune and felt himself again become the person that he needed to be. He leaned the ukulele, unstrummed and silent, against the wall and then walked back to his own office, where the postdocs were nervously waiting for him. "There's a problem," Kalina said, and Dr. Grind smiled, unintentionally or not, at having something else to deal with.

"I talked to one of the night nurses," Kalina continued as they all stepped inside his office, "and she told me that when Ellen Tilton had been on duty in the sleep room, at around one A.M., she walked over to Marnie's crib and picked her up. Marnie had been sound asleep, but Ellen jostled her awake until she cried and then she rocked the child until she fell back to sleep and then held the baby in her arms for two hours, while other babies needed to be fed or changed."

"Understandable," Jill offered. "We talked about this happening. She just wanted some extra time with her own child."

"It's understandable," Dr. Grind admitted, "but that's not how the family works. I'll talk to her about it."

"How?" Jill wondered. "You'll just say, 'You need to stop paying so much attention to your baby'?"

"No," Dr. Grind said, having grown used to Jill's tendency to argue a position just to see how Dr. Grind might react, as if testing his own confidence in the project. "That would be a terrible way to go about it. I'll remind her about the goals of the project and the need for us to function as a singular family."

"You'll be very sensitive and very charming," Kalina offered, and Dr. Grind nodded.

"And if she refuses and says that she wants unlimited time with her own baby?" Jill asked.

Dr. Grind threw up his hands. "We've talked about this, Jill. We'll intervene, collectively."

"That will be the most awkward intervention I've ever heard of," Jill said, almost smiling at the thought of it.

"I'll talk to her," Dr. Grind said with some finality and they moved on.

After the postdocs left, Dr. Grind's thoughts were on Ellen. She had a history of depression, the only parent in the project who had been clinically treated; the staff had been prepared for the possibility of post-partum depression among the mothers, but they had been lucky thus far. They hoped that the collective aspect of the project had lessened the individual responsibility of each parent, though Dr. Grind now worried that Ellen could be finding the unique circumstances to be overwhelming. And yet, as he dealt with most crises, he believed in the best possible scenario, that Ellen had simply wanted to hold her daughter for a few hours, a one-time event, something that Dr. Grind could admittedly understand. He imagined his conversation with Ellen but could not make it coalesce in his mind. He would save the details for later; he would wing it.

At dinner that evening, as the parents gathered with their children, Dr. Grind watched Ellen, who was standing with Jeremy as the two of them played with Eli, Jeremy's son. There was nothing out of the ordinary in Ellen's actions, and her happiness was evident, the way she and Jeremy kept the boy entertained with little more than facial expressions and hand gestures. He waited for the right moment to walk over to Ellen, but he kept avoiding the moment; he had the slightest fear that addressing this small problem would uncover massive errors in planning, that the whole thing would fall apart around him. If Ellen left, so would Harris and Marnie. If one family learned that they could leave, who else would follow? He had made something wonderful, he believed, but he also knew how precarious it was, especially in these early stages. Callie walked over to Ellen and Jeremy and the three of them began to talk, the baby now starting to walk away from them, taking the shakiest steps imaginable but possessing a motor that would take him as far as he wanted to go. Dr. Grind started to get up in order to tend to Eli, but Asean quickly perched beside the baby and encouraged him to keep walking, as if cheering on a runner in the Olympics, and Dr. Grind returned to his seat.

Izzy walked over to Dr. Grind, holding Cap in her arms, and Dr. Grind felt slightly odd as the woman and her child both regarded him with emotions that he could not quite decipher.

"Hello, Izzy," he said.

"I heard that Cap said his first word today," she told him.

"He did. We're very proud of him."

"Daddy," Izzy said.

"That's it," Dr. Grind agreed.

"I wish I had been there to hear it," she admitted. She stood over him, her emotions seemingly tamped down, her demeanor always a source of some mystery to him. She was talented at holding her feelings just below the surface, where they dissipated and became easier to manage. It reminded him of his own makeup.

"Izzy," Dr. Grind finally said. "I hope that word, *Daddy*, isn't too strange for you."

"It's weird," Izzy replied, her face darkening; she seemed to be choosing her words carefully, as if being interviewed by the police, and wanting to be anywhere else. "But I think about how, if I'd been raising him by myself, trying to take care of him, how that word would never have entered into his vocabulary, at least not for a long time. I guess it's good in the end that the project made it possible for him to use that word and to understand it and to mean it." By the time she finished speaking, her face was calm and there was the slightest hint of a smile, though Dr. Grind did not entirely believe it was genuine.

"That's a good point," Dr. Grind said.

"I'm handling it much better than if he said *Mommy* to someone else, you know?

"*Daddy*," Izzy whispered to Cap, and the baby looked at her with great fascination. "*Daddy*," she said again, and the baby, emboldened, replied, "*Daddy*," his eyes fixed on her face.

She turned to Dr. Grind and smiled. "These are going to be the most perfect, weirdest kids ever," she said, and this, finally, made Dr. Grind laugh.

When the meal had ended and it was time to prepare the babies for bedtime, he stayed behind to help clear the table, while Ellen and Asean loaded the dishwasher and listened to some unidentifiable, sloweddown southern rap, everything rounded off and rolling easy through the kitchen. When they had finished, Asean rushed off to help put his daughter to bed, leaving Ellen and Dr. Grind to finish the last few tasks in the kitchen before turning off the lights.

"How are things, Ellen?" he asked her.

"Fine," she said.

"I want to talk to you about something, if you have a second," he said and she seemed to freeze, her eyes widening.

"What's wrong?" she asked.

"Nothing's wrong," he continued. "I just want to check in and see how things are going. We've reached almost a year together, so I'm wondering how you feel about your role as a parent."

"It's complicated," Ellen admitted. "I know this is the best place for Marnie, for all of us, but I can't pretend that it's not strange. It seems like a lot of the other parents don't have issues with any of it. Maybe it's because I'm older than most of them, but I sometimes need a little more time to get used to all the new changes that pop up. I want to be a good mother."

"You are a good mother," Dr. Grind said.

"I think so," she said, "but who knows? This is my first time. I don't have enough evidence to know for certain. I'm just trying to do my best."

"That's what we're all doing, together, trying to do our best," Dr. Grind offered.

"It's easy to say that, this idea that we're all in this together, but, honestly, Dr. Grind, some things are private and I have to deal with them on my own. I talk to the other parents. I talk to Harris. I talk to the psychiatrist. I talk to you. And that's fine, but no matter how many people tell me this is the best thing for all of us, I am not totally convinced yet. I just need time, I guess. My life has been such that, when I think things are okay, they start to fall apart. I guess I'm just wary of things when they seem like they're working. Sometimes I need a little reassurance. Sometimes I need to reassure myself, in my own way."

"That's fair," Dr. Grind said. "I can appreciate that."

"Good," Ellen said.

There was a pause between them, both of them looking for the next thing to say and finding nothing before Ellen finally said, "This is about me holding Marnie, isn't it?"

"Partly," Dr. Grind said, slightly taken aback by the honesty of her statement. "Well, actually, yes. Entirely."

"I figured as much. I knew it even when I woke her up. I knew it was going to get me in trouble, but I just needed to do it. I needed to hold her a little longer."

"Okay," Dr. Grind said. "I understand that, Ellen, you have to believe that I understand that desire."

"But you still don't want me to do it," she said matter-of-factly.

"Not under those circumstances. I want everyone to follow the procedures as we've established them, to ensure that everyone is taken care of and that we continue to adjust so that we're prepared for whatever comes next."

"Okay," Ellen said, waving her hand in surrender. "I know you don't enjoy this. I know I'm making things complicated. I'll figure it out."

Ellen touched her forehead, as if she was looking into the future and unhappy with what she saw. Finally, she looked up at Dr. Grind and said, "You know what you're doing, right? This will all work out?"

"It will, Ellen," he replied.

"I think I believe you," she finally said, and then she walked out of the kitchen, leaving Dr. Grind alone in the room.

Knowing that sleep was not a possible outcome, not even the skittering, patchy sleep to which he was accustomed, Dr. Grind changed into his workout clothes and walked the length of the complex, the courtyard illuminated by solar lights. It was bracingly cold, the sky vast and clear above him. He could see some of the families already in their homes, watching TV or typing on their laptops, and then instantly felt creepy to be watching them, as if he wasn't enough of a constant presence in their lives. He swiped his key card and entered Main 2, heading to the exercise room, where he planned to get on the treadmill and run himself into a kind of uneasy exhaustion. He had Julie Howser's novel on audiobook and he was halfway through it, a dense, complicated book about several generations of rabble-rousers in the American South. The language was so artful, the sentences unwinding in such complex rhythms, that he found he occasionally lost the thread of the narrative and had to skip back on his MP3 player.

When he got to the gym, Jeffrey was already there, moving quickly through a series of exercises, curling dumbbells before tossing them down and doing a set of jumping jacks, then lunges, his face a perfect mask of unhappiness. When he noticed Dr. Grind, he stopped his routine and nodded.

"I thought you might come here," Jeffrey said. "How did it go with Ellen?"

"I'm not sure," Dr. Grind admitted. "We acknowledged the issue and I think we agreed to try to deal with it in the future."

"So, no need for a collective intervention?" Jeffrey asked.

"No, thank god," Dr. Grind said, and then walked over to one of the treadmills and turned it on. Before he could start running, he noticed that Jeffrey was standing in front of the machine. "What?" Dr. Grind asked, wanting to burn off his anxiety, his legs already warming up to the idea of motion.

"This is going to keep happening," Jeffrey said. "It's natural that the parents are going to gravitate toward their own kids."

"I know that," Dr. Grind said. "We anticipated that. That's why we have structures in place to help mitigate those circumstances."

"No matter what we do, especially in the beginning, we're going to see this problem. It's just a fact."

"What do you want me to say, Jeffrey? Do you think I'm being heartless? I'm not preventing anyone from loving their child. I'm just asking them to expand their emotions to include other people."

"It sounds good when you say it out loud. I'm just saying that, in practice, it will be more difficult."

"Well, I agree with you there. We've moved from theory to practice, and we'll adjust as necessary."

"You know that I was really skeptical about this project at the beginning. I didn't see how it would work out, but I wanted to give it a shot. It was a good opportunity for me. And now, I've been here a year, and I truly think something amazing is happening. Whenever you compare the results to the anticipated outcomes, we're surpassing them. The kids are healthy and happy and cared for in ways that wouldn't be possible otherwise."

"But?" Dr. Grind said, feeling his heart rate increase, as if he was already running.

"It's the parents we have to worry about," Jeffrey finally said. "The kids are going to be great; the parents are the unstable element. You've got to watch them."

"We don't want to turn into Big Brother, Jeffrey. We have to give them some freedoms within the project. I can't watch them twenty-four hours a day. I don't want to."

"I don't either. My focus is on the kids. And maybe this all starts to work itself out when the parents head off to their jobs and school and all that. Once their life outside the complex expands, maybe then they'll be more comfortable within the family. I hope. I'm just voicing a concern."

"I hear you," Dr. Grind said.

"That's all I wanted to say." Jeffrey grabbed a towel that he had hung on one of the exercise machines and wiped the sweat from his face. "I'm going to bed," he said. "I've got the first shift in the morning with the kids."

"Have a good night," Dr. Grind said.

Once he was alone, Dr. Grind turned on the treadmill and began to walk; it seemed like every time he put his foot down on the treadmill, it was like stepping in tar. His muscles were twitching. He turned up the speed until he was jogging at a fair pace, but even that didn't get rid of the nerves that were causing his muscles to harden and atrophy. He turned the machine up even faster, and then a few more clicks, until he was running as hard as he could. He knew that if he slipped up or stopped, the force of the treadmill would send him crashing through the wall behind him, so he kept running, feeling his lungs contract, his legs burn. He named every single child in the family, and then named every parent, as if the sequence was a code that would unlock something in his brain. "Marnie, Eli, Cap, Eliza, Ally, Lulu, Gilberto, Jackie, Irene, and Maxwell," a song without music. "Izzy, Harris, Ellen, Julie, Link, Asean, Nikisha, Kenny, Carmen, David, Susan, Paul, Mary, Benjamin, Alyssa, Carlos, Nina, Jeremy, and Callie." Even then it did not end. "Kalina, Jill, Jeffrey." He ran and ran. "Marla . . . Jody." How was it possible to hold all of these people in his heart? What were they even doing there? Over the course of a year, he had brought all of these people together and now he felt the pressure that, if he did not hold on to them tightly enough, they would slip away, spread out across the map and never return. He finally slapped at the console of the treadmill and the speed began to decline in increments, until Dr. Grind finally remembered that his legs were a part of his body, until he was once again simply putting one foot in front of the other, his footsteps not making a sound.

Sleep was not going to be possible tonight, not a single minute. He stepped off the treadmill, feeling like he was now on the surface of an inhospitable planet. He felt the urge to go to the sleep room, to check on the babies. Instead, he walked out into the open air, the chill instantly attaching itself to the sweat on his arms and legs. He seated himself on a bench in the middle of the courtyard. He looked up at the sky, at the stars, and let his body adjust to the temperature. After a few minutes, his mind wandering, nothing that he could focus on but the fact that he needed to go back inside, he heard one of the doors of the houses open. He tensed up, so clearly visible, and then he heard Carlos call out, "Dr. Grind?"

"It's me, Carlos," he said, waving to the shadowy form standing in the doorway.

"You okay?" Carlos asked.

"I'm fine," he said, now worried that his voice would wake the other parents.

Carlos walked back into the house and then, a few seconds later, returned, now wearing a coat and a pair of sneakers. He jogged over to the bench, and Dr. Grind had the immediate desire to simply take off, but he remained where he was.

"It's cold out here," Carlos said, and Dr. Grind agreed.

"What are you doing up?" Dr. Grind asked him.

"Nina was pumping; I always get up with her, get her water, and then she goes back to sleep and I'm always wide awake. I was looking up stuff on the Internet and then I saw you out here." He looked at Dr. Grind and then said, "You should be inside."

"I will, Carlos," he replied. "I was just about to motivate myself to get back to my office, but I was enjoying the quiet."

"Okay," Carlos said. They were silent for a few seconds and Carlos looked up at the stars. "We like it here," he told Dr. Grind. "I really thought I would hate it, being cooped up with a bunch of strangers and ten crying babies, but I don't. I like everything about it."

"I'm glad," Dr. Grind said, patting Carlos on the shoulder, grateful for this small kindness.

"Thanks for everything, Dr. Grind," he said, and then gave Preston a quick hug, the intimacy startling the doctor. "Thanks for watching out for us."

Dr. Grind simply nodded, too embarrassed to speak, and Carlos hustled back to the warmth of his home, waving just before he quietly shut the door. Dr. Grind stood and walked slowly back to Main 1. He had no idea what would come next, but maybe if everyone around him thought he did, it would all work out. As long as they thought that he was taking care of them, nothing bad could happen. He would give them everything they wanted, even things they didn't know they wanted, and they would all be okay in the end.

When he returned to the main building, he saw one of the night nurses waiting for him in the hallway. "What's going on?" he asked, noticing the tight look of inconvenience on her face.

"We have a slight situation," the woman said. "Ellen is in the sleep room, but she's not scheduled for tonight. She's been there for about thirty minutes now."

"What is she doing?" he asked. "Has she woken up Marnie?"

"No," the woman replied. "She's just standing over her crib. We told her she should get some sleep, but she won't say anything. And we don't want to escalate the situation and wake the babies."

"Call Harris," Dr. Grind said. "Wake him up and tell him to come over."

Dr. Grind charged up the steps, all the certainty and calm from his meeting with Carlos now vaporized. He swiped his card, making a note that perhaps he should program the reader so that it would not allow anyone who wasn't scheduled to enter the sleep room, and found the parents on duty and the other nurses standing at a good distance from Ellen, who was, as the nurse had said, simply standing motionless over Marnie's crib. Dr. Grind nodded at the silent group, who looked like hostages in a crisis, and slowly walked over to Ellen. He put his hand on her shoulder and, without even looking back at him, she replied, "I know this is bad."

"It's not bad," he whispered to her. "It's totally understandable."

"I tried not to come in here," she said. "But then I did."

"Let's move away from Marnie so we don't wake her, Ellen," he said, gently guiding Ellen from the crib, from the other parents, who watched in stunned silence, from the room itself, until the door clicked shut and the two of them stood alone in the hallway. Almost immediately, Ellen slumped into his arms and he held her up. "I can't help but feel like I've made a terrible mistake," she said, her teeth now chattering.

Just then, Harris stood at the entrance to the stairway, holding out his arms as if waiting for direction. Dr. Grind held up a hand to ask for a few minutes alone.

"You haven't made a mistake, Ellen, I promise you that," he said. He could feel something inside him opening up, a kind of black hole that was slowly rotating and sucking in any emotion that might spill out of him. "Being a parent is the hardest thing you'll ever do. We're all adjusting to that. We're all trying to do our best."

"I don't think my best is going to be enough," she said.

"It will. I know with absolute certainly that it will be more than enough."

"Harris thinks so," she said. "He said this was where we needed to be. He said this place was going to be so good for us, for Marnie. So I guess it's just me."

"Everyone has doubts," Dr. Grind said.

"Even you?" she said.

"Yes," he admitted. "Of course."

Her teeth stopped chattering and she slowly let her own body support its weight, pulling gently out of Dr. Grind's grasp. Dr. Grind motioned for Harris to now come over.

Just before Harris stepped into earshot, Ellen leaned into Dr. Grind and whispered, "Even if this all turns out to be for the best, Dr. Grind, I still kind of hate you."

Dr. Grind accepted this comment with a slight nod; he thought for a brief moment that Ellen was going to kiss him, but then Harris put his hands on her shoulders and Ellen smiled. "I won't do it again," she said, and Dr. Grind was certain that she meant it. She had needed this transgression, perhaps, to test the limits, and would make a greater effort to fall in line with the structure of the complex. Or not, Dr. Grind also allowed. Perhaps she would simply be the leader of a revolt that would burn the complex to the ground. All he could do now was squeeze her hand in sympathy and watch as she and Harris disappeared from view.

Dr. Grind looked through the window of the sleep room and nodded toward the other parents, who had been watching from a distance. He flashed a thumbs-up gesture and immediately felt ridiculous, as if he thought he was a navy SEAL who had just defused a bomb. He walked into his own apartment, shut the door, and stood there for a minute, breathing deeply, arranging his emotions. And then, with great sadness, overwhelming sadness, he walked to his bedroom and took off his clothes until he was only wearing a pair of underwear. He then opened the bottom drawer of his nightstand and removed a small, black, leather pouch with a zippered closure.

He sat cross-legged on the floor and opened the pouch to reveal a plastic box of Wilkinson Sword razor blades, a dozen or so alcohol wipes, a travel-size box of tissues, a tube of Neosporin, and a box of butterfly closure Band-Aid bandages. He took one of the razors and unwrapped it from its thin protective paper. He stretched out one of his legs and examined the skin of his thigh. He took the razor and, as he took a deep inhalation of breath, he drew the blade across his skin, a steady pressure, and watched a thin line of blood slowly appear, like a conjured-up ghost. He exhaled and felt the toxins, entirely imagined but nonetheless tangible to him, seep from somewhere deep inside him.

He placed the razor blade in the slot on the back of the razor blade box, for used blades, and then removed a single tissue. He laid it on the wound and watched as it absorbed the blood, the deep red spreading across the pristine white tissue. He closed his eyes and remembered what Ellen had said to him, her breath hot on his face. The bleeding, after less than a minute or two, had begun to subside; he had been careful not to cut too deeply. And, soon enough, he found that Ellen's words had turned into a foreign language, a lost language that would never be translated. The words meant nothing to him, and he felt calm and silent and assured of his place in the world. He cleaned the wound with an alcohol wipe, placed a bandage on the wound, and then put the supplies back in the leather pouch. He returned the pouch to the nightstand drawer and, as he closed it, he promised himself, once more, that he would never again use it.

It had started when he was nine years old, the memory faded and tinged with a dreamlike quality that made it feel both more and less real to him. With the Constant Friction Method, his parents trained him by creating moments of disaster and conditioned him to handle it with a minimal amount of emotion. He was good at it; they were so proud of him, the way he continually proved their methods to be sound. But there were times when a few days had passed without a manufactured incident, everything calm and happy, and, to Preston, it was altogether terrifying and unbearable. He lived in a state of expectation, always wondering when the next test would come. His parents would sometimes stretch out the spaces between events, forcing him to be ever vigilant, to control himself even in moments of peace. Every interaction seemed a possibility for ruination, and, finally, Preston could handle it no longer. On a particularly lazy Sunday, his mother and father reading in the library, leaving him to his own devices, he could not ignore the strange rhythm of his heartbeat, as if his own internals were waiting for something to happen. He finally walked into the bathroom, took a razor blade from his father's drawer, a Wilkinson Sword, and awkwardly slashed at his arm. He walked into the library, blood trickling from his fingertips, and he then offered his arm to his mother and father. "Can this be it?" he asked. "For today?" He had never seen the look on his parents' faces, a curiosity mixed with admiration at his ability to surprise them. A complication had entered into their study, and they slowly knelt before their son, holding him, kissing him, and told him that this was not his fault but their own. "We're sorry, Preston," his mother said, and he relaxed in her embrace, knowing that, for a few minutes at least, he was truly safe.

The cutting would continue for the rest of his childhood, perhaps two or three times a year, when he felt overwhelmed with anticipation, but his parents never recorded these events in their findings. Preston, for his part, kept the cuts in places that were hidden from view. The one time he had cut too deeply, he had even stitched up the wound himself with a needle and thread to prevent a trip to the emergency room, and his parents had been ostentatiously grateful for his kindness. But, for the most part, the cutting became a way to occasionally assert that, despite what his parents thought, they did not entirely own him. He would slice into his skin, show his parents the result, and they would know what it felt like to be shocked by the actions of someone you loved.

He had stopped in college, once he found Marla, and so it made sense to him that, right after the funeral for Marla and his son, Dr. Grind drove to a drugstore and purchased the supplies necessary to continue the practice. When he felt the overwhelming emotions take control of him, the pain greater than the training he had learned from the Constant Friction Method, he would cut into himself and find that weird peacefulness, almost druglike, that came over him and made it possible to get through another goddamned day. He had brought the pouch with him to the complex, a compulsion that he could not eliminate, and he now felt a sense of pride that he had made it this long before needing it.

Dr. Grind changed into his pajamas, though he had no designs on sleep. He wanted so badly to walk back into the sleep room and pick up one of the babies, to hold their warmth against him, to ease them back into sleep. He understood, without much effort, what Ellen had wanted when she took Marnie into her arms. When you felt adrift, when you wondered if you were doing the right thing, there was nothing better than holding something small and defenseless and telling them, over and over again, that you would care for them, that nothing bad would happen as long as you were there. Instead, Dr. Grind simply lay in his bed and waited for the rest of the world to awaken, when he could walk freely among his family and do whatever was needed to keep things together.

chapter eleven

the infinite family project (year two)

zzy, as hungover as she'd ever been in her life, bourbon swirling through her bloodstream, stirred crumbled bacon and diced jalapeños into her cornmeal and flour mixture as a photographer from *Time* magazine took pictures of the process, as if Izzy were a celebrity chef and not some kid trying to make an entire meal from scratch for her family. All she was worried about was keeping her own sweat out of the food, which was more difficult than she had expected, but the photographer kept asking her questions about the complex, the babies, the parents, the weird AstroTurf buildings, snapping another picture after every question, Izzy certain that every photo would show her grinding her teeth in agitation.

The details of the night before, hazy as a dream, kept returning to her, stabbing her with embarrassment. Her creeping paranoia made her expect a visit from Dr. Grind, telling her that he knew all about her actions last night and that she needed to pack up her belongings and leave the project. Her son, Dr. Grind would inform her, would stay with the Infinite Family.

It had been Alyssa's birthday, and Izzy, even with all the expectations of the party for *Time*, had made a cake, German chocolate, Alyssa's favorite. The whole family sang "Happy Birthday," the kids cackling, their fingers wriggling, wanting only to eat something sweet. Afterward, Izzy and some of the other parents cleaned up the kitchen and then helped prepare the children for bed. Izzy had immediately returned to the kitchen, going over the menus, doing prep work, rethinking each recipe. By the time she looked up at the clock, it was nearly midnight, and she instantly felt exhaustion flood her system. She cleaned up her station, wiped down the counter, and walked out of the kitchen to find that the lights were still on in the TV room. Izzy crept down the hallway and peered through the window to find seven of the parents still awake. Benjamin, who was holding a cocktail shaker, saw Izzy and smiled, inviting her inside. She shook her head, but then Alyssa and Ellen also noticed Izzy and emphatically gestured for her to join them. Izzy, so stressed about tomorrow's party, saw that all the parents held a drink in their hands and decided she needed to unwind.

"Izzy!" Alyssa shouted. "Benjamin is making whiskey smashes. We'll have to pump and dump, but it's totally worth it. Have a drink."

Before she could respond, Benjamin handed her a glass, filled to the brim. Without hesitating, Izzy took a huge gulp and felt the sweetness and burn of the cocktail. She was unused to alcohol, but she welcomed the way it smoothed out her nerves. Her milk, yes, would be ruined, but there was always more milk, a never-ending supply of milk; she needed something for herself right now.

She felt at ease in this room, drink in her hand. Benjamin, barrel-chested and imposing at first glance, was a great conversationalist, always finding ways to draw people out of their shells, able to hold up his end of any topic. Part of this must have been his previous job as a car salesman, his ability to walk up to any person and instantly know what they wanted, what they would give him in exchange. One night, while the two of them washed dishes after dinner, Benjamin had spoken so frankly of his childhood, moving from foster parent to foster parent, abused and unloved, that Izzy had, without meaning to, told him all about her mother's death, the debilitating sadness that came in the aftermath. This was his gift, to give you enough of himself that you wanted to repay it with interest.

His wife, Alyssa, was quiet but assertive, staying silent through an entire dinner before making a casual observation that seemed perfectly constructed and true. She often looked, to Izzy, to exist in two states, the physical world of the complex as well as some secret parallel universe that was much more interesting.

Ellen was by far the prickliest member of the project, never missing an opportunity to speak to her confusion at how things worked in the complex. It was clear to Izzy that Ellen did not fully believe in Dr. Grind or the project as a whole. "If I had known . . . ," Ellen would always say when faced with some new facet of the project. She would drift off, never once saying what was understood. Tonight, however, she seemed so emboldened by the cocktails that she acted as if she could think of no better place in the world than this strange complex.

Along with Ben, Alyssa, and Ellen, there were also Jeremy, Callie, Asean, and David. Asean and David were intently watching a mixed martial arts event on the TV, but the other parents were restless, laughing at the slightest provocation, trying to think up party games but too inebriated to remember the rules correctly. So, excited at being up so late when the rest of the complex was fast asleep, they just kept drinking. And Izzy did her level best to keep up. She thought that if she drank enough, she would forget about the party tomorrow and, when she woke up the next morning, it would be a grand surprise. She finished her second whiskey smash and Benjamin was already shaking up another batch. Callie and Ellen went to the kitchen to get the rest of the birthday cake. The fight on the TV now over, even Asean and David turned their focus to this impromptu party. Izzy watched Asean play a few hands of poker with Jeremy and Alyssa, smiling, taunting the others when he laid down a straight flush, sweeping a load of imaginary chips to his side of the table and miming stacking all of them up.

Izzy realized the interesting fact that perhaps the three most reserved people in the project, by far the shyest in the group, herself, Asean, and Callie, were all here. And yet the party seemed not to suffer from it. She turned to watch Callie eating a slice of cake with her hands, her teeth black with chocolate crumbs. Benjamin offered to top off her drink, but she shook her head. She had no practice. She was already drunk.

It was now three thirty in the morning, and the party was losing momentum. They had spent the last thirty minutes watching an info-mercial for a hand-cranking vacuum cleaner that, through some minor adjustments, could turn into a leaf blower. "Can we get Dr. Grind to buy us one of these?" Ellen asked. All of them were sunk deep in the cushions of the couch, so drunk that they kept leaning against each other. When the infomercial gave way to a religious program, Asean turned off the TV and they all started to pull themselves together to return to their own beds.

"This was nice," Alyssa said. "I feel like this has helped me feel closer to you guys than anything we've done since we've been here."

"I love all of you now," Ellen said.

"It's weird," Benjamin said. "I understand how our relationship works with the kids. We are all their parents. Each one of them is our child. It takes some getting used to, but I get it now. But it's never been super clear on how it works with all of us, the adults. What are we to each other?"

"Brothers and sisters?" David offered.

"Maybe more like second cousins," Benjamin said.

"I think it's more like the cast of *Gilligan's Island*," Alyssa said. "We're these random people who ended up stranded on an island to-gether."

"And once we get off the island?" Izzy asked, trying so hard to keep up.

Alyssa shrugged. "Who knows?"

Jeremy then said, "There was a lot of sexual tension on that show."

"What?" Ellen said, laughing. "No, there wasn't."

"It was there," Jeremy said. "You just had to know where to look."

"That makes sense," David said. "If you're stuck on an island, it's bound to turn sexual."

This made everyone go quiet for a moment.

"What does that mean for us?" Alyssa said.

"That's not what I meant," David replied, blushing.

"But it's true," Ellen said, starting to perk up. The logical end of the party had come and gone, and now they were stuck in a kind of riptide. It was pulling them . . . somewhere, and Izzy was too tired to fight it.

"There's no doubt that there's sexual tension at the complex," Ellen continued. "But we can't act on it, right? That would be awful. It would ruin everything. But it seems crazy not to acknowledge it."

"Okay, so we acknowledge it," Benjamin said. "And that's that."

"Everything here is so calculated," Ellen said. "Emotions don't matter. It's what's best for the kids, for the family. Everything is an experiment; whether Dr. Grind admits it or not, he's kind of making it up as he goes along, right? So why can't we experiment, too?"

"It's late," Callie said, but Ellen kept going, not leaving enough time for anyone to agree and then disband.

"We should interact with those desires, but in a controlled way."

"How?" Benjamin asked, leaning forward.

"Spin the bottle?" Ellen offered, and the statement clattered so loudly to the ground that Izzy swore she could hear the sound.

David, who Izzy now realized was drunker than he had originally seemed, said, "But that's not really fair, right? Depending on the unknown variables of the bottle spinning, someone might never get kissed while someone else might be constantly kissing other people."

"And women might have to kiss another woman, and vice versa," Alyssa said.

Izzy couldn't decide if she was the least or most drunk person in the room. It was too difficult to parse.

"A lottery!" Ellen shouted. She took a pen and a piece of paper and wrote down some numbers. Then she tore them into separate pieces, placed them in two distinct piles, facedown, and pointed to her work. "Guys draw from here. Girls from here."

No one moved, not even Ellen. Izzy looked around the room. If one person stood up, said they had to go, Izzy knew that the whole thing would fall apart. She waited, but no one moved. She looked at Asean, at Callie. They could not possibly want to participate. But, still, no one moved. Izzy realized, with shock, that she could be the one to break this up, to save everyone from their poor decisions, but she could not do it. And she could not determine, in her inebriated state, if it was because she was too shy to call attention to herself, or if she really wanted to see what it would be like to kiss someone else in the project.

Benjamin finally reached for a piece of paper. Ellen did the same. Then Alyssa and Jeremy and David and Callie. Asean, hesitating, finally took the last number from the men's pile. Everyone looked at Izzy. Ellen was smiling. Izzy reached for the last piece of paper and held it to her chest.

"Okay, turn over your piece of paper," Ellen said. Ellen had always had a little more power than most of the other adults. She was perhaps the most skeptical of the project, and therefore the one least inhibited to discuss it. And now they followed her cue.

Jeremy and Ellen. Callie and Benjamin. David and Alyssa. Asean and Izzy.

"Perfect," Ellen said. "It was entirely possible that the two couples could have been matched up, which would have been boring."

"Now what?" David asked.

"There are four couples. Four corners of the room. Maybe we just each go into a corner?" said Benjamin.

This was so absurd, so stupid, but Izzy watched everyone move to opposite corners of the room. Izzy and Asean still sat on the couch.

"We don't have to do this," Izzy said. Asean nodded, but then looked around at the other couples, who were waiting for them.

"I think it would be weirder not to do it at this point," he said, not able to look at her. He took her hand and they walked to the last unoccupied corner of the room.

"Okay," Ellen said. "Go."

Asean was the tallest man in the project, but Izzy was the tallest woman, so it wasn't as awkward as it could have been. They leaned into each other, embracing. It felt nice to be held, Izzy could at least admit this. She remembered how Asean had told Izzy how, his entire life, coaches had tried to recruit him for football, and how he had always declined the invitation. "I don't want to hurt anybody," he told her. "I like putting people together more." He had instead become the team trainer in high school, learning how to wrap an ankle, when to apply ice and when to apply heat. She imagined the strange sight of Asean, taller and more muscular than anyone in pads, jogging onto the football field during a time-out, picking up an injured player and carrying him easily back to the sidelines. She thought of what he had said, not to hurt, but to put back together. He was good at it, he had assured her.

She then tilted her face toward his and they kissed. It could have been two seconds or two hours. Izzy had no concept of time in this moment. She simply kissed Asean and was amazed by how easy it was. Then she became terrified; it was so easy. She pulled away and Asean nervously rubbed her shoulder. Against their better judgment, they looked toward the other corners of the room and saw each couple kissing, hesitant and slow, but most definitely making out.

"Let's just wait for them to finish," Asean whispered, and Izzy agreed, though she could easily have been convinced to do it again. She found that the kissing had burned out every drop of alcohol in her system and already, holy shit, she could feel the hangover rattling around in her empty head.

Finally, the other couples finished, and they all sheepishly moved back to the middle of the room. They smiled, awkwardly shifting their feet. "Does anyone want another drink?" Benjamin asked.

"It's late," Callie said again, and she pulled on Jeremy's arm, who nodded and walked out of the room without another word. David silently followed them out.

Ellen looked at the rest of them. "Was it bad? Was that a mistake?"

"Maybe," Asean offered, his voice so soft it sounded like a lullaby.

"Well, that's the nature of this project," Ellen admitted. "It's how life works in general. You only know after the fact whether or not it was a good idea."

Alyssa and Ben stayed with Ellen to straighten up the room, and Asean and Izzy walked out together.

"I wish I hadn't done that," Asean said.

"I know," Izzy replied.

"Not because of you, you know?" Asean corrected himself.

"No, I know."

"I wouldn't have wanted it to be anyone else," Asean said.

"Thank you," Izzy said, unable for a few moments to meet his gaze until, finally, she looked at him. He was so handsome, so gentle, the kind of partner she'd hoped for. And here he was, in front of her, living with her, sharing the same spaces. But these were the limits of the project, no matter how much they talked about being a singular family. Asean was not hers and, even if they wanted each other on some level, they could not have each other. Izzy found herself less sad about this than she expected. She was okay with limits, some boundaries. If there would always be this strange electricity between herself and Asean, so be it. It would not ruin them.

"I better get back," Asean said. He offered his hand to Izzy, and she awkwardly shook it, as if he had just sold her a very generous life insurance policy. "Good night," he said.

"Good night," Izzy replied.

Back in her house, under the covers of her bed, knowing that she would not sleep, she kept wondering if Asean, with Nikisha staying in the children's room that night, would find his way back to her house, knock on her door, and whether she would let him in. She hoped, a million times over, that he would not, that nothing would ever come of this night. She wished so hard that her head ached and ached, but by the morning, she found that perhaps the mistake had been so small, so much a dream, that it would never matter, that nothing had changed or would change.

She added the buttermilk mixture to the bowl and stirred until everything looked correct; she kept glancing at Chef Nicole, but she was reading a magazine, her feet propped up on one of the prep tables, either confident in Izzy's abilities or wanting to disassociate herself from the entire enterprise. In the courtyard, a whole hog was cooking in the smoker that Gerdie Kent had, without batting an eye, rented for the occasion, a Meadow Creek smoker on its own trailer, so big it looked like a submarine from the Cold War. The pig had been bought from a local farm, a perfect specimen, another miracle on Gerdie's part.

It had been almost two years since she'd prepared a hog for the smoker, but it seemed instinctual after so many days working with Mr. Tannehill. It was the rest of the meal that worried her, traditional southern sides that she and Chef Nicole had spent the past week figuring out how to make more interesting, more flavorful, more unique. The collards would be cooked for barely even a few minutes in bacon fat, instead of simmering for hours in a pot. The deviled eggs were to be pickled in beet juice so each egg turned the brightest shade of purple and was flavored with that vegetal tang, then topped with candied bacon. And Chef Nicole remembered a recipe from the restaurant WD-50 in New York where a traditional baked beans dish was instead made with pine nuts, which the two of them tried to replicate over several attempts until they got it just right. "You want it to be surprising," Chef Nicole told her, "but still have the essential properties of the traditional thing that they love." Like the Infinite Family, Izzy immediately thought, and she had spent the last fifteen minutes trying to figure out an organic way to give this quote to the reporter.

Through the window, as if she could control the temperature of the smoker with her mind, Izzy stared at the activity in the courtyard; the babies, all of them now mobile and powered by some internal nuclear engine, moved with great purpose around the playground, always right on the verge of falling on their faces, while the parents took photos of them with their cameras and hoisted them onto various pieces of equipment. Every month, a different parent compiled dozens of photos of the Infinite Family that had been taken in the past thirty days and had photo albums printed and delivered to everyone in the complex. Izzy had these slim, flimsy photo books, stacked in chronological order, in the bookcase next to her bed, and she consulted them often, feeling somewhat guilty that, on every page, she immediately searched for Cap's face.

At the edge of the activity, Izzy watched the reporter from *Time*, a rugged-looking adventurer type who seemed mystified by the dimensions of the family, as if he'd stumbled upon an unknown tribe, talk to Dr. Grind and Dr. Patterson. One of the babies, Maxwell, walked over to Jill and reached for her hand, imploring her to join in the fun, and she bent over and shuffled to a mini merry-go-round and began to spin it for the child. It looked like a block party, something normal and middle American. This was what Dr. Grind kept stressing to them in the days leading up to this visit. He had seemed slightly annoyed by the fact that the magazine was coming to write about them at all, but, as Izzy learned from Kalina, this was the work of Brenda Acklen, their mysterious benefactor, who wanted the work at the complex to be noticed, to be a part of the national consciousness. "We're not going to highlight what's different about our project," Dr. Grind told them over dinner a few nights before the visit. "We're going to highlight what's just like everyone else in the world."

"Why?" Julie Howser asked. "Why not highlight why we're so different?"

"Because," Dr. Grind replied, smiling, gesturing to encompass every person around the dinner table, "that will be wonderfully obvious after they spend some time with us."

Apologizing to the photographer, she ran out of the kitchen and down the stairs to the courtyard to check on the temperature of the smoker. She added some more wood and then mopped the entire carcass with a vinegar sauce, slightly different from that at the Whole Hog, her own recipe, and closed the heavy lid of the smoker, which clanged shut like a prison door. Asean and Alyssa both came over to the smoker to see if it was ready yet, and Izzy assured them that it was almost finished. Feigning great interest in the smoker, the two of them finally looked at Izzy. "We know it was a mistake," Alyssa admitted. "It was stupid. We were drunk. What's important now is that we don't talk about it. What's done is done, right?"

Izzy looked to Asean, who nodded. "We know that it didn't mean anything, but others might not," Alyssa continued, the longest Izzy had ever heard her talk at one time. "Dr. Grind, can you imagine what he would say? It's done, it's over, and we'll just keep it to ourselves."

"Okay," Izzy said.

"I'm so hungry," Alyssa said, looking back at the smoker. "I'm starving." Then the two of them walked away, Izzy watching them return to the fold with perfect composure.

Izzy knew she should head back to the kitchen to finish the sides, but she wanted to be with the kids. Disco was playing on the boom box and the children were wiggling without any regard for the actual beat, simply acting out the sounds as it fired in their brains. The photographer was now back outside, snapping photos of the children. She watched Cap and Ally roll an oversize beach ball back and forth and occasionally try to climb it. Gilberto, unattended at the edge of the playground (even with so many adults around, it was still so strangely easy to lose track of a child), toppled over and started to cry, and Izzy scooped him up and rubbed the reddening bump on his forehead until he crumpled in her arms and went quiet. Nina came over and checked on them, and Izzy handed the boy over to her; as soon as he was transferred, a smile returned to his face and he wriggled with impatience until Nina placed him back on the ground and he crab-walked back to the action. It amazed Izzy the way the children rushed through so many complicated emotions without space between each one. Everything rose so quickly to the surface and then subsided, like firecrackers, and what had originally been so jarring to her, their unguarded emotion, now filled her with great comfort, that anything, no matter what it was, would eventually give way to something else.

She wished this was how it worked for adults. She thought again about Asean, that kiss, the sight of the other couples in the corners. Why the hell had they all moved to the corners of the room like they were being punished? For a brief second, just long enough that it made sense, she thought of running out of the complex, driving as far as she could get. She wondered how long it would take before anyone noticed that she was gone. But she knew her absence would be noticed immediately, the way she was connected to them. What troubled her, the fantasy already turning into something dangerous, was how long it would take before they got over her, how quickly they would move on, would simply keep going as if she had never been there.

The reporter noticed Izzy and whispered something to Dr. Grind, who nodded and then smiled. As Izzy turned to flee back into the kitchen, the reporter came alongside her and said, "So you're the youngest person here?"

"Except for the kids," Izzy replied, wanting to shake him before she returned to the food.

"And you're the only single parent?" he asked.

"Well," Izzy said, feeling slightly irritated, "that's the whole point of the project. I'm not alone. It's why I'm here, so that I have a group of people to help me."

"And there's nothing about this that seems strange to you?" he asked.

"I can't really answer that," Izzy replied, thinking of last night, how strange it had been. "It doesn't feel strange to me because it's my life. It's my family."

"But surely you can—" the man said, but Izzy cut him off. "It's unique, not strange," she said. "That's why we're all here, to try something new, to have access to things that we wouldn't have otherwise."

"Are you dating anyone?" he asked and she immediately blushed.

"No," she said.

"If you did start dating someone, how would you explain this place to them?"

"I'm not dating anyone, so I don't have to worry about that," she said, and she walked back into Main 1, swiping her key card and then pulling the door shut before he could follow her.

Izzy was now in her second semester at the university, taking courses in literature and history, bored out of her freaking mind. The work wasn't especially difficult, though it did take up a necessary part of her brain, but it did little to excite her. The problem, she had determined, was that she had taken such a liking to her work with Chef Nicole. After talking so much about theoretical ideas, metaphors, and themes, there was something wonderful about taking a slab of salmon, the flesh so pink it looked like something in a children's fantasy novel, and poaching it until the wine and dill infused the flesh of the fish and, when served, everyone thought you'd conjured up the flavor by incantation. She liked prep work, cutting all the vegetables to Chef Nicole's exacting standards. After working with the cleavers to pound barbecue into irregular chunks, she loved how quickly she could now turn a bowl of onions into something precise and perfect with the deft movements of her knife.

Chef Nicole was strict and not very chatty in the kitchen, but she pushed Izzy into a million different methods with an assured manner that made Izzy want to please her. It helped that Chef Nicole thought nothing of making a simple dish of mashed avocados for the babies' breakfast but then whipped up a delicate foam of strawberries and cream to top it, the flavors perfectly balanced. The babies, however, simply ate whatever was placed in front of them, no matter how outlandish, and it became an experiment in the kitchen to see what they could get away with, what they could sneak past the babies' palates.

Now back in the kitchen, Izzy pulled the muffins out of the oven and then quickly cooked the collard greens in batches until the leaves just barely wilted, the bacon fat leaving a perfect gloss on the dish. She broke the candied bacon into tiny pieces and sprinkled it over the purpled deviled eggs, so many of them it felt like a White House Easter egg hunt. She and Chef Nicole placed these and the other side dishes into the wheeled food transporter and took it down to the courtyard, where the casters bounced unevenly along the ground, the sound producing a reaction in the parents like children hearing the jingle of an ice-cream truck.

While Chef Nicole set out the children's meal, Izzy let Asean and Link distribute the side dishes on the picnic tables and then she returned to the smoker, where she asked Jeremy to help her place the finished pig on the chopping block. Some of the parents lifted the children up and let them observe the now steaming carcass, its skin the most perfect color of fine leather. The children's eyes were wide, and Izzy felt embarrassed when she shoved her gloved hands into the pig and began to tear it apart, deconstruction at its finest, the children engrossed in the act. In less than ten minutes, she had separated and then chopped up a fair portion of the pork and the parents now filled their plates with the meat. The reporter came over to the chopping block and took a chunk of pork and placed it in his mouth, a look of instant surprise forming on his face. "This is incredible," he said. Izzy looked down at the meat, unable to return his gaze. "Thank you," she said, and she was once again grateful for this project that she'd lucked into, the opportunity, over and over again, to do something that someone, anyone, would notice, to have people think she was special.

Praise for Izzy's pork came from every member of the family, each person more enthusiastic than the last. Paul proclaimed, after his third helping, that it was the best thing he'd ever eaten. The photographer hovered over the remains of the pig, snapping photo after photo as if it were a crime scene. Even with the awkwardness, the surreal experience of being watched by outsiders, the party was a great success, the food disappearing from the tables, everyone happy. The children particularly loved the deviled eggs, the pretty color and the softness of the whipped egg yolks. All of their fingertips were stained the faintest shade of purple and their faces were smeared with the mashed yolk mixture. Izzy herself, so nauseous from the night before, did not eat and not one person noticed.

Once the children were freed from their seats, Dr. Grind hooked up the complex's iPod to the sound system and shuffled the music. The iPod held a playlist specifically for the children, new songs added daily based on what they were listening to in the nursery. The songs usually had some kind of dance or action associated with them, and Izzy was always shocked to watch the children, still babies almost, so young, instantly performing their own variation on the dance, as if each child was in their own music video. The reporter and photographer from *Time* seemed fascinated by the spastic dancing as the playlist shifted from the Wiggles' "Taba Naba" to Pretty Tony's "Get Buck." After only a few songs, the children had moved on to other interests, but they occasionally stomped their feet in appreciation of a song they particularly liked.

As the party wound down, Izzy prepared a plate of food for both the reporter and photographer to take back to the hotel. "I'm sure you can understand why I was intrigued by this place," the reporter told her as she handed over his covered dish of food. "It just sounds so strange in practice. But it was really wonderful to witness. You're a part of something special here."

For a split second, she felt an unknown and yet unmistakable dread settle in her stomach and she wanted to tell the reporter that Jeremy didn't want Eli to have his nails painted pink with the other kids, or that Carlos and Nina had brought up several times that they thought it wasn't fair that the kids couldn't play with weapons like swords or toy guns and that they thought it cut them off from a necessary part of childhood. Or that sometimes the children all sounded exactly the same, their cadence and vocabulary like a professor's lecture that's been given many times with great success, and the parents, late at night, worried that Dr. Grind was going to somehow make all their children in the Infinite Family supremely autistic. She wanted to tell him that her mother had struggled for her entire adult life with mental instability and morbid obesity, and she worried that the stress of living with all these strangers would somehow pull these aspects out of her genes and ruin her. She wanted to tell him that sometimes everything was so perfect, that she worried that the rest of the world might have been wiped out in a nuclear event, and no one had told them. She wanted to tell him how terrified she was of what would happen when it was over, that this project would both save and ruin her. She wanted to tell him how stupid they all were, how easily they could break the delicate thing that they all held in their clumsy hands. Instead, she simply said, "I think so. It's really special."

"Best of luck," the reporter said, and as he left, walking side by side with Dr. Grind toward the entrance of the complex, Nina and Susan came up to her. "You're going to be the star of the article," Nina said, poking Izzy in the ribs.

"Just don't read the comments," Susan said.

"I know, I know," Izzy replied.

She had made this mistake enough times in the past; every person in the project had clicked on to a site whenever the Infinite Family was mentioned online in articles or blog postings. Izzy had scrolled through nearly 1,500 comments on a Yahoo cover story and felt both angry and intensely embarrassed by the vitriol of the commenters.

> Way to fuck up your kids, LIBTARDS
>
> 2 to 1 odds that Doctor is fucking all the women in that place
>
> How mentally handicapped would you have to be to bring your own child into something like this? This is why our country is falling apart. No more traditional family values.
>
> The women are ugly as dogs, bet on that.
>
> This project could work, but you can't mix up the races like that. It needs to be pure.
>
> The kids are all gonna be transgender vegan serial killers.
>
> This is socialist propaganda; this is the future, people. A welfare state for lazy poor people.

Izzy now avoided social media and the Internet, preferring to stay in the complex, where everything was clear and thoughtfully arranged. Still, she worried, there would be a time when she would leave the complex and return to the world where all those commenters currently lived, waiting for her to come back.

"You'll have dudes from all over the country wooing you," Susan added.

"Best of luck to them," Izzy said. From time to time, Susan, Nina, and several other women in the complex seemed intent on getting Izzy to admit that she wanted to find a man. And though they never believed her when she said as much, Izzy really wasn't interested. So much of her time was given over to the family, still getting used to the unique aspects of each person, that it seemed overwhelming to try to date someone and have to deal with learning all of their own quirks. And sex, though the women joked with Izzy frequently about it, to her embarrassment, wasn't something she thought about much. She'd first had sex right after her mother died, the connection between the two events so obvious that it made Izzy feel so simple, so psychologically trite. There had been four different boys, one after the other, and then it was as if the process had been demystified and there was no need for it any longer. At least, this was true until she met Hal, when she again became infatuated with the act. But perhaps it was the sadness that accompanied that relationship, or just her own disinterest now, but she rarely thought about sex and it was simply easier to handle it herself than to imagine a series of events that would lead to an outsider coming into the complex to sleep with her. And, finally, there were the children. They took up so much of her time, so much of her emotions, that it seemed like sex was something available to people without such complications. Whatever the reason, Izzy wasn't interested and this seemed to drive the other women crazy.

But there was the kiss, Asean's hand on the small of her back, holding her close. There was something pleasurable in that. But, no, it wasn't pleasure. It was just an experiment. No emotion behind it. An experiment that had failed, she hoped.

"Eventually you'll get tired of us," Susan said, "and you'll want someone in bed at night to talk shit about us."

"Is that what you and David do at night?" Carmen asked.

"Not yet," Susan admitted.

"I'll have time for guys and relationships later," Izzy said, for what felt like the thousandth time. "When we all leave the complex and set out on our own. Then I'll look for someone."

"That's a pretty damn long time, Izzy," Carmen said.

"It'll happen faster than you think," Izzy said, hoping that this wasn't true.

"I still can't believe we'll have the kids with us in the house in a few more years," Carmen said, and Izzy felt the atmosphere around the three of them grow dense and staticky. They all knew it was coming, when the children would move out of the sleep room and live full-time with their birth parents, but it seemed so unnatural, strangely enough, that they tried not to think about it. Or, rather, they tried not to think about it until they let their guard down and admitted that they thought about it all the time. Izzy couldn't wait for the chance to have Cap in her own house at night, to know that it was just the two of them sharing the air in that space. And then, in her fearful moments, she thought of the possibility that she could not handle it on her own. This whole experience, she reminded herself, was to prepare her for that day, to take care of her son as if she knew exactly what she was doing.

"Can I ask you something?" Susan suddenly asked. "Something personal?" It was a rare night when beer was served with dinner, and Susan, an admitted lightweight, had two bottles, enough that it made Izzy grow tense with worry about what she would say. Had David told her about last night? Still, she and Carmen both nodded, the instinctual desire to give another member of the complex what they wanted.

"Do you ever feel like you might love one of the other children more than your own?" Susan asked, her eyes already welling up with tears, her expression like a ruined surprise birthday party.

"Sweetie," Carmen said, immediately moving to Susan while Izzy remained frozen in place, as if Susan's admission had directly entered into her nervous system. "I know exactly what you're talking about, but you're thinking about it all wrong. We're with the kids all day, every day. And kids, especially toddlers, have good and bad days. So it's easy to have favorites from day to day. It's not the same thing as loving one more than another."

"That's not what I'm talking about," Susan said, shaking her head vigorously. "I mean, what if I told you that I love a few of the other kids more than I love Irene. I just have such a hard time connecting with her most of the time. She's not very affectionate, which is fine, but then there are kids like Eliza, who is so cuddly and sweet. Or, shit, even Maxwell, who I just love being around, the way he gives me high-fives with the back of his hand every time he sees me, like it's our special thing."

Carmen visibly stiffened, at least by Izzy's estimation, at this admission, but she continued to rest her hand on Susan's.

"It's normal," Izzy finally said, as if the words had been pushed through layers and layers of cobwebs. "It really is, Susan."

"None of this is really normal, though, is it?" Susan said, and Izzy knew these things had simmered in her brain for at least a few months, had sat unchallenged until they became fact.

"It's normal enough," Carmen said. "It's working. Most of the time, it is definitely working, and I know you believe this, too. I know Izzy believes this."

"I just wonder if we went into this in order to avoid all the problems that were waiting for us," Susan continued, unable to stop, "and we ended up just creating other problems, problems that no other parent outside the complex could even understand."

Izzy immediately turned to Carmen, as if Susan was starting to make sense and she needed her friend to set both of them straight now. Carmen seemed to sense this, Izzy felt, because she took a deep breath, smiled, and then talked very calmly and slowly, looking back and forth between Izzy and Susan.

"Let's not pretend that we weren't, in a lot of ways, kind of fucked when we found out we were pregnant. I know I was. My first, second, third, fourth, and fifth thought about it after I took the pregnancy test was that I was going to get an abortion. I just couldn't fathom any way that this was going to work. But Kenny really wanted it to work, and then, the longer it took me to decide, the more I wanted it to work. But that didn't mean that we could have made it happen on our own. We needed this family. We needed Dr. Grind to choose us. And it is working. Kenny and I are so happy and we're going to be ready for the world when this thing ends. And it won't really end, you know. We'll stay in touch, so it'll just keep going, but in a different way. And, Susan, if your problem that other parents don't have to deal with is that you love other kids as much if not more than your own, isn't that kind of amazing? Isn't it awesome that you're such a part of Maxwell's life that he loves you like you're his mom?"

"Isn't that bizarre as shit to you?" Susan asked.

"It is one million times better than the alternative," Carmen admitted. She gestured for Izzy to move, to get close to them, damn it, and so Izzy crouched down beside Carmen and took hold of Susan's other hand. If any of the other members of the family had walked in on this, Izzy was certain they would assume something sexual was about to happen.

"This is good," Carmen said, and, finally, as if this was the final piece of coding that made the program function correctly, Susan nodded her assent. "It is," Susan said.

Carmen looked over at Izzy and nodded toward Susan, her eyes opening wide. Izzy, as much as Carmen made sense, could not help but agree with Susan. She had worked so hard in that first year to simply not lose her mind, and now she felt an irritation with Susan that she was just now figuring out the strange aspects of the complex. Izzy felt herself being pulled into that doubt once again. She wanted to be strong and certain like Carmen, but, especially with the reporter and all of his questions, it was harder and harder to feel certain about anything. Carmen, however, kept staring at her.

This was perhaps the first time that Izzy truly felt the cultlike elements of the project, which she had always worried about but never encountered. Susan was thinking about leaving the fold and it was up to her and Carmen to pull her back, to keep her connected to them. Because if they lost Susan, they lost David. And they also lost Irene. And if they lost the three of them, who else could leave? And, Izzy realized, she did not want to leave, so she had to keep Susan here with them.

"It is good," Izzy said. "It's really good."

"And you will love Irene when the time comes," Carmen said, not missing a beat, "you love her right now, actually, but you'll love her even more later."

"I will," Susan said.

"Okay," Carmen said, looking over to Izzy. "Are we good?" There was a temporary slackening of Carmen's expression, as if she was admitting to Izzy that she, too, had no idea what she was doing and she needed Izzy to reassure her.

Izzy nodded. Perhaps this was just the way it would always work. Everyone would have their doubts, feel that they had made a mistake, but they would hold on to each other tightly and hope that it wasn't true.

"I'm drunk," Susan said. "I'm sorry."

"It was good to talk about it," Izzy said, not meaning it at all, and the three of them stood, still holding hands, and then they hugged; and, because there was nothing else to do, they separated and headed to their own homes.

It wasn't awkward to Izzy, after such an emotional moment, to walk into an empty house, because she knew that the next day would bring them back together. And still, perhaps it was all the talk, all the awkward honesty, but as she lowered herself onto her bed, not even bothering to shower or brush her teeth or even change out of her clothes, she did think that it would be a little bit nicer, just the slightest bit easier, if there were someone in the bed waiting for her when she slipped between the covers. Not Asean. Not another parent. Someone far removed from the complex. But then she tried to imagine this person, the circumstances that would bring him here, the attributes that would make him plausible, and she decided, though perhaps it was just the exhaustion of the day, that it wasn't worth the trouble. And, she surmised, beyond the empty bed were so many people just feet away from her. In an adjacent building, her son was soundly sleeping, watched over by an army of people who loved him. This was good enough, she decided once again. Better than good. She slept so soundly that night that she awoke the next morning convinced of her sound reasoning.

A new rumor moved quickly through the family, a weird game of telephone that traveled around and around the complex until everyone thought they understood the weird thing going on.

The first time Izzy had experienced it, in her third month at the complex, it had been disorienting, the way several different people, all believing they were the first to tell Izzy, sidled up to her after dinner or while she was walking through the courtyard, to inform her that David and Susan had made friends with a couple outside the complex and had met with them in Nashville several times.

"Who has time for other people?" Nina had wondered after David and Susan had driven to the city to see a movie with this couple, the husband a friend of David's from college. "Should we tell Dr. Grind about this?" Kenny asked, and Carmen replied, "Why?"

"Shouldn't he know that, I don't know, members of the family are hanging out with other people?"

"That sounds really weird, Kenny," Carmen informed him. "Like something a stalker would say."

Nina jumped in. "Maybe, but it's still weird. I know we're not all gonna be best friends or anything, or even like each other, but it feels like a slight to choose them over us."

"Maybe it's different because we're family, but they're friends," Izzy offered and Carmen frowned.

"C'mon, Izzy," she said. "Dr. Grind's not around."

Nina continued, "I mean, there isn't someone in the complex that they'd like to spend time with?"

"Your feelings are hurt?" Carmen asked.

"Yes," Kenny and Nina said at the same time, and then Kenny again said, "Should we tell Dr. Grind?"

The next day, Kenny did tell Dr. Grind, who only said that it was a process, getting used to the complex and the kind of life within it, and he said it would work itself out. And it did, Izzy discovered. After a few months, David and Susan stopped seeing their friends and when Nina casually brought it up at dinner one night, Susan said, "It was nice at first; it felt like nothing had changed in our lives, but then we kept talking about things going on here, the kids and the complex, and they seemed to get weirded out by it. They started trying to get us to admit, every single time we met, that we were in some kind of cult, and so we just stopped responding to their e-mails and then they stopped asking."

"We were getting worried," Kenny then said.

"What? That we would leave this place?" David asked, smiling.

"Maybe," Kenny allowed.

"We're here," Susan said. "Don't worry about that."

A few seconds later, after everyone went back to their meals, Kenny said, "Good," so softly Izzy thought only she had heard it.

Now, the rumor was that Benjamin and Alyssa were having problems with their marriage. One night, Link had gone to the makeshift studio that he'd set up in one of the rooms in Main 2 to work on some music, when he noticed a light on in one of the empty rooms adjacent to the studio. He knocked and Benjamin sheepishly opened the door, revealing a sleeping bag, a pillow, some potato chips, and a book. "Trouble in paradise," Benjamin had said, shrugging.

Link had stayed up most of the night talking to Benjamin, but he told Julie about it the next morning, who had told David and Susan, and then it spread around the complex. Link and Julie were closest to Alyssa and Benjamin, spent the most time hanging out by virtue of age and interests, and they admitted to the other parents, who now talked of the matter whenever Benjamin and Alyssa (and Dr. Grind) were out of earshot, that Benjamin sometimes disappeared when Alyssa needed help, always watching a movie or checking the Internet, barely listening as she recounted her day.

"But he doesn't think he's done anything wrong," Link offered, and Ellen rolled her eyes and said, "Anytime a man says that they don't think they've done anything wrong, they've definitely done something wrong, but I also believe that they don't think that they have. You guys are so stupid."

"Well, Alyssa kicked him out and said he has to straighten up, be a part of this family, or, I guess, their family, or she doesn't want to be with him."

"Who would leave the complex?" Izzy asked.

"Both?" Ellen offered, and then Link shook his head and said, "Probably Benjamin."

"We should tell Dr. Grind," Kenny said.

"Ben would be mortified," Link said, shaking his head.

"We all have to see a therapist anyway," Julie then said. "Why not a marriage counselor?"

At dinner, Benjamin and Alyssa would sit at opposite sides of the table, and Izzy would frequently look at Dr. Grind to see if he had any inkling, but he merely smiled in that soft, patient way, focusing mostly on the children. At the end of the night, when the parents went their separate ways back to their houses, Izzy would watch from her window until Benjamin, twenty or thirty minutes later, would slip out of the house he shared with Alyssa and stroll toward Main 2. She had thought to buy some magazines and make some cookies to leave by the room where he now slept, but worried that would be creepy. She would climb into bed, staring at the ceiling, and imagine what Benjamin was doing, so far from everyone else, somehow separate from the actual family, and then she wondered for the millionth time if this was how the rest of the complex felt about her, watching her walk into her own house each night, alone. For the entirety of the trial separation, or whatever the Infinite Family might call it, Izzy slept fitfully, her dreams uneasy.

"Dr. Grind knows," Link said a month later, while a group of parents were playing cards in the TV room.

Carmen immediately looked at Kenny and said, "You told him, didn't you? Even after I told you not to."

Kenny shook his head, then frowned. "Well, no, not exactly. I mean, I told him about it, but he already knew. He said Alyssa had come to him immediately, telling him that she and Benjamin were having problems and she wasn't sure what was going to happen."

"And?" Carmen asked.

Link then interjected, "Benjamin told me that Dr. Grind said today that they would both stay in the Infinite Family, that the project would continue and would want both of them to stay. He said that if the two of them decided to separate, Dr. Grind would open up one of the empty apartments in Main 1, and Benjamin could stay there. Ben said that he wanted to stay in the room in Main 2 for now, because it made everything feel less permanent."

"I'm curious," Julie said, "whether there's anything we could do that would make Dr. Grind get angry with us. Would he ever kick any of us out?"

"If we killed somebody else in the family," Kenny offered, his facial expression one of apology for even mentioning it.

"Not out of the realm of possibility," Link admitted, "come year five or six."

"I think we're safe," Paul said, who was on the sofa, watching a football game. The others turned toward him, not realizing that he had been listening. "Dr. Grind needs us just as much as we need him," he continued. "Maybe more."

Izzy wondered if this was true, but couldn't make her brain tabulate the facts in a way that made sense. She would take it on faith that this was true, hoping that she never had reason to find out.

A week after that conversation, as the parents and children played in the dining hall before dinner, Izzy watched from the kitchen when Ally and Gilberto and Jackie all scrambled over to Alyssa and, pulling her by her arms with great purpose, dragged her over to Benjamin, who was watching all of this from across the room. Jackie then instructed Benjamin to stand up. She held on to each of their hands and the two adults listened to Jackie as she tried to tell them what was in her head, the two of them never once looking at each other. Soon, more of the children ran over to the couple, surrounding them. They both nodded and then swung Jackie by her arms, swinging her back and forth, the two of them supporting the child as she giggled, kicking out her legs. After Jackie, Ally broke in to swing with them and, once Ally tired of the game, each child asked for a turn. Alyssa and Benjamin looked at each other, and they had to know that the entire family was watching them in this moment, trying to decipher the slightest of emotions. It was as if the other seventeen parents were trying through sheer force of will to keep the two of them together. Izzy needed to strain the pasta, but she kept watching, searching the room for Dr. Grind, who was holding Cap in his arms; even he was turned toward the couple.

They didn't speak, only looking at each other, before Alyssa turned and walked back toward the table, seating herself, waiting for dinner. Benjamin sat back down and read his magazine that he kept rolled up like a baton in his hand. They did not speak at all during the dinner, the entire meal a subdued affair.

Once the children were put to bed, the parents on duty staying behind, the rest of the family walked into the courtyard. Even though they had to understand that everyone in the complex already knew of their marital troubles, Benjamin and Alyssa still walked together into their house, Benjamin only leaving again after everyone else had dispersed. And, as always, Izzy sat by the window, the lights out in her house, watching. Thirty minutes passed and yet Benjamin stayed in the house. Thirty more minutes passed, then another thirty minutes. Finally, the light in the house went off. Izzy waited a few more minutes, with no sign of Benjamin's retreat, and then she ran for her phone, calling Carmen.

"What's up?" Carmen said.

"It's okay," Izzy said. She understood how much she needed these other parents to stay together, for the family to remain complete. She needed all of this to work out, to overcome her constant worry that it would implode, and so she had to rely on people who, just a few years earlier, she did not know existed. She had to place her trust in people who might not deserve it, but perhaps that's what others thought about her, the weakest link in the bond, the only one alone. So, she would do it, would put her life with theirs.

"What's okay?" Carmen said, her voice turning serious.

"Everything," Izzy said, unable to fully articulate what was happening. "Benjamin and Alyssa. Ally. All of us. It's okay," she said.

"Izzy . . . ," Carmen said, pausing for a solid second, before continuing, "are you drunk?"

"No," Izzy assured her.

Carmen said that they would talk in the morning and then hung up.

Izzy watched the stillness inside Benjamin and Alyssa's house, resting her head on the windowsill, until she could no longer hold off sleep, though she felt that the minute she closed her eyes, it would all fall apart again. It was strange, to believe that she had some kind of power over everyone else in the complex, but she was too tired to dispute what she imagined every other member of the family also thought.

Two weeks later, after some of the family made a trip to Chattanooga to visit the aquarium, the children hypnotized by the swirling light and colorful fish that seemed to watch them as they swam past, Izzy had received permission to break off from the caravan of motor vehicles and head back to Coalfield. She was going with Cap and Maxwell (so as not to, in Dr. Grind's words, "overwhelm Cap with the singular focus of the moment") in order to visit Mr. Tannehill, the first time she had seen him since Cap had been born.

The two boys sat happily in their car seats, covering their arms and faces with a seemingly infinite number of smiley face stickers that Izzy had found at a gas station. When they pulled into the parking lot of the Whole Hog, she could see Mr. Tannehill standing out back, sorting pieces of wood, talking to himself. She called out for him and he shaded his eyes and smiled, opening his arms as if to embrace the world. Izzy freed the boys from their car seats and watched as they waddled toward Mr. Tannehill, as if instinctually knowing that he would be kind to them. Mr. Tannehill gingerly lowered himself to the ground, resting on one knee, and held out the index finger of both hands to greet the boys. Maxwell and Cap stopped just short of Mr. Tannehill, observing him, their heads slightly tilted, as if he were a puzzle that their eyes could not quite decipher. Suddenly, Cap reached for Mr. Tannehill's left index finger and gripped it, a child's handshake. Maxwell immediately followed suit, and Izzy realized that she was frozen in place, had not taken another step in this entire greeting. She wished she had a camera, had forgotten the ease of living in the complex, where there was always at least one person ready to document the proceedings. Mr. Tannehill let the smile on his face broaden into something all-encompassing, a happiness that could not be manufactured. Izzy finally moved toward the boys, who were examining the hair on Mr. Tannehill's arms, as if scientists experimenting on a heretofore unknown species.

"Cute kids," Mr. Tannehill said.

"That's Cap," Izzy said, pointing to her son, "and that's Maxwell."

"Pleased to meet you boys," Mr. Tannehill said. He pointed to the small recording devices that hung around the children's necks. "What are these?" he asked.

"A few days a week, the kids wear them and it records everything that they say and everything that someone says to them. And then Dr. Grind and the fellows analyze the recording to tally all the conversations that take place among the kids and then the conversations that occur with the kids and the adults. It's complicated. I'm not sure I totally understand it."

"So my voice is gonna be on there?" Mr. Tannehill asked, and Izzy nodded. "You're part of the study now, I guess," she told him, and they both laughed.

He then looked up at Izzy and continued to smile, his face readjusting to contain another kind of happiness. "You look good, Izzy," he said.

"I've missed you a ton," Izzy replied.

"Same here," he said. "The letters and pictures have been just about the happiest part of my days, honestly."

Izzy remained silent and watched as Mr. Tannehill lifted both boys into his arms and stood up, his posture slightly unsteady until he readjusted his grip on the children and it seemed entirely natural for him to be holding the boys. She was grateful that Cap, who was sometimes anxious around strangers, had allowed Mr. Tannehill to hold him.

"These boys eat barbecue?" he asked Izzy.

"They eat everything," she answered.

"Let's eat, then," he said, gesturing toward the restaurant. Izzy once again felt the sluggishness of her own legs, which she overcame with loping, awkward steps in order to catch up to them, as if Mr. Tannehill would take her two boys into the restaurant and disappear into an entirely new life that awaited them inside.

True to Izzy's word, the boys did eat whatever was presented to them. More than the barbecue, Cap seemed to love the salty broth of the collard greens, his face dotted with bits of leafy green, while Maxwell crunched on the burnt ends of the pork. While the boys ate, Izzy told Mr. Tannehill more about the complex, about all the members of the family, while the old man nodded and furrowed his brow. "I believe I need a notebook and a pencil to keep track of all these people, Izzy," he said.

"It can certainly feel that way," Izzy said. "The first few months I was there, I would always say *hey, you,* or *hi there* to everyone because I was terrified of getting their names wrong. After a while though, it just becomes second nature."

"And you really seem happy there," Mr. Tannehill said, a statement but one that had the tiniest element of a question creeping along the edges.

"I am. And Cap is, for sure."

"That's good to hear," he said. He paused for a second, peering into the parking lot as if searching for conversation. "Have you seen your father yet?" he asked.

"No," Izzy said.

"You plan on it?" he then asked.

"No," Izzy said again. She had sent her father numerous letters and pictures in the first months of living at the complex, though she'd never gotten a response. She called him a few times, but she could hear the way the alcohol dulled all of his responses; he could barely remember Cap's name. After a while, Izzy had simply given up on staying in touch. Her father was now simply a person from her past, and she understood how strange it was to trade in one family for another. But this was how it was for other people in the project. The few who did have family with whom they stayed in touch did so sparingly, sending e-mails to siblings or parents or cousins who didn't really seem interested in what was going on in their lives. "I guess I didn't realize how little was holding us together," Alyssa said of her sister, twelve years her senior, barely a part of her upbringing. "She seems almost relieved that I'm not a part of her life."

Most of the people in the complex were either estranged from their own families, or their parents were dead. They knew this was one of the reasons that they had been chosen for the project, which made Izzy feel weird, the idea that they could join the Infinite Family because no one else wanted them. No one would miss them if they disappeared and no one would be there for them if it all fell apart.

"He's in a bad way, near as I can tell," Mr. Tannehill said. "Sometimes I go into the market and a full aisle is empty because he's forgotten to restock. I found him asleep in there once. And I know he's been robbed already this year."

"You want me to go see him," Izzy said, another statement of fact that felt like a question.

"No," Mr. Tannehill said. "I'm just your friend. We're just talking. You're an adult now. You got a kid of your own. You know what you're doing, Izzy. I just thought you should know."

"Okay, then," Izzy said, happy to let the whole matter drop. Just then, Maxwell started pushing himself out of the high chair, and Izzy stood up to hold him. He squirmed out of her arms and started to prowl around the nearby tables, which prompted Cap to want to get up. Mr. Tannehill lifted the boy out of the chair and set him gently on the floor.

"They can't go more than a few minutes without wanting to run around," Izzy explained.

"I know how it is," Mr. Tannehill said.

"You must think this is so strange," Izzy admitted.

"I do," Mr. Tannehill replied, smiling, "but the best kind of strange. You're a different person, Izzy. You look good; your boys are sweet boys.

If it takes this Infinite Family place to take care of you, then I think it's great."

"You're still the best person I've ever met," Izzy said.

"I'm not," Mr. Tannehill said, his face blushing. "I used to be a pretty damned awful person. I drank too much and ran off my family. But you helped me realize that I could still be a decent person and so I try to be when I can. Ask anybody at the restaurant, though. They'll tell you I can be a real sonofabitch."

"Bitch," Cap said, and then he and Maxwell repeated it, "bitch, bitch, bitch, bitch."

"See now?" Mr. Tannehill said, but Izzy leaned over and hugged him.

"Good to see y'all," he said, "real good."

On the way out of town, Izzy passed by her father's market, the cinder-block building so squat and ugly, and so familiar. She remembered her father letting her take a package of candy cigarettes, all the soda she could drink. She remembered sleeping under the counter while her father worked. At the last possible second before she would cause a fairly substantial accident, she pulled into the parking lot at the corner of the building. From the car, she could see into the market, the counter in the middle of the building, and there was her father, wearing a flannel shirt that she recognized as his uniform. He was resting his head on his fist, reading a magazine. She knew that the right thing would be to step out of the car and introduce Cap to his grandfather. But what would she do with Maxwell? What would she say to her own father? She felt the uncertain terror that her proximity to her father could pull her back into her old life, totally alone, with no hope of something better.

And yet, there was her father, now making change for a group of teenagers, as close to her as he had been in two years. She could simply run into the market, give him a hug, and then drive home.

Maxwell started to whine, growing restless in the parked car, and Cap joined in, at a higher pitch, his annoyance even greater than his brother's. Izzy felt something hazy grow in her brain; her tongue felt fat in her mouth. Suddenly, she felt so far away from her past life, as if it had all happened to someone else, as if she had arrived at the complex with Cap in her arms and no history to speak of.

But, strangely enough, she also felt disconnected from the Infinite Family. Here in her car, back in Coalfield, the complex felt like it was a million miles away and there was nothing that connected her to it. In this moment, who knew how long it would last, she was entirely free of her past, present, and future. It was just her, Izzy, in space, entirely at peace. And then she looked in the rearview mirror and saw Cap and Maxwell. She had the two of them, her two sons. She could go anywhere, do anything, and no one would ever know. No one would ever look for them, not her father, not Dr. Grind, no one.

She started the car, backed out of the parking lot, and got back on the highway. She was driving south, away from Coalfield, but also away from the complex. She would head south, as far down the coast as she could go, until she hit Key West. She would rent an apartment and get a job waitressing or tending a barbecue pit. She accelerated, the car now going eighty miles per hour in a fifty-five-mile zone. She was putting miles between her and the entirety of her life up to that point. The boys had fallen asleep in the back. Kenny and Carmen would not begrudge her having taken Maxwell with her. They still had eight other children to love. Dr. Grind would not begrudge her disappearance. He still had so many people to take care of. It would not matter. The project had to anticipate some measure of loss during the duration of the study. They would let her go.

She was breathing so rapidly, it felt like she was sprinting, as if she was moving the car forward by her own sheer force of will. Forty minutes later, she was in Georgia. No one had called her. No one knew where she was. She could not believe she was doing this. She reached across to her purse in the passenger seat and took out her wallet. She had eighty dollars. If she stopped at an ATM soon enough, she could probably take out a few hundred more without anyone knowing. She would be the best mother. She would love Maxwell and Cap as much as everyone else in the project combined. It could work, she kept reassuring herself. It would work.

And then Cap started to cry, fussing and fidgety in the car seat. He kept grunting, trying to get Izzy's attention. "It's okay, honey," she said. "It's okay."

Then Maxwell awoke from his nap and began to fuss. "Izzy," they both said. "Izzy!"

Izzy put her foot on the brake, slowed the car down, and pulled onto the shoulder of the road. A truck passed by, shaking the car. She took off her seat belt and turned toward the two boys. They held out their hands for her. She climbed into the backseat, barely enough space for her to fit between the two car seats. She unbuckled them, pulled them into her lap. She hugged them, whispering to them sounds that were not words, just musical notes to calm them. They held tightly to her.

She could not do it. If they had slept the entire way, maybe she could have managed it. The faster she ran from her past and present toward a new future, the present was always right there, always on top of her. There was no way she could separate the three of them from the larger family; the lack would be too intense. She did not know where she was, on a road in Georgia, her two boys in her arms. She slowly placed them back in their car seats. She climbed into the driver's seat and started the car. Temporary insanity. That's all it was. She would never mention it. No one would ever know.

She turned the car around and started back for home, for the complex. She sang "The Wheels on the Bus" to Cap and Maxwell and by the time the doors on the bus went open and shut, they were quiet and happy once again and she felt sure of her decision.

Back at the complex, the family getting the children ready for bed, Izzy kissed Maxwell and Cap and signed herself back in before she started to walk back to her own house. Dr. Grind appeared and held out a Tupperware container.

"We had Nicole's peanut butter and dark chocolate pie for dessert tonight," he said. "I know that's your favorite, so I saved a piece for you."

Izzy smiled and took the offering with great pleasure. She hugged him quickly and then walked back toward her house.

"Everything went okay on your trip?" he called after her.

"Great," she said. "As great as I could have asked for."

"Glad to hear it," Dr. Grind replied.

In her house, Izzy sat on the floor of the kitchen and ate the pie in three huge, quick bites. It was so delicious it left her momentarily dizzy. She sat on the floor and replayed the events of the day in her head. She thought of Mr. Tannehill. She thought of her father standing behind the counter of the market. She thought of that race to the ocean, nothing around to stop her but her own heart. And she thought of Dr. Grind, holding that piece of pie, offering it to her like a bouquet of flowers. She thought of Cap and Maxwell, now probably lying in their own beds. She finally stood up, washed the Tupperware container and the fork, and went into her bedroom.

After the visit to the aquarium, the children clamored for fish, for a tank the size of a football field, stocked with all manner of brightly colored specimens. The children's thought journals were filled with elaborately detailed drawings of sharks and stingrays and piranhas. At the weekly meeting between the staff and the parents, Dr. Grind brought up the possibility of buying an aquarium with some fish.

"I'm actually a little stumped that we didn't do this earlier," he told the parents. "It has so many benefits. The children can learn about aquatic life and its environment, they can gain the experience of having a pet with minimal responsibilities, and there are studies that show that observing fish in an aquarium can greatly reduce anxiety, which would help the children further explore relaxation therapy, which, as you know, we're doing more and more with the kids."

"I could go for that, too," Link offered.

Everyone agreed that pet fish seemed like a great idea and Dr. Grind tasked Susan and Asean with researching types of fish and aspects of care and equipment.

"We also have another reason for the fish, one that might be a little more alarming at first glance," Dr. Grind continued, still smiling, which made his remarks seem slightly disconcerting, as if he were an evil scientist explaining the experiment he was about to perform on you. "We're in the very early stages with the children, but we are interested in how they line up with the averages when it comes to certain concepts and their ability to grasp them. One of these concepts is, well, death."

"I don't like where this is going," Ellen said, looking around for support; Izzy noticed that the faces of quite a few of the parents seemed to suggest that they agreed.

"It's fairly harmless," Dr. Grind replied. "In studying how death affects children, their ability to understand death, typically children under three have no real concept of how death works or even what it is. But by age four, children start to understand irreversibility, the fact that once something dies, it cannot come back. Between ages five and seven, they figure out *nonfunctionality,* the idea that a dead body cannot do things that a living body can. For instance, a dead person or animal cannot still eat. Then, finally, children learn *universality,* that everyone and everything dies."

"I'm really uncomfortable with this," Ellen said, her voice slightly trembling. "I don't want Marnie to think about the fact that she's going to die."

"She might already be thinking it," Link offered, not as helpfully as he might have imagined.

"Well, it's not quite as problematic as you might think. When we buy these fish, there is a distinct possibility that one or more might die. This will allow us to talk to the children about death and gauge how much they understand. We won't press the issue and we won't fill them with existential dread. We'll simply ask them questions about these deceased fish to see what they know."

"But if the children ask you if they are going to die someday, what are you going to tell them?" Carmen asked.

Dr. Grind shrugged so softly that it seemed more like breathing than uncertainty. "We'll tell them that, yes, everyone dies—"

"Oh, god," Ellen said.

"But," Dr. Grind continued, "we will explain that this will typically not occur for quite some time."

"What about heaven?" Izzy asked, knowing that the project had been upfront about the fact that religion would not be a guiding principle in the study, which all the parents, all of whom were lapsed Christians or nonbelievers already, had agreed to support. "If they ask if there's a place that they go after they die?"

"No," Dr. Grind said. "We're staying away from abstract concepts."

"Death seems like a fairly abstract concept to me," David said. "I mean, I still don't fully comprehend the universality of death. Or perhaps I willfully avoid comprehending it so I don't lose my mind."

"This is a necessary component of development," Dr. Grind told them. "It's difficult, but we do it so that we will be better able to anticipate the needs of these children, to help them as they grow up."

With some reluctance, the parents agreed. As the meeting was about to end, Izzy thought of something and said, "What if the fish don't die?"

Dr. Grind looked at her with a kind of skepticism. "What do you mean?" he asked.

Izzy felt her face heat up, knowing that she was blushing fiercely, but she continued. "I mean, I know that fish die. I can grasp that concept. What I'm asking is, what if the fish don't die very soon? What if they outlive the project?"

"Well, that's tricky, Izzy." Dr. Grind seemed pained, as if she was forcing him to reveal a secret that he had withheld for her own good. "If, after six months, a fish does not die, we will remove a fish from the tank and begin the process of talking about death with the children."

"But you won't kill the fish, right?" Julie asked.

Dr. Grind laughed. "God no," he said. "We'll return it to the store."

Harris, who seemed bored by the discussion, said, in a distant tone,

"Store probably won't give us a refund on a fish that's been here six months."

"That's okay," Dr. Grind said.

"Maybe store credit though," Harris said, and Ellen jabbed her elbow into his side.

"So it's settled. The children get their fish," Dr. Grind said, and he walked out of the room, followed by the three fellows, leaving the parents to discuss the particulars of a fish funeral, in preparation for the fish's death, an animal they did not even possess yet.

Dr. Grind's parents had brought home a puppy when he was a child, a sweet dog who instantly took to Preston. The parents took all manner of home movies and videos. The dog, Huck, slept with Preston, and he walked the dog daily on a black leather leash that, later in his childhood, Preston would use with some other provided materials to fashion a way out of a deep hole in which he had been placed. The presence of another living thing seemed to add lightness to the family, and his parents also pampered the dog, allowed it to sleep on the sofa while they worked. It was a kind of stability that Preston, despite his training, believed would last.

Two weeks later, he woke to find that Huck was gone. He was not alarmed, had anticipated this possibility. He went downstairs to find his parents at the breakfast table, drinking coffee, reading magazines.

"Where's Huck?" he asked.

"He's gone, sweetie," his mother said.

"Is he," Preston said, then paused, hoping for the best, "is he dead?"

His father looked down at him and then put down his coffee. He knelt beside Preston and hugged him. "Oh, no, champ, not at all. He's not dead. He's just gone."

Preston let himself go limp in his father's strong embrace. "Will I ever see Huck again?" he asked.

Preston's father looked over at his mother, something unspoken occurring between them, the experiment expanding. His father looked back at Preston and smiled. "We don't know, champ. We just don't know."

Preston breathed in, tightening his stomach muscles, and made his sadness, his worry for Huck, break apart, slowly shattering. And then it was gone. Preston nodded to his father and then went over to his mother and hugged her tightly. "Okay," he said, and his parents, nodding, both smiled.

Dr. Grind never saw Huck again, had no idea of where he ended up.

Two weeks later, the complex had its aquarium, stocked with various tetras, so colorful that they seemed like a low-level acid trip as they darted around the water. One week later, three of the fish were dead, scooped out of the tank by Kalina and placed in Ziploc bags filled with water. After the funeral that evening for the fish, small stones erected to mark the spot in one of the gardens, each child putting their own rock over the burial site, Dr. Grind informed the parents that he and all three of the fellows talked to the children about what had happened, allowed them to observe the dead fish. Once the children had moved on to new activities, the fellows and Dr. Grind took the children, one at a time, and met with them to allow the children to ask questions and discuss what had happened.

"It was enlightening," Dr. Grind said, though Izzy wished that he wasn't quite so eager to discuss the findings of an experiment on their not-yet-three-year-old children. "We simply explained that the fish weren't moving any longer because they had died. The children accepted this without question. Several of them, when we said that we would not see these fish again, waved to the fish and said, 'Bye-bye, *fish*.' And, in most cases, that was that. When we asked them if they understood that the fish could not come back, more than half of the children, through our discussion, showed that they understood the irreversibility of the event, while the others thought that there might be some procedure or even magic spell that could bring the fish back. That is, though it's simply more data to add to our larger study, a fairly significant number compared to the averages of studies like this."

"So our kids are advanced when it comes to death?" Kenny asked.

"In some ways, yes," Dr. Grind responded.

"Well . . . good, I guess," Kenny replied.

"Not good or bad," Dr. Grind said, "simply another way that we can better serve these little children and help them."

The parents simply nodded, and Izzy wondered what had opened up, what doors in their children's brains were now unlocked and could not be closed up again.

Nikisha then asked, "You said that the kids moved on fairly easily *in most cases*. What do you mean? Did some of them not handle it so well?"

Dr. Grind looked at his fellows, paused thoughtfully, and, frowning, looked back at the parents. "Well, some of the children, a very small sample, two of them, were emotionally affected by the deaths in stronger ways. They cried. It took a fair amount of time to calm them."

"Which kids?" Nikisha asked.

"Well, we can't say. As you know, we have to keep the results private until we accumulate more data."

"Why do you think those kids cried?" Paul asked, and Izzy knew that, like her, everyone in the room was wondering if their own child had been distressed by the death of the fish.

"Well," Dr. Grind said, dragging the word out to worrying lengths. "Well," he said, trying again. "Those two children understood the irreversibility of death. But they also, through their own questions, mind you, understood the nonfunctionality of death, and . . ." Dr. Grind looked around the room. "They also understood the universality of death. This is, mind you, incredibly mature thinking on the part of these two children. It's fairly uncommon."

"So those two kids understand that everyone dies?" Paul asked.

"That's right," Dr. Grind replied.

"So they understand that they will die?" Paul continued.

"Yes," Dr. Grind said.

"That's really troubling," Paul said, "really troubling. I feel like maybe we shouldn't have killed these fish."

"Okay, again, we didn't kill the fish. They died a natural death. And, truthfully, your children are in the best place they could be if they're going to have these kinds of epiphanies. They receive round-the-clock care, top-notch psychological care. We're moving slowly, in small increments. We adjust as we go on. I can assure you that this will not have adverse effects on their development. If anything, it shows how quickly, with the right care, with all of your help, they are becoming really wonderful children."

"I'm just saying," Paul then said, his foot tapping the floor during Dr. Grind's speech, "that I'm uncomfortable with this."

"Well, that's understandable, Paul," Dr. Grind said.

Izzy thought of her own mother, those months after the funeral when she believed that her own thoughts, her frustrations with her mother's instability, had caused her mom's death. She then remembered how she had behaved so poorly for a few weeks in the aftermath, shoplifting, making C's on assignments out of spite, having sex with boys who didn't deserve her, hoping that if she misbehaved enough, her mom would come back to this life and straighten her out. And, then, as time passed, she accepted that she had nothing to do with her mother's death and could not overturn it. That depression, that acceptance, was worse for her than the actual death of her mother. It had taken so long to recover from it, if she had even now fully done so.

After the meeting, she looked through the window at the aquarium, on one of the tables in the children's room, at the glow of the water, the colors moving in darting passes in and around each other. She hoped that none of the children thought they were at fault for the death of these beautiful, goddamned fish.

The next day, Izzy went to play with the children and sat down with Cap and Eliza and Ally as they rolled a ball back and forth. Izzy, not able to help herself, and her curiosity at what they had done to these kids, pointed to the tank of fish and said, "Aren't they so pretty?" The children looked and nodded. Eliza said, "I name them."

"Me, too!" said Cap and then Ally said, "Me, too!"

"What are their names?" Izzy asked, and she then nearly fell back as the three children rattled off the names of the fish, none of them matching up. *Boing-boing* and *Janky* and *Mutt* and *Boba* and *Fishy* and *Dumdum,* until it seemed that the children had named every single fish in the ocean.

After they all laughed and went back to the ball, Ally now sitting in Izzy's lap, Izzy asked, "What about the fish that died?"

"No names," Eliza said.

"Yes names," Cap said.

"They're dead," Ally said.

The kids all fell silent for a few seconds and Izzy could see their brains making tangible things.

"But we don't die," Eliza said.

"No," Cap said. Ally then said, "No."

They all looked at Izzy and she smiled. She grabbed all three of them, though they squirmed to get away, laughing, having moved on, their immortality assured. Izzy was pleased that they weren't advanced enough yet, that death had not seeped into their bones. She kissed the children and said, "We don't die," not caring one bit if Dr. Grind tried to correct her.

chapter twelve

the infinite family project (year three)

Izzy carefully arranged a series of wooden letters, each one small enough to fit in the palm of her hand, along the floor of the complex's studio, a thin film of sawdust coating everything around her. As she laid them out, making a sentence, she checked each letter for obvious imperfections. She returned to the band saw, a ridiculous expenditure that Dr. Grind, or a magician or Santa Claus or some other kind of benevolent god, had rented for the complex simply so Izzy could continue working on this project. With a steady hand, a trait that she admired in herself more than almost anything else, she moved the wood around the whirring saw blade, following the deep black lines that served as her guide, until she had a *c* that was nearly perfect. She placed the letter on the floor and observed her sentence, *I want arsenic,* before she scooped up all of the letters and dumped them into a blue plastic fifty-five-gallon drum, which was nearly half full of other letters. She took a black marker from the worktable and walked to one of the walls, which was covered in sheets of paper. She found the sentence on the corresponding page and crossed it out with the marker. She looked at the next sentence, *The druggist looked down at her,* and returned to a fresh piece of wood and a set of stencils to trace the next letters, a chain of words that felt endless to Izzy, though she knew deep down that this was a story and, like all stories, it would eventually end.

Though she found most of her time was devoted to her work in the kitchen, Izzy had, perhaps stupidly, declared a major in art. She wasn't so clueless that she didn't understand, on some level, that this was connected to Hal and his influence on her in high school, but she found that she still desired the specific pleasure of creating an object that existed beyond something as ephemeral as food. Her current art course, where she was the only student who wasn't a senior, having begged the professor to let her in, focused on three-dimensional work, and Izzy was now feverishly working on her final project. While other students were making intricately knitted covers that would fit over a truck or making plaster casts of dead animals to be suspended from ropes, Izzy had focused on woodworking, a talent she had continued since joining the Infinite Family.

Her original plan was to take a famous poem and then whittle individual letters that she would affix to a large wooden plank to be hung on a wall. However, there were two problems that seemed to work against each other as Izzy started on the project. First, she was not as skilled a whittler as the work required. It seemed impossible that she would be able to whittle the letters necessary to complete the poem. Second, the work seemed too small, too minor, not impressive enough to make up for the fact that she was pretty much making a cut-rate physical representation of a Joyce Kilmer poem about trees. It felt embarrassing, now that she looked back on it, to imagine how silly it would have looked at the art show, her family standing around her, praising her in the most polite way possible.

Jeremy had told her about band saws, the way she could more easily make the necessary curves of each letter. "Heck," he said at dinner one night, using his knife on a piece of beef tenderloin to demonstrate, "you could knock out a lot of letters in the time it'd take you to whittle just one." Izzy spent long hours in the general sculpture area of the university studio, working with the school's band saw and her professor until she could make each letter from the stencil set with some ease. The next step was to expand the work.

Eliza, Link and Julie's daughter, had awoken one morning from a dream and told Izzy about it while they were playing in the pool. "I dreamed that I was on a boat," the little girl said to Izzy, her voice calm and measured, "and I put my hand in the water and I pulled out all kinds of stuff. I pulled out a star and then I pulled out a little bird and then I started pulling letters out of the water, until my boat was filled with stuff." Izzy immediately had a vision of dipping her hands into a lake and the water turning into wooden letters, so many possible words and sentences. She imagined that the lake was a story and each letter contributed to it. She hugged Eliza, who accepted the affection without surprise, as if every recollection of a dream should be met with hugs. She needed something larger. Not a novel, not *Moby-Dick*, but something more than a poem.

Izzy started thinking of her favorite stories, books she'd read at the library on summer breaks. There was "The Lottery" by Shirley Jackson, her mother's favorite story, as if the actions of this fictional village more than proved her own agoraphobic tendencies. Her mother also loved "Hands" from Sherwood Anderson's *Winesburg, Ohio,* which was devastating and lonely. Were all of her favorite stories about fucked-up groups, lonely people living in broken-down villages?

It didn't take long for Izzy to think of Faulkner's "A Rose for Emily," which had terrified her in the eighth grade, the story of a spinster and her isolation from the town, ending with her death and the revelation that she had been sleeping with the decomposing body of her former love. Izzy had always loved the story, rereading it over and over even as it scared her. And, wonderfully, the story was told in the first person plural, using a "we" voice to encompass the entire town of Jefferson, Mississippi. It reminded her of how everyone in the complex began to use "we" in place of "I," the way it seemed that your own desires were somehow those of the people around you. She downloaded a Word document of the story and used the word count feature to check the number of characters in the story. When the number came back, more than fifteen thousand, a quick shock of breath flew from her mouth, as if she had been pricked with a pin, and yet she did not turn away. She would do it, she decided in that moment. She imagined all the children of the complex reaching their hands into a pile of letters, letting them fall from their fingers like coins.

To be truthful, Izzy was grateful to have the art project, something that seemed completely separate from the day-to-day events of the complex. The children, ten divine constellations at birth, had turned into something altogether feral, ten hyenas after sunset. Cap had begun an awkward phase of biting any available piece of human flesh, as did several of the other children. Even the most innocent of games ended with scratches or unintentional injuries as the children swarmed over each other to recover a ball or a stuffed animal. They became defiant, which stunned the parents and caused them a greater sense of awkwardness as they realized that these children, while born to separate parents, were raised collectively. It was easy to hug another person's child, to rock them to sleep as they smiled in their dreamlike states. It was altogether something else to punish another person's child after they had dug their claws into your face. They handled this with what they believed was great patience, stern but fair, all the while silently holding grudges, blaming the parents of the child, no matter how collective the project was. "Genes," Carmen once whispered to Izzy, "genes still count for something." And Izzy tried to smile, knowing that her own DNA was as frayed and flawed as anyone else's.

Dr. Grind seemed unconcerned. Or, rather, Dr. Grind was certainly concerned with the children's progress and behavioral shifts, but he didn't seem to think the recent developments required any hand-wringing or revisions to the program. "I remember, one time, Jody bit Marla on the cheek when she refused to give him an M and M," he said, a strange smile on his face. Izzy had been shocked to hear Dr. Grind speak of his son and wife; he was always so careful not to mention them, and the rest of the family made a point not to bring it up in conversation for fear of upsetting him. As if realizing he had opened a door, Dr. Grind took a deep, controlled breath, but continued smiling. "I don't remember the point of that story," he admitted. "I think I was building toward reassuring you that the kids are fine. They are doing so wonderfully in so many ways. They'll be fine, Izzy. I promise."

On campus, her art class just ended, a group of students were heading to the coffee shop. David, who was smoking a cigarette so casually that he seemed like he might be more interested in setting something on fire, came over to Izzy and said, "We're gonna hang out for a while; you wanna come with?"

David, a senior, was the darling of the art department. He made the most traditionally beautiful objects, amazing vases and bowls, but then he would film himself smashing it into tiny pieces with a hammer. Once the object was ruined, he went about gluing it back together as best he could. His final piece would consist of photographs of the original work, the video of him smashing it, and then the crudely repaired object. When she had first seen one of his pieces, she had instantly remembered Hal on the first day of art class, the vase he had set in front of the class. It had taken her breath away, as if Hal had somehow sent David into her life to remind her of him.

David was also incredibly handsome, had olive skin and dark hair, and would sometimes make casually flirtatious comments to Izzy during class, to the amusement of his friends. He was twenty-one, but seemed like he was much, much younger. All the students in her class seemed so young to Izzy, which she was quite certain would be irritating to them, as if Izzy was looking down on them from some mountain of experience.

"I better not," she said. "I have to get home and make dinner."

"Aren't there, like, fifty of you living there?" David asked, flicking ashes on the ground near her feet, which seemed so rude to Izzy. Since the *Time* article and various Internet stories, which Izzy no longer even bothered to read, people recognized her as being part of The Infinite Family Project.

"Not that many," Izzy replied. "And I like cooking. Thanks though."

"Come on. One hour," he said, pulling on her arm in fake pleading. "How can you be a real artist if you don't drink coffee and smoke cigarettes and talk about art? Don't you want to be a bohemian?" Izzy could not tell if he was joking or not. She looked at him, the cigarette in between his long, slender fingers, the smoke reeking of European incense. She stared at his bright blue artist's jacket, made in France, the kind worn by Bill Cunningham. He was not, she was now certain, joking at all. She looked at his dark brown eyes, which held the certainty of being someone important. How, he must be wondering, could she resist him? And how could she?

At the coffee shop, Izzy listened to David and his friends talk about famous artists whom they hated because they had always been hacks or, worse, had turned into hacks because of success. Then they talked about parties, what the last one had been like and when the next one would be. She tried to be present, to hold on to the fact that there were many things that connected her to these people, but it was a losing battle. She smiled, followed the conversation, but silently counted the minutes until she could reasonably leave them behind. Just then, one of the girls, a Gothy, sarcastic girl named Meggy, asked Izzy about the Infinite Family.

"You've got a kid, right?" she asked Izzy, who nodded.

"Kids kill art," David offered casually, "they really get in the way of becoming a true artist." It was as if David thought that this advice would compel Izzy to jump into a time machine and never have Cap. David seemed to consider his statement and then amended it. "Well, that's how it is for men, at least. It might be different for women artists."

"But, like, it's not really your kid, right?" Meggy continued. It was hard to tell if she was just curious or being antagonistic. "It's, like, everyone's kid, right?"

"It's complicated," Izzy admitted. "He's mine. We just raise all of our kids together."

"Like brothers and sisters," David said, showing that he understood.

"Kind of," Izzy allowed.

"And the parents? How does that work?" Meggy asked.

"Like a kind of extended family, maybe?" Izzy offered. She still, even though Kalina had spent hours coaching them on how to deal with these kinds of encounters, couldn't quite articulate how the Infinite Family worked to someone on the outside.

"Do you sleep with each other?" Meggy asked.

"Jesus, Meggy," David said, growing bored with the conversation.

"I'm just trying to figure it out. It's weird to me."

"It's weird to me, too," Izzy said. "Actually, I better get going. I have to make dinner."

"I'm sorry if I made you uncomfortable," Meggy said. "If I were in your shoes, I'd be talking about it all the time."

"You don't have to talk about it," David said. "There're so many other interesting things to talk about."

"Okay," Izzy said. "Thanks, guys. See you in class."

They waved good-bye, even Meggy, and Izzy walked out into the parking lot, David following her.

"Sorry about that," he said. "Meggy is nice, but a little tone deaf."

"It's okay, really," Izzy said, getting her keys from her bag. She wondered if maybe all college students were tone deaf.

"Listen," he said, "I really would like it if we could hang out. Do you want to have dinner sometime?"

"I can't right now," Izzy said. "I have—"

"No, I know you have to make dinner tonight. I meant some other night. Sometime in the near future."

"I better not," Izzy said.

"Are you dating somebody?" he asked, genuinely puzzled by having been rejected in even this minor way.

"No," Izzy said quickly. "It's just, my life is complicated and I have to focus on the kids right now."

"You can't focus on your own happiness?" David asked. "You've got real talent. Can't you make time to be around people who care about that kind of thing? I'd be good for you, I think."

"I don't know," Izzy said. "I just don't have time right now for anything like that."

David kissed her quickly, which struck Izzy as something he'd seen work out in a movie. She, on the other hand, hated the presumption that she would change her mind if she only made out with him. She tasted clove or juniper on his breath, filling her mouth. His lips were as soft as anything she had ever felt in her life, until she felt his hands on her face, which seemed ghostlike enough that they could pass through her body without resistance.

When he let her go, his point made, he fished around in his artist's jacket for another cigarette.

"You should make time for normal human interaction," he said. "You're still young. You should enjoy life." He walked away, seemingly confident in his assertions, so he didn't hear Izzy reply, as she opened her car door, "I am enjoying life." And she meant this, no matter how defeated she sounded.

Izzy had also made her first enemy in the Infinite Family, a disorienting separation in which she realized how fragile the connections in the family could be, how easily it could fall apart. She had been playing with some of the children in the gym and had gone into the closet for more soccer balls, when she returned to see Mary, the only other adult with the kids, grab Maxwell and swat him hard on the bottom, the force of it bringing Maxwell's feet off the court.

Izzy shouted, "Ungh," like she'd been punched in the gut, and immediately clamped her hand over her mouth, as if the action could call back the sound she had already made. Mary wheeled around and locked eyes with Izzy. She let go of Maxwell, who slumped to the ground, more aggrieved than hurt, and pointed at his bottom and then jabbed wildly at Mary, making pained sounds of betrayal. Mary's eyes were wild looking, her teeth gritting in such a way that Izzy felt she could hear it across the court. Izzy, finally in control of her own body, ran toward the scene and scooped up Maxwell in her arms.

"That . . ." Mary paused, biting back whatever expletive she had originally planned on using. "He scratched Lulu because he wanted her damn ball."

"Mary," Izzy said. "We can't hit them. Ever."

"I know that, damn it," she said, shaking her head.

"We can't curse either, not in front of the kids."

"You are just so perfect, aren't you?" Mary said. "Little Miss Perfect, in every single way."

Izzy was so shocked by the venom in Mary's voice that she could only stare in silence before she finally returned to Maxwell, the boy burrowing into her chest.

"We're going back to the room," Mary shouted to the other kids in the gym. Mary kicked a soccer ball so hard that it made a resonant whoomping sound as it hit the far wall. "Let's go," she shouted, and the kids nervously followed her out of the gym. Izzy, unsure of what else to do, held Maxwell on her hip and collected the balls to return to the closet before she walked back to the room to rejoin all the children and caregivers who had stayed behind. Mary was talking to Nina, smiling, and when Izzy walked in and placed Maxwell on the mat to play with the other kids, Mary stared her down until Izzy finally signed herself out and went into the women's restroom, sitting in a stall for fifteen minutes, afraid that Mary might come after her.

Mary was from the mountains of East Tennessee, her body thin and wiry and her eyes always darting around as if looking for predators and, at the same time, for easy prey. She had the mannerisms of a type of girl that Izzy knew well from high school, the girls from the farthest edges of the county, who chewed tobacco and handled firearms with ease and treated any outward display of femininity with great derision. These girls had always terrified Izzy, the casual cruelty they handed out to anyone they deemed weak or useless. Izzy, who thought of herself as trash when compared to the rich kids in her school, preppy and confident, seemed like royalty when next to these feral teenagers. Mary, always quiet, always with a look of slight irritation on her face, stayed clear of Izzy, though she had never assumed it to be personal. Now she thought about what Mary had said to her, Little Miss Perfect, and it caused her such embarrassment that the only way she could combat it was to punish Mary in the only way she knew how.

A day later, Izzy told Dr. Grind about the event while they were alone, drinking coffee, and he thanked her for reporting it to him. "This is incredibly serious, Izzy. It goes against all the work that we're doing here at the complex. Mary is struggling with being overwhelmed when she has to deal with a lot of children at once. She and I will talk it over, and I'll stress to her how important it is that we never strike the children, under any circumstances. Now, Izzy, did you tell Kenny and Carmen about what Mary did?"

Izzy shook her head.

"That's probably for the best, if only to keep further unrest from setting in. I'll talk to Maxwell to reassure him that no one will ever hit him again, tell him that it was not his fault. We'll solve this." And Izzy felt the satisfaction of things being made right, the edges of a puzzle piece fitting neatly into another, the picture becoming whole again.

That evening, however, while Izzy worked on her letters, Mary came into the room and shut the door behind her.

"I'm sorry," Izzy said immediately. "I'm sorry, but I had to tell him."

Mary's jaw was set so tightly that it seemed like her head might explode from the pressure. "I lose my temper one fucking time, and you just have to tell the world about it." She stared at Izzy with such anger that Izzy knew there was nothing to do but shut her mouth and take whatever was coming.

"I've known people like you my whole goddamned life," Mary continued. "I know you're a piece of white trash just like me. I can hear it in your voice, how hard you try to cover up what kind of a hick you are. I hated girls like you, who thought they were better than me even though they were just as poor as me, sometimes even worse off. Thought they were going to leave me behind and become something better, somebody important."

"That's not true," Izzy said, instantly regretting it, but Mary stepped closer to Izzy. "We don't have to like each other," Mary said. "I know how it works. We have to love each other, for the good of the family, but we don't have to like each other. And I just want you to know that I don't like you. I won't ever like you. I'm here, same as you, trying to do right for my kid. So don't you judge me or think that you're better than me. We'll have to work together and live together and all of that, and I'll be good to you, but you better know that I do not like you one bit."

Mary walked out of the room, and Izzy finally took a breath. Her head was buzzing from the adrenaline, and she looked at the letter in her hand, a *d* that now seemed so tainted by the interaction with Mary that Izzy tossed it into the trash and started over with a new piece of wood. Even then, she found that her hands were shaking so hard that she couldn't continue. She swept up the room, dumped the sawdust into the trash, and turned off the lights. The entire walk back to her house, she felt the creeping dread that Mary was waiting for her, hammer in hand, ready to send her forever out of the family.

The next day, though, Mary was talking to Carlos and Jeremy when Izzy happened to walk by. Mary smiled and waved to Izzy. "Hey, Izzy," she said. "I made coffee if you want some." Izzy couldn't speak, only frowned at this kindness, and she watched as Mary's smile never wavered. She also noticed that Jeremy and Carlos seemed puzzled by Izzy's silence, and, as she walked past all of them, she could feel the group staring at her. She wondered, startled by how deeply she wanted to know the answer, how many people hated her. Or worse, she wondered how many people, under any other circumstances, would think nothing of her.

One night, unable to sleep, Izzy walked barefoot to the studio to continue the never-ending work on the letters. As she reached the door, she could hear the buzzing of the saw in use and was temporarily confused, wondering if she was somehow dreaming this. When she pushed open the door, she saw Jeremy working on the band saw and Ellen sorting the fresh letters on the ground, a black Magic Marker sticking out of the pocket of her work apron. When Jeremy looked up from his work, he instantly held up his hands as if he was being robbed. Ellen was occupied with a single letter, worrying it with a piece of sandpaper, but soon she, too, saw Izzy and her face became red with embarrassment.

"Hey, Izzy," Jeremy finally said, and Izzy took a few tentative steps toward them. She looked up at the pages of the story on the wall and noticed that almost an entire paragraph was newly blacked out.

"What are you guys doing?" Izzy asked.

Ellen handed the wooden letter to Izzy, a perfect *g*, and replied, "We wanted to help."

"We figured, with you working by yourself, you might never finish the piece in time. We thought we'd help. I know we should have asked, but I thought you might worry that you had to do it all by yourself or it wouldn't count."

"Warhol had all kinds of assistants help him make his art," Ellen offered, her face still bright red.

Izzy placed the wooden letter on the floor and then gave Jeremy a hug. She did the same to Ellen. "Thanks so much, guys," she said. The truth was that, yes, she wanted to do this project entirely on her own. It had been her idea, her strange vision, and it was meant to be something separate from the rest of the family. But as she noted the worried but slightly manic looks on the faces of Jeremy and Ellen, she realized the futility, within the complex, of keeping anything entirely to yourself. If someone placed their hands on your child as if it was their own, what in the world would stop them from touching a wooden letter?

It was one of those moments when Izzy again realized how cultlike the project could be, but she knew this was unfair. Or was family, in any formation, its own kind of cult? Finding a partner, bringing a child into the world, surrounding yourself with people you cared about, all of these things required a reorganization of your brain, an expansion of what the world could be.

But no, Izzy finally decided. She could be disappointed that Jeremy and Ellen were here, making letters, even if she was happy that they were part of her family. Pettiness, jealousy, secrecy, these were aspects of her makeup, and she would not erase them. It did not matter right now, though, Izzy knew. Ellen and Jeremy were not leaving, and so she rolled up her sleeves and got to work with them.

David had e-mailed Izzy, asking her to meet up with him at the studio. *I need your help with my piece,* he wrote, and she gave in to her curiosity, feeling genuinely intrigued by David's work, why someone who could make something so beautiful would want to smash it into something ugly.

David was wearing a tank top that said JAPAN in bright red letters, his right shoulder bearing a tattoo of a hammer and a paintbrush crossing over each other to make an *X*. His pants were too short to be pants, but too long to be shorts. He was standing over the table in the middle of the room, rolling a joint. Next to him was a ceramic vase, pure white, with a dozen black birds in flight. It was so wonderfully made that Izzy would have believed it was over a thousand years old.

He noticed her and waved her over. "It's beautiful," she said, gesturing to the vase, but he merely shrugged. "Not yet," he replied. "It'll be beautiful when we're done with it."

"What did you want me to help you with?" she asked.

He held up the joint, perfectly rolled. "First we're going to smoke this," he said. "And then you're going to smash this fucking thing with a hammer."

"Oh, no," Izzy said. "No thank you."

"No thank you? Do you mean the joint? Or the hammer? Or both?"

"I don't know," Izzy admitted. "Both, I guess."

"C'mon, Izzy. If you're an artist, then make art."

"I'm not an artist," she said. "I just make art sometimes."

He leaned in and kissed her, once again without her permission, but this time she gave herself over to it because it felt so good. As they continued to kiss, she could sense that he was reaching for something, his hand scratching at the table. When they broke the kiss, he held up the joint.

"I promise that you'll like it," he said. "There is nothing better than getting high and smashing shit to pieces."

"Okay," she said, still recovering from his mouth on hers. "Okay then."

David lit the joint, took a deep hit, and then passed it to her. She held it for a second, observing the bright orange glow. She thought of Dr. Grind, his disappointment in her, but she brought the joint to her lips and took in as much smoke as her lungs could hold, enough to obliterate her nerves. She was young, wasn't she? She was allowed indiscretions, stupid decisions. She was allowed to be around people her own age, who didn't have children, who didn't live in a woodland complex funded by a billionaire, whose lives weren't some grand experiment. As she held the smoke in her lungs, she thought of her wild period, after her mother's death, and how thrilling it had been to do something bad and realize that no one was going to try to stop you. Izzy blew the smoke in one long, unbroken plume right into David's face, which made him smile. They made out again, this time on the floor, and he put his hand down the front of her pants and rubbed his long, slender fingers against her, making her shudder, sending flashes of colored lights just in front of her eyes. "Let's slow down," Izzy said, removing his hand from the waistband of her panties, tapping the palm of his hand as if calming a skittish horse.

David smiled and shrugged. "We can do more of that later," he said, and then he reached for the hammer. "Now, let's make art."

David recorded the moment with his phone, while Izzy, so stoned, put on a pair of safety goggles and then gripped the hammer, testing the heft of it. She looked at the vase, the way the birds seemed to be moving, and she looked to David for reassurance. He nodded his approval, his permission to ruin what he had made. Though Izzy knew she would hate herself for it later, she raised the hammer and brought it down on the lip of the vase. Shards of ceramic skittered across the table, the vase still recognizable as a vase, but badly damaged. She brought the hammer down on it again, then one more time, then one more time, and now it was nothing but broken pieces, unrecognizable. With his free hand, David mimed more hammer blows, but Izzy shook her head. This was as much as she could do, a black cloud in her stomach, so many pieces around her, no idea how she would put it back together again.

"That was great," David finally said, putting his phone back in his pocket. He reached for what was left of the vase, the base of it still intact, and he smiled. He set it down, looked around at the shards of ceramic on the table and the floor, and nodded, as if he was putting the entire thing back together in his mind. He went into his bag and grabbed some Krazy Glue. "This isn't as much fun," he admitted, "but it's the most important part of the process." He relit the joint and took a few more hits, offering it to Izzy, who declined, still so damn high. When he was done, he started picking up the pieces of the vase, holding them up to the light. Finally, he found a piece that fit the base. He applied glue and held it in place. After a few minutes, though it felt like an entire day to Izzy, he let go of the piece and it stayed connected to the base. "Okay," he said, nodding. Then he resumed his search among the shards.

"How long does this take?" Izzy asked.

"Days. Weeks. Forever," David replied. It was as if he had forgotten she was still here, his attention entirely on the vase. She watched him sort through the pieces until he found another one that fit. "I have to be high to do this," he said. "No other way to do it."

Perhaps it was unavoidable, the way that she saw Hal in David. She imagined that watching David provided some strange window into Hal's life before Izzy had ever known him, when he was still young and in thrall to his talent and convinced of his future fame. The intensity of David's focus, the way Izzy felt as if she had disappeared from his mind, reminded her of Hal, those moments when he was right next to her but so, so far away. And then it was simply too much, the pot, the ghost of Hal, David. Were they dating now? What was happening? She took a deep breath, as if it would expel the haziness from her brain. It did nothing.

She looked at her phone and realized how late it was, that she was supposed to be back at the complex, helping with dinner. "Oh shit," she said. "I have to go."

"Bye," he said, not looking up. Izzy fumbled for her keys and began to hurry out of the studio.

"There's a party this weekend," he said, still not looking at her. "Let's go to it."

"Maybe," Izzy said, not really thinking, just wanting to get in her car and go home.

"Definitely," he said, and then Izzy left.

Back at the complex, Izzy ran into the kitchen, her gait entirely foreign to her, the pot still impeding every single action, to find Chef Nicole and Carmen working together. "I hate tardiness," Chef Nicole announced. "You should know that by now."

"I know, Chef," Izzy replied. "I got caught up at school. I'm sorry."

Chef Nicole pointed to Carmen. "Lucky for you Carmen's so good at this. You might be in danger of being replaced." Izzy felt her stomach drop, and Chef Nicole finally noticed her alarm and smiled. "I'm just kidding, Izzy. You're fine."

Izzy stood there, unsure of what to do, how to return to normalcy. Carmen put down a bowl and walked over to Izzy.

"David?" she asked, smiling. Izzy had shown David's pictures on Facebook to Carmen, who nodded with each picture. "Oh, yes," she said. "That kind of beauty is *infuriating*."

Izzy nodded. "I got caught up with him. We *made out*."

Carmen frowned. "Are you high, Izzy?" she whispered.

Izzy nodded, unable to lie.

"You kind of reek of it," Carmen said. "Go get a shower. Take a break. I've got the kitchen stuff handled."

"I'm sorry," Izzy said, blushing.

"Go on," Carmen replied, smiling again. "You're bad."

"No," Izzy said, shaking her head, but Carmen had already returned to the prep work for dinner. "I'm good," she said to no one.

* * *

A few days later, Izzy held Gilberto and Jackie in her lap, the two children squirming to get comfortable, talking about the meal they had just eaten, which Izzy had prepared, things returning to normal after her dalliance with David, when Izzy opened to the first page of *Go, Dog, Go*. Once she began reading, the children instantly quieted, listening to Izzy describe the various dogs in various circumstances. Gilberto placed his finger on the picture of a blue tree and then traced a line to the word *tree* on the page. Izzy smiled and nodded. Jackie pointed to the word *yellow* and sounded it out slowly, not unsure but careful. "Good job, sweeties, but let me read the story one time and then we'll go back and you two can read it," she said, turning to the next page, as the pages would fill with more and more unique dogs. After a few more pages, she turned to look at Paul, who was holding his own daughter, Lulu, and reading *Lyle, Lyle, Crocodile* to her. Her own son, Cap, was supposed to be reading the book with Lulu, but he had apparently lost interest and was about to destroy a tower of blocks that he had just built. As she lingered over the image, feeling the slightest irritation that Paul was not giving his attention to Cap, Jackie patted her knee and pointed to the next page, saying, "Party!" over and over, which got Gilberto worked up as well. "Yes," Izzy said, finally returning to the two of them, "a big dog party."

Of course, it was very rare for children this young to be reading words off the page. Still, Izzy wished that Cap was one of the five children who could already read. While he loved to listen as someone read a book, and he also understood, as Jill Patterson kept assuring her, that the printed words on the page were creating the story that he was hearing, he didn't seem interested in translating those symbols into words. He knew the alphabet, but preferred to keep the letters separate, single letters that he could spit out one by one and then forget. Benjamin, whose own daughter, Ally, could also not yet read, once confided to Izzy and a few other parents, "I see these kids doing these incredible things and I worry that I'm doing something wrong. And then, fuck, I realize that Ally is not our kid, or not just our kid. She's everybody's. It's not anything that I did. It's all of us. And then I don't know if that makes me happy or sad."

Dr. Grind reiterated over and over, "The goal of the Infinite Family is not to create tiny superheroes, an army of baby geniuses. Of course, we're doing everything we can to help these children develop and feel confident in their abilities. But that ultimately doesn't matter as much as if they're happy. We're providing them with love and support. If they start walking at seven months instead of twelve months, it doesn't matter in the least bit to us. We just want them to feel safe and secure and happy. Everything else will follow." Izzy could not help but notice, especially now that she spent most of her evenings carving out letters for a story that spoke in the first person plural, that Dr. Grind said, *we* instead of *I*.

Things were easier at night now that the children weren't breast-feeding. The evenings felt less regimented; while there was still a chart of who was on duty for those sleeping hours, it was easier to hang around the children, to help out wherever you could fit yourself into the action. And even though Izzy was elated when she was paired up with Cap, she admitted there was a certain happiness in finding how easily she could adapt to any permutation of the family. One night, she would scoop up Irene and Marnie, and Asean would fall into step with her as they helped dress each child in their pajamas. Though she hadn't seen Asean all day, perhaps hadn't spent a single minute that week alone in his presence, it was reassuring to see how easily they understood each other in that moment, the way they each tugged gently on Marnie's shirt until her head pushed through the opening. But then, all the children asleep, Asean would hug Izzy and say good night and then drape his arm around Nikisha and they would retire together to their house. And Izzy would walk to the studio to make a story that had already, long ago, been written.

On Saturday afternoon, she received a text from David. *Party tonight. Come.* It was the first time he'd contacted her since she had been with him in the studio. She had made herself scarce on campus, embarrassed by how she'd lost control, even briefly. She thought of what the party would be like, red Solo cups and music that she did not recognize but could still sing along to. She thought of David, his delicate hands, and then she texted back, *I can't*. She waited for his reply, but hours passed and there was still no word from him. Later, on the playground with some of the kids, she wrote *Sorry* and texted it to David, but still nothing. And, like that, Izzy imagined that she had missed her window for a normal life, doing things that kids her age did. She looked at the children, running wild, and she wanted to do the same, to run until her legs gave out, collapsed in a heap, someone else's job to take care of her.

After dinner, Izzy was clearing away the dishes when Gilberto ran up to her. "I pooped," he said, and Izzy immediately put down the dishes. "In your pants, sweetie?" she asked, and Gilberto nodded, smiling. "Oh, no," she said. "Let's go get cleaned up."

The less she remembered about the experience of potty-training ten kids at once, the better. It had been a kind of war zone, poop and pee everywhere, the paranoia that, at any given time, at least one of the children was having an accident. At one point during the training, five of the kids were running around the bathroom, naked, and Nina had yelled, "Infinite. It's infinite piss and shit. That's what this place is." And yet somehow they had made it through, another milestone passed, their lives that much easier, except for these occasional accidents.

In the bathroom, she pulled down Gilberto's pants and carefully removed his underwear, so ruined that Izzy could only think to throw them away. While she reached for the wipes, Gilberto suddenly grinned mischievously and said, "I'm gonna pee in your face."

"Don't do that, Gil," Izzy said, absentmindedly, trying to get a single wipe from the pack.

"I am. I'm gonna pee in your face," he said, giggling.

"Don't, please," Izzy replied, and then Gilberto peed in her face, in her open mouth.

"Fuck," Izzy said, and Gilberto laughed. "Help," Izzy yelled. "Help!"

Carmen ran into the bathroom. "What is it?" she asked, and Gilberto said, "I peed in her face," and Izzy said, "He peed in my face."

Izzy looked up at Carmen, who was trying not to laugh. "I need to get out of here, Carmen," she said, suddenly overwhelmed. "I need a break."

"Okay," Carmen said, suddenly turning serious. "Where will you go?"

"There's a party. David asked me to go."

"Okay," Carmen said. "But be careful. Don't drink and drive. Call me if something happens."

"Thank you," Izzy said.

"Seriously, Izzy," Carmen said, steadying Izzy with serious vibes of big sisterhood. "Be careful. Don't do anything that you'll regret."

Izzy nodded, not truly listening; she was already walking out of the bathroom, leaving the stained underwear on the floor, Gilberto still not cleaned up, and had already pulled out her phone and was texting, *Yes party. Send directions.*

Five minutes after her arrival at the party, a bunch of cars scattered along a field, kids swimming in a stagnant pond, Izzy wanted a drink. She couldn't find David anywhere and she was surrounded by people she vaguely recognized but not enough to strike up a conversation. She had decided, on the drive here, that she would fuck David tonight if he asked. Getting peed on by a three-year-old had left her in need of some excuse to feel sexy, to feel sexual. She did a loop around the party and still no sign of David, having texted him three times already, and she settled herself at the edge of the pond, watching people jump in and then squeal at the pond scum and mud that attached itself to their bodies. They climbed out of the pond, looking like swamp creatures, poured a beer from one of the many kegs that seemed to have been randomly air-dropped from a cargo plane, and then dove back into the slime and muck.

More than forty-five minutes had passed since she arrived at the party, and she stood up, unsteady on the soft ground, and walked to one of the kegs. She found an empty cup on the ground and filled it halfway with beer. She did another loop, amazed at how easily she went unnoticed by every other partygoer; David, she decided, was either sunk beneath the pond, forever lost, or having sex in one of the cars. She texted: *Where R U?* but did not expect a reply.

She returned to the same spot at the edge of the pond and took a few tentative sips of the beer. It tasted like fermented skunk. She'd never enjoyed the taste of beer, and yet she forced herself to drink more of it for reasons that her brain couldn't actively unpack. Eventually, she realized that even if she drank the entire contents of the cup, it wouldn't be enough to get her drunk, and she dumped out the beer and vowed to sit for fifteen more minutes and then leave. Just then, she heard someone shout, "Hey, bitch!" and, startled, Izzy turned around to see three girls running toward her. She put up her hands to defend herself from the screams of the girls, who suddenly stopped short, momentarily sobered. "Oh, shit," one of the girls said. "We thought you were someone else." One of the other girls leaned close to inspect Izzy and then slurred, "Someone we know."

"Sorry," Izzy said.

"Maybe she went into the pond," the first girl offered.

"Here hold this, please," the drunker girl said, placing a lit joint between Izzy's fingers. Izzy instinctually began to refuse, but the weirdness of the *please*, which sounded out of place coming from someone so drunk, caused her to relent. She took the joint and the girls tore off toward the water, not even bothering to shuck off their clothes.

"Are you guys coming back for it?" Izzy asked, feeling like she'd been tricked into taking on a high-interest loan. The girls did not respond, were already shrieking at their bad decision, boys circling them to keep them from running back out. She put the joint to her lips and took a deep puff, holding it so long in her lungs that time stopped and then restarted. She took two more hits, her body immediately easing into inactivity. She watched the party swirl around her, two boys trying and failing to set a hay bale on fire, a girl throwing up into the pond and no one getting out or even caring. Without any sense of how long she'd been there, she flicked the rest of the joint into the pond and, though it took a few minutes, made her way to the truck that she'd signed out from the complex. She pulled onto the dirt road and tried to put as much distance as possible between herself and the party. As soon as she found the highway, slightly more buzzed than she had thought, her phone vibrated and there was a fresh text from David: *R U Here?* Izzy just kept driving, making her winding way back home.

When she made it home, driving five miles under the speed limit the entire way, she knew it was pointless to try to go to sleep. Instead, ravenous from the pot, she put on some fresh clothes and went into the kitchen. She then made herself some scrambled eggs and pureed some avocado, using the blowtorch to char it, Izzy showing off even without Chef Nicole to witness it, before mixing it up with the eggs. She made herself an iced coffee and took the food into the studio to continue working on the art project, but found Dr. Grind inside, his hands held behind his back as if being careful not to touch anything, looking closely at the tacked-up story by Faulkner. When she opened the door and made herself known, he turned to her without surprise; Izzy, knowing a lot more now about his childhood upbringing and his parents' thoughts on development, imagined that they had trained him to treat any possible surprise with calm, reasoned actions. He smiled, gesturing to the story. "Sorry," he said. "I was just doing some light reading."

She set her plate of food and the iced coffee on the table and then stood beside him, looking at the story that she had now memorized and was almost entirely blacked out with marker at this point.

"I knew that everyone has been helping you with the project and so I decided that I should be a part of it as well. Then I spotted the saw and it looked rather complicated, and I was afraid to touch any of the letters for fear of ruining them. I thought it better to just observe."

After Jeremy and Ellen had convinced her to accept outside help, other people had chipped in when they had free time. Julie, who was working on her novel, said that it really helped her writer's block to carve out a few letters, toss them on the pile, and then go back to her computer and keep writing. Izzy had hidden the final page of the story in her house so that she could be assured of finishing it on her own.

"Have you read the story before?" she asked him.

"No," he replied.

"It's pretty sad," she told him.

"I gathered as much," he said, pointing to the first legible sentence, which read:

She died in one of the downstairs rooms, in a heavy walnut bed with a curtain, her gray head propped on a pillow yellow and moldy with age and lack of sunlight.

"Does it say something about me that I chose this particular story?" she asked, and he smiled and shook his head.

"Nothing that would hold up under scrutiny," he answered.

"I'm stoned right now, Dr. Grind," Izzy said, surprising herself with this admission. Would she have to inform someone every single time she got high? It was predicated in no small part on the idea that Dr. Grind already knew and it would be worse not to acknowledge it.

"Well, Carmen said that you had been invited to a party. I suppose this was one of the possible outcomes," Dr. Grind replied.

"I don't do this normally," she admitted. "Certainly not around the kids."

"I am certain of that, Izzy," Dr. Grind said, his voice betraying no sense of disappointment or surprise.

"Have you ever been stoned, Dr. Grind?" she asked.

"Yes. Several times. My parents made pot brownies for me sporadically through my childhood, just to test how it might affect my abilities to handle conflict. I did not enjoy it."

Izzy realized once again that if she wanted a normal conversation, a life of understandable experiences, then Dr. Grind was not the person to talk to. And, still, this was what drew her to him, the understanding that, whatever strangeness had befallen him, he had somehow made it out alive.

Dr. Grind's face was so open and inviting, the way he seemed to always find her to be worthy of fascination. David, when he looked at her, seemed to be looking only at her outline, as if there was nothing about her that truly held his attention. Continuing to compare the two men, she tried to imagine what it would feel like to kiss Dr. Grind, and, without thinking, she leaned over to Dr. Grind and kissed him.

He received the kiss the way she had anticipated, with tenderness and at a slight remove. He did, however, she believed, return the kiss. It had depth to it, she felt. She had an idea that a good kiss, held long enough, could be felt in the feet. And her feet certainly were doing something down there. When she broke the kiss, Dr. Grind either too polite or too involved to turn away from her, simply smiled, shaking his head.

"That's not a great idea, Izzy," he said. "That's quite bad, actually."

"I won't do it again," she said, immediately feeling ashamed, like a child. "I'm just . . . I'm high, you know?"

He nodded. "My responsibilities . . . ," he said, though he seemed unsure of how to proceed and the words just hung there.

"I understand," Izzy said.

"Good," he replied, and he winced for a split second before returning her gaze.

"Do you want to make something?" she asked, desperate to change the tension in the room. And to her surprise, after a brief moment where he seemed to be thinking about it, he nodded. As if nothing had happened, he took a step away from her and leaned over the letters once more.

They spent the next two hours working on the letters. Dr. Grind would trace, while Izzy used the saw. Izzy resolved that she would not try to kiss him again, and, she was certain, Dr. Grind would never mention this moment again. It was, she decided, a fairly good compromise, better than being kicked out of the complex, and as the time passed and she further sobered up, she appreciated the fact that Dr. Grind, unlike almost any normal human being, would not hold this against her. He would be flattered and yet firmly principled and would forget it had ever happened. After they had finished a sentence, they took a break, and Izzy finished her coffee while Dr. Grind sat on the floor and looked closely at the wooden letters.

"Cap's father was an artist?" he asked her, his voice steady and gentle, knowing the potential for sadness this would create.

"He was," she said. "He was a painter, but he seemed more interested, once I met him, in more experimental forms of art. I think it was because his career didn't really work out the way he had hoped, so he started to dismiss traditional art as boring. I thought his paintings were pretty wonderful, though. He hated them. He mostly did portraits but he did them on old doors, so they were really big and unwieldy. He had all these painted doors stacked up in his garage, not even covered or anything, just gathering dust and fading."

"What do you think happened to them?" Dr. Grind asked.

Izzy realized that she had no idea, had never thought to ask. "I don't know," she said. "I hope they didn't get thrown out, but I feel like that's probably what happened. I wish he'd given me one to keep."

"That would have been nice," Dr. Grind admitted. "Marla was in a band and I sometimes listen to their album and it's reassuring in some way."

"And sad in other ways, I bet," Izzy offered.

"Yes, that, too," he admitted.

"When I think about Hal—" she said, suddenly stopping when she realized that this was the first time she'd said his name in a long time, that his identity had been kept out of the records of The IFP. She looked at Dr. Grind, who waited patiently. She decided, ultimately, that it didn't matter. She could say his name. It wouldn't hurt anyone. "When I think about Hal, I get really angry that he killed himself. And then I think that I probably wouldn't be here now if he hadn't. And that makes me feel so strange, so unsure of myself. It's awful, but sometimes I think it was for the best."

Dr. Grind was silent for a few seconds; he traced a circle in the sawdust on the floor, and Izzy immediately felt that she had made a mistake. Because he made it so easy, she often thought of Dr. Grind as just one of the other participants in the Infinite Family, not the person in charge. It was also the same kind of uncertainty that she felt in these moments, when it seemed like he was courting her, the way he made himself available. She understood that this was simply the kind of person he was, his skill at making everyone think they were the most important person in the complex, combined with her own loneliness, but it still left her confused at times. Now she wished only that he would say something, move past her admission.

"It's not awful at all, Izzy," he finally said, but did not continue. He kept tracing the circle in the sawdust, the circle slowly widening. Izzy was about to stand when Dr. Grind, still looking at the circle, said, "Marla and our son died in a car wreck. Did you know that?"

She nodded.

"Marla became very interested in my parents' work with child development. She became slightly obsessed with the Constant Friction Method." He then realized that Izzy might not know of this method and he looked up at her to explain, but she waved her hand and said, "I read about it. We all did some sleuthing on you before we came here."

"I assumed that would be the case," he said. "Well, Marla was very interested in it. She kept saying that, if the process had created me, then maybe it wasn't so bad. Of course, I told her the various reasons for why I didn't approve, and she knew these reasons herself, but she still seemed attached to it. So, a few times, I would find Marla with Jody and she would be intentionally putting him in harm's way, doing something slightly dangerous. Nothing too severe; perhaps she would be playing with matches with him or tripping him when she didn't think I was watching. We talked about it a lot; she even went to therapy to work it out. Things got better, and I stopped worrying about it. And then they died."

Dr. Grind stopped talking and again stared at the floor. Izzy knew that if anyone else in the complex was telling this story, she would give them comfort, but she could not bring herself to touch him. If she did, she knew with certainty, she would kiss him again. She simply waited for him to continue, if there was anything left to say.

"I'm sorry for telling you this," he said.

"It's okay," she admitted. She was amazed that he had said this much, and it felt good. There was a fuzziness inside her, better than being stoned, warm and pleasant, because the doctor had opened himself up just for her, given her a window into the life he had before the complex.

"Well, I often wonder, especially late at night, times like this when I'm awake and everyone else is asleep, if the car wreck wasn't intentional. I wonder if Marla intended to drive off the road to shock Jody and then actually lost control of the car in the process. I wonder if, good lord, she drove the car intentionally into the tree, thinking they would survive it. And then I think that Marla wouldn't do that. But that's the problem, isn't it? We're mysteries to each other, no matter how hard we try to prove otherwise."

This time, Izzy did reach out for him, touching his shoulder as gently as snow falling, and Dr. Grind seemed slightly embarrassed by the gesture, but he grasped her hand and squeezed it. Then he stood and walked toward the door. He stopped and turned to Izzy.

"No matter what happened that night," he said, "it doesn't change the fact that I loved Marla very much. Even if I'm furious with what she might have done. That's what emotions are, I think, complex and shifting, and yet we think that any deviation from what we're supposed to feel makes us a bad person. We're good people, Izzy. Hal was a good person. Marla was a good person. But they're gone and so we do the best we can."

He walked out of the studio, and Izzy felt so bereft, so strangely saddened for Dr. Grind and herself, the two people in the Infinite Family who had experienced such a loss, that all she could do was go back to the band saw and continue her work. Even if it amounted to nothing, even if it was tossed aside the day after, she had to believe that it meant something now. That it mattered. And so she made the letters and arranged them and read the words aloud.

The next time she saw David, he grabbed her arm and asked, "Why didn't you wait around for me?"

"I did," she said, pulling her arm away from him. "I waited for more than two hours. Where were you?"

"Working," he said, shrugging with great irritation. "Making art. Doing something important."

"That's fine," Izzy said, "but I am making art, too. I'm doing all kinds of things, but I still went to the party to see you."

"I'm not trying to be rude," he said, so effortlessly being rude that he didn't have to try, "but your art is not my art. You're just copying a story that someone else made. You're making letters."

She thought of Hal's assertion that everything was art. She now realized that he had never stated that one kind of art was better than another. It pleased her, in this moment, to think of him as being more open-minded than David.

"Then I guess there's no need for further discussion," she said.

"Do you want to go get high?" he asked her. "Make out?"

"No," she said.

"Have sex?" he said, smiling.

"I better go," she said.

"How long are you supposed to live at that place?" he asked her.

"It's ten years," she replied. "Total."

"When it's over, the whole world will have passed you by," he said. "You'll have missed out on everything."

"Maybe," Izzy allowed.

"You'll have missed out on me," he told her.

"Oh god, David," she said, "I don't fucking care about you." She realized that David's beauty was the kind that allowed him to be an awful person and still get everything that he wanted. But not her. He could not touch her life. She held up both hands, middle fingers extended. It was so juvenile, but it felt fucking right to her.

"Well," he said, unsure of how to proceed. "Bye, then."

"Bye," she said, and she walked to her car, wondering what she'd lost and what she'd gained and thinking, maybe, she had come out entirely even. An hour later, pulling into the complex, she thought to herself, *No.* She had come out ahead. She had come out way, way ahead.

Izzy was reading the Dr. Seuss book *And to Think That I Saw It on Mulberry Street,* long a favorite of all the children, in the day care center. All the parents took turns signing up for times to read aloud to the kids, which Izzy always looked forward to. The kids cheered as each successive rendition of what was happening on Mulberry Street became more and more fantastic. Maxwell had started a tradition where, with each new object or person or animal that the story included, the kids would shout, "Yes," and point their index fingers in the air. As Izzy looked over the top of the book at the kids, she watched them mischievously grinning, their fingers pointing out from their heads like devil horns, waiting for yet another new thing on Mulberry Street. "Yes," the kids shouted to a Chinese man who eats with sticks (the parents were encouraged not to say the book's term *Chinaman* for obvious reasons), to a big magician doing tricks, and to a ten-foot beard that needs a comb. "Yes, yes, yes," they said, gesticulating wildly. And then the book returned to its quiet beginnings, a plain horse and wagon, and the kids all groaned dramatically and fell to the floor.

When the book was finished, Izzy asked the children what they would like to see on Mulberry Street, and the kids gave their own fanciful versions. Ally said she would like a polar bear on roller skates holding a big birthday cake. Jackie wanted to see a fancy car with princesses inside. When it was Cap's turn, he said that he wanted to see himself and Izzy riding together on a motorcycle. "That's it?" Maxwell asked, and Cap nodded, smiling. Izzy smiled so hard back at Cap, her son but not quite yet her own son, that her eyes began to well up with tears, and even the kids understood it was a good thing.

Izzy popped kernels of corn on the stove, machine-gun fire rattling inside the pot, while Carmen made hurricanes, toxic red and syrupy.

Chocolate chip cookies baked in the oven. They were watching *Mahogany* on DVD, but mostly they talked over it, recounting their week, the numerous weirdnesses of their lives.

The two of them got together at Izzy's every Wednesday night if they could manage it. Of all the people in the project, Izzy felt the strongest connection to Carmen, found it easiest to talk to her, and Izzy was pleased that Carmen confided in her above everyone else. Izzy felt like Carmen's younger sister, constantly striving for her approval, sure that Carmen had experience where Izzy didn't. And Carmen, if not her older sister, gave Izzy enough attention and care that she felt most like actual family.

Carmen had grown up near Memphis. Her parents divorced when she was only three, and her dad took Carmen's brother, who was nine at the time, and moved to Texas; she never saw them again, heard not one word from her dad or brother. "For all I know," she told Izzy, "they're both dead. Or on the moon. Or still in Texas, not thinking a thing about me."

Like Izzy, Carmen was thirteen when her mother died, a swift and inoperable lung cancer, and Carmen moved to Memphis proper to live with a distant, older cousin who already had a family of her own. She did that until she was sixteen, when the cousin and her family moved to Florida, and Carmen spent the next two years living with friends, until she graduated from high school. Then she'd met Kenny, who'd been working at a garage where Carmen, one of her two jobs, worked the register. They married two months after getting together. "We loved each other," Carmen admitted, as if Izzy had doubted her, "but we also were just so happy to be with somebody who wasn't going to up and leave as soon as they had the chance. Both of us had a bad history of getting left behind, and so we thought we'd do much better if we held on to each other." Two months after Carmen had decided to enroll in nursing school, a step toward the future, she got pregnant, and now here she was, so much further into the future, on Izzy's couch, the two of them slightly drunk, talking about Izzy's love life.

"So it's not going to happen with David?" Carmen asked.

"I don't know that it ever was, but it's definitely not going to happen now," Izzy replied, her teeth stained red from the hurricane. "I've shut the door on that."

"His loss," Carmen said. "There are lots of other guys for you."

"I can't imagine starting anything with them. They seem very, very young to me."

"You old soul," Carmen said, shaking her head.

"Well, I have a kid. I have responsibilities. I don't begrudge the fact that they don't. But I don't have time for them."

Then Izzy, just buzzed enough, spoke before she could consider how smart it was. "What do you think of Dr. Grind?"

"What do you mean? Romantically?"

"I guess," Izzy replied, knowing she had made a mistake.

"Izzy?" Carmen said, and then laughed loudly, a quick burst of surprise. "You have a crush on Dr. Grind?"

"I don't know." Izzy's face, she could feel, was blazing hot. But there was no point in turning back. "I guess I do."

"He's cute enough, I guess, though he looks so much like a little kid. Plain, but not unattractive. He's sweet. He's too earnest for me, though. He talks to everyone like they're a purebred dog that might bite. Always wearing that tie. Kind of spooky, the way he moves so quietly through the complex."

"But he's kind," Izzy offered, suddenly feeling the need to defend him.

"Is that all you need, kindness?" Carmen said. "Dr. Grind doesn't look like he's spent a single minute of his life thinking about sex."

"I think kindness is sexy," Izzy said quietly, now grasping at straws.

"You'd make a cute couple," Carmen allowed, reaching for another cookie.

"It doesn't matter," Izzy said, thinking back to the kiss. "It couldn't happen."

"No, I guess not," Carmen said. "Not while he's running the show."

"So there's no point in talking about it."

"You brought it up, Izzy."

"Sorry."

"I wonder if he dates," Carmen said. "Do you think he has some Internet girlfriend that he talks to?"

"Let's just finish the movie," Izzy said, feeling sick at the possibility.

They watched Diana Ross on the TV, the lines almost memorized by this point. After ten minutes of quiet, so much time passing that Izzy assumed the conversation was over, Carmen rubbed her shoulder and said, "It's okay to want somebody, Izzy. Dr. Grind's a good guy."

"Maybe someday," Izzy said, just to end the conversation. She leaned against Carmen, suddenly tired, and Carmen snorted. "That tie," she said. "Those sneakers."

Izzy closed her eyes, unable to keep herself from smiling.

After Carmen went back to her own place, Izzy went upstairs and sat in her bed, suddenly unable to sleep. She reached into the drawer of her nightstand and retrieved a gray velvet box. She didn't open it, merely held it in her open hand. It was one of the few objects she'd brought with her to the complex, something she couldn't get rid of, and so here it was, in her hand again.

For her birthday, Hal had given her an antique emerald ring, the kind of jewelry that could not be mistaken for anything other than priceless, old world beauty. It fit her finger perfectly. "I can't wear this," she told him, immediately tamping down the joy she felt upon seeing the ring.

"Why not?" he asked, smiling, still proud of the perfection of his gift.

"Because someone like me, who doesn't have five dollars in her purse and has to wear clothes from Goodwill, does not get to walk around school with this kind of ring on her finger. People will want to know who gave it to me."

"Well, you wouldn't have to tell them the truth. Say it was your grandmother's ring."

"My grandmother, on both sides, married a farmer, sewed her own clothing, and died with the exact same amount of money she started with. Even if you go a dozen generations back, I don't come from any kind of family that would own this ring."

"Well," he said, looking at her, Izzy felt flushed to understand, with the kind of affection that suggested she was made for beautiful things, "you can keep it here and wear it only when you visit me."

"This is turning out to be less of a great gift, Mr. Jackson."

Whenever she wanted to needle him, whenever she wanted to see his ears tint red, she called him by his teacher name. She did not like foolishness for the most part, but she thrilled at the wickedness of this small act.

Hal did not even register the needling; he was so focused on her, and she again felt the strange sensation of being witnessed, something she worked so hard to avoid in most cases. "Pretty soon, Izzy," he then said, "if you still feel like it, you'll have so many nice things like this that you'll make up restrictions on them just to make them special again."

She did not allow her emotions on the surface to change but she felt the swell of his consideration of the future. Their future. She could never figure out, and it felt childish to ask, what he expected from this relationship. She simply dug her nails into herself and hoped that the marks would remind her, years from now, of a time that was good.

"I don't know how a person gets tired of this," she said, and then carefully put the ring back in its box, placed it on the coffee table, and willed herself to forget that it existed.

Now, in bed, holding the box that she had still not opened since Hal died, she knew that she didn't want to see what was inside. She wondered if it was even still in the box, or if it had disintegrated as soon as Hal left her. She could see the ring clearly in her mind, more defined than she could see Hal, who had grown hazy in her memories. If she put the ring on, would it bring Hal back to life? She considered the box for a few seconds and then placed it, unopened, in the drawer. She lay back in bed and dug her fingers into her arm, the sensation so pleasing, the slight pain, that she fell into a deep sleep.

* * *

On the night of the exhibition for her art class, nearly the entire Infinite Family came to the gallery, even the children, who had to be carefully shepherded around the precariously arranged works of art. As they sipped punch, the adults stared with polite but confounded expressions at a six-foot-long string of plaster molds of shrimp arranged like Christmas lights around a fake tree. Finally, Marnie pulled on Izzy's arm, shocking her back into coherence, and asked her, "Where is yours, Izzy? I wanna see Izzy's art." Izzy pointed toward the second room of the gallery and said, "It's in there." Everyone in the family turned and, instead of observing all the artwork as it was set up, made a beeline for the next room.

It had taken Izzy hours to load up each plastic drum, filled with wooden letters, into the van, requiring the help of several other adults. But she alone did the arranging in the gallery. Now she was glad she had refused their help because the piece had become new to the family, even though they'd seen the rough elements dozens of times in the complex.

"Izzy," Nina said, holding on to Izzy's hand and squeezing it. "It's beautiful. It's weird, too, but it's beautiful. It looks like real art."

"Thank you," Izzy said and they both stared at the mountain of letters, taking up nearly the entire room, spilling out in all directions. On the wall, blown up, were sheets of paper that held the story of "A Rose for Emily" in its entirety. But it was obscured by the letters, so many of them, impossible to count.

Dr. Grind and Jeffrey knelt down with two of the children and they put their hands in the pool of letters, picking some up and letting them fall like rain down onto the floor. Dr. Grind looked back at Izzy, who nodded her approval, and he smiled back. Though the signs said PLEASE DO NOT TOUCH, Izzy had hoped this would happen, all the children of the Infinite Family picking up the letters that she, and many others, had made. Her teacher had said that they were interested in adding the piece to the permanent gallery across campus, and she was happy to hear it, though embarrassed to be so young and have her professors say nice things to her, even if out of politeness.

Pretty soon, Maxwell, one of the wildest of the bunch of kids, started throwing letters at Marnie, and a few of the attendants, other students in the art department, ran over to stop him. Izzy said, "It's okay," and the attendants shrugged and let the action continue. A crowd formed, not just the Infinite Family, and they watched as all the kids reached for handfuls of letters and sent them flying across the room, skittering across the floor. Izzy saw David, his face so contemptuous—true art was nothing like what she had made of her life. The other kids from her class were also watching Izzy and her family, and their faces were slightly numbed with confusion at the chaos around them, but she turned away and watched her own family. She watched as Cap and Ally carefully picked up the letters that made their own names, and laid them out on the floor. They ran over to Izzy and showed her what they had made and she said how beautiful it was, how perfect it was, this thing they had made with their own hands.

chapter thirteen

the infinite family project (year four)

Dr. Grind returned to his office after a thirty-minute walk through the woods beyond the complex to find that Kalina was standing in his doorway. He smiled and then realized that she had been, or perhaps still was, crying. He walked over to Kalina, but she took a few steps back and then stuttered, "I-I'm sorry, Doctor. I'm really sorry about this."

"It's okay," he replied. "Well, I don't know what's wrong yet, but I assure you that it's okay."

"I'm pregnant," she said. "I'm with child."

Dr. Grind could not process the statement as he had no frame of reference, no institutional memory to make this understandable. Instead, he waded through the way he always did, deliberately, until he reached dry land.

"That's nothing to cry about, Kalina. This is something to celebrate."

"I know; that's why I feel so bad."

"Sit down, Kalina. Let's talk."

"It's complicated," she said, as if this would encourage him to call the whole thing off and just pretend it had never happened.

"Tell me," he said, sitting down beside her.

"I'd gotten close to someone, really connected with them," she started, her voice slowly gaining its composure.

"I had no idea," Dr. Grind replied.

"I know. I never told you. The research fellows all felt it was better to keep that part of our lives private when we came to the complex. We didn't want to have our relationships outside the family impinge upon the work we were doing here."

"So, do Jeffrey and Jill have boyfriends or girlfriends, too?" he asked, genuinely mystified as to why he had never really pursued this in the past.

"Jill has a partner, a really nice woman who lives in D.C. They've been together since before the study. Jill sees her during every break she gets. Jeffrey, well, I'm not entirely sure. I know he's had a few girlfriends since we've been here, but nothing too serious. When I first got here, I'd been dating Marco, who I met at an art gallery in Nashville. He's a barista but he's also a really talented artist." Kalina was speaking so quickly, as if the words had been dammed up for months and only now could come out. "He does coffee portraiture."

"What is that?" Dr. Grind asked.

"He manipulates the milk and coffee in a latte and makes portraits of the people who order. He's semifamous on the Internet."

"Well, I can't wait to meet him," Dr. Grind said, not knowing what exactly to say about coffee portraiture that wouldn't sound condescending.

"No, see, we broke up last year. Since then, nothing for me, but then I met someone. He's really kind and understands me and my work and how complicated it can be. We really connected in a way that I haven't with anyone else."

Kalina started to cry again, hiccupping gulps that seemed unintentionally rhythmic. Dr. Grind handed her his handkerchief and she gratefully accepted it. "I don't know what to do now," she said. "I got pregnant, so stupid, and I don't know what to do."

"Well, you should get married. You should have a baby."

"I can't!" she said, almost wailing, as if Dr. Grind did not understand her problem, or saw only one part of it.

Suddenly, Dr. Grind felt a realization crystallize in his brain, an understanding of Kalina's despair. "Kalina," he now asked, dreading the answer. "Is he part of The IFP?"

Kalina's eyes widened. She recovered, steadied herself, and simply nodded.

"Is it one of the parents?" he asked, this time knowing the answer.

"It is," she admitted.

"Who is it?" he asked, trying to keep hold of his frustration. Now even the people hired specifically to help him achieve his goals were actively sabotaging the project.

"I can't tell you," she said. "It doesn't matter anyway."

"It matters quite a bit, Kalina," Dr. Grind replied. He rifled through an imaginary Rolodex in his brain. Kenny? David? Perhaps Link? Any possible name seemed entirely impossible and, at the same time, perfectly reasonable.

"I mean, it's over now. It was a one-time thing. We were both in the gym one night and things just got out of hand. Immediately afterward, we knew we'd made a mistake, and we never did it again. When I told him that I was pregnant, he said that he couldn't leave his wife, the project, but I was never going to ask him to do those things. He was very adamant that I not go through with it. And I'm not even really mad at him. I had no illusions about some kind of fantasy life with him."

"But you want to keep the baby?" he asked.

She nodded. "I've spent so much time taking care of other people's children, helping them become better parents. I feel like I deserve this opportunity to take care of my own child. I have so much to offer a child. The situation with . . . with the father was doomed to fail, I understand that. But maybe something good came out of it. An opportunity for just me."

"Well," Dr. Grind said, considering the situation. "Then you need to have this baby."

"But I don't want to leave the project," Kalina said, again nearly wailing.

"You don't have to leave the project," he said quickly, reaching out to calm her. Then he realized that maybe she would have to leave. What would it mean to have one of the research fellows pregnant? How would it affect the dynamic, especially when the unknown father also lived in the complex? Would they even live here in the complex? Would the baby become part of the study? One of the main requirements of the project, discussed at length before the parents signed on, was that they would not have another child for the duration of the project. It was a way, perhaps unfair, to keep the focus on the ten initial children, to prevent any issues that, he now realized, Kalina's pregnancy might bring up.

"I can stay?" she said, brightening up. "How?"

"Well," Dr. Grind said, trying to backtrack, to figure out how to proceed. And then he realized that Brenda Acklen had given him ultimate power over the study, had tasked him with making something incredible. If he wanted Kalina to stay, and he most certainly did, as she was a vital part of the project, one of the best researchers he had ever encountered and the best at working with the parents, though he now allowed perhaps too attached to one of the parents, then he could simply let her stay. "Well, we can talk to the rest of the family and figure this out. Then, um, I suppose you'd have the baby and he or she would be a part of the family as well. Not officially, you understand, not part of the study, but your child would be cared for and loved by everyone."

"That's incredible," Kalina said, her face slightly puffy, though she was at least smiling now. "It's perfect."

"Okay," Dr. Grind said, "whenever you're ready, we can announce the news and I think you'll find that everyone will be very supportive. Well, almost everyone. I can't imagine how the father will react." He wondered if even his initial statement was true, how the parents might feel about another child in the complex, one who would have a specific parent from the get-go. And was he really going to jeopardize the entire project by allowing Kalina and her child to perhaps complicate the lives of the family? What if the child looked exactly like one of the fathers? Why let this time bomb live inside the complex? Deep down, he knew that he simply couldn't let anyone leave, could not lose one person from the project, or else he'd feel like he'd failed. The only way this would work, he told himself over and over, was to keep everyone as close to him as possible.

All he could hope for was that he had built up enough goodwill with everyone, having never denied them anything he had promised, that they would accept Kalina's new status and things would be fine. He was certain this would not be the case, but he let himself believe it in order to move on to the next step.

Jeffrey and Jill appeared in the doorway; Jill immediately knelt beside Kalina and embraced her, while Jeffrey remained at the door, a solemn expression on his face.

"It's okay," Kalina assured Jill. "Dr. Grind said I could stay."

Jill smiled at Preston. "We would have left if you had said no," she told him, and Jeffrey quickly said, "Well, we discussed that possibility. It wasn't set in stone or anything."

"Jeffrey," Jill said, "he already said yes. It's fine."

Kalina stood and Jeffrey gave her a hug. The three fellows, arm in arm, walked out of Dr. Grind's office, and Preston understood that the family had expanded yet again and wondered if, as the project continued, how many other people would come on board, how else the world he had created would start to slowly transform into something beyond his control. It was, he knew from experience, not unlike a real family, the ways you accepted the uncertainty and kept your heart open for whatever might follow.

That night, after everyone had eaten and the children had been put to bed, Dr. Grind awkwardly invited the parents into one of the common rooms to discuss, as he called it, "a family matter," instantly feeling that this phrase sounded overwrought and silly, but he did not amend it. The parents arranged themselves on sofas and beanbag chairs, or leaned against the wall, a few of them holding wineglasses as if they were attending an open-mic poetry reading. Dr. Grind took a seat on one of the sofas and then felt too obscured and stood up to address the parents.

Just as he was about to speak, Harris said, "Are you shutting down the project?" Dr. Grind, dumbfounded, looked over at Harris, who was so pale it seemed that he had lost half of the blood in his body.

"No," Dr. Grind replied. "Absolutely not."

A few of the other parents audibly breathed out in relief and readjusted their positions in their seats. Harris, who Dr. Grind remembered had lost his last business to bankruptcy, then said, "You should always make that immediately clear when you call a mysterious meeting."

"Sorry," Dr. Grind said. "It's nothing like that, though. It's good news, truly. Dr. Kwon is pregnant." He noticed the looks of surprise on the faces of some of the parents, but he was more curious about the parents who seemed entirely unsurprised by this news. Julie, in fact, had her arms folded across her chest and merely nodded.

"It seems that some of you already knew this," Dr. Grind said. He then looked around the room as five or six parents nodded in agreement. "Kalina told you?" he asked. Julie shook her head and then said, "I just knew. You guys try so hard to keep your private lives separate from us, but we know things. We're observant." Nina then nodded and said, "It wasn't that hard to notice." Jeremy admitted that he'd had no idea, and Dr. Grind noticed that Julie rolled her eyes, which he filed away for later examination, as any possible signs of fracturing in the family.

"Well," Dr. Grind continued, slightly unsteadied by the reception to his revelation, "just so we're all on the same page, Dr. Kwon is pregnant, which signals a rather interesting shift in the dynamics of the family."

"Who's the dad?" Carmen asked. "Is she getting married?"

Dr. Grind scanned the room, looking at all the men, but one of them had an excellent poker face. "Well, that's complicated. The father will not be in the picture. Kalina will be raising the child on her own."

Link then raised his hand, and Dr. Grind, feeling awkward, gestured toward Link, who then said, "I'm confused. Is she going to stay?"

Dr. Grind hesitated for a second, trying to parse the emotions within that question. Was he the father? Did he want Kalina out of the project in order to keep his infidelity a secret? Finally, he said, "Well, that's what we're here to talk about. I'm afraid I didn't entirely plan for this possibility, but it strikes me as an extension of the work we're doing here. In my opinion, we should welcome Dr. Kwon's new child into the complex, to be an important component of our family."

There was a palpable silence in the room, and Dr. Grind felt that tinge of expectation, the knowledge that the bad thing was about to strike, too late to prevent it, but enough time to feel the dread of impending pain.

"I disagree," Link finally said, now standing up, his hand resting on Julie's shoulder. "A few of us have been talking about this development for a little while now, and I don't want to force anyone else to have to speak, but we agreed that it would not be in the best interests of our family, meaning the nineteen parents and ten children, the Infinite Family, to have this unknown element in the complex. You have to admit that it brings up quite a few difficult challenges to the project. As a researcher, I would think you would be a little more resistant to adding this unknown element into the project."

Dr. Grind then said, genuinely curious, "Link, when you say *unknown element,* do you mean Kalina's unborn child?"

"Yes," Link said. Link was perhaps the most easygoing member of the project, a man who radiated drum circles and *All Things Considered* and pot brownies. Dr. Grind, who'd naively assumed he could immediately sense the emotions of his family, quickly scanned the room and thought he could see agreement plain on the faces of at least five or six other parents. And he could feel the haze of confusion give way to a kind of righteous anger, a belief that he had given these people everything and they still weren't happy. It wasn't generous or empathetic, but Dr. Grind felt it hardening into fact, a black cloud that turned into a diamond.

"I'm mystified, honestly," Dr. Grind said, though he was doing everything he could to control his microexpressions, never letting his unhappiness curve the shape of his features into something that could be interpreted as anger. His face was flat and unknowable, but he knew it wouldn't last forever. "The whole point of the project was to create a larger, more inclusive family in order to be stronger."

"That's what we signed up for," Susan said. "We've made strong bonds and we've done what was asked of us, no matter how much it worked against our own instincts. But now you're changing the parameters. You're asking us to take on another child, even though we've been told that we could only have one child for the duration of the study. What happens to Dr. Kwon's child? Does she get her own set of teachers and caregivers? Do we go back to the sleep room in shifts to watch over the baby? It feels like there are a lot of exceptions that will be made for this child, when our own children were a collective that operated as a singular body. I don't know that I'm comfortable with that."

"And that's what you want me to say to Dr. Kwon?"

Link then said, "We are the Infinite Family. We are the family, Dr. Grind. Dr. Kwon and the other fellows, the caregivers and teachers, Gerdie, even Mrs. Acklen, help facilitate that family. But they aren't a part of it in the same way."

Dr. Grind could not bring himself to ask if he was inside or outside that Infinite Family. It was shocking to him, the fact that he had always considered the Infinite Family to radiate outward, not inward.

"This is what I'll say. I believe that Dr. Kwon is most certainly an important part of the work we're doing here. Her contributions have been invaluable in so many ways. She is directly responsible for a number of you even being here in the first place. She has found happiness, a child, and yet she wants to continue her work with the project. I cannot think of a good reason to tell her that, because she is having a child, she cannot participate in the same way. There is nothing, legally, in her contract that stipulates that she could not have a child."

"We're not telling her that she can't have a child," Julie said, speaking up. "We're saying that if she has a child, she'll need to move out of the complex and take on fewer responsibilities with the family. I don't think that's as cold as you're making it seem."

"Here is what we're going to do," Grind said, not even bothering to respond to that line of reasoning, wanting nothing more than to get the hell out of this room. "If this is a family matter, then you will vote on it. All nineteen of you get one vote. A yes means that Dr. Kwon stays on in her role as a fellow, and we make accommodations for the baby. A no means that Dr. Kwon will move out of the complex and I will change the nature of her work with the project."

"We're going to vote right now?" Nikisha asked.

"Yes," Dr. Grind said. "I need to tell Kalina the decision. I think to draw it out would be cruel." Dr. Grind reached into a drawer and retrieved a notebook and a box of pens. He tore out nineteen sheets of paper, taking absolutely no care to make them ordered and even, and handed these ragged sheets to each parent. "This will be anonymous. I'll wait in the hallway. Izzy, if you'll collect the votes and call me back into the room, we'll make our decision."

"No chance of a tie, at least, with nineteen of us," Link offered, which made Dr. Grind want to punch him in the face, a feeling he immediately regretted. Link was one of the best parents in the complex, so giving of his time, so kind. It mystified Dr. Grind that he was leading this charge; he could not conceivably believe that Link was Kalina's secret lover, his devotion to Julie was so complete. Was it just simple jealousy then? He wondered how many of these parents were secretly worried that their own place in the family, their own children, would be threatened by change.

Dr. Grind sat in the hallway and, nearly ten minutes later, so long that Dr. Grind had no idea how it would contribute to the outcome, Izzy opened the door and called him into the room. On the coffee table were nineteen folded sheets of paper. Dr. Grind scooped them up, rearranged them into a neat pile, and then tabulated the votes in the notebook. The first four votes were all no, and Dr. Grind nearly ripped through the paper as he notched each vote with his pen. But then a flood of yes votes came in until, a miracle that unfolded right in front of Dr. Grind, the yes votes overwhelmed the no's and the final tally, thirteen to six, meant that Dr. Kwon would stay.

"It's yes," Dr. Grind said. He saw Izzy smile and then quickly return to her serious expression. Link stared at the ground and then, in a manner that suggested an elasticity that Dr. Grind wasn't sure was entirely human, he smiled and looked back at Dr. Grind. "Okay," Link said. "That's all I wanted, a family decision. I'm fine with it."

The rest of the parents talked in whispers, slowly rising from their seats, the decision final. Link then said, as they walked out of the room, "I mean, I *like* Kalina. She's great. You know?" And though he was sheepishly smiling, Dr. Grind knew this was an event that would nag at Link, and whoever else voted to keep Kalina out of the family, especially the father of Kalina's child. Or had the father voted to keep her here, wanting to keep track of the child's development, to still be a part of the baby's life without anyone knowing his secret? It was too much to consider right now; all he knew was that the family was in danger of falling apart and he had to do everything that he could, even against his better judgment, to keep it together.

Dr. Grind stayed in the room. He went through the votes again, counting them out another time, thirteen to six. He counted again, thirteen to six. He tried not to imagine what would have happened if the votes had been reversed. It was a family decision, all nineteen parents. But Dr. Grind knew, deep in the secret places of his heart, that no matter what these nineteen parents decided, whether they liked it or not, they were his children, they were all his children, every man, woman, and child who resided inside the AstroTurf-covered buildings of the complex. And if they were his children, he was their father.

He would never tell Dr. Kwon what had transpired in this room. He would tell her, in the morning, that the family had enthusiastically agreed that she should remain a part of their family. He would keep everyone together, whether they wanted it or not. He thought about the time, when the duration of the project had ended, when he would extend his arms and let all of his children wander into whatever came next. He thought of how difficult that moment would be, but perhaps, a darker part of him wondered, it wouldn't be nearly as difficult as he thought. Perhaps, by the end of their time here, he would never want to see any of them again.

He carried the votes into his apartment and ripped them into confetti, the process taking far longer than he had expected, but he was fully committed to the action. He dumped the scraps of paper, a blizzard of paper, into the trash can. Then he walked into his bedroom, retrieved his dopp kit, and exorcised whatever demons he thought lingered inside him.

Dr. Grind placed a marshmallow on the table and Cap, sitting in a chair, watched it with great interest, as if it were a crystal ball that could tell him his future. "Now, Cap," Dr. Grind said, gesturing toward the marshmallow, "you can eat this marshmallow if you would like. Or, if you wait fifteen minutes, I will give you another marshmallow. So you will have two."

Cap nodded, understanding perfectly the terms of the experiment. "Now, I'm going to leave you alone, and I'll come back in fifteen minutes." Cap smiled and waved good-bye to Dr. Grind, who then stepped out of the room, into the observation room, where they could watch Cap through the one-way glass. Before Dr. Grind had even closed the door, Jill said, "He's already eaten the fucking marshmallow." Dr. Grind quickly turned toward the glass and looked as Cap chewed with great happiness, his face angelic. "Half a second," Jill said, observing the timer.

The Stanford marshmallow experiment was as basic and fundamental as you could get with regard to child development. The idea, cooked up in the 1970s, was that a child would be offered the immediate gratification of a marshmallow. However, if they could wait for fifteen minutes without eating the marshmallow, they would be rewarded with a second. The study had found significant correlations between those who could delay their gratification and their success later in life. Simply put, the kids who couldn't resist the immediate gratification of the first marshmallow trended lower in several categories than those who waited.

As the research fellows went through their research, with Dr. Grind serving as a mentor, they were now publishing articles in scholarly journals, developing data to support the foundational beliefs of The Infinite Family Project. Dr. Grind also wrote summarized examinations of these studies for publications like the *New York Times* and *Time* magazine and *Parents* magazine. In almost every study, the children were charting higher in many significant aspects than their peers outside the project, sometimes to such a degree that it wasn't entirely clear that the project itself was responsible. So when the children were finally of the age to undertake the marshmallow experiment, none of the researchers had thought much of it with regard to the outcome. They had talked of which children would excel and which children might find it more difficult. The fellows had even set up a rather complicated chart on which they bet on the children, which Dr. Grind discouraged but did not abolish. Dr. Grind himself had pegged certain children to be more likely to excel at the experiment. So, it was very disorienting to realize, now having tested all of the ten children, that not a single one of them had resisted the impulse to eat the marshmallow immediately.

The first child, Gilberto, had said, when questioned later by Dr. Grind, that he really only wanted the one marshmallow and he didn't think it would make sense to wait fifteen minutes for a marshmallow that he didn't want. And so, even if the outcome had not been what they had suspected, the researchers all seemed to justify Gilberto's actions as falling in line with mature, responsible logic. The experiment, they believed, was still sound.

However, Ally, the next child, had told him that she did not actually believe Dr. Grind would withhold the second marshmallow from her, even if she ate the first one before the time limit was up. She seemed genuinely mystified as to why he hadn't already given her the second one, and Dr. Grind had to work hard to not go ahead and give it to her anyway. Jackie had said that, if she wanted another marshmallow later, she would just ask one of her parents and they would probably give it to her. The other children had said much the same thing, that if they truly wanted another marshmallow, no matter what they did, they would not be denied.

After the fifteen minutes had passed, Dr. Grind returned to the room and Cap smiled and said, "It was a good marshmallow!" Dr. Grind nodded, trying to keep the grimness out of his demeanor, and then asked Cap why he hadn't waited for the second one.

"Because I really love marshmallows, and I really wanted to eat it," he said, almost laughing.

"But, Cap, because you didn't wait for the fifteen minutes, you won't get a second one."

Cap frowned. "What?" he said.

"You could have had two delicious marshmallows, but, because you didn't wait, you only got one."

"Could I try it again?" he asked.

Dr. Grind thought for a second. "Cap, if I put another marshmallow on the table and said you could have another one if you only waited, what would you do?"

"I would eat the marshmallow."

"Right away?" Dr. Grind asked, incredulous.

"Yes," Cap said, smiling.

"Why?" Dr. Grind asked.

"Would I be able to try the test again after that?"

Dr. Grind shook his head, shrugged, and then sent Cap back to the classroom with his friends. He turned to the mirror, unable to see the fellows, and again shrugged, genuinely mystified.

"So what do we do now?" Jeffrey asked.

"It's clear that they don't entirely adhere to the parameters of the experiment because they don't believe the parameters will hold up against their own desires," Dr. Grind said.

"They're spoiled?" Jill asked. "They're delusional? They're so used to living in a utopian ideal that they don't understand the concept of working for something?"

"No," Dr. Grind said. "All of our other testing shows that they are quite patient and have more than enough willpower under normal circumstances. They're able to share. They do chores in return for points, so they understand the value between work and reward."

"So, what's the explanation?" Kalina asked. "Have you simply found an experiment that the children are immune to? Did they break the experiment?"

"It broke us," Jeffrey admitted.

"I don't know," Dr. Grind said. "I don't think we have enough information to say."

"But to an outside observer, this does not look good for our work, for the children," Jill said. "They aren't capable of delaying their gratification for even two seconds. And they believe that the rules don't apply to them. That's bad."

"Under those limited circumstances, yes, it doesn't look good," Dr. Grind allowed.

"What do we do, then?" Jill asked.

Dr. Grind considered the options. He could send the results to Mrs. Acklen and to the various members of the advisory council for the project, could allow Jill to add the findings to the article that she was already planning on childhood development. They could administer the experiment again to determine if this was an anomaly. There were many possibilities, but Dr. Grind felt a gnawing irritation with all of them.

"We're going to hold off on this experiment," he finally said.

"Lose the data?" Jill asked.

"No, not at all," Dr. Grind continued. "We're not getting rid of the data. We're just holding on to it until it makes more sense. We're just going to take our time with it, keeping it among ourselves, until we know the proper context and how to best present it."

"That sounds problematic," Jeffrey said.

"It is," Dr. Grind said. "But we know these children. We know the framework that we have constructed to support them. And this experiment's outcome does not entirely make sense. So we're going to hold on to it until we find enough data that helps explain it."

"Okay," Kalina said. "We'll do the marshmallow test next year. And again after that. We'll see if the children develop a proficiency for the experiment, or if they continue to exhibit these same traits."

"Exactly," Dr. Grind said, feeling great relief to have someone else say it. "This is year one of a multi-year experiment."

The fellows nodded in agreement, though Dr. Grind wasn't sure exactly what else was implicit in the gesture. After everyone else had left, Dr. Grind continued to stare through the one-way mirror at the empty seat in the other room. Had he made a mistake? Were the children too protected, too spoiled? Was he alone responsible for any outcome? He reminded himself that he could not allow the luxury of doubt, the idea that he could simply try something else with this family.

And yet, here was a moment. Not enough time had passed that things were ruined. If there was doubt, he could pull the plug on the whole enterprise. It would take some explaining, and there would be hurt feelings, maybe even lawsuits, but he could stop it. But, he reasoned, either way, yes or no, there would be repercussions. And in one scenario, he would be alone again, even if he had made the right choice. In the other scenario, right or wrong, he would still be here, in the complex, with this family. It was not, he decided, worth the effort of contemplation. Whatever he had started, he would have to see it through until the end.

Three weeks later, Dr. Grind focused his attention on Brenda Acklen's visit to the complex. She had made it clear that, after her first visit, before the parents had come to the complex, she would stay away from the project, content to fund it and to hear from Dr. Grind about the state of the children's development and its effect on the parents. "You've made a family, Preston," she told him once over the phone. "Best to keep the money separate from that."

Still, for the benefit of both, they had included a clause that would allow either of them to back out of the project at the halfway point if things were not progressing in a way that made them comfortable. It had seemed a good idea at the time to Dr. Grind, who was worried about forcing himself to stick with the project even if the children and the parents didn't seem to benefit from the arrangement. It allowed him to admit defeat and not waste more of his life on a family that would ultimately fall apart. For Mrs. Acklen, it allowed her to pull the funding if she felt that the project wasn't fulfilling the goals she had outlined, however vague they were. The thought of losing the funding, if Dr. Grind slept regularly, would have kept him awake at night.

As a result, he had often entreated her to visit, wanted her to meet the members of the family, and he updated her every three months on the development of each child, substantial packets that included all the information that he and his fellows shared with each other. Nevertheless, she declined his invitations. "I'm getting slow in my old age," she would say, "it gets hard to go from the bedroom to the kitchen. I barely leave the house anymore." Still, she sent gifts to each of the children on their birthdays, vintage toys like Holly Hobbie rag dolls and Star Trek Inter-Space Communicators, so strange it was as if they had fallen out of some wormhole and into the complex. Each one came with a card that said, "With love, Aunt Brenda."

Now, as they approached the halfway point of the project, the parents soon to be reunited with their children for a more permanent familial arrangement, Dr. Grind argued to Mrs. Acklen that it was important for her to visit the complex to get a sense of what life was like, before she decided for or against continuing the project, especially since things would change dramatically in many ways once they moved on to their second-half goals for the project. Brenda finally agreed, saying she would come, along with her granddaughter Patricia, whom Dr. Grind had heard was being primed to take over as CEO of the company in the near future. "She wants to know what I've been spending all my money on," Mrs. Acklen told Dr. Grind. "I've kept most of my intentions close to my heart. Didn't want my own family to feel like they had disappointed me and I needed to make a new one."

Now that the day had arrived, a Sunday when all the members of the family were present, Izzy was again preparing a lavish picnic for the entire complex. The children played a game of lawn memory, where each of the children had made two identical giant poster-board works of art, set up facedown on the lawn. Benjamin and Asean served as the card flippers, and two teams of children directed them to different cards as they tried to match them up. The other parents listened as Link played guitar and Mary sang folk songs. There was also a group of some of the complex's specialized tutors, who worked with the kids and seemed fairly invested in the Infinite Family as a whole, as they sometimes would hang out during their off hours, playing with the kids, socializing with the parents, chipping in with chores when time allowed. It was, Dr. Grind admitted, a fairly compelling ad for the work he was doing. It seemed completely in line with the values of Acklen Super Stores, even if they were not exactly the kind of family that fit neatly into the demographics of Acklen Stores, Inc.

When Brenda Acklen arrived at the complex, Dr. Grind, who received a text message alerting him to the fact that she was in the driveway, didn't want to worry the others just yet, and so he simply slipped away from the party and walked out of the complex to greet her. The last time he had seen her in person, she had seemed youthful, below her actual age, a kind of rodeo gal who seemed entirely in control of her world, which extreme wealth could always provide. So it was shocking to see the driver open the passenger door, with a walker at the ready, and help Mrs. Acklen to her unsteady feet, her body swaying as she adjusted to being upright once again. She had lost a significant amount of weight, her western clothes hanging off her frame, but, as he walked closer to greet her, he saw the clarity in her eyes, the way she immediately steeled herself for his embrace. A smile came to her face, and she nodded at Dr. Grind. "Can't take my hands off this walker at the moment, so you'll have to do all the work here," she said as Dr. Grind gave her a cautious hug. Just as he was about to speak, he noticed a woman in her forties, dressed in a seersucker jacket and a vibrant orange scarf, hurry to Mrs. Acklen's side. "Hello, Dr. Grind," she said. He shook her hand and Mrs. Acklen said, "This is my dearest Patricia. Smartest person in the whole family."

"After you, Gramma," Patricia replied. "I'm very interested in the work you're doing here, Dr. Grind. I begged Gramma to let me see it firsthand."

"Welcome to the complex," Dr. Grind said.

"You're so young," Patricia said, as if Dr. Grind had lied on some form, her expression open but critical. "I expected someone much older."

"I told you that he was a kid genius," Mrs. Acklen said, as if irritated by Patricia's comment, and as if Dr. Grind weren't standing right there.

"I don't feel that young, unfortunately," Dr. Grind responded. "Certainly not when I'm chasing after ten little kids all day."

"I'd like to tour the facilities," Patricia said, looking past Dr. Grind as if he was hiding the children behind his back. He always avoided the impulse of making instant assessments, but he was unnerved by the focus of Patricia, the way she seemed to be silently making decisions about the future of the complex. It was in direct opposition to Brenda Acklen's ease and faith in Dr. Grind.

"Well, I need some food first," Mrs. Acklen said. "Food and a comfortable chair. Then we can meet these children."

There had been a serious discussion, in the week before the dinner, about serving another barbecued pig and how it might serve as a necessary lesson for the children. Jeremy had mentioned that he had some experience in slaughtering hogs and wondered if the children could see the entire process, from life to death to table. "The kids could really understand how connected we are to the food that we eat. How grateful we should be for the food that sustains us," he said, as if he had a pamphlet in his back pocket that would explain more if you wanted to learn.

"I don't want my kid to watch a pig get shot in the head and then make her eat it," Julie said, shaking her head.

"You don't shoot them," Jeremy said, his voice soothing and solicitous. "You cut their throats."

"No," Julie said.

"It's more humane than I'm making it sound," Jeremy offered, and then Ellen said that she thought it seemed like a good idea. "It feels like the way our forefathers would do things," she said. "And farm to table is very popular stuff right now."

Dr. Grind then said, "Ordinarily, I think we could talk through this more deliberately, but I want to bring up one aspect that perhaps we're not considering. If we kill the pig, and the children observe the act, we need to remember that our benefactor and her granddaughter, who is in some ways a stranger to the work we're doing here, will be here. I think we need to be careful about how we promote the complex to the larger, perhaps more skeptical world. While we might think this is a helpful lesson for our children to learn, we have to realize that we're representatives of the work we're doing here. If the children cry or are distressed by the event and they haven't shaken it by lunch the following day, how might outsiders, without the proper context, consider this event?"

"They'd think we were fucking up our already fucked-up kids even more," said Benjamin.

"The most unkind people would phrase it that way, perhaps," Dr. Grind said.

"It was just a thought," Jeremy said.

"Well, let's vote," Dr. Grind offered, and, though not as overwhelming as he had suspected the vote would be, the complex decided to table the idea of slaughtering pigs for the children's enrichment.

"I'll put together a menu that doesn't have any animals," Izzy said, more to herself than to anyone else, but Dr. Grind nodded his approval.

Izzy led Dr. Grind around the table, loading up a plate of food for Mrs. Acklen. "I can make her something else if she doesn't like any of this," Izzy told him as she spooned a serving of German potato salad onto the plate, already loaded with food. "It would be criminal to make something else with all this food," he replied. "You should give her the plate," Dr. Grind said, "since you made the food," but Izzy shook her head. "I'm not ready to meet her yet," she told him.

"She's the most normal and down-to-earth billionaire you will ever meet," he said, and gave her a gentle nudge toward the picnic table where Mrs. Acklen and Patricia were waiting. The three research fellows were making small talk with the two women, and Dr. Grind cleared his throat and handed each of them a glass of water spiked with cucumber. "This is Izzy, one of the parents. She made all the food."

Izzy set the plate down in front of Mrs. Acklen, who whistled long and low.

"I can make you something else if you'd like," Izzy stammered, but

Mrs. Acklen shook her head. "If I can't find something on this plate to eat, that's my fault," she replied. She lifted her fork and indiscriminately poked it into a mound of food. She took a small, careful bite and she seemed instantly relieved. "This is so good," she said. "What is it, now?" As she asked, she offered a bite to Patricia, who politely, but firmly, declined.

"It's grilled tofu with a wasabi-soy dressing," Izzy answered.

"It is so much better than that sounds," Mrs. Acklen remarked. She took another bite and then regarded Izzy. "I've heard a lot of good things about you, miss," she told her, which made Izzy blush. "You're an interesting case, I remember that from the beginning. I'm glad to hear things are going well for you."

"They are," Izzy said forcefully, as if she couldn't figure out how to accurately explain this to Mrs. Acklen.

"Keep it up," Mrs. Acklen said, then returned her attention back to her plate, and Izzy walked over to the rest of the parents, who were now keeping the party going, playing with the children, while also craning their necks to watch Mrs. Acklen.

Finally, as the fellows and Patricia awkwardly watched Brenda Acklen take tiny bites, steadily, never stopping, of everything on the plate, Dr. Grind noticed that Cap and Eliza and Marnie had broken away from the rest of the family, cards in their hands, and gestured for him to listen to a secret. The children seemed to be vibrating with excitement. Dr. Grind knelt and then Marnie whispered into his ear, "We made stuff for that old lady. They said we hafta wait, but we're going do it anyway."

Dr. Grind nodded in agreement. It seemed useless to try to keep the two parties separate any longer. He stood and then made eye contact with some of the parents, who had managed to wrangle and hold back the other children, before waving them over. The rest of the children came running, holding their cards like tickets to the greatest event in history.

"Lord have mercy," Mrs. Acklen said, smiling, slightly shocked, as the children approached her. Cap, in the lead, now seemed suddenly shy, as if his card was not actually worth of all this fuss. "You have something for me, sweetie?" Mrs. Acklen asked him, and he handed the card to her and then looked down at his feet. "We all have cards!" Marnie shouted. "They're beautiful!"

Patricia helped Mrs. Acklen open Cap's card, a watercolor of a giant, Godzilla-size woman assembling a skyscraper. "What's this, now?" Mrs. Acklen asked Cap. "It's you," he said quietly. "You're making our house for us."

"I love it," Mrs. Acklen said. "What's his name?" she asked Dr. Grind, who nudged Cap and the boy replied, "Cap."

"I love it, Cap." She gave him a hug, which made Cap smile, and he slipped away from the crush of kids, a dazed look on his face. One by one, the children handed their cards to Mrs. Acklen, who delighted in each one, especially Jackie's picture of a stick figure shooting dollar signs from her hands into the open mouths of little-kid stick figures. "She's busted it down to the bare essentials," she told Dr. Grind.

Patricia took the picture from her grandmother and frowned. "It's a little crass, though, even for a kid, Gramma," she said. Brenda Acklen waved off her granddaughter. "Patricia is a little skittish around children," she said to Dr. Grind, who could only nod. Patricia looked slightly sheepish and then shrugged. "They're very unpredictable," she admitted, as if she were talking about the stock market or tigers kept as pets.

When it was all over and the kids had been introduced to Mrs. Acklen, Ally returned to the table with another card that she had just made and handed it to Patricia. "What's this?" Patricia asked. "Another card for Gramma?"

Ally shook her head. "It's for you," she said. "So you can have a card, too." Patricia opened the card and then thanked the girl; Ally then ran back to the other children to play. Mrs. Acklen, watching the whole thing, announced that she was quite certain she had made a wise decision to fund this project. "These darn kids are so sweet, it makes you want to cry," she said, and Patricia nodded. Dr. Grind reminded himself to secretly give Ally a very expensive toy in the near future.

* * *

That evening, as the parents prepared the children for bed, Dr. Grind met with Mrs. Acklen and Patricia in his office. He and Kalina and Gerdie had spent almost a week creating a PowerPoint presentation as a last-ditch effort in case Mrs. Acklen decided to pull the funding and shutter the project. He turned his computer screen toward them and started the presentation. The project's revamped logo, a Möbius-strip-like design of stick figures holding hands, started to slowly spin on the screen, and Mrs. Acklen waved her hands as if surrendering just before a battle began. "Dr. Grind, I am so darn tired. Those kids wore me out, and I hardly even stood up. I just want to get back to the hotel and sleep and then get back to Knoxville. You do not have to sell me on anything else. I'm in. I'm still doing this. You have the full funding and the project will continue."

"Thank you so much, Mrs. Acklen."

"Mere formality. I had decided as much almost immediately after the project started. I know you're doing something special here, Dr. Grind. I had a vague idea of what I wanted, but you've taken it much further than I ever anticipated."

"Thank you, again."

Patricia then motioned to Dr. Grind and said, "But I would still like to look over this information, just to see exactly how the money is distributed and, if you'd like, I could offer my own suggestions from an outsider's perspective."

"Of course," Dr. Grind said.

"I'm so happy, Preston," Brenda said, smiling. Dr. Grind was about to thank her when she continued. "The problem, unfortunately, is that I am dying," she said, not even the slightest change in her voice, the most beautiful and calm assertion of her own mortality. "I've got cancer, quite a bit of it, and it's going to be awful."

"Gramma, it's going to be okay."

"Well, I have enough money that I might survive, but it's going to be awful either way. If we're being honest, Dr. Grind, I probably won't survive till the end of this project."

"I'm so sorry, Mrs. Acklen," Dr. Grind said. He felt a deep, disorienting fuzziness overtake him, as if he had just finished holding his breath for three minutes. He focused and tried to stay present in the moment.

"It's fine. I've had the best life of probably anyone in the entire history of the world. It's been very good for a very long time. The reason I'm telling you this, Dr. Grind, is not to make you sad or to worry you. It's to let you know that, even if I die before the project ends, it will continue to be funded. You will have complete control over the project and can continue to run it as you see fit. On our end, Patricia is going to help deal with the particulars. I've stressed to her how deeply I feel about this project."

Patricia then spoke up, saying, "I see real potential for The IFP, something that shifts the paradigm in ways that will be beneficial for all involved."

"So," Mrs. Acklen continued, "no matter what happens, you'll be safe. Patricia will be your liaison and she'll make sure you get what you need. I do wish you the best of luck. It's unique, what you've made here, so I hope you can keep it going."

"I'll do my best," Dr. Grind assured her.

"And what about the postdoc fellows?" Patricia then asked.

"What do you mean?" Dr. Grind replied.

"When would I talk to them? It seems that it's necessary for me to have contacts with the people who work for you, to receive some sense of how you're performing."

Dr. Grind stiffened; it seemed disrespectful to be discussing this before Brenda Acklen, who was dying, was actually dead. "I guess that could be arranged," he allowed.

Brenda interjected, "This is Dr. Preston's show; he chose the families and he chose the fellows. Everything comes through him. That's how we've done it and I aim to keep it that way. He's the one I trust."

"Okay, Gramma," Patricia said, smiling so hard that it erased the frown Dr. Grind could see if he looked hard enough. "You're the boss. We do it your way. I was just trying to open lines of communication for more effective management."

"Never mind that," Brenda said, done with the subject. There was a moment of silence, the awkwardness settling in the air.

"What will you do when it's over?" Patricia suddenly asked him, as if she'd been waiting to offer this question the entire day.

"What do you mean?" he asked.

"What are your plans once the project ends and the families disperse?"

"I haven't thought about it very much, to be honest. I suppose I'll look into continuing the study, setting up more rigorous testing to decide the outcomes. And the families won't truly disperse, I believe. They'll stay in contact with each other, remain a large part of each other's lives. That's the hope."

"And you'll continue to be a part of their lives?" she asked, as if the idea was slightly troubling to her.

"In some way, perhaps," he said, embarrassed to be saying this aloud. He had truthfully not discussed the end of the project with any kind of definitive outlook for the future. He had avoided the strangeness of what would happen to these children, to their parents, once the families left the complex and began their own lives.

"Of course he'll be a part of their lives," Mrs. Acklen said, smiling, reaching for Dr. Grind's hand. "It won't end, will it, Dr. Grind? It will keep going, just in different ways."

"That's right, Mrs. Acklen," Dr. Grind replied.

"I wondered if *Infinite* was just a kind of grandiose word," Patricia said.

"It's not," he said, surprising himself by how certain he sounded.

chapter fourteen

the infinite family project (year six)

Izzy woke to find Cap sitting on the floor by her bed. He was reading a book, taking bites of an apple, completely oblivious to her presence. Izzy leaned over the bed and rubbed his hair to get his attention. His hair, sandy blond and wild, hanging down over his face, hadn't been cut in years. Izzy remembered when the children had experienced their first haircut at age two, driving them all to a hair salon in Murfreesboro. One by one, the children had climbed into the chair and watched, almost stricken with bewilderment, their own reflection in the mirror as the stylist clipped their hair into new shapes and styles. Each child was then given the clipped hair in a plastic bag for their memory boxes. Izzy remembered that Cap, on the way back home as he placed his hand inside the open plastic bag, rubbing the hair between his fingers, had forcefully declared that he did not want to experience a haircut ever again. And since the children were still being collectively raised, no single parent to decide that their own child needed a haircut, the decision had been left to the children. Some of the kids wanted monthly haircuts, while a few, Cap being one of them, opted to never have their hair cut again. As a result, Izzy had always loved watching Cap's hair whip around when he played with the other children, the way he would frantically sweep his bangs out of his eyes as he chased after another kid. He looked slightly feral, but his calmness, his thoughtfulness, belied that wild look. Now, Izzy lifted his bangs so that she could make eye contact with him. Looking into his light brown eyes, she smiled, and he returned the expression.

"How long have you been there, buddy?" she asked him, and he thought for a moment and then flipped through the pages of his book. Holding the read pages between his thumb and index finger, he held up the book for her inspection. "This long," he said.

In the first month after being reunited with Izzy, Cap had trouble sleeping on his own, which was a common problem for all the children, so used to sleeping in the communal bedroom with each other, and so he would often crawl into her bed at some point in the night. A therapist had worked with all the kids, using a Sleepeasy program involving books and night-lights and noise machines and "sleep zones," but the children were used to the sound of ten bodies sleeping in unison, of waking to find their brothers and sisters surrounding them. As Dr. Grind emphasized, only the passage of time would alleviate the stress and, in time, it did. The first time Cap slept through the night in his own bed, Izzy was surprised by how saddened she was to not find him beside her, however necessary the development was.

Izzy lay on the bed, watching her son as he returned to his book. They had a little more than an hour before Izzy would take him to the main building to meet up with the other children, all of them now in kindergarten, for their lessons. "You want some breakfast?" she asked him. He nodded and then offered, "Fruity Pebbles?"

"When did you have them last?" she asked him.

"Last week," he said, and so she nodded. Though the complex stressed healthy eating, and Izzy herself was responsible for setting up the weekly menus, she had managed to bring a box of Fruity Pebbles into the house, her favorite cereal as a child, and shared it with Cap, who was instantly mesmerized by the radiant, neon colors of the cereal. A single bowl of the cereal was more sugar than he'd probably had in his entire life up to that point, but she had wanted something special for him, a treat. And it wasn't as if sugared cereals were forbidden. There were no restrictions on diet, but most of the parents seemed set on continuing the healthy eating that had been stressed when the children were living communally. No candy or fast food, obviously, but Link and Julie admitted that they gave Eliza Kit Kat bars on special occasions and Irene once informed some of the family that her dad had given her a packet of Pop Rocks one time and the other children were immediately jealous. Of course, this was the new way of living, the way the children and their parents, while still part of the larger family, had made a hidden life for themselves within the complex's homes. And so, Izzy allowed Fruity Pebbles and felt no less a good mother for it.

"Fruity Pebbles it is," she said, and Cap cheered, jumping to his feet and running to the kitchen. Izzy swung her feet onto the floor and followed her son, listening to him hum "You Are My Sunshine" as he gathered the bowl and spoon and a napkin to set the table. Izzy reached into a cabinet and, in the very back, she retrieved the box of cereal and poured a generous amount into the bowl, the skittering sound making Cap shake with excitement. Izzy returned to the table with the almond milk and soon Cap was powering his way through breakfast, still humming, his legs pumping. Izzy made herself a cup of iced coffee with concentrate from the fridge and she sat at the table with Cap. The breakfast table was strewn with Magic Markers and paper, as Cap had been drawing the night before, several pictures of an idea he had for an amusement park where kids wore jet packs and flew around. She held up one of the drawings, the sign for the park announcing it as FLY WORLD. One child's jet pack had apparently caught on fire and the child was hurtling to the ground, but there were staff members waiting with a trampoline to catch her. "It's a good thing you made sure there were trampolines at Fly World," Izzy said to Cap, pointing to the faulty jet pack in the picture. Cap shrugged as if to say, *Of course you need trampolines if you're going to run a successful jet-pack amusement park.* "Even though the jet packs sometimes blow up," he said, so earnestly that Izzy felt her heart flutter, "nobody ever dies at Fly World."

At the mention of death, Izzy waited to see if Cap would once again bring up Hal. For the past seven months, ever since Cap had been reunited with Izzy and he had realized that it would be only the two of them instead of the traditional families of the other children, Cap would often ask about his father. And Izzy was dismayed and slightly embarrassed to realize that she didn't have much to offer in the way of answers to Cap's questions. He would ask what Hal's favorite food was and Izzy, who honestly had no idea, would try to remember any food that Hal ever ate. It was like walking through a fog into a world that Izzy could not entirely believe had really existed. Her time before the complex, before the Infinite Family, felt, for better or for worse, like a punishment that she had endured and was now free of. She did not even have a picture of Hal when she moved into the complex, but had found a few pictures online and printed them off for Cap. She had considered e-mailing the Jacksons and asking for more pictures and details of Hal's life, but decided that involving Mr. and Mrs. Jackson in her new life, especially since they had never once contacted Izzy after Cap's birth, would be a mistake. And so Cap and Izzy made their way with what little Izzy remembered of Hal. His penchant for soda in glass bottles. His fondness for the Velvet Underground. His easy humor and genuine kindness in the classroom. Whatever she gave Cap, it did not seem to be enough. Before, he had nine other dads, plus Jeffrey and Dr. Grind and all the other male staff members who would come to the complex, but now, in the transition, it was as if he had lost a permanent claim to those men, and now it was just Cap and Izzy, no father to speak of. A few times, Cap, making peace with his new situation as best as he could, would say to Izzy, in confidence, that he would sometimes make-believe that Dr. Grind was his father. "I know he's not my real dad," Cap then admitted, "but he's, like, my number one pretend dad." Izzy had no strength to argue or try to find a sensitive way to expand the topic. She merely nodded and said, "I know exactly what you mean."

Now that Izzy had graduated from college, with a bachelor's degree in art that she could not imagine putting to any use, she had moved into the kitchen at the complex to work full time. Chef Nicole had decided to leave to start her own restaurant, and Izzy had taken over as the head chef, and she loved the idea of staying close to home, to be near Cap and the other children.

Of course, now that the families had broken into individual units, the work was a little less involved. Families ate breakfast in their own homes, so Izzy was only responsible for the children's snacks and lunches and the entire family's dinners, which were still a communal affair. She missed Nicole, who had given Izzy a new set of knives as a present when she left, but she enjoyed the quiet of the kitchen and having access to any ingredient she could want and all the freedom to make the menus.

The children's snack was due at 10 A.M., so Izzy baked some seasoned kale chips, chopped carrots into sticks, and scooped out individual portions of cashews. She also used the juicer to make a beet squeeze juice that the kids loved, a mixture of beets and apples and ginger. Once she had arranged the food and drinks on trays, she took them into the classroom, where the children were waiting.

They were lifting various toys using a fixed pulley, as the science teacher, who came three times a week to work with the kids, watched over them, cheering as each child lifted the toy of their choice with the pulley. When the children noticed Izzy, or, more important, the snacks she was holding, they cheered. Irene let go of the rope and a sock monkey flopped back to the floor. "Snack time," the teacher yelled, and she went over to her desk to prepare the next project while Izzy sat on the floor, the children surrounding her, and handed each of them a bowl of food and a cup of juice. Cap and Jackie sat in her lap as they ate their snacks. Even with the separation of the children, Izzy was happy to see the ways in which the kids still treated the other adults with such affection. And she was also pleased, in moments such as this, where she held on to both Cap and another child, splitting her attention, that Cap was more than willing to share her. As they all finished their snacks, Irene showed Izzy her new pair of glasses, pink and white stripes, and Izzy told her how wonderful they looked, which made Irene smile. The teacher came back to the group and called them to attention. Each child gave Izzy a hug and placed their cup and bowl back on the tray.

"Say thank you to Izzy," the teacher instructed the children, and Izzy felt so happy to hear the chant, in unison, of "Thank you, Izzy," with the slight disruption of Cap, who said, "Thanks, Mom."

Just as Izzy was about to leave, she heard Marnie come up to the teacher and inform her that she had forgotten to bring her observation journal from home. They were about to begin a new series of experiments, so Izzy volunteered to retrieve it. The kids waved good-bye and Izzy returned the tray to the kitchen before she jogged down the stairs and ran across the courtyard. The weather had turned overcast, gray, with impending rain, and Izzy watched a string of prayer flags flutter in the breeze from atop one of the play spaces.

Izzy came to the house of Ellen and Harris, and knocked on the door. Harris was at work, but Ellen was home; Izzy had seen her this morning from the front steps as Marnie joined the group of kids to head to school. After thirty seconds, Izzy knocked once more, but still no one came to the door. She looked through the window and saw the journal lying on the coffee table, Marnie's book decorated with neon paint and so much glitter that it looked radioactive.

The family was fairly informal when it came to boundaries, having grown used to the preponderance of communal spaces, so that it sometimes bled into their own houses. Izzy never locked the door of her own house and Carmen or Link would often walk in unannounced to borrow ingredients or check to see if their child was playing with Cap.

Izzy tried the door, found it unlocked, and walked into the living room. Just as she picked up the journal, she heard the sounds of moaning, someone in the throes of nausea, the volume of it troubling, suggesting an emergency. Before she could keep herself from it, she called out, "Ellen?" She heard all sound immediately cease in the bedroom. And Izzy would later wonder why she remained in the living room, still holding the journal. She wondered what she thought was going to be on the other side of that bedroom wall. "Harris?" Izzy then said, now feeling like a kid detective on a case that was way beyond her abilities. The bedroom door opened, and Ellen appeared, wearing a sweatshirt and no pants, her face Mars red. Behind her, kneeling on the bed, completely naked, was Jeremy.

Ellen shrugged, and the motion caused the bottom of the sweatshirt to rise just enough so that Izzy could see the bush of Ellen's pubic hair. "You know, don't you?" she asked Izzy, and Izzy shook her head. She held up the journal, as if it could exorcise demons. "Marnie . . . ," she said, and then fell silent.

Ellen shook her head with disgust. Izzy started to retreat to the door, but now Jeremy was pulling on his jeans and stood with Ellen in the living room. "Come here, Izzy," Jeremy said. "Let's talk about this."

Izzy saw that Ellen was now crying, her tears so silent, almost without effort, that it unnerved Izzy to the point that she was paralyzed, could not retreat to the door or come to a love seat, where Jeremy was motioning for her to sit.

"No," Izzy finally said, unable to say anything else, feeling a sick kind of certainty, suddenly wondering why something like this hadn't happened sooner.

"This is exactly what it looks like," Jeremy said. "I'm not denying anything. I just want you to listen to us. We need to talk to you."

"You can't tell Dr. Grind," Ellen said, and then she immediately looked at Jeremy. "She's going to tell him. I know it."

"Sit down, Izzy," Jeremy said. "Please? Izzy? Please fucking sit down and listen."

Izzy finally moved to the love seat. "How long has this been happening?" she asked.

"Two years," Jeremy said, and Ellen nodded.

"Who else knows?" Izzy asked, hoping, strangely, that everyone else already knew, that she was the last to find out.

"No one else," said Jeremy. "Well, Harris and Callie know. We never kept it from them."

"And they're okay with it?" Izzy asked, incredulous, feeling like she was improvising a soap opera.

"Yes," Ellen said. "We're not hurting anyone, okay? You can stop staring at us with those goddamned Precious Moments eyes."

"We're all adults and we're all making our own decisions," said Jeremy.

"This is temporary, until the project ends. We want Eli and Marnie to have all the opportunities that they deserve, but we deserve our own happiness, don't we?" Ellen said. "Then, when the project is over, Jeremy and I will take Marnie and Eli and we'll start a new life and—"

"Ellen, please," Jeremy interrupted. "Not now."

"Why does it matter at this point?" Ellen said.

"Just please, Ellen," Jeremy said, resting his face in his cupped hands, breathing deeply.

There was silence in the room, all three of them unable to continue. Izzy gripped the journal so hard that she thought it might burst into flames. She prayed for it to burst into flames, to provide a distraction so that she could run out of the house.

"You can't tell anyone," Ellen said. "Not Dr. Grind. Not Carmen. No one."

"Okay," Izzy said, saying only what she thought would get her out of this situation.

"Do not be the reason that we all get kicked out of the project, Izzy," Jeremy said. "Do you want to be responsible for Eli and Marnie having to leave the family? Do you want to break this family apart?"

"No, of course not," Izzy said, feeling very much like the entire affair had been her fault, that her carelessness, not Ellen's and Jeremy's, had caused this.

Ellen finally laughed, a ragged little breath of irritation and wonder. "You just had to come see me today," she said to Jeremy. "You couldn't wait until tomorrow when I'd come to the farm."

Jeremy looked very much like a man who was just now realizing the choices he had made in his life; he looked so much older. "Ellen, please," he said, once again.

Ellen looked at Izzy. She seemed almost grateful to have someone else to talk to. She waved off Jeremy with the flick of her wrist and then said, "I remember when we first moved here, a lot of us women were not exactly thrilled that you were coming to the complex, a single mother, like you were some kind of free agent. Some of us worried that you would try to take one of our husbands. It was kind of a thing for a few months and then everybody realized that you were really sweet and not a psycho and it was going to be okay." Ellen laughed and then said, "Honestly, I was the one who was most upset about the possibility of you stealing Harris from me."

Izzy looked back at those first few months at the complex, but couldn't remember any tension with the other men and women in the family. Perhaps it was because that first year was so strange, regardless of whether people were worried about her status as a single woman, everyone trying to get used to the idea of being a new parent, of adjusting to life in the complex. Still, she felt the residual embarrassment of having been talked about, of being singled out, and then she reminded herself that the real issue was with Ellen and Jeremy.

"I have to go," Izzy said, holding up the journal, forever holding up that fucking journal. "I have to get back to the kitchen."

"I told Marnie not to forget her journal," Ellen said, shaking her head.

Izzy left Ellen and Jeremy on the sofa and walked out of the house. As she closed the door, she did it so carefully and quietly, as if she was sneaking out of the house undetected, that she had not been discovered, that she had not discovered them. Outside, the wind had picked up and the prayer flags were flapping crazily; they looked like people falling out of the sky, rag dolls suspended in the air.

Izzy returned the journal to the classroom; Marnie gave her a hug in thanks, but Izzy could not bear to return it. She stood in the hallway, all alone, the walls vibrating with the sounds of the children expanding into the world. She looked toward Dr. Grind's office, knew he would be in there, and she started toward it, but then pulled up short. She could feel her heart expanding and contracting. She thought about the entire family, a collective, a single form. It was a mistake to keep it a secret, would only delay the inevitable. One day Callie or Harris would grow angry with the situation. Marnie or Eli would discover Ellen and Jeremy and tell all their brothers and sisters. Or one of the other parents would find out, as easily as Izzy had, and they would go straight to Dr. Grind. But Izzy wanted only to hold on to what was good in her life. She would not be the one to potentially ruin it. She returned to the classroom and watched the children, furiously scribbling in their journals, rubber balls bouncing across the room, so much motion that it felt like it was the children, and the children alone, who kept the world spinning on its axis.

A short time later, back in the kitchen, Izzy was checking over the ingredients for that night's dinner when Callie knocked on the door. Izzy felt the revelation of Jeremy and Ellen seize up inside her before she recovered and waved her in. Callie held up a basket of green beans from the farm, as well as some soft-neck garlic. While Jeremy and Callie had originally worked the garden at the complex, they had saved up enough money from Jeremy's construction work and Callie's odd jobs to buy some acreage a few miles away to start their own farm, selling their vegetables and meat, all organic, to local restaurants and farmers' markets. Izzy was one of their best customers, using whatever they had harvested in her dishes, finding the quality to be unmatched.

Callie, so shy and reserved, simply pointed to the invoice that she'd placed on the table, and Izzy nodded and signed off on it after checking over the vegetables. Callie turned to leave, but Izzy, as if overcome by a muscle spasm, reached out for Callie's arm, which made the woman flinch. She remembered what she'd said to Jeremy and Ellen, her promise to keep it a secret, but Izzy could not resist, needed to know for herself what the stakes were.

"Callie," Izzy said. "Are you okay?"

Callie finally made eye contact with Izzy and held her gaze for a few seconds. Finally, stuttering, she said, "You know, don't you?"

Izzy nodded and Callie backed away from her before she seemed to weaken, the tenseness in her shoulders finally relaxing, and she walked over to the counter and leaned closer to Izzy.

"Who told you?" she asked.

"No one," Izzy replied. "I found them. In . . . in bed."

"Who else knows?" Callie said, her stuttering becoming less pronounced.

"Just me," Izzy said.

"Jeremy is a real complicated person, okay? He is a good man, but he has his own issues. He hasn't really been the same since he lost his family's farm. He became a lot more closed off after that, kind of wounded. I was the one who begged him to come join the project. I thought it would help us to be around other people. And he did get better, happier, and then I found out why."

"What are you going to do?" Izzy asked her.

"What we've been doing since it started," Callie said, shrugging.

"Really?" Izzy asked, confused.

"You're not going to tell Dr. Grind or the fellows, are you?" Callie asked, a flash of something wild in her eyes, her stutter returning with force.

"No," Izzy said.

"Not even the therapist," Callie continued. "I don't know if she reports to Dr. Grind or not."

"She can't tell anyone else, Callie," Izzy said, believing that the therapist all the parents met with monthly had to abide by doctor-patient privileges. "So you haven't even told her about it?"

"No," Callie said. "But Ellen wants to, of course. She wants to tell everyone. She wants Jeremy all to herself. She wants Eli, too. But she won't get them. Or she won't get them to herself. She doesn't understand that Jeremy has enough space in his heart for more than one person. We'll just wait until the project is over, to do what's best for Eli, and then we'll move on to what's next."

"That's a long time to wait, Callie."

"I'm patient," Callie answered.

Izzy, knowing now that there was little she could say or do, simply nodded and returned to the vegetables. Callie, however, remained standing in front of Izzy, staring at her. Izzy, unnerved, finally looked up again.

"We've started saving up for a house to build on our farmland," Callie said. "When the project ends, Jeremy wants to have the families stay together, to live together, and share the responsibilities. He's got it all worked out in his head. You'd be welcome to join us, if you wanted. It'd be good for you and Cap. Jeremy thinks the world of you, Izzy. You wouldn't be left alone when all of this is over."

This was the most talking that Izzy had ever heard from Callie, perhaps more than during the entirety of their time in the complex up to this point. And now Izzy, herself unaccustomed to revealing much of herself to another person, found it difficult to respond. There was something cultlike in what Callie was proposing, the way she seemed to be an agent for Jeremy's own desires to take control of the Infinite Family, but Izzy also thought she was perhaps being paranoid. To an outsider, the project itself seemed like a weird commune, so who was she to question what Jeremy and Callie might be planning for the next stage in their lives? But Izzy knew she wanted nothing to do with it. And yet there was Callie, still standing there, the only other woman who was nearly as tall as Izzy, waiting for a reply.

"I'll think about it," Izzy said, which was as close to the truth as she could muster up, knowing she'd be thinking about Callie and Jeremy and Ellen and Harris and Eli and Marnie and, goddamn, the entire family for quite some time to come.

Callie turned and walked out of the kitchen, leaving Izzy alone, now realizing that she needed to get lunch ready for the kids. She considered the green beans and garlic in front of her and then pushed them aside, feeling embarrassed that the food from Jeremy and Callie's farm would now seem slightly tainted, ominous. Still jittery from the morning, wanting only to return to her own house with Cap in tow, Izzy instead turned to food, one of the few things in her life that made everything tolerable, or at least easier to ignore.

By the time the children came into the dining hall, Izzy had taken the lunches to the table and found Dr. Grind and Dr. Patterson already there, interacting with the kids, listening to them explain another science project they had performed as to whether boys or girls were more ticklish on their feet, recording the results in their science journals. Izzy sat down next to Maxwell, as Cap was already next to Dr. Grind and Jackie, and listened to the conversation.

"Boys are less ticklish on their feet," Cap pronounced. He held up his science journal and showed a page that had pictures of stick-figure boys and girls, as well as a fairly good drawing of a foot. Then there were numbers and check marks in various boxes, as well as a graph that didn't seem to correspond to any of the figures. Dr. Grind accepted the journal and looked over the data very carefully.

"Interesting work," he proclaimed to the kids. "We'll need more data, of course, but this is a great start."

"Can we tickle *your* feet?" Jackie asked, and the other kids shouted with joy.

"For science," Eli shouted, and the other kids joined in.

"SCI-ENCE, SCI-ENCE, SCI-ENCE," they all chanted, Dr. Patterson now joining in, patting Dr. Grind on the back. Izzy watched as Dr. Grind's face quickly reddened and he looked around the table for help, finding none.

"Well," he said, fumbling for something to say. "Perhaps not while we eat."

The kids groaned. Izzy kept staring at Dr. Grind. *Right now,* she kept thinking. *I will tell him right now,* but then the moment passed, a new moment already occurring, and Izzy would again muster up the courage to tell him only to have it deflate.

The buzzing in her ears was so loud that Izzy wondered if the children could hear it. To remove herself from her own anxiety, Izzy spoke up. "You can tickle my feet after lunch," she said, and the kids cheered.

Jill then said, "Me, too!"

Dr. Grind finally put down his fork and shook his head. "And mine as well," he allowed.

He looked over at Izzy and smiled. "For science," Izzy said, shrugging.

After lunch, the three adults slipped off their shoes and socks and the kids chose Ally to do the tickling. Cap kept the records of the experiment in his journal. It turned out that Jill was quite ticklish, almost immediately pulling her foot away from Ally, giggling loudly. Dr. Grind, of course, wasn't ticklish at all, allowing Ally to run her fingers up and down the sole of his foot without even the slightest change in his demeanor. When it came to Izzy, she relaxed her body and the children craned their necks and bunched together to watch Ally slowly tickle Izzy's foot. The sensation ran up her leg and she began to smile, her leg slightly shaking, and she started to laugh. The children hooted and hollered, and Cap furiously scribbled in his journal. "Girls are more ticklish," he said to the adults, who nodded, unable to refute the evidence.

The children then took their trays back to the kitchen and Izzy, Jill, and Dr. Grind began cleaning up the dishes from lunch. Jill wiped down the counter and talked about a concert that she had attended with a few of the staff members the night before, while Izzy and Dr. Grind washed and dried the dishes, Izzy handing off the plates to Dr. Grind, who dried them and carefully returned them to the cabinet.

Later, Jill left the kitchen to retrieve one of the children for some individual testing, and Dr. Grind then leaned against the sink and told Izzy that he had some news for her.

"I talked to Nicole yesterday. Her restaurant is doing well, finally making some money, and she asked about you."

"That's kind of her," Izzy replied. She had taken Cap and Maxwell to the restaurant, Golden Apples, a few weeks after it had opened, and Izzy had been mesmerized by the adventurousness of the menu, and yet how delicious it had been; even the boys had happily eaten everything served. Nicole had come to their table and seemed wired, smiling more than Izzy had ever seen her do at the complex. "It's destined to fail," Nicole had told her. "Running a restaurant is a different beast than being a personal chef, but it's so much fun. It's constant madness, which I like. And, who knows, maybe it will last."

Dr. Grind then said, "Nicole wondered if you might like to take on an apprenticeship at the restaurant. She said it would be a chance to gain experience in a real working kitchen."

Izzy was surprised by the offer, but could not help but wonder about the work. She was already handling the kitchen duties at the complex. She also had Cap in her life, and didn't want to lose that time, see him even less than when he was part of the larger family.

"How would that work?" Izzy asked.

"Well," Dr. Grind continued, "you could work a few nights a week, whatever would fit your schedule."

"But what about the kitchen here? What about Cap? I'd be out most of the night. Where would he stay?"

"We can help out," Dr. Grind reminded her. "We can all chip in with dinner on the days that you're away. As for Cap, he can stay with other parents on those nights."

"Then I wouldn't be with him when he woke up. He'd be in another house."

Dr. Grind thought about this for a moment. It seemed obvious by his now worried expression that he had not expected this response. "Well, I could stay with Cap," he finally offered. "In your house. I'll just bring my work with me and stay with him until you get back from the restaurant."

"I can't ask you to do that," she said.

"You know I don't sleep anyway," he said. "I'll stay with Cap and get him ready for bed and watch over him."

"It's very kind of you," she said, reaching out to touch his arm. "But I don't think I can do it. I'm just getting used to the changes in my life. I like cooking for the family. I don't want to take on too much work and lose what makes this place so special to me and Cap."

"I just don't want you to turn down opportunities, because you're the only person here without a partner to help you," Dr. Grind said.

"I don't feel that at all," she replied, though of course it was an ever present concern; she couldn't figure out how to explain that to Dr. Grind, who had done so much to help her that it seemed greedy to whine about it. She imagined coming home from Nicole's restaurant, at two or three in the morning, and looking in the window of her house to see Dr. Grind waiting for her, reading a book, sitting on her sofa as if he lived there, Cap safely asleep upstairs. She thought of it and it felt like the best kind of dream. It was natural, she imagined, to love Dr. Grind, to want him to be a part of her life in such a way, and she couldn't help but feel, especially with his offer to watch Cap, that he perhaps felt the same way. She wondered, knowing she would never do it, what would happen if she leaned over and kissed him. She then thought of Jeremy and Ellen, the slight fractures already forming in the family. It wasn't clear if their indiscretion would be seen as worse than Izzy making out with the founder of the project. She didn't wish to find out.

"Well, if you change your mind," Dr. Grind said, trying to smile, slightly disappointed, "the offer stands. From both Nicole and myself."

"Thank you, Dr. Grind," she answered,

This was the moment, Izzy knew. If she didn't tell Dr. Grind about Ellen and Jeremy right now, this very moment, she would lose the chance. Of course, she knew that she could tell him later, but it wouldn't mean the same thing. It would still be a kind of betrayal, though she wasn't sure exactly who would be betrayed and how. All she knew was that Dr. Grind expected and encouraged honesty, the easiest way to solve a problem, and she had a planet-size problem. But she knew she would say nothing. She simply let the moment pass, the easiest action in the world, and, the kitchen now clean, nothing left to do, the two of them turned off the lights and went their separate ways.

That evening, after dinner, all ten of the children crouched on the floor and silently watched as Kalina and her daughter, Grace, rolled a red rubber ball back and forth to each other. If the ball slipped away from Grace, one of the other children would frantically rush over, scoop up the ball, and bring it back to the other nine kids, who would wrestle over it until Izzy, who watched the whole thing with teeth-gritted embarrassment, would walk over to them, arms open, and demand the ball. They would begrudgingly hand it over. "You guys can play with Grace, you know," she told them, but they pretended not to hear. Izzy handed the ball back to Kalina and smiled. "Tough crowd," Kalina said, though Izzy could see the pain on her face. "It'll pass," Izzy said, but she honestly wasn't sure.

Though everyone had hoped for a seamless transition for the new family in the complex, and even if the parents had for the most part allowed for the change, the children had balked at the presence of a new baby. When Kalina had presented Grace, wrapped in a blanket, radiating pink, so tiny, the children had looked with great trepidation at the child. Izzy had heard Maxwell whisper, shaking his head as he slouched away, "Ugly baby." Whenever Grace cried at dinner, the children would all dramatically place their hands over their ears and mime irritation. "We're all one family," Dr. Grind once told them, as if this would solve anything. The children all nodded, like "duh," and went back to sullenly eating their food.

One night, Izzy had asked Cap why he was so opposed to Grace's presence in the complex. He had ignored her, kept coloring at the table, until she took the crayon out of his hand and asked again. He wouldn't look at her, but he replied, "One is not better than ten. One is not more special than ten." Izzy then said, "But isn't eleven better than ten? Isn't that how you should think of it?" Cap merely shook his head, too aggrieved by this suggestion to even argue with her. "Mom," he said, exasperated, shaking his head.

While there were fewer moments of outright hostility, and some of the children could be affectionate and kind with Grace when they were alone with her, there seemed to be an impossible resistance to expanding the family. And so, six weeks later, Kalina quietly enrolled Grace in a play group in Murfreesboro; when she finally revealed the shift to the rest of the complex, she said, "I think Grace would be happy to broaden her connections, to have kids her own age."

"That sounds like a really good idea," Jackie said, and the other children wholeheartedly agreed. And, with that, the family receded just slightly, but enough to understand the excision that had occurred.

Izzy couldn't help but feel like they had failed Kalina and Grace, that the entire point of the project was to open themselves up to the possibilities of family, that by increasing their numbers, the love would compound and everyone would benefit. And yet, there was little Izzy could do to stifle the competing feeling that she could not share her family more than she already had, that maybe her heart was finite.

As the parents cleared the table and washed dishes, Link caught Izzy's attention and gestured toward the edge of the dining hall, so they walked to the empty space. Izzy had always liked Link, his good humor and laid-back, slightly stoned demeanor. Since he was a stay-at-home dad and helped out a lot with the children during the day, she saw him often throughout the week. He pointed to Cap, who was clapping his hands, watching with delight as the ball ricocheted around the circle.

"You've got a little prodigy on your hands, I think," he told Izzy.

"Really?" Izzy asked.

Link had volunteered to teach the music classes and they had moved from drums to piano to stringed instruments.

"He did really well during the month we studied the piano, but he didn't seem overly interested in it. The drums were the same. But once we started the ukulele, he was super intense about it. He picked it up faster than any other kid. He can do actual songs now."

"That's incredible." Izzy said. "He never really talks about it."

"Well, you know, I'm working with Eliza on the piano individually because she has a real aptitude for it. And Ally and Gilberto are meeting with me outside classes to work on the drums, but I wondered if you might want me to work with Cap on guitar."

"I'll ask him," Izzy said. "But I think that would be great."

"These kids," Link said, shaking his head. "They're scary good at stuff."

"Better than us," Izzy admitted.

"I'm scared of the day they don't need us," Link said. After a sudden pause, Link started to tear up, his expression one of complete shock.

"Sorry," he said, but Izzy embraced him and told him it was okay.

She looked back toward the crowd of people and saw Ellen watching her and Link, which made Izzy break the embrace, suddenly self-conscious.

"Ask Cap to play something for you," Link finally said. "He's awesome."

Once the kitchen was clean, the parents each found their child and walked together into the courtyard, the families disappearing into their own separate houses. Izzy and Cap hung back, walking slowly, hand in hand, until they were the last people in the courtyard. She looked back at the main building and saw Dr. Grind watching them from the entrance. She waved to him and he waved back. When Cap saw the doctor, he broke from his mother, ran back to Dr. Grind for a hug, and then sprinted back to Izzy. Finally, they stepped into their house, all the lights on, as if someone was waiting for them to return.

After bath and story time Cap sat on the edge of his bed, while Izzy sat on the floor facing him. He strummed a few chords on the ukulele and then took a deep breath. "'You are my sunshine,'" he sang, his fingers easily making the simple chord changes, "'my only sunshine. You make me happy when skies are gray. You'll never know, dear, how much I love you. Please don't take my sunshine away.'"

And suddenly, as if someone had layered her past memory over this moment and marveled at the similarity, she remembered a moment with Hal, lying in his bed, when she had noticed a guitar sitting in the closet of his bedroom. "Do you play?" she had asked him, and he shook his head, seemingly irritated that the guitar had made its presence known, as if it were a stray dog that kept invading his space.

"Not really," he said.

"But you play some?" she asked him.

"I guess," he said, and she could see his face scrunch up, the tiny tics moving across his skin, his aggravation with the whole damn world, and she quieted and rested her head on his chest to calm him. After a few minutes of silence, he said, "You want to hear something?" and she nodded. He swung his feet onto the floor and gently picked up the guitar. He returned to the edge of the bed and quickly tuned the guitar before he expertly strummed the strings with such precision that it seemed to Izzy it was a kind of magic trick. In a soft, but gruff, voice, not Hal's real voice at all, he began to sing, "'Oh, I'm sailin' away, my one true love. I'm sailin' away in the morning.'" He played the entire song, about a man and a woman, about separation, Spanish boots of Spanish leather. It was, to Izzy, the most beautiful thing she had ever heard. When Hal finished, he placed the guitar back in the closet, softly closed the door, and stood over Izzy. "That was so beautiful," she told him. He shrugged. "Not that beautiful," he said. "That motherfucker leaves her, doesn't he?" and Izzy realized that she hadn't really listened closely to the song, and she wanted him to sing it again. But she was afraid to ask. And, she now realized, she never heard him sing another song, not another note strummed on that guitar.

Cap frowned when he finished the chorus and then paused for a second. "The rest of the song is kind of sad, actually," he said, his face so serious, as if he did not think that Izzy could handle the lyrics in her current state.

"That's okay," she assured him, wanting only to hear him continue to play; as she stared at the concentration on his face, the seriousness of his actions, she could see Hal so clearly. Was this a new development, she wondered, or was Hal always there in her son and she chose to ignore it to save her heart from breaking? So much of Cap came from Izzy, her genes so insistent on possessing her son entirely that they had taken over the construction of the boy, but there was Hal staring back at her and, though of course it made her sad, it felt like a gift that she would never have given to herself, one that she would always love.

"I'll just sing the chorus a few more times," he finally allowed, and Izzy nodded her approval, trying to keep from tearing up until he returned his attention to the song, and then Cap played the chorus once again, then a second time, then three times. Each time he reached the end, Izzy would smile and clap, which would start Cap again. He sang the chorus for the fourth and fifth time, then a sixth. Izzy felt like they could stay like this forever, just the two of them, forever each other's sunshine in the middle of the night, and she clapped and clapped and then Cap asked her to sing with him and so she did. They sang in unison, and sometimes Cap would speed up the music and other times slow it down to a funeral dirge, before returning to the normal rhythm. Finally, long past the point that Izzy kept track of the song, Cap stopped strumming. "My fingers are a little sore," he admitted, and Izzy leaned forward and embraced him.

"I love you," she said.

"I love you, too," he replied, holding the ukulele away from his body to keep it from getting in the way of their hug.

"You are an amazing boy," she told him.

"Am I?" he asked, genuinely curious.

"You are," she said.

"Good," he said, satisfied with her assessment.

She took the ukulele from him and placed it carefully on his dresser. Then she turned off the lamp and she leaned against his bed. In only a few minutes, she heard the easy, steady breathing of her son, already asleep. She knew she needed to leave the room; she still had work to do, but she lay against the bed until she began to drift into sleep, knowing that, when he awoke, she would be right there.

chapter fifteen

the infinite family project (year seven)

Ten members of the Infinite Family Project claimed two rows of chairs at Parnassus Books in Nashville, each of them holding a copy of Julie's new novel, *An Artificial Family*. Link was standing in the back with a camcorder and several children were hanging out in the children's section of the bookstore, playing with a train set and reading picture books about dragons, a newfound obsession of the family. Izzy sat next to Dr. Grind and watched as Julie sipped from a water bottle and talked to some of the audience members in the front row. The bookstore was nearly filled with people, some of them, Izzy noticed, openly staring at the Infinite Family, smiling at them as if to show that they were progressive enough to approve of their situation.

Izzy returned her gaze to the novel in her hands, a hardcover book with a light blue cover featuring a wooden dollhouse filled to overflowing with Fisher-Price Little People figurines from the '70s. On the back of the novel, there was a picture of Julie, standing in front of one of the AstroTurf-covered buildings of the complex, looking more serious than Izzy had ever seen her in real life. The photographer had wanted to include all the members of the Infinite Family in the background, but several of the adults had balked at this idea, the weirdness of it, as if Julie had adopted them or ruled over them. The ad copy on the back cover began: *A novel about a unique kind of family, from one of the members of The Infinite Family Project,* which had given Julie fits at first, the way the publisher demanded that her status in the project be part of the promotional materials. "I was a writer before the project, you know," she said, exasperated, at dinner one night.

The novel itself was about a woman in her forties who has inherited a fortune after her parents pass away in a plane crash. Without any family now of her own, no husband or wife, no children, no brothers or sisters, she decides to hire a group of actors to play her family. Soon, she hires more and more actors, until she has an extended family of thirty people, some of whom she only sees once a year. She eventually falls in love with one of the actors who plays her brother and they end up marrying and having children of their own.

To Izzy, who had read, like most of the Infinite Family, galleys before the book had been released, it was a weird kind of postmodern fairy tale. It was also, thank god, fairly removed from the actual Infinite Family, which had been a worry of many of the members of the project when they heard the title of the novel. "The publisher wanted that title," Julie informed them immediately after showing them the cover, her face pink with embarrassment. "It's pretty darn close to the Infinite Family, isn't it?" Harris asked, his face smiling in a Silly Putty way, but no one else commented on the similarity. At least not at the table, not in front of Julie.

And yet, there were enough people in the family who felt ill at ease with Julie's book, not only from outright jealousy but also from a feeling that Julie was using the Infinite Family as a promotional tool for her own career, no matter how often she said otherwise, the way she was, whether they wanted it or not, pulling them into the spotlight.

"When you get down to it," Nikisha said to Susan and Izzy one night, "she and Link were the two people who needed the project the least. They weren't poor, Eliza wasn't an accident, they already had their own careers." Nikisha ticked off each detail as if she were a lawyer in the midst of a closing argument. Nikisha was, to Izzy's mind, one of the smartest people in the family, had an uncanny ability to recall perfectly anything that she had read, was unbelievably capable and seemingly impossible to unsteady, so Izzy could not help but fall into agreement with her, even if, hours later, alone, she realized that she actually didn't think that way.

"It's like the project is their own experiment," Nikisha continued, "one that just Link and Julie are conducting, and we're just lab rats."

"I don't know," Susan said. "They had just as many reasons as we did to join, and Julie's always been one of the biggest cheerleaders for the project. Should she give up writing because it might make us uncomfortable?"

"I like Julie," Izzy offered quietly.

"What if this project was just a long-term investment in her career? She becomes the most visible member of the Infinite Family; it becomes her brand. If someone is going to write a book about this place when it's all over, who do you think is going to do it?"

"Are we allowed to write a book about it?" Susan asked. "Legally?"

"Even if it's not a memoir. What about another novel? Don't you think she's been taking notes?" Nikisha offered, not bothering to answer Susan's question. "Do you think we'll turn out to be characters in her next book?"

After one of the bookstore employees introduced Julie, she stepped up to the podium to fairly boisterous applause. The book, only out for two weeks, was already at nine on the *New York Times* bestsellers list, well reviewed in numerous newspapers and magazines. There was talk, Julie admitted, of film rights being negotiated. Julie, wearing a plaid shirt and blue jeans, her red hair pulled back in a ponytail, read from the first chapter, where the main character, Anna, one year after her parents have died, puts an ad on craigslist for two actors to play her parents. Once she finished reading, she took questions from the audience. One woman in the front row asked if living at the complex and participating in the project had helped her writing. Julie frowned, thinking over the question, and then said, "Well, it gave me more time to write as a new mother than I would have had otherwise. But, on the other hand, there were times when I wanted to focus on the book and there were just so many people around, so many wonderful people, I might add, that it was hard to find time for myself. I don't think of the project as something that helped me as a writer; I think of it as something that helped me as a person."

A man then asked if she would be sad when the project ended. "Yes," she said, looking at the group of people from the Infinite Family, smiling. "But I'll also be happy to see what comes next. I think it will be a good thing, too." She then shrugged, as if to apologize for her honesty, but Izzy completely understood what she meant, the appreciation for the larger family, but the feeling that there was an unknown future that would only open up after they left the complex for good. It seemed, now that they were more than halfway through the project, that it was harder and harder to avoid the understanding that the Infinite Family, despite its name, would eventually end. And it was even more difficult to properly analyze how they felt about this, if they should be guilty for wanting to move on to what was next or if they should be terrified to be leaving their family behind.

Once the Q and A ended, Julie signed books and the rest of the family members hung around in the children's section with the kids, finding it very strange to stand in a line to have Julie sign their own books. The kids were beginning to grow bored in the bookstore, their bodies needing some new distraction, and so the adults promised them doughnuts, even if it would spoil their dinner. The five children, Irene, Cap, Eliza, Gilberto, and Jackie, all cheered and began to put away the shocking number of books they had pulled from the shelves and scattered across the floor. Dr. Grind walked behind them and plucked every third or fourth book to purchase for the complex's library. Link sneaked over to Julie to tell her to meet them at the Donut Den after she had finished meeting with her fans, and the rest of the family walked out of the bookstore, all of them holding books, excited to be out in the city on a weekend afternoon, as if it was an adult version of a field trip.

At the Donut Den, the children all chose the pink sprinkled doughnut, each one warmed in the microwave, pink icing smudging the fingerprints of the kids. The adults chose coffee and glazed doughnuts, though Asean tried a maple-bacon doughnut and Izzy, slightly embarrassed but determined to get what she wanted, ordered a pink sprinkled doughnut for herself and was instantly gratified by her decision. Julie joined them, giddy from the reading, and Link handed her a doughnut as if it were a Pulitzer Prize. Izzy and Nikisha stood with the children who were, a single doughnut in their systems, already becoming slightly manic from the sugar, so happy and elated to be out in public. "It's been a good day," Link said, his tone that of a man who always expected happiness, and Izzy admitted that, even with her innate anxiety to never expect things to work out, she would not deny the string of good days that stretched out in front of her.

They arrived at the complex, and the children immediately ejected themselves from their booster seats, climbing over the seats to burst onto the pavement, running toward the doors of Main 1. Izzy walked slowly, hanging back with the adults. She had been given the night off from kitchen duty, and she enjoyed listening to the other parents talk about the bookstore and how well Julie had read from the novel. Suddenly, Izzy looked down and realized that she had left her copy of Julie's novel back at the Donut Den. And, once again proof of her ease in this world that had been constructed for her, she did not begrudge the loss for even a second.

It was controlled chaos in the dining hall, the children who had stayed at the complex now listening to the children from the excursion describe the pink frosting on the doughnuts as if bringing back stories of strange beasts from an undiscovered country. Ellen walked up to the parents from the field trip, her face smiling so hard it looked as if a device had been implanted in her mouth. "Jeremy and Callie are making dinner," she said, her voice high and quavery. "Just the two of them." The parents, except for Izzy, simply smiled and nodded, and, when no one spoke, Ellen shrugged and then said, "They look so damn happy in there!" She then walked away, moving through the children as if they were currents of warm and cold air. Izzy immediately searched the room for Harris, who was sitting at the table, alone, drinking a beer. She watched him for a few seconds and noticed the way he kept scanning the room for Ellen, his eyes narrowing before he took another swig from the bottle of beer. Ellen then walked back toward the kitchen, peeked in, and exclaimed, "How's it going in there? Smells good!"

Izzy found Carmen and took her aside. "Does Ellen seem like she's acting strangely?" she asked. Carmen looked around the room until she finally saw Ellen, who was now standing behind Harris, though neither acknowledged the other one. "No," Carmen said. "Why? Is she acting strangely?"

Izzy shook her head. "I don't know," she lied. "I guess not."

Carmen looked at Izzy, cocked her eyebrow. "You seem to be acting a little strangely," Carmen said.

Izzy laughed as authentically as she could manage. "I ate a doughnut," she said. "I think it had a lot of sugar in it."

"You didn't bring any for the rest of us?" Carmen asked, and Izzy simply smiled and walked back to the children, not composed enough to actually interact with them. They were playing a makeshift game of kickball, and Izzy gave them enough distance to stay out of harm's way. She wanted so badly to pull the fire alarm and evacuate the entire building. She wanted to go to Dr. Grind and tell him that there was a bomb in the dining hall that was going to go off. But she realized that she had lost the opportunity to share her secret. It was too late. And nobody else, save the two couples caught up in the affair, knew what was coming.

"Dinner's served," Jeremy shouted as he and Callie emerged from the kitchen, holding up a baked ham as if it was going to be baptized. The children and parents all clapped as Jeremy carried the ham to the table. Callie awkwardly held three baskets of fresh-baked bread, and, as soon as Jeremy had placed the ham on the table, he retrieved two of the baskets from Callie and kissed her forehead. Watching closely, Izzy noticed that Callie did not smile at this affection, only nodded in assent. Izzy, as if watching a tennis match, then swung around to see how Ellen would respond to Jeremy's action. Ellen, still smiling in such a painful way that Izzy wanted to rub her own cheeks, slowly backed out of the room, taking tiny steps, as if practicing a dance she'd only heard about secondhand. Just as she reached the doorway, Harris stood up and gestured for Ellen to join him at the table, but she shook her head and disappeared. Izzy waited for someone to retrieve her, but Harris merely sat down next to Marnie, helping her order her silverware, and Jeremy and Callie helped serve the rest of the dishes that they brought from the kitchen. "Sit down, Mom!" Cap shouted, and Izzy smiled. She tried several times to make eye contact with Harris, but he would not meet her gaze, though Izzy had no idea if this was intentional or not. She sat between Cap and Gilberto, the two boys each demanding that she butter a slice of bread for them, and soon she was caught up in the activities of the meal, food being passed around, the garbled happiness of the children's nonsense.

Occasionally she would look over at the head of the table, where Jeremy was sitting, Eli and Callie on either side of him. Callie was not eating, only taking infrequent sips of water, and she kept her hands in her lap. Izzy caught Jeremy reaching under the table at one point, to take her hand, which Callie allowed, though she closed her eyes. He stared at her until she opened them and they both smiled.

As dinner was winding down, dessert mere minutes from being served, Ellen returned to the dining hall, her arms rigidly held at her sides, her eyes puffy and red.

"Ellen?" Dr. Grind said, rising from his seat.

"I love you," Ellen said, staring at the head of the table. Izzy looked to Jeremy, who shook his head and stared down at his empty plate. Callie kept her eyes closed, hands still in her lap.

Harris finally stood up, said, "Okay, Ellen, that's it," but Ellen moved closer to the table and said, "I love you, and I don't understand why you don't love me anymore." Jeremy still wouldn't look up, though he now reached again for Callie's hand and held it tightly.

"Ellen, please," Harris said, now standing next to her; Dr. Grind was now standing as well. "Ellen," Dr. Grind said, "let's do this away from the children."

"I have to leave the family," Ellen declared. "I can't be around all this if I don't have him."

"No one has to leave," Dr. Grind said. "I don't know exactly what's happened, but we can work it out."

"Mom?" Marnie said. "Why are you crying?"

"I took a lot of pills, those pills I got after my dental surgery. I took all of them," Ellen said, her face temporarily brightening with the certainty of her action.

Dr. Grind took hold of Ellen, held both of her arms at the wrist, gripping her tightly, as Jill and several of the parents ushered the children out of the room; the children were now shouting that they didn't want to go, that they wanted to stay.

"Harris," Dr. Grind said, "help me take Ellen to the hospital. Everyone else stay here, watch over the kids. No one else leave. We have to sort this out."

"What's to sort out?" Ellen said, her voice far away and dreamy. "We were supposed to run away, take the kids and start over, but he got scared or something. He couldn't leave Callie; he couldn't leave Dr. Kwon, who he fucked, did you know that? He couldn't leave his little garden. He chose all of you over me."

"That's not true," Jeremy said, his voice loud and indignant. "She's lying. I never slept with Kalina."

"Jeremy, please," Dr. Grind said.

Dr. Grind looked genuinely mystified, as if the members of the family were all much more complicated and yet much dumber than he had ever thought possible. Harris and Dr. Grind were now awkwardly walking Ellen out of the dining hall, and Izzy ran toward them.

"Can I come with you?" Izzy asked.

Dr. Grind declined her offer. "I think you better stay with the children. With something like this, the more people available at the complex, the better."

Izzy wanted to tell him what she knew, the details of Ellen's situation, but she imagined his disappointment, the chance that Izzy had caused all of this to happen with her silence, and she instead simply nodded and stood rooted to the floor.

"What the fuck?" Asean said to Jeremy, who shook his head, constantly denying something that no one else fully understood, and took hold of Callie as they walked out of the dining hall.

Izzy saw a group of people standing in the children's classroom; the kids were now arranged around Marnie, who was sobbing, both of her parents now gone, as she sat in a beanbag chair in the middle of the room. Without speaking, the children maintained a protective barrier around Marnie and held hands, sometimes resting their heads on each other, their bodies calm and quiet. Jill was sitting on the sofa with Jeffrey, watching the proceedings, while the parents gathered in groups to talk. Jeremy and Callie were nowhere to be seen.

"Ellen and Jeremy?" whispered Kenny, looking around at the other parents for reassurance that this was bizarre. Kenny turned to Paul, Harris's best friend in the project, and said, "Did you know?" Paul held up his hands in surrender. "No way," he said. "I mean, Harris talked a lot about trouble with his marriage, that things weren't getting better, but he never said anything about an affair."

"Did anybody else know?" Kenny asked, but no one said anything. "How do you miss something like this?" he asked, dumbfounded. Finally Carmen rubbed his shoulders and said, "Maybe we can talk about this later."

Jeremy and Callie showed up, each of them holding a duffel bag. Jeremy held back at the end of the hallway while Callie walked over to the other parents.

"Callie," Carmen said, "are you okay?"

Callie didn't respond to the question, only said, "We're leaving for tonight. We need to be alone. We've got a little yurt that Jeremy built at the farm; we'll stay there. I'm just going to get Eli. We just can't be around this right now."

"Maybe Eli should stay here," Kenny said, but Callie was already past him, walking into the classroom. The other parents followed her into the room.

"Eli, let's go. We're going to camp out tonight," Callie said, clearly uncomfortable with how many people were watching her. Her stutter was pronounced and nonstop.

"No way," said Eli, retreating into the crowd of children, who shielded him from Callie. "Please, sweetie," Callie said, nearly crying.

"I don't want to leave my family; you guys hurt Ellen and I'm not leaving until she comes back," Eli said, who had never fully given himself over to Callie after the formal introductions, who had always wanted Ellen more, and this made Jill stand up. "Let him stay here tonight, Callie."

"Jeremy thinks we need to be together, just the three of us," Callie said.

Jeremy now pushed his way past the other parents and walked into the classroom. "Eli, let's go. Now," he said sternly.

"No," said Maxwell, who put himself between Jeremy and his son. Marnie took hold of Eli and the two of them held each other. Now Asean and Paul walked up behind Jeremy and put their hands on his shoulders. "C'mon, Jeremy," Asean said, "don't do this."

Jeremy shoved his hands into the mass of children, as if reaching into a river to retrieve a fish, but the kids slapped at his arms, and Asean pulled Jeremy, nearly lifting the man off his feet, away from them. "That's it," Asean said, carrying Jeremy away from the children, Jeremy's feet dragging soundlessly across the floor. Even in the tense atmosphere, Izzy was awestruck by how effortlessly Asean moved Jeremy toward the door.

Finally released, Jeremy pushed away from Asean. "I didn't mean for this to happen," he said.

"You should have thought about that before you fucked Ellen," Paul said, anger blazing on his face.

Now Jill and Jeffrey were pushing all of the adults out of the room. "Out, now!" Jill shouted, and the children started to wail. The adults spilled into the hallway and Jill shut the door, the two fellows tending to the children. Jeremy, surrounded on all sides by people who suddenly hated him, backed away, Callie next to him. "This place," Jeremy muttered, gesturing to the walls, the sky, all of the other parents, "it's so confusing." Then he and Callie turned and disappeared down the stairs. The hallway was crowded with all the parents, like the floor of the stock exchange, everyone revolving around and around, reminding themselves of what was left, of their new situation.

Just as the parents were about to return to their children, Jill stood in the doorway and then shushed the parents into silence.

"Okay, here's the deal. They don't want you guys around right now. The best way I can put it is that they feel betrayed. Some parents brought some real shit into their world and now they want all of you away from them for a while until they figure out what to do."

"Well, I'm staying here," Julie said, and Link agreed, as well as a few others.

"For now, guys," Jill said, "let's give them their space. I'll let you know as soon as something changes."

Izzy turned to head out of the hallway, and the others soon followed, Julie the last to leave. They holed up in the dining hall, each of them sitting around the table that now felt empty and pockmarked.

"They don't want us," Kenny said, shaking his head with disbelief.

"Can't say I blame them," Paul replied, his face red with embarrassment.

Finally, after 10 P.M., Jill came into the dining hall and faced the parents. "Okay, they're leaving the room, but they want you guys to stay here for a while," she said, but Julie and Link immediately ran out of the room and down the stairs. The other parents followed, over Jill's protests. The parents stood in the courtyard and watched as each child went into their own house, Ally staying with Marnie, and returned with sleeping bags and pillows and flashlights, each one shining in the darkness of the courtyard. They marched past the parents, who were now stunned into silence, and walked back into the main building, up the stairs, the parents following them as if in a trance. The children opened the door to the room that had once been their communal bedroom, which had now been turned into a music room, due to the soundproofing of the walls. The parents hovered around the window that looked into the room and watched as the children moved all the chairs and tables and instruments to the outer edges and then laid down their sleeping bags in the middle. Cap came to the door and taped a sign that read KEEP OUT to the window. Then the children turned off the overhead light and lay in their sleeping bags, each one so close to the other that they seemed to be sleeping on top of each other.

The parents slumped against the walls of the hallway, couples embracing, except for Izzy, who was, as always, the only parent on her own, no one to hold on to.

Against the silence inside the communal bedroom, the parents kept their voices low, keeping their sadness from radiating too far from their own bodies. Izzy felt the strange mixture of exhaustion and anxiety putting her in a state of near hypnosis, unable to focus on much of anything that was going on around her, though the other parents seemed touched by the same feelings, everyone slightly drugged and yet unable to close their eyes.

Dr. Grind finally returned to the complex, Izzy hearing his footsteps on the stairs. He appeared before the parents, looking as tired as Izzy had ever seen him, his red tie no longer around his neck, his hair ruffled and sticking up like a child's on Christmas morning.

"She's okay," he finally said, his voice soft and clear, the slightest hint of emotion wobbling the words. "They pumped her stomach and she's in no danger at the moment."

"Where's Harris?" Paul asked.

"He's staying at the Hospitality House there at the hospital," Dr. Grind answered. "He's going to be with Ellen tomorrow and then the hospital is going to release her and she's going to check herself into a mental health facility to deal with her situation."

"Which is what exactly?" Susan asked. "I still don't understand what's going on."

"Well, Jeremy and Ellen have been having an affair," Dr. Grind said.

"We know that much," Carmen offered, but Dr. Grind seemed not to hear her.

"It's been going on for a while, but apparently Ellen has been pressuring Jeremy to leave altogether. She wanted to start a new life away from the complex. She wanted to take Eli and Marnie. When Jeremy refused, Ellen became a little more antagonistic, according to Harris, who has been aware of this for some time, by the way. Tonight, when she saw Jeremy and Callie making dinner, it caused her to make an attempt on her life."

"What happens when she finishes her time at the facility?" Julie then asked. "Does she get to come back to the complex?"

"In a perfect world, yes," Dr. Grind said. "To remove Ellen from the family would remove Harris and Marnie. I don't want that to happen."

"Well," Julie said, emotion breaking her voice into a higher octave, "I don't know if I want Ellen here, to be honest. I don't know if I want Jeremy here either."

"We're a family," Dr. Grind said, "an imperfect one. I think we're testing the limits of what that means, unfortunately."

"I think we might be past that, Dr. Grind," Julie then said.

"Let's try to think of the present moment," Dr. Grind said. "Let's try to be kind, as much as we can be. We need to make our kids—"

"*Our* kids," Julie said.

Dr. Grind paused, wincing at the wording. "Of course. Your children need to feel safe, and so we need to try to stick to our routine as much as possible, to make them understand that, while bad things happen to those we love, we can rally around each other to make us all stronger."

"They won't even let us in the room," Asean said.

"And I see that you are all respecting that," Dr. Grind replied. "That's fine. Be ready for when they do want you to come back to them. It could be tomorrow or it could be days from now, but we have to show them that we can be there for them."

Izzy had not fully understood this particular problem of collective parenting. It was wonderful when a child could look to every adult in the project and think of them as their parent. But, for Izzy, it suddenly dawned on her with a hopelessness that she could not control that if one parent betrayed a child's trust, then, in the eyes of the children, every parent had betrayed them. No matter how good a parent Izzy might be, if one of the other parents fucked up, it would be her fault, too. Equal attachment, she understood, worked both ways.

"I'm going to get us some blankets and pillows," Jill said, and Jeffrey went with her. The parents returned to their spots on the floor, leaning against the walls, while Dr. Grind, taking deep breaths, trying to be calm, walked past them and disappeared from view, gone to his own apartment or perhaps to wander the grounds, as Izzy had seen him do countless times in the past.

After Jill returned with an armload of blankets and pillows, she and Jeffrey now returning to their own apartments, the parents began to settle into their spots on the floor. Nikisha, however, suddenly stood up and ran down the hall to the art room. She came back with a piece of red construction paper and a black marker. She knelt on the floor and drew a large heart and the words, *We love you kids so much*. She then signed her name. She handed it to Asean, who signed it, and then passed it to the next parent. Eventually, everyone had signed his or her name. Nikisha then took the paper and slid it under the door of the music room. "It's something," she offered, and the other parents, now exhausted, agreed. Just when it seemed, having done all they could think of to win their children back, that they would begin to fall asleep, they found themselves too wired to get comfortable.

"Should I get some booze?" Link offered.

"Maybe that's not a great idea, sweetie," Julie then said.

"I'll make some coffee?" Kenny suggested, and then Susan stood and said she would make some popcorn and get some chips. The rest of the parents now stretched, afraid to leave their spots in the hallway for somewhere more comfortable, in case the children came out of the room. Izzy, however, still too jittery from what she knew and her own guilt, told the others that she wanted to take a walk, to burn off some of this energy. They nodded and Carmen gave her a hug, and then Izzy was off. She took a few steps down the stairs and then stopped. She sat down and thought of Dr. Grind, knowing he would still be awake. She thought of that moment, when Julie had reminded him that he was slightly outside the experience that the parents were undergoing, the way he had been momentarily stunned by the admission. She went back up the stairs, past the hallway where the parents were now talking softly, and she stood in front of Dr. Grind's door. She tapped as lightly as she could, as if testing the thickness of a sheet of ice, and waited for a few seconds before the door opened. Dr. Grind was standing in front of her, his hair combed back into place, his tie, having been removed before, now in place and properly knotted.

"Izzy?" he said.

"I need to tell you something," she said, walking past him into his tiny living room. It was the first time she had ever seen the inside of his apartment. The walls were entirely bare, no TV or stereo, the entire room empty except for a sofa and a coffee table, which was covered with folders and files. The carpet was so properly vacuumed, the lines so precisely military, that it seemed as if no one walked on it, as if Dr. Grind hovered an inch above the ground, and suddenly Izzy was afraid to move.

"What's going on?" Dr. Grind said, folding his arms across his chest, his head slightly tilted as if he was hard of hearing. "Now is not the best time, perhaps, Izzy."

Izzy stared at the rigid tension of his jawline, his eyes darting back and forth from her to his bedroom, the door closed. She looked at his arms, which were crossed over his chest, and then she noticed his right hand, twitching slightly. It was streaked with blood, staining the cuticles of his fingers.

"You're bleeding," she said, reaching for him.

He shrugged and then took a step back. "It's nothing," he said, wiping his hand on his pants, leaving the slightest stain, his hand not actively bleeding, which made Izzy even more uncomfortable, having walked into something private, when she had all but assumed that there was nothing in Dr. Grind's life that required secrecy. It unnerved her in such a way that she blurted out, "I knew about Jeremy and Ellen."

"What?" Dr. Grind asked, his face impassive.

"I knew that they were having an affair and that Ellen wanted to leave the complex with the kids."

"Oh, Izzy," he said, nodding as if he understood her own worries.

"I didn't tell you because I was afraid of what would happen," she continued, feeling a weird lump forming in her throat, that hated sensation of impending tears, the way she had to screw up her face to make the words coherent. "I didn't want the family to fall apart, so I just didn't say anything. I hoped it would all resolve itself and things would stay the same. And now Ellen is in the hospital and the kids won't talk to us and I feel like it's my fault. I did something terrible." She barely finished speaking before she started tearing up, which angered her because she wanted to be clear and straightforward with Dr. Grind, and she pushed the edges of her palms roughly against her eyes, pressing her hands against her face so hard that it felt like sandpaper, as if she could strip away her own emotions if she simply applied enough pressure. Just when she thought Dr. Grind might walk over to her, to comfort her, she heard him shout, loud enough that it temporarily stopped her tears.

"Fuck! Goddamn it, Izzy," he said, louder than she'd ever heard him speak. "Fuck!"

He held out his hands, as if to apologize, but then he kept speaking. "I do so much to keep this thing going, to keep this fucking family together, millions of little parts that have to be attended to. I do it all. And then you people actively try to ruin it. It's like you can't keep yourselves from ruining something perfect."

"I'm sorry," Izzy said, but Dr. Grind didn't seem to hear her.

"Fuck!" Dr. Grind again shouted, as if he was performing a magic trick and this was the word that was supposed to unlock the spell. Then, as if the gravity in the room was temporarily haywire, his body seemed to fold in on itself and he bent at the waist, and then returned to his standing position, his face now calm, slack.

"Of course, it's not your fault at all, Izzy," Dr. Grind said, still standing apart from her. "It's a big family. It's impossible to control it. We hope for the best. We do our best. Sometimes things fall apart. You and I probably know this better than anyone else, right?"

Izzy removed her hands from her face and looked at him. It was as if he did not remember having yelled at her. Could unkindness be so foreign to him that he imagined it to only be a dream? He now smiled at her and she, against her own instincts, smiled back.

"I remember when I got the news about my own family," he continued. "There was that realization that I had not done enough. That I had not been able to keep what I loved safe. It was such a deep existential unhappiness. I am feeling that right now, that same frustration."

"Me, too," Izzy said.

"I'm so sorry for how I just acted. Of course, you had nothing to do with what happened to Ellen. This is the business of Ellen and Jeremy and Callie and Harris. It affects us, because we share this space, but we can't control other people, no matter how much we want to."

"I just don't want this to end," she said. "I don't want it to fall apart. I need this place. I need the family. I need you."

Dr. Grind finally stepped closer to Izzy, placing his right hand on her shoulder, and Izzy shrugged out of his grip, and pulled him close to her and kissed him. He immediately disengaged, and she noticed something in his expression that had not been there the first time she kissed him, his emotions cracked open for a brief moment. Dr. Grind, a lifetime of training, absorbed conflict and uncertainty and unhappiness and burned it off immediately within his body, the surface never changing. Even when he learned of Ellen's suicide attempt, whatever shock waves had pulsed within him did not change his demeanor. And now, having kissed Dr. Grind, a man she knew with great certainty that she loved, she saw genuine desire. She saw him running through the events that marked their time in this family, and she saw him come to terms with how this had come to pass, her in his room, her mouth on his.

"Izzy," he said, but she wouldn't let him finish. Whatever he said next would be proper and measured and he would try to put distance between this moment and their lives moving forward. He would calm her down and this moment would pass and, if they both worked hard, nothing would come of it. She had a few seconds, she knew this, to disrupt the moment, to have what she wanted. She kissed him again and she felt him relent and then return the affection. And when it was over, the two of them stood there, unable to speak, unsure of how to proceed. Izzy looked down at the floor, at the indentations that her shoes had made on the carpet. She had left some kind of imprint, she understood this. If her family was falling apart, was it wrong of her to try to hold on to another person and make it last? She smiled at him and, before she could get a response, she opened the door to his apartment and walked out, closing the door behind her as quietly as she could.

She walked out into the courtyard and stared up at the smeared clouds above her, not a star in the sky. She wanted to find a way into Cap's heart, reach all of the children in that room, but knew that she could not invade their space with her own presence. Instead, Izzy went into her house, remembering the pneumatic tubes that ran throughout the complex and all ended up at the former communal bedroom of the children. The glass door that held the canister had been easy to ignore these several years in the house since there was no longer any need to send milk to the bank. She opened up one of the drawers in her kitchen and grabbed a handful of lollipops, enough for all of the children to have more than one, and she dropped them one at a time into the canister before sealing it shut. She placed it in the tube, shut the door, and pushed the button, wondering if the tubes still worked. There was a soft hum, a whoosh of air, and then the canister shot out of view, through the walls, through the complex, and she imagined it ending up in the room where her child now slept. She imagined the clunk as it settled into its new destination and the tiny red light that would blink on and off until someone removed the canister. She wondered if the children would even see it, if anything that Izzy did from now on really mattered. After a lifetime of trying to do the exact opposite, had she ruined her own child? No, she knew she hadn't. None of the children, so impervious and brilliant, could be ruined. The parents, however, had become ruined, or had simply dragged their already broken bodies into the complex and let them rupture all over again. She felt like it would take thousands of pages of official paperwork to ever deserve Cap, but some miracle had simply given him to her, no questions asked. She hoped she could keep him, whatever came next.

She packed her duffel bag with her swim cap and suit and goggles and went to the pool. She kept all of the lights off and lowered herself into the water of the main pool, the temperature just cold enough to alert her muscles to the fact that they were needed. She swam lap after lap, the room echoing with the sounds of her movements, the world completely closed off to her, nothing but blackness. She loved the sensation, though, of pushing her way through the water, entirely blind, and finding, every single time, the solid edge of the pool against her fingertips, reminding her that she had once again found her way home.

After nearly an hour of swimming, her body finally felt accepting of sleep. It was now 4 A.M., but she changed into a pair of sweatpants and a T-shirt and crept across the courtyard and back into the main building. She found the parents still in the hallway, a weird rhythm of snoring and breathing and slightly whining murmurs coming from the pile of them. She stepped over a few parents and found a tiny unoccupied spot and fit her body into it. She made her own breathing match the people around her and, before she even knew it was happening, she was asleep, her waking life so bizarre that she dreamed of nothing but the sound of waves, beating against a shore that she could not see.

chapter sixteen

the infinite family project (year seven)

D r. Grind could not help but think of his own parents, long dead, as the world around him started to fall apart. He no longer debated whether or not they loved him; he had long ago determined that they had loved him, in their own way, no more or less than other parents he had encountered. What he now wondered, thinking back to those experiments, carried out over such a long period of time that they were not really experiments to him but the events of his life, was what exactly his mother and father were preparing him for. What darkness could they have imagined that would require such steadfast resilience in the face of it? And yet, his wife and child, his world entire, had died, and he had somehow kept going. Were his parents to thank for this? Perhaps. But now, as his new family, the Infinite Family, threatened to splinter into pieces that could not be put back together, he did not think that his parents, as strange as they were, could have ever imagined the scenario in which he found himself. And perhaps, he finally decided, that was the point. Parents do everything they can for their children, unable to conceive of the child's future, hoping only that they've done enough to protect them. Right now, looking at a chart that outlined each member of the Infinite Family, Dr. Grind only knew that he had not done enough, and his family was now leaving him behind.

Not long after Ellen had moved into the mental health facility, Jeremy and Callie had taken Eli and moved permanently to their farm, having already constructed the yurt and some basic conveniences to sustain themselves while they worked the land. Dr. Grind had tried everything he could think of to keep them, had looked over the legal contracts that they had signed and found, though he already knew it, that there was very little that would keep the families in the complex if they did not want to stay. It had always been a fragile situation, but the project had given the families so much that they never questioned the fact that they could leave. They hadn't wanted to. But now, with one family already gone, Dr. Grind knew there would be a greater awareness among the members of the family, the realization that they, too, could become a singular family.

Kalina had wanted to call child services on the Gipsons, but Dr. Grind knew that there was no real legal way to bring Eli back to the complex and there was nothing to be gained by making problems for Jeremy and Callie. They needed to keep the lines of communication open. The complex would still purchase fruits and vegetables from the family, and Dr. Grind had even allowed that Eli could commute to and from the complex for his schooling, but Callie had told him that she would now be homeschooling Eli and that they also wanted him to spend more time working on the farm.

On the night Callie took Eli from the complex, Jeremy having never shown his face since the night Ellen tried to kill herself, there had been no mention to the other children that Eli would be leaving. After dinner, when the families returned to their own houses, Callie and Eli had simply hung back with Dr. Grind and the fellows. Eli hugged Dr. Grind, who told Eli that he could visit any time that he wanted, though Eli seemed to disbelieve this offer, merely frowned and turned back to Callie. Jill was crying and Kalina was holding on to her as Callie and Eli walked to the driveway, where a truck was idling by the curb, waiting for them. Jeffrey shook his head and spoke of how this development would affect their studies, how it would create instability in the outcomes, but Dr. Grind barely listened. He focused instead on the taillights of the truck as it disappeared down the long driveway, the trees swallowing it up. Now, not by magic or careful design but rather the imperfect nature of all human interaction, the family was less by three people.

In the morning, when the children saw that Eli was no longer there, the fellows had anticipated another outburst, the children locking themselves in a room or refusing to eat food, but they seemed to accept the diminishment without emotion. Their world, Dr. Grind understood, had been damaged, and the children seemed to understand, earlier than he had ever hoped, that more woe would probably follow.

"We're leaving," Harris Tilton informed Dr. Grind. A month had passed since Ellen's hospitalization and she was now due to be released and returned to the complex.

"Of course," Dr. Grind answered, showing not the slightest bit of surprise, "you have to know that I think this is a bad idea."

Harris nodded. "I appreciate everything that you've done for us. I know that Ellen's situation is not your fault in any way, and you've made our lives so much better than they would have been without you, but this place is toxic for Ellen, even with Jeremy gone. She doesn't want to come back; she doesn't want to be reminded of what happened and she doesn't want to see the other members of the family. She wants to start over. She needs a fresh start with her real family."

"What about Marnie?" Dr. Grind asked. "It will be a huge change for her, to lose her brothers and sisters, to lose access to the other parents."

"I've been talking to her. She understands what's going on. She misses her mother. She's willing to trade the complex in order to have Ellen back."

"Why should she have to choose, Harris?" Dr. Grind asked, a hint of desperation now entering his voice.

"Because," Harris said, starting to cry, "everyone has to choose at some point. You can't have everything, Dr. Grind, right? Why does it matter if we leave tomorrow as opposed to a few years from now? This wasn't intended to last forever."

"Well, the intention was that the members of this family would stay in contact after the project ended, to form a network of support even beyond this place."

"No reason that still can't happen. I care about this place, Dr. Grind. I hope you know that. I love those kids and I really care for the people I've met while we've lived here. But, and I hate to say this because I know it might upset you, they are not my real family. Ellen and Marnie are my real family, and they have gone through some really unpleasant shit and my responsibility is to fix that."

"And you don't want our help?" Dr. Grind offered.

"Not now," Harris said, having collected himself, his eyes still red.

"When will you leave?" Dr. Grind asked.

"I've rented a house in Murfreesboro, near my work. Marnie and I will move in five days. Then Ellen will be released a few days after that. I've already enrolled Marnie at an elementary school. My insurance from work will cover Ellen's continuing treatment. We'll be fine, I promise."

"When do you want to tell the other members?" Dr. Grind asked.

"I was hoping you would tell them," Harris offered, as if he was giving Dr. Grind a thoughtful gift. "After we leave."

Dr. Grind could not even manage to stand; he merely shook Harris's hand and watched as the man walked out of his office. Jill walked by his door a few minutes later, holding up her hands as if to ask what the outcome was, but Dr. Grind shook his head and Jill understood that now was not the time to discuss it. Dr. Grind removed a piece of paper from his desk, a crude family tree that contained all the members of the Infinite Family. On the sheet, where Jeremy and Callie and Eli had been penciled in, Dr. Grind had cut out their names with an X-Acto knife, leaving a hole in the paper. He now took out the knife and carefully, with great precision, cut out the names of Ellen, Harris, and Marnie. He took the square that he had cut out and placed it in the drawer of his desk, next to the Gipson family's square. He laid the sheet flat on his desk and traced his fingers along the lines that connected the remaining families. He felt the odd sensation of his fingertips touching the slick surface of his desk through the holes he had cut from the paper. He returned his gaze to the box that held Izzy's name, circling it with his finger, over and over, as if hoping he could make a halo of light appear around her, illuminating the room.

After she had kissed him, Dr. Grind had expected Izzy to retreat from his presence; she was so stoic, so careful with her own emotions, that he imagined she realized her actions were an accident brought on by a traumatic event and that she would spare him the humiliation of informing him that she had made a mistake. Instead, Izzy had become more confident in the wake of their kiss. She stared at him with open curiosity, which left him more flustered and unable to concentrate than even the impending loss of the project's subjects. She did not shy away from his presence, but she also did not mention the kiss or try to explain herself. Izzy merely proceeded with the day-to-day routine, continuing to make the meals, to help with the children, to swim her endless laps in the pool. And Dr. Grind found, with a secret satisfaction that he kept compartmentalized and hidden, that when he saw her for the first time each day he was incredibly gratified, was relieved that she, too, had not left.

Two days after Harris, Ellen, and Marnie left the complex for good, Dr. Grind received a phone call from Patricia Acklen. He had kept the details of the Infinite Family's disruptions from Patricia, had not mentioned that they were now missing six members of the project, a fairly substantial loss that had definite repercussions with regard to their studies. He was afraid that any signs of dysfunction would jeopardize the remaining members of the family. And, if Dr. Grind was being entirely truthful with himself, he had a small hope that he could somehow convince those departed families to return before Brenda and Patricia Acklen realized they were gone. He imagined that they would see what life was like outside the complex and they would come back to the fold and they could proceed as if nothing had happened. Now, however, with Patricia Acklen on the phone, her voice slightly stiff and formal in a way that denoted no sign of her southern manners, Dr. Grind realized how stupid he had been, how irresponsible he had become with his own work.

"Dr. Grind," Patricia continued, their formal pleasantries dispensed with, "I'm afraid I have some bad news."

He almost cut off Patricia in order to apologize for not telling her about the defections, but he remained silent, realizing that there was no point in delaying the inevitable.

"I'm outside the complex," she continued.

"Excuse me?" he replied, the fingers on his right hand quivering suddenly, as if awakened by electricity.

"That's not the bad news, actually," Patricia said. "I just wanted to let you know that I came here to deliver the bad news."

"Where are you now?" he asked, still not sure of what was going on.

"I'm in a car just outside the complex. Come meet me."

Preston's first instinct was to hide under his desk and hope that Patricia gave up and went back to Knoxville. But he knew, even from his limited exposure to Patricia Acklen, that she would never fucking leave until she got what she wanted. So he walked down the stairs and exited the building to find a BMW idling in front of the complex. As soon as he stepped outside, the driver got out of the car and opened the door for Patricia Acklen. She waved to him, the kind of limp wave that looked a lot like shooing something away. Preston, still shocked, could not even raise his hand to acknowledge her.

"My grandmother has died," Patricia said once they had seated themselves back in his office, not a single pleasantry to blunt the impact of this statement. "She died two days ago, bless her, but we haven't released any details to the media as of yet. It's all being kept very quiet to respect my grandmother's privacy. But we will be releasing the news tomorrow at three P.M. I've spent the last day and a half talking to people who worked with my grandmother, to let them know about this in advance."

"I'm so sorry, Patricia," Dr. Grind finally managed. "Brenda was an exceptional person. I'm honored that I got to know her."

"She felt the same way about you, Dr. Grind, I can assure you," Patricia said, some warmth now returning to her voice, the bad news delivered.

"I know what my grandmother said to you, regarding the project, as I was there that day and I have talked to her many times in the past year about the project, but I do believe there are ways that we can improve upon the initial work."

"Whenever you'd like," Preston replied. "Please know that we appreciate everything that Mrs. Acklen did for us here and how much we appreciate your support."

Patricia looked at him for a brief moment, a strange smile on her face, as if she were listening to a song that he could not hear.

"You don't know, do you?" Patricia finally asked him.

"Know what?" he asked.

"Dr. Grind," she continued, "I have read about your upbringing, about your special capabilities when it comes to emotion and stress. And I honestly cannot read you. I admire that in you."

"What do you mean?" Preston asked.

"I imagined that Jill might have said something," she remarked, more to herself than to Preston.

"Dr. Grind," Patricia continued, her voice lowering in volume, deliberate pauses between her sentences, "I know about the Gipson family and the Tilton family. I know they are no longer with you. And I'm a little sad that you did not deem that important enough to share with me."

"I'm so sorry, Patricia," Dr. Grind responded, not a sign in his voice that his body felt like it was falling off a cliff. "I've been trying, in my own way, to manage the fluctuations in our dynamic and I've not had time to focus on keeping you and your grandmother up-to-date."

"My grandmother was content to sit back and let you run the project as you saw fit. I loved my grandmother, but we have slightly different ways of managing our assets. I believe very strongly in the Infinite Family, and, as a result, I want to make sure that it's proceeding in a way that best represents my grandmother's wishes."

"Absolutely," Dr. Grind agreed, realizing, because he was an intelligent enough person and because he was attuned to the uncertainties of all things, that he had officially lost control of his own project. He had imagined, for so long that he had accepted it as gospel, that these people were his family. That he had, somehow, brought this family together. But how had he made it happen? With Brenda Acklen's money, with her complete and utter belief in what he was doing, even if he himself didn't always know what he was doing. Now that she was dead, that would all change. He was a researcher and he was conducting an experiment. And the findings, which were being funded at a considerable expense, were not his property. At any moment, he realized, the family could be taken from him, which was worse, he decided, than if the family slipped away from him by his own failures.

"God bless you, Preston," Patricia said. "I'm going to be entirely honest with you, because I think you deserve it. Even if you didn't believe that I deserved that same honesty."

Preston didn't respond, though he had immediately wanted to thank her; against his better nature, he would not be polite in this moment.

"I'm ending this particular study, Dr. Grind," Patricia finally said, not smiling, but it was clear to Preston that she was happy to finally say it out loud.

"Patricia," Dr. Grind said. "It's been almost seven years of nearly flawless work, so I don't think it's so easy to just call it quits at the first sign of disruption."

"You really have no idea what's going on, do you?" she asked. She seemed genuinely curious, her head tilting to properly observe his reaction.

"What?" he asked.

"The work here is finished. I've got the legal power to do it; I've gone over this countless times with my lawyers."

"I don't understand why you'd want to end it," Preston responded, suddenly angry. "It feels entirely selfish to shut down a project that could have a huge impact—"

"Dr. Grind, I am not shutting down The IFP. I am expanding it. I am doing more with it than you ever considered possible. What you're confused about is that I'm doing this without you."

"I made this family; I built the whole thing, Patricia."

"With my grandmother's money. With my money. And, regardless of my grandmother's hopes for this project, we can't just give away money to solve society's ills. Why is that Acklen Super Stores' responsibility? If the government wants to incorporate the findings of The IFP into their own initiative, then I won't stop them. But I'm working to preserve the legacy of my grandmother. I'm working to preserve the legacy of the work that we've done. And you, frankly, are detrimental to that legacy."

"So what are you going to do?" he asked.

"The project, our project, Preston, has been incredibly useful as a measure of how a communal structure can improve the development of children. You've gathered more than enough data to support that theory; allowing the project to continue would only jeopardize those findings. Once these defections occurred, the suicide attempt, it could only harm the brand, could reduce our claims of success. The key, what is truly important at this stage, is to move on to new families, to offer it to more people."

"But that's what I'd like to do, Patricia. We're working toward the same goals."

Again, she looked at him with curiosity. "I cannot read you at all, Preston," she said. "No, we're not working toward the same goals. You have some kind of social agenda that may or may not prove successful in a measurable way. My concern is to take the positive publicity that you have thus far generated for the project and begin to open IFPs all over the country, beautiful houses in gated communities with their own schools and playgrounds and whatnot. It will be an opportunity for new families to ensure that their child receives the kind of exemplary care that they deserve."

"This is my family. Even if you want to expand, why not let me keep this family?"

"Dr. Grind, this is not your family. It never was. Ask those parents. You were a supervisor. You were not their father. It's troubling that you continue to think otherwise."

"You're wrong."

"The Infinite Family Project is going to be a paradigm shift in the way children are raised. It's going to be revolutionary. We're going to make a huge profit, yes, but, more important, we're going to be at the forefront of something that will define our society from here on out. I can't have you jeopardizing that."

"You want to be the mother now," Dr. Grind said. "To replace me."

"No, I would never want that. You should never have wanted that. I'm going to be their CEO."

"So this is all about money, then?" Dr. Grind asked.

"Lord, Dr. Grind, please give me a break. This is about more than money. It's about ensuring that my grandmother is remembered for being the innovative, charitable, forward-thinking woman that she was. It's about protecting her dream for childhood development from the obviously poor candidates that you chose to make up this project. You chose deficient people, Dr. Grind. You picked people who were accustomed to nothing and you overwhelmed them with so many possibilities that they sabotaged the project. We are not going to make that mistake again. Ever. We're going to help people who have the means to help themselves. There's nothing wrong with that. I won't apologize for this. We're going to make something special out of The Infinite Family Project."

"Please don't do this, Patricia."

"I'm sorry, Dr. Grind," Patricia said.

Dr. Grind resisted the urge to smash the desk into a million pieces, to yell, to waste his emotions on something he could not control. Instead, he compressed everything, pulled all of his emotions into a ball, pulled it into his heart, and then let it reside there, undisturbed. He stared at Patricia Acklen, the light in the room turning wavy and uncertain. It was somewhat reassuring to be a world unto himself. And then, by tiny degrees, he returned to the present moment.

"And how did you know about the suicide attempt? The defections?" he asked, now genuinely curious, no longer believing he could effect any change.

"Right after I came to visit the complex with my grandmother, I got in touch with all three of your fellows. Of course, I told them that they were doing incredible work and I had plans for them to further the research, to take a greater role in the project. I simply asked them to keep me informed on the day-to-day operations of the complex."

"And did they?" Dr. Grind asked, understanding a little too late for it to matter.

She nodded. "That's how I knew about the Gipsons and the Tiltons. And Kalina and Jeffrey will now be leading their own Infinite Families, the pilot programs. It's an incredible opportunity for them."

"What about Jill?" Preston asked.

Patricia shook her head. "I'm afraid that she doesn't entirely fit the model for our future goals."

Preston nodded and then tapped his desk, as if expecting it to be made entirely of smoke, as if the whole complex was a dream. "I appreciate your honesty, I do, Patricia. How long do I have until the project is shut down?"

"Well, I have to get back to Knoxville. I'll send you more information, but I think you'll be more than happy with the provisions that I've included, not just for you but for the entire family. And, Preston, I do think you made something truly unique. I do admire you, whether you believe me or not."

She stood and, without waiting for Dr. Grind to acknowledge her, walked out of the office. Dr. Grind went to the large window that looked over the entrance to the building and watched until Patricia Acklen had returned to her car and it pulled away, disappearing from view.

When he turned around, Jill was standing before him.

"Do you know?" she asked, and Preston only nodded.

"I told them to fuck off," Jill said, smiling through her tears. "She called me a few days ago to tell me that she wanted me to head up one of the new projects."

"You told Patricia Acklen to fuck off?" Preston asked.

Jill nodded. "I don't have any interest in helping rich people further the gap between them and poor people. I don't think they need more ways to improve their situations. This whole project was set up to help people in need, to help children develop in ways they wouldn't have otherwise. These Infinite Family gated communities are going to be status symbols, a way for rich people to separate themselves from other rich people. I didn't get into this to make money. I did it to, you know, help fucking kids."

"And Jeffrey? Kalina?"

"They're in. They're totally in. I don't blame them; well, I guess I do, but I love them so much I'm willing to forgive them. It's a lot of money, Preston. It's a really good gig for them, I guess. Whatever."

It was as if the ground beneath him kept opening up, always yet another level before hitting the very bottom. He wondered how easy it was for Kalina and Jeffrey to accept, if there was even hesitation. He thought of their recent interactions and could find no trace of secrecy or weirdness. And yet these were the people he had assembled, had entrusted with so much, passing him by without a word. They had spent this time spying on him, on the family, silently separating themselves from the project, knowing that soon they would have their own family to watch over.

Jeffrey's decision he could almost anticipate, the single-mindedness he brought to the work; why would he turn it down if offered the chance to run his own project? But Kalina? He could not quite numb the pain of that betrayal. He thought of his fight to keep her as a part of the family; she had always been the most supportive of the fellows, the one most fervent about the possibilities of the project. And that, perhaps, was why, when threatened with losing it, she chose the project over him.

He could not imagine what he would say to them when he next saw them, how he could communicate the loss he was feeling.

"Thank you, Jill," Dr. Grind said.

"Did we outlive our usefulness?" she asked him. "Do these families not need us anymore?"

"Maybe not," Dr. Grind admitted. "But it's not over. It doesn't end, right? It keeps going after they leave us."

"They're still going to be our family after they leave," Jill said. "It's nice to believe that, isn't it?"

"I do believe it, Jill."

"Then you're a good person, Dr. Grind," Jill said. "You've always been the best parent."

She hugged him and he held her as she sobbed.

"Okay," she finally said, pushing away from him. "This is when I walk back to my apartment, get extremely high, and watch TV until I pass out."

"That's a good plan," Dr. Grind said.

"It was nice while it lasted," Jill admitted. "I guess now we have to do the next thing."

"What's that?" Dr. Grind asked her, genuinely curious.

"Start our own families," she said, walking away.

And perhaps that would be easy for Jill and her partner, to embark on something that, for Preston, had ended in abject failure. But he could not figure out where to go from here, how to build something else.

All he could do, in the brief time that was afforded him, was hold on to what he had made and hope that, years from now, they would all remember him with something that resembled love.

chapter seventeen

the infinite family project (year seven)

zzy reached into the box and randomly pulled out a Christmas ornament, a snowflake made of Popsicle sticks and decorated with Magic
Marker. Every ornament for the Christmas tree had been made by the
children of the complex, rickety and fragile crafts that could fall apart
with the lightest dusting of snow. On this particular snowflake, Izzy saw
Marnie's name written in blue marker, while Marnie herself had van-
ished from the complex, living only a half hour away but, to Izzy and the
other members of the Infinite Family, it was as if she had been teleported
to another dimension, never to be seen again. She thought about putting the ornament back in the box, but she decided against it. Marnie,
whether she was here or not, was still a part of the family, and if she
wasn't here to hang her own ornament, Izzy would be the one to do it.

At the long table in the dining hall, the remaining children worked
with a needle and thread to string lines of popcorn; from years of practice, they had created an assembly line of sorts and, despite the holiday
music echoing from the speakers, they did not look excited about the appearance of Santa Claus. They looked like factory workers trying to meet

a quota. It was to be expected, as even the children now understood that this was their last Christmas in the complex, their last time as a family. Izzy hung the snowflake on the tree and felt the tiniest measure of happiness that the ornament held its shape, would last one more year.

Jeremy, Callie, and Eli had now been gone for almost six months, Harris, Ellen, and Marnie having left not long after. A few months later, Paul, Mary, and Lulu were gone.

The day that Mary left the complex, everyone now so numb to the experience of saying farewell, Mary walked over to Izzy and asked to speak with her in private. Ever since Mary had accosted Izzy in the early years of the project, they had steered clear of each other, an intricate dance so subtle that perhaps no one else in the project understood what was happening. To Izzy it felt like they were two actresses on the same TV show who hated each other, and it was up to the writers to figure out creative ways for the show to continue without their actual interaction. Izzy, before walking into a room, would instantly scan for Mary, so quickly that it no longer even caused her anxiety, and Mary, if she sensed Izzy's presence, would slowly fade out of the scene. Izzy had often wondered how spouses stayed together, shared a house, a bedroom, even after they had fallen out of love, but she no longer thought it odd.

Izzy followed Mary down the hallway but hesitated for a second when Mary opened the door to the music room and gestured for her to go in. "What's going on?" Izzy asked. "Come on," Mary said, walking into the room. Izzy followed.

"We're leaving," Mary said.

"I know," Izzy said. "I'm sorry."

"I guess," Mary said, but then stopped. She frowned and then looked up at her, as if frustrated with Izzy for putting her in this situation. "I just wanted to say that I was sorry for the way things happened between us. I hated you so much when we first got here."

"Mary," Izzy said, holding up her hands in supplication.

"Just . . . let me finish here. I hated you, but we had to stay together and that made me angrier. But then, time passed, and I realized that you weren't so bad, or not as bad as I had thought. But it was hard to apologize, so I just let it keep going between us. So I'm sorry, now. I'm sorry that we didn't get along better."

"I'm sorry, too," Izzy admitted.

"I'm not going to pretend that I'll stay in touch. I will probably never see you again, and I don't really have a problem with that. But I didn't want to leave and have you think that I hated you. I don't. Okay?"

"Okay," Izzy said. Izzy wondered if they were going to hug, but then she realized that this was Mary, and there would be no affection in this room. Mary nodded to Izzy and walked out the door. And that was indeed the last time she saw Mary, or Paul, or Lulu ever again.

A few days after that, Dr. Grind and Jill Patterson, the only supervisors who remained now that Jeffrey and Kalina had left the complex to begin preparations for their own versions of the project, called a meeting. It was strange to watch only the two of them at the front of the room, and Izzy felt the stab of loss from Kalina's departure, the one who had found her, had brought her to the attention of Dr. Grind. She could not, in good conscience, begrudge Kalina taking on a new version of the project, but it had hurt Izzy deeply that Kalina had left the family before it had come to its natural close. If even the people paid to stay in the complex couldn't do it, Izzy felt less and less sure that anyone else would.

And then, as if reading Izzy's mind, Dr. Grind had informed the rest of the family that Patricia Acklen had made the decision to prematurely end The Infinite Family Project. On December 31, The IFP would officially close down. Legally, she had the power to do so, Dr. Grind assured everyone, having looked over the legal documents himself. She had allowed that each family would receive a payment of $100,000 to help cover the costs of relocation and reentry into the "real world," but there would be no further affiliation with the original families. "It's a transition," Dr. Grind admitted. "But we still have each other, and some time to continue our work here."

"What would it matter to Ms. Acklen if we stayed the full time?" Asean asked. "What harm would it do to keep the project going, the way you had planned it, Dr. Grind?"

"I don't think it would matter to the bottom line," Dr. Grind admitted, a touch of anger in his voice, though perhaps only Izzy could hear it. "It's purely a managerial decision, which, unfortunately, we cannot change."

"What if we just stayed?" Asean asked, and Nikisha leaned over to whisper to him, but he shook his head. "What if we just refused to leave?"

"I can't imagine anything good would come from that, Asean," Dr. Grind said, "though, honestly, I am so invested in this place, in all of you, that I'd be willing to try."

"I think," Julie said, fuming, "that we should burn this place down when we leave."

"Okay, well, that's problematic," Dr. Grind offered, realizing perhaps what he had started. "Look, the real issue is that Acklen controls the money that funds this project. And they have legal barriers in place to prevent us from benefiting from the study after it has been deemed unnecessary. They are being generous, in their own way, by letting us stay here a little longer. They are giving you a fairly hefty severance package, as it were, which they are not obligated to do. They could even, if they wanted to use enough of their lawyers to do so, find ways in which we were in breach of contract, and ask us to pay restitution for those things. Right now, they think they are being kind. So you cannot imagine what it would be like if they decided to truly be nasty to The Infinite Family Project."

"I still say we burn down the place," Julie said.

"I hope they turn it into a museum," Kenny said, "leave it exactly this way, and we can come back every year and look around. We could all bring the kids and they could see their old home."

"There'd be a gift shop," Carmen added, smiling.

"A food court," Susan said.

"Free and open to the public," Dr. Grind finally said. "Perhaps."

"Though without us," Kenny sadly admitted, gesturing to those who remained, "it wouldn't be very interesting."

And then Carlos, Nina, and Gilberto informed the rest of the family that they were moving to St. Louis, where Nina had a cousin who'd offered her a job working in the accounting department of a very successful start-up company. They left in November, leaving only six families.

It was a heartbreaking experience for Izzy, for the entire month of December, to walk around the complex and find it ghostlike and empty. Even if the people who had left had never been her closest confidantes (Carmen and Link and Susan were still here), they had created the framework that allowed Izzy to feel like she was a part of something larger than herself. Moreover, she felt a creeping dread around the edges of her consciousness. With fewer people populating the complex, the woods that surrounded the buildings seemed to be pulling closer, inches at a time, swallowing them up. When she walked through the courtyard at night, the safety she had always felt had given way to a need to be alert; the real world was seeping into the complex, and she did not feel safe in the open air.

The children attended classes, went on field trips, swam in the pool, but they also seemed haunted by the defections, as if, at any moment, another one of them could be taken away. Dinners were now muted affairs, as everyone was thinking about the next step, finding a new place to live, looking at school systems for the children, but not wanting to talk about it in public. They were huddled together, sharing this doomed space, unable to imagine a world without each other, with no other choice but to move on.

Izzy was still unsteadied when Dr. Grind was around. If he was near her, Izzy would force his gaze, staring at him until he truly looked at her, and she would quickly search for some small clue that he had relented, would give himself to her, but she could find nothing in his demeanor other than the apologetic sadness that seemed to glaze his expression these days. His boyishness, so unreal and disconcerting at times, was finally starting to give way to his actual age, stubble that roughened his face, a pale grayish hue around his eyes. She promised herself that there would be no more outbursts on her part. She had made her intentions known, had embarrassed herself; if something was going to happen, he would be the one to do it.

One morning, while Izzy was preparing lunch for the children, Dr. Grind came in, asking if Jill had been in the kitchen. Izzy shook her head and returned to her work, expecting him to move on, but he lingered in the doorway, and she looked up and smiled.

"We're doing some more research," he admitted. "Jill and I aren't quite sure what to do anymore; it's not like Patricia will want any further data from this project, but we can't just sit around, waiting for the end. Pretty soon, we'll lose the kids; it hurts to think about it. We're trying to do all we can in the meantime."

"What kind of research?" Izzy asked him.

"Oh, we resurrected an old experiment. Do you know about the marshmallow experiment?" he inquired.

Izzy nodded. She had watched clips of it on YouTube, had wondered how Cap would have reacted to the experiment.

"We tried it the fourth year. It was not a success, or not in the obvious ways. The children could not hold off from eating the marshmallow, not a single one of them. A lot of them simply assumed that, no matter what they did, they would still be rewarded. It was a problematic experiment at a key time in our work here at the complex. We tried it the following year and got the same results. I made a call to discontinue the experiment. And . . . I hid the results from Brenda Acklen." Dr. Grind shrugged when Izzy showed surprise. "It was not my finest moment. But I didn't want anything to prevent the work we were doing from moving forward. It seemed like such a silly experiment, and I've come up with dozens of reasons why the testing itself is quite flawed and not really predictive of anything."

Dr. Grind thought for a second, debating something, and Izzy tensed, waiting for whatever he said next.

"With Jody, who was such a beautiful boy, so sweet and open to the world, I gave him everything that he wanted, even before he knew that he wanted it. I know part of it was because of my own upbringing, and I didn't want him to ever feel the lack of something, but I spoiled him, we both did. Even when my own research and my work with children said otherwise, preached limits, I couldn't do the same with my own son. And he was wonderful. He turned out to be a perfectly well-adjusted child." Dr. Grind pulled up short, obviously recognizing the fact that Jody was no longer alive and was forever that child Dr. Grind remembered. Izzy let him contemplate the loss.

"So maybe I just did the same for these children, knowing it would be okay," he said, wincing in a way that mixed happiness and sadness, a look that Izzy understood well.

"Still," Dr. Grind continued, "the outcomes of the experiment were a sore spot for us. So today we gathered the children and we performed the test again." He paused, looked over at Izzy, who smiled.

"How did they do this time?" she asked.

Dr. Grind smiled, but there was little emotion behind it. Izzy could sense that he had started this conversation because he needed to talk about it, but he had wanted to talk to Jill, not one of the parents. But Izzy was the only one here, and so he continued.

"They were able to wait the full time. Every child easily waited in order to get the second marshmallow."

"Well, that's great," Izzy said. "It's progress."

Dr. Grind paused for a moment and then said, "When we gave them the second marshmallow, to go with the one already on the plate, I noticed that a few of the kids didn't eat either marshmallow. So I asked them why, and they said that they wanted to hang on to them. That, since they were leaving the complex soon, they wanted to save everything for when they might really need it."

"Was Cap one of those kids?" she asked him.

"He was," he replied.

Izzy kept herself from crying by sheer force of will; she reminded herself that this was her kitchen, her space, and no one else had more power in here than she did.

"He's losing so much," she admitted to Dr. Grind. "I guess I understand his thinking."

"I suppose I do, too," Dr. Grind said. They stood in silence, and then, just before Izzy once again made a fool of herself, Dr. Grind nodded and then walked out of the kitchen.

The week before Christmas Eve, Carmen had visited Izzy with some real estate options printed out from the computer. She seemed to be vibrating with excitement, which was a marked difference from the atmosphere in the complex. "I've got something good," she said, opening Izzy's cabinets. "Do you have any booze?" she asked, and Izzy produced a bottle of vodka and they made screwdrivers and Carmen laid out the pages on the coffee table.

"There are two houses for sale," Carmen said, "right across the street from each other. They need some work, but they're in a good neighborhood and they're affordable, which is rare in East Nashville right now."

"Okay," Izzy said. "Are you going to buy one?"

"I talked to Kenny about it. We've got the money to do it. We're buying this one," she said, pointing to a cute one-story house with a nice yard. "And," she said, smiling as she pointed to the other house, a two-story cottage, "we think you should buy this one."

"Really?" Izzy said.

"Wouldn't it be perfect?" Carmen said. "We'd stay together. At least a small part of the family."

"I'd love that," Izzy said.

"I think of you as family," Carmen said. "I want us to stay close. Maxwell and Cap, they're closer to each other than actual brothers. I cannot imagine a world where Maxwell doesn't see Cap every single day."

"You've looked out for me the whole time we've been here," Izzy said.

"Yeah, but that's nothing special," Carmen said. "Family, right?"

"I didn't think so before this place," Izzy said.

"That's why we're here," Carmen said, and both Izzy and Carmen realized that in less than two weeks the entire complex would be empty.

Once the tree was decorated, Izzy returned to the kitchen and made a batch of eggnog and started to bake the cookies that the children had cut into festive shapes earlier that evening. By now the children had wrapped the popcorn strings around the tree and were checking over the presents, identifying the recipient of each package. Now that it was almost nine o'clock, the remaining parents, as well as Jill, began to wander into the dining hall, ready for their last enactment of the complex's Christmas tradition. As the clock rolled over to nine o'clock, the kids perked up at the sound of jingle bells coming from the hallway. They ran to the door just in time to meet Dr. Grind, dressed as Santa Claus, weighed down with a sack of presents. Izzy brought out the cookies and eggnog, spiked with even more rum than usual, and watched as each child waited for their turn on Santa's lap to receive their one gift on Christmas Eve, a special treat to hold them over until the morning. The parents sipped from their cups and used their phones to take pictures as each child stepped up to Dr. Grind, the festivity of the situation finally easing some of the tension in their bodies.

This year, the gift was a customized photo album of the past seven years, showing each child from birth to the present, with their names printed on the glossy covers. Jill and Dr. Grind had worked on the presents for more than a month, Dr. Grind doing most of the work while everyone else slept. Each book was entirely unique, an assortment of the thousands and thousands of photos that every member of the family had taken. It was, Dr. Grind had told the family one day, halfway into the project, like excavating the artifacts of a grand and heretofore unknown civilization. As each child received their gift, they ran over to their parents to show them their bounty. "Merry Christmas!" Jackie shouted, and Dr. Grind, fiddling with the itchy fake beard, gave a resounding "Ho, ho, ho," and the children all clapped as he exited the room, only to return a few minutes later in his regular clothes, wondering what all the fuss was.

The cookies consumed, the stockings hung with care, each child hugged and kissed by every member of the family, Izzy turned off the lights and returned with Cap to their own house. "It was the night before Christmas," Cap stated, and Izzy couldn't tell if he was starting the poem or simply making a very obvious statement. "The last one," he then said.

"Just the last Christmas at the complex," Izzy reminded him, and he smiled weakly, allowing her correction, too tired to explain what they both knew he really meant.

A few minutes later, just as they had begun to get ready for bed, someone knocked on the door. Cap ran to answer it and they found Dr. Grind standing there with a large, awkwardly shaped present.

Cap ran back to the coffee table and retrieved the photo album before running back over to Dr. Grind; Cap gave him a hug, holding up the photo album and begging him to look through it with him.

"Is this okay?" Dr. Grind, placing the present next to the sofa, asked Izzy, who nodded at the same time that Cap, still smiling at Dr. Grind, exclaimed, "Sure it is!"

The three of them sat on the couch and flipped through the album, Izzy shocked at how vividly she remembered nearly every image.

"You're in hardly any of these pictures," Cap said to Dr. Grind.

"Is that so?" Dr. Grind replied, seeming genuinely surprised by this observation.

"Not enough," Cap said.

"We'll remember you anyway," Izzy told him, and Dr. Grind blushed before, as if by magic, it disappeared from his skin. He would not meet her gaze and instead said, "I have something for you, Cap," as he awkwardly reached for the present on the floor.

"I don't have to wait until tomorrow?" he asked, suspicious.

"You can open it now," Izzy said.

He tore into the wrapping paper and then paused as he observed the black banjo case. "I know what this is going to be," he said excitedly, and then flipped open the case to see a banjo that seemed both ancient and brand-new at the same time, so perfectly designed that even to Izzy's untrained eye it seemed more expensive than a car.

"Awesome," Cap shouted.

"It's a Gibson Mastertone," Dr. Grind informed him. "I went to Gruhn Guitars in Nashville, and they assured me that this banjo was worthy of someone of your talent."

Cap plucked the strings and it sounded like pure silver, the tone so perfect that Izzy felt like it would reverberate for years if allowed to do so.

"It's mine?" Cap asked.

Dr. Grind nodded.

"Thank you," Cap said, hugging Dr. Grind as tightly as he could.

"It's time for bed, sweetie," Izzy said to Cap, who nodded.

"Can I bring this to bed with me?" he asked, and both Dr. Grind and Izzy nodded their approval.

"Merry Christmas to all," Cap said, and then he kissed Izzy and went to his room.

Once he was gone, Izzy watched Dr. Grind, still smiling, his gift so well received.

"Do you want a cookie? Coffee?" she asked.

"No thank you," he said. "I should get back."

But before he could rise from the sofa, she grabbed him by the arm, as if pulling him underwater, sinking back into the Infinite Family, the one that would soon disappear.

"I love you," she said.

Here he was, she thought, maybe the last chance that she would have. He was in her house, beloved by her son, so perfect for her. He was about to walk out of this house, back to his own lonely apartment, and she wanted only to hold on to this moment for as long as she possibly could. She wanted only to stretch this moment out into infinity.

"I'm going to say this once and I'll never bring it up again. Everyone is going out into the world, or ready to do it. Every time the younger women and I get together at night, they all talk about what's coming next, about getting their own house and having another kid even. And they can because, even when the project ends, they'll still have a family. They'll have each other. When it ends, it's just going to be me out there, trying to find my way. And when this ends, it'll just be you out there. And what will you do? Start up another project? Just do this for the rest of your life?"

"I don't know, Izzy," Dr. Grind remarked. "It's hard to think about what comes after all this ends." He paused, considered something for perhaps the hundredth time, and then said, "I suppose it was an act of pure hubris to call it The Infinite Family Project."

"It wasn't hubris. It was hope," Izzy said. "And it won't really end. Most of us, when we do discuss the end of it, already know we're going to try to live in the same neighborhood, to move to Nashville and have our kids in the same school and spend vacations together. And that may fade with time, but I don't think it will. I think we'll be together for the rest of our lives, in some essential way, like any real family."

"That's reassuring," Dr. Grind admitted. "It's what I'd hoped for."

"But," Izzy said, her own coffee now finished, the table between them, "you'll be alone when this ends. And I'll be alone when this ends. And why should that be, Preston?"

"I don't know," Dr. Grind said, now looking at Izzy.

"I love you," Izzy said. "I truly do."

But Dr. Grind stood and began moving toward the door. He put his hand on the doorknob and then hesitated, his hand retreating as if a tiny static shock had moved through him. He turned back to her. "I love you, too," he said.

"You do," she said, feeling so certain of herself, so happy, thinking to herself, *Yes, you do, goddamn it,* wanting to hear him say it again, to make him her own.

"I do, truly," he said. "I guess I should stop denying it. I feel like I've spent my time here constantly trying to live beyond my capabilities, to do what's right for the project, for the memory of Marla and

Jody, for my parents' work, for everyone but myself. But you are wonderful, and you have always been wonderful to me. If nothing else, all my failings, the project brought us together, and I don't want to leave it without you."

She walked toward him, pressed herself against him, and they kissed. It was an awkward kiss, unsure, their mouths not quite matching up, two people with little practice and hyperaware of their discomfort with their own bodies, but it was still better than she had ever hoped. It was a decent enough kiss, she allowed, and then she willed herself to stop thinking about it and be happy.

"Let's be together," Izzy said once they finished. "Whatever happens next, let's stay together."

"Okay," Dr. Grind said. Every word he spoke now seemed to make him dizzy, as if he had suddenly learned a new language and was testing it out.

"What is going to happen next?" Izzy asked.

"I suppose we find a way to make a life together."

"You and me and Cap?" she asked him and Dr. Grind nodded.

"A family," she said, and he nodded. "Yes," he said.

And even though she knew how fragile a family truly was, how quickly it could disappear and ruin you, Izzy smiled, willing to undergo any uncertainty for the chance to be happy.

Izzy held his hand. "Do you want to come to my room?" she asked him.

"Oh. Well, do you think that's a good idea?" he replied. "At this moment, I'm still running the project. You're still a member of the study."

"That's fair," she said, but in her mind she was thinking, *JEE-SUS CHRIST, Dr. Grind*. She had professed her love for him. He had done the same. The rules were broken. There was no need, in this little space, to pretend otherwise. Still, she allowed him his uncertainty.

"I'm also a lot older than you," he added.

"Ten years," Izzy said, shrugging. "Not that much. Less than my last relationship."

"Point taken," Dr. Grind replied.

"Still, come upstairs," she said, tugging gently on his hand, and he agreed, his feet keeping time with her own steps.

When the world fell apart around you, when the walls of your home cracked and crumbled, Izzy now had some idea of how to keep living. You held on to the person you loved, the one who would be there in the aftermath, and you built a new home.

The next morning, Izzy woke to find Cap standing over her. "It's Christmas!" he shouted, his arms in the air. She shot up, searching for Dr. Grind in the bed, but there was no sign of him. He did not sleep, she knew, but she had expected him to at least stay in the bed.

"Merry Christmas," she finally said, hugging Cap, pulling him close to her. She got out of bed and the two of them walked down the stairs to the living room, which was pristine, swept and straightened and shining. In the small kitchen, they saw Dr. Grind, making waffles, as precisely and expertly, to Izzy's mind, as most everything he did when it seemed to matter.

"Merry Christmas," he said, and the three of them ate their breakfast, Cap saying nothing about how strange this moment was, merely eating the waffles that Dr. Grind had made as if this happened every single morning of his young life.

"Cap," Izzy finally said, her voice returned to her. "I want to tell you something now, something important."

"Okay," Cap said, finally able to look up from the banjo in his lap.

"When we leave the complex in a little while, Dr. Grind is going to come with us."

"He is?" Cap asked, frowning.

"I want to," Dr. Grind then said. "I want to live with you and your mom and stay with you guys."

"Forever?" Cap asked, still uncertain, looking back and forth between Izzy and Dr. Grind.

"Yes," they both said.

Cap thought about this. "And you're my mom," he finally said, pointing to Izzy, "and you would be my dad?" He pointed at Dr. Grind, who nodded.

"If it's okay," Izzy said. "We want all of us to be together."

"I wished for this," Cap said, his face so serious. "And it came true."

Izzy could appreciate this sentiment, the alchemy that seemed to have made this moment happen.

Cap went to Izzy and hugged her, Izzy wrapping her arms around him so tightly, this person who, a lifetime ago, she had hoped would save her.

"It's Christmas," Cap said.

"That's right," Izzy said.

He held on to Izzy, his body shaking softly. "I don't want to leave," he said.

"You don't have to," Izzy told him. "Not yet."

Then she stopped, lightly stroked her son's hair, and looked over at Dr. Grind, who she had to remind herself to call Preston now, and said, "I don't want to leave either."

He reached for her free hand and squeezed it.

It was, Izzy could not deny, a strange life. There was nothing normal about her circumstances, how young and stupid she had once been and how much she still felt connected to the teenage version of herself, completely lost and with no possible chance of happiness. It wasn't fate that she felt in this moment, no sense that any of this had been ordained. She felt the chaos of the world, how easily she could have ruined her life and the life of her son, and how some miracle had changed it. She thought of that day when Dr. Grind had come to visit her at the barbecue joint, and how she had signed her life over to him, had decided that she would not settle for anything other than a happy life. She was, which she rarely admitted because of her own discomfort with emotion, so fucking strong. She had made this happen through sheer force of will, and she would never, ever, let it go.

The three of them, together, listened to the quiet of the room, the warm air circulating through the house, everything silent and still. When they returned to the world, this moment past, and it would happen soon enough, the three of them would stand up, hand in hand, and walk into the courtyard to greet the new day and whatever mysteries that it held.

epilogue

the infinite family project (year ten)

I zzy and Mr. Tannehill stood side by side and pulled the meat from a pig, their motions so in tune, even after those years apart, that their hands never crossed each other up. By the time they were finished, they had a tray filled with steaming pork. Though Mr. Tannehill had slowed down some and Izzy had taken over a good portion of the work with the pigs, he was still strong enough to lift a whole hog on his own and he still inherently knew the exact time to cook a pig, the perfect rub, a wealth of knowledge about barbecue that, to Izzy, was unequaled. He carried the barbecue out of the kitchen and to the porch of the restaurant that he and Izzy co-owned in Nashville, Swine Before Pearls. They had also branched out to ribs and brisket, though Mr. Tannehill had worried over the shift, and their restaurant, since it had opened two years ago, encountered lines running out of the building, people waiting for more than an hour for Swine to open, the barbecue running out before the lunch shift had even ended, customers turned away only to show up earlier the next day.

They had recently won a James Beard award in American Classics, which had only served to increase the lines that waited for their barbecue and Izzy's strange twists on classic southern sides. Izzy and Mr. Tannehill had been featured on several TV shows, standing with looks of complete befuddlement beside famous chefs-turned-hosts. Today, however, a Sunday, they were officially closed; even so, the first Sunday of every month was the Infinite Family Reunion, and Izzy was excited to find that seventeen of the twenty-nine members of the family had gathered at the restaurant for lunch.

The walls of the restaurant were covered with small wooden letters, a holdover from Izzy's work in college. To unwind, her hands jittery from hours working in the kitchen, after Cap went to bed, she would spend an hour in the garage, her bare feet covered in sawdust, using a band saw, bringing yet another story into the world, making it tangible, a ghost in reverse. With each letter, sanding it carefully, she could feel the tiny threads that connected her to all aspects of her life. She would touch the smoothness of the wood, and feel her life stretch out to Hal, the emphatic way he asserted that art was necessary, and she could feel it stretch to her mother, long dead and yet always within fingertip reach, watching her daughter with great approval as she created something strange and beautiful, and she could feel it return to the complex, to each and every member of the family who had spent time with the band saw to help Izzy.

She had chosen *Jane Eyre,* a book that she had come to love, her connection to Jane, her weird acrobatics that turned Preston into Mr. Rochester. It was a never-ending project; Izzy admitted that she might never complete it, but the letters had spilled out of the garage, into their house, and it had been Cap who finally suggested that she hang the letters on the walls of the restaurant. She had agreed, though she placed the letters in random order, each week bringing in a new batch to cover the bare parts of the walls, answering questions about the letters with a shrug, as if she was crafting a hidden code that only she would know the answer to.

* * *

On the porch, Link tuned his guitar along with Cap on banjo, Maxwell on stand-up bass, and Eliza on mandolin. Cap, for the past year, had been playing in a couple of bluegrass bands in Nashville, easily the youngest member by decades. In the audience, Izzy saw Carmen and Kenny, who lived right across the street from Izzy and Preston, as well as Julie and Link, who lived in the same neighborhood in East Nashville and who Izzy saw at least weekly. And there were Benjamin, Alyssa, and Ally, who lived in Franklin, Tennessee, both Benjamin and Alyssa working for a computer company, and who came frequently into town. She was also happy to see Asean, Nikisha, and Jackie, plus their baby son, Desean, in town for the weekend, now living in Memphis, where Nikisha had just been appointed library director at Rhodes College. David, Susan, and Irene and their newest daughter, Michelle, only a few months old, were also in town for the day, David now a high school teacher in Murfreesboro.

Preston, who had married Izzy as soon as the project ended, had been worryingly adrift, spending day after day sitting around the house, waiting anxiously for Cap and Izzy to return. He spent hours at night creating elaborate bento boxes for Cap's lunch, became really interested in composting, and spent a lot of time on eBay buying rare punk rock records from Europe. He continued to wear his uniform from the Infinite Family, his tie now tucked into the middle of his dress shirt to avoid stains, his sneakers replaced with slippers. Izzy found his leather pouch in the back of their closet. He had of course told her about his scars, his process, before they married, and he had vowed to quit. She forced him into the car, placed the pouch in his lap, and they drove twenty miles to a Hardee's fast food restaurant, and she made him shove the pouch into a trash can just outside the entrance. "Nothing is changing for you," she said, and he agreed, the rest of the ride back home in total silence.

And then, one evening, he received an e-mail from a man who had been raised using the Constant Friction Method. The man said that he had never quite recovered from the experience, had been in therapy since adolescence, rarely if ever saw his parents, and, when he did, it ended in screaming and arguments. He could barely hold down a job. The man, Charlie, who also happened to live in Nashville, wanted to know if Preston could give him some advice, since Preston had gone through the same experience and seemed to have managed to live a life without incident. "All I'm asking for is a few tips about how you deal with that weird buzzing in your head, that moment where it seems like clairvoyance, that you know something bad is about to happen and you can't stop it from happening," Charlie had written, which Preston had read to Izzy that same night.

"Buzzing?" Izzy asked.

"It's not untrue," Preston admitted. "It's a kind of malfunctioning spidey sense that you can't rely on. I haven't thought about it in some time."

"There's a buzzing in your head?" she asked Preston.

"A kind of buzzing," he admitted, his voice just above a whisper, his attention entirely focused on the e-mail, reading and rereading it.

Over the next few months, Preston met three times a week with Charlie, while also searching message boards and blogs dedicated to adults who had been raised using his parents' method. He started reaching out to them, discussing his own methods for dealing with the fallout from that particular childhood experience. He began traveling around the Southeast, meeting with people, inviting them to become part of a new study that he was only beginning to outline. It wasn't going to focus on the effects of the Constant Friction Method, which had been done numerous times by researchers better than him; the results of these studies were tainted by biases and improper methodology. What Preston was interested in was creating a method to deal with the aftereffects of the Constant Friction Method, a way for adults to find their way clear of that upbringing, a support system that would override what their parents had done to them.

Now two years into the study, Preston had amassed data from more than 350 adults, had developed a network that covered most of the Southeast. He was also, as a way of funding his work with this new project, writing a memoir of his childhood, an examination of his parents and how he fit into their lives. He had retrieved a good deal of his parents' journals and notes from his childhood, and was discovering just how conflicted they were about the method the longer it progressed. "We can't stop now," his mother had written in one of her journals, "we can only hope we've done the right thing. And if not, we pray that Preston is strong enough that none of this sticks." The book, *A Constant Fiction: A Portrait of a Normal Family,* had sold in the high six figures, and Preston was working on a second draft, the pages of which he read to Izzy each night, Izzy learning details about her husband, and the in-laws she had never known, the sensation like discovering a sealed-up room in a house you had lived in for years.

As the food was served, Izzy finally took a seat beside her husband, who called the kids over to the table. "To family," he said, raising his glass, and everyone happily shouted, "Family!" in response. They ate and talked and it felt like, though it would never be the same as it had been at the complex, a close approximation that allowed them, if they tried hard enough, to pretend that things had never changed.

After lunch, the makeshift bluegrass band played songs and the parents and children danced on the porch, twisting and twirling. Izzy danced awkwardly with Mr. Tannehill, who had become the closest thing to a grandfather for Cap, and who, most nights, enjoyed dinner with Izzy and her family.

Cap, only nine years old, sang in a high lonesome voice, and the other players struggled to keep up with the virtuosic way he played the banjo. Mr. Tannehill then handed Izzy off to Preston, who swung Izzy around the porch, neatly avoiding the other families. And, not for the first time and not for the last time, Izzy marveled at the sheer luck of her life, the family she had prayed for and somehow received.

It wasn't always easy, life away from the complex. Cap, along with the other kids from the Infinite Family, was way ahead of the other students in their grade, but Izzy didn't want him to skip ahead and be surrounded by older kids because he was, still, so naive in social situations. A life lived around only nine other children, his brothers and sisters, had left him wide open to the world, so trusting that it nearly ripped out Izzy's heart each time he learned, once again, that not everyone wanted to be his friend, that not every child was his sibling.

Izzy herself felt overwhelmed in the grocery store or waiting to pick up Cap from school, so many people swirling around her, people she did not and would not ever know moving in and out of her life. And then, alternately, there were nights with Izzy and Preston and Cap, the three of them at the dinner table, when Izzy wanted to scream; how strange it seemed that their family, which had been legion, had shrunk to this final iteration. It would never again be how it once was, she understood that, and though she was happier than she had ever imagined, she knew that those years in the complex had been a magic trick, and it was only natural to want to see the trick performed, again and again, until you truly understood how it worked.

Now, however, surrounded by her loved ones, every person she needed in the world, she danced with Preston. She listened to her own son's voice sing, "'there's a better home awaiting,'" and she spun away for a brief second, everything blurry and unsure. And then, falling back into proper alignment just before she broke free and lost her way, she spun right back into Preston's arms. And she was home again.

acknowledgments

Thanks to the following:

Julie Barer, my friend and agent, who has made this writing life for me, for which I am eternally grateful, and who shaped this book in so many important ways.

Zack Wagman, for championing this book and helping me find out what it was and what it should be.

Ecco, with special mention to Allison Saltzman and Emma Janaskie, for all their work in getting this book out to the world and for continuing to support my writing.

Kelly and Debbie Wilson, the greatest parents, the earliest supporters of my work; Kristen, Wes, and Kellan Huffman; Mary Couch; John, Meredith, Warren, Laura, Morgan, and Philip James; and the Wilson, Fuselier, and Baltz families, for their love and kindness.

Ann Patchett, for reading an early draft of the novel, for a lifetime of good advice, for her constant support and friendship.

The Rivendell Writers' Colony, which provided me, several times, with the space to continue my work on this novel. Thank you to Carmen and Michael Thompson, and with gratitude to Mary Elizabeth Nelson.

St. Mary's Sewanee, for the use of the Hermitage, where I wrote parts of this novel.

The University of the South, especially the amazing students with whom I've had the honor of working over the past eleven years (especially Annie Adams, Kilby Allen, Jessica Barber, Aaron Browning,

Caroline Byrd, Liz Childers, Catherine Clifton, Sarah Cumming, Lily Davenport, Kat Dembergh, Ellen Doster, Norris Eppes, Daniel Fortner, Eli Gay, Anna Grishaw, Hallie Gladstone, Meg Hall, Becca Hannigan, Kelly Hines, Sarah Horton, Brandon Iracks-Edelin, Reed Jackson, Kate Jayroe, Sara Kachelman, Zoey Kortz, Robin Lee, Lara Lofdahl, Jacob Moore, Sarah Pinson, Chris Poole, Thomas Sanders, Charlotte Seaman-Huynh, Param Singh, Justin Smith, Leah Terry, Bea Troxel, Kathryn Willgus, Laney Wood, and Lena Yarbrough), and with special gratitude to the English Department, particularly Kelly Malone, Lauryl Tucker, and Elizabeth Grammer, for their mentorship and friendship.

My friends Leah Stewart, Matt O'Keefe, Sam Esquith, Cecily Parks, Isabel Galbraith, Lucy Corin, Claire Vaye Watkins, and Caki Wilkinson.

Ally Syler and Eliza Griffey, two of the most wonderful kids I know, for allowing me to use their names in this novel, and for their amazing parents and my best friends on the mountain, David and Heidi Syler, and Betsy Sandlin and Jason Griffey.

Finally and most emphatically:

Griff Fodder-Wing Wilson and Patch Halcomb Wilson, my sons, perfect little worlds.

Leigh Anne Couch, my cowriter, my best and truest love, every single good thing I have.